REINHART'S
WOMEN

NOVELS BY

THOMAS BERGER

REINHART'S WOMEN

A
NOVEL BY
THOMAS BERGER

DELACORTE PRESS/SEYMOUR LAWRENCE

Published by
Delacorte Press/Seymour Lawrence
1 Dag Hammarskjold Plaza
New York, N.Y. 10017

An excerpt from this book originally appeared in *Playboy* magazine.

Manufactured in the United States of America

First printing

Designed by Oksana Kushnir

Library of Congress Cataloging in Publication Data
Berger, Thomas, 1924–
Reinhart's women.

I. Title.
PS3552.E719R4   813'.54   81–3271
ISBN 0–440–07408–8   AACR2

To Emma Berger Jewett
and in memory of
Joseph F. Jewett III

REINHART'S
WOMEN

CHAPTER 1

Reinhart was preparing brunch for his daughter and his new girl friend. He and Winona had lived together since his divorce from her mother, ten years before. The friendship with Grace Greenwood was a recent development.

At the moment he was slicing little *lardons* from a stack of bacon strips. Grace was not due for another quarter hour. Winona appeared in the doorway to the kitchen.

"Is this O.K., do you think, Daddy?" She turned sveltely in her figured dress of turquoise, green, and blue. With amber eyes and chestnut hair, and a person that was not less than exquisite in any particular, Winona was as lovely a creature as Reinhart had ever seen, and though she was, technically speaking, but half his creation and took her coloring from the maternal side, in spirit she was nothing like her mother. The nice thing about Winona, as one of her admirers had explained to Reinhart, was that though a beauty she seemed to believe herself unattractive. The combination quite devastated this prosperous young lawyer, who had offered her his heart and his considerable goods of life. Among her other suitors had been an up-and-coming, middle-of-the-road politician and a forty-two-year-old department-store executive who professed to be ready to dump his wife and kids for her hand.

Winona's habitual response to male attentions was first disbelief, then amusement, but with the executive she had been outraged.

"Daddy," she had said through tears of anger, "he's *married*. How can a man be so disgusting?"

"It really turns one's stomach," said arch-hypocrite Reinhart, an old frequenter of whores extramaritally, but then his wife had been a real bitch at the time—indeed at all times. "Of course there may be extenuating circumstances, Winona. He's probably not a criminal, but it's not the worst strategy to consider all men as conscienceless brutes." That he was here being a traitor to his own sex gave Reinhart no qualms: he could not remember the last time a man had done anything for him, anything, that is, that did not militate to the advantage of the giver.

"What," Winona asked now, "is Grace's favorite color?"

Reinhart had finished his neat knifeplay, having transformed a half-pound of slab bacon into an accumulation of little strips measuring half an inch by an inch and a half.

"Favorite color," he said speculatively. "Now, I don't mean to offend you, but that would seem a very female question."

"Daddy," said Winona, "how could you offend me, since I *am* female?" She said this with her habitual sweetness, being incapable of irony.

Reinhart always kept a supply of chicken stock in the fridge, but anxious as he was to make the best impression on Grace Greenwood, he had earlier that morning cut up a three-pound bird, immersed the pieces in water to which he had added a sliced carrot, a diced onion, and a quarter teaspoon of dried thyme, brought it to a boil, and simmered it, partially covered, for an hour and a quarter. Then he removed the flesh, putting it aside for another use, and strained the fragrant liquid, which of course was in itself a bouillon. Only half a cup was needed for the Eggs Meurette.

He turned up the gas under a saucepan full of water: the slab bacon had a good strong, smoky flavor that was first-rate with an American breakfast, hen fruit sunny side up and home fries, or with flapjacks (though little pork sausages had the edge here), but eggs poached in red wine and chicken stock, with mushrooms, had a flavor that obviously would be stained by any hint of smoke, nor would the excessive salt in which bacon is cured be welcome.

The point was that Reinhart was about to blanch the bacon— which Winona brought home, for it was she who supported them while he served as housekeeper.

"Daddy, you're like all men," his daughter told him now. "You never look at anybody." She said this in a tone of affectionate reproach.

"Why, of course I do, Winona. But it *is* more like a woman than a man to notice colors. Whether or not that is based on some biological difference I couldn't say."

"Oh, I think it is," she said with vigor. No unisex theories would be entertained by Winona. Of course Reinhart, at his age, was gratified by his daughter's failure to be up to date. In truth the two of them saw eye to eye on almost everything, with the notable exception of food.

Winona had been a glutton until the last year or so of her teens, stuffing her then-stout person daily with sufficient carbohydrates to sate the Sumo wrestler she was on her way to resembling. But when she reformed, her efforts were not niggardly. In fact, what she had done was simply to reverse the coin and eat hardly enough to sustain life. The doctor assured Reinhart that her about-face was not abnormal in an American adolescent, and further he suggested that Reinhart himself, who had not then seen his own belt buckle in years, might do worse than follow his daughter's lead.

It was at this time that Reinhart had really begun to take a serious interest in food, after having gorged on it mindlessly for half a century. But despite his efforts to prepare such delicious meals that small portions exquisitely flavored would fill the role earlier performed by mountainous servings of sweet-and-salty blandness, he could claim no great success with Winona. Nowadays she simply ate almost nothing at all but wheat germ and yoghurt.

True, his leverage of argument was feeble. The slimmer she became, the more robust her health; whereas as a fatty her colds, laid end to end, had embraced the year, and of the common nonlethal complaints of all the popular organs she had evaded few. But the real clincher, unanswerable, was that Winona's dwindle in girth was accompanied by her gain in height, and by the time she had finished her eighteenth year, which coincided with her completion of the last term of high school, she stood five feet eight and she weighed a hundred twenty, and in no time at all she had become a fashion model and supported her father in a style he had never known! Their apartment, for example, was in a high-rise overlooking the river, five rooms furnished with expensive blond wood and chromium and glass, and Reinhart had a kitchenful of appliances. He supposed that it was in his interest *not* to feed Winona much. Yet cooking was the only thing in life he had ever done well.

Once he had wryly made that point to Winona herself. Her response, truly unexpected, had sent him behind the closed door of the bathroom: for, despite all the feminist propaganda, Reinhart continued to believe it unmanly to weep before others.

"Maybe it is a thing you've done *well,*" Winona had said in a solemn, even owlish style, "but what you've done *great* is being my dad."

Imagine having a daughter like that!

"Darling," he said now, "whichever color is Grace's favorite, she's going to fall in love with you. Now, I know that's a man's answer and that you're still going to worry about how you're dressed, because even though you're the leading model in town, you're female, and that means you're more anxious about other women than about men when it comes to your attire."

"I wonder why that is?" Winona asked.

Reinhart placed a dozen and a half of the button mushrooms in a colander and plunged the perforated vessel into a potful of cool water. He lifted it out, dripping, and then plunged it back. He decided to add another half-dozen fungi, did so and rinsed the lot once more, then removed the colander and emptied its burden onto paper towels.

"I suppose it makes sense, all in all," he said to his daughter. "Persons of the opposite sex look at each other with a totally different kind of interest from what they have when they see their own kind. They measure themselves against their fellows—they're in competition, aren't they?"

"Well," Winona said, moueing, "so are male models with us, I can tell you."

Reinhart snorted. "But is that the most manly of professions?" In justice it did occur to him that perhaps keeping house for a young woman, when you were not *that* old, might be seen as a failure of virility—but that the woman was a daughter made, as anyone would agree, a substantive difference.

"Anyway," he went on, "Grace has seen your pictures in the paper, and of course I've told her all about you. She couldn't be more impressed than she is, you know! You're a celebrity, Winona."

"Oh, come on, Dad." She hung her head, then raised it and chided him: "You are the most awfully unreliable person to ask about anyone's opinion of me! You always say it's fantastic. If I believed you, I couldn't get my hat on."

Winona was the only truly modest person Reinhart had ever known. He wondered whether it was really for the purpose of being sweet to him that she used so many of his own old-fashioned phrases: she never wore a hat, for example. She was also wont to say something was on the fritz or somebody had gone haywire or took the cake. On the other hand, the once-bygone "nifty" had been resuscitated by the world but was never used by Winona.

"It doesn't flatter my ego," said Reinhart, "but I strongly suspect it was because of you that Grace found me at all interesting."

"Now, Dad!" Winona said. "You're a fascinating fellow, and also a handsome dog." She approached him.

"Careful of your clothes, dear," Reinhart warned, though in fact his striped butcher's apron was not soiled.

"Well, I'm going to kiss my dad!" Winona cried in mock petulance. "I can always get another dress." She bussed Reinhart on the cheek. "Listen," she said, "if I could find a guy who was just like you, I *might* want to get to know him better. But he still wouldn't, he couldn't, know as much about me as you do! So how could I possibly make a life with him?"

Though this sort of expression was habitual with Winona, Reinhart himself was never blasé about it.

"You mustn't be too discouraged," he said lamely. "You just haven't met Mister Right as yet. When you do—and you will— everything will be different. You'll see."

Winona grimaced, and it was all Reinhart could do to keep from joining her. The idea of her being associated intimately with some squalid little ape was unbearable to him, if the truth be known; and by definition any male admirer whose affection was requited by her could be so characterized. Reinhart was well aware of his bias. But we cannot in justice be blamed for having our prejudices: all that matters is how they affect our actions. Therefore, secretly gritting his teeth, he invariably praised her gentlemen callers. But could he have done so if she herself had not disparaged them?

She drifted out of the kitchen now, in an abstracted mood. The water was boiling, and Reinhart plunged the little strips of bacon into it. When the boil returned from its brief setback he reduced it to a simmer. The mushrooms were small enough to cook whole, but without at least one flat surface the little buttons could roll on the plate, perhaps even tumble off. The potential mobility of food was to be inhibited. With his big chef's knife, which often could be put to defter use than a midget paring blade, he halved each button. It was a bit early for this, especially if Grace were to arrive late, and the cut mushrooms would darken unless sprinkled with lemon juice.

While he was squeezing a lemon half Winona returned.

She had changed her attire. Now she wore beige slacks and a shiny black blouse.

"Don't you think this is better?"

He inspected her with deliberation, then asked her to turn so that he might do the same from the rear perspective. Not that he saw anything with an eye that was at all competent in women's fashion, but Winona needed someone to turn in front of and to ask for approval. At such times he always felt a little twinge of guilt. A mother was the only proper audience for this sort of performance, as a father was the correct parent before whom to punt or throw a screwball.

She had already chided him today about overpraise. He might be restrained now with profit.

He said almost severely: "I think it strikes just the right note, Winona." He turned back to his counter top. "Of course, as I always say, dear, I think it's pretty ironic that I should be rendering a judgment on what our leading model wears."

"Dad," said Winona, in her most naïve manner, "didn't I ever tell you that I don't choose what to wear on a job? Gosh, to all intents and purposes we're not much different from window dummies, you know. And I'm not 'leading' anybody. I just work here in town, not in New York or Chicago or anyplace important."

Reinhart shook his head. "But you had a New York offer. And if you *had* gone, you would be famous from coast to coast." His conscience was clean: he had not stood in her way. Winona really had no ambition for spectacular success and little attraction to any way of life that could be called glamorous.

She started away from the kitchen, murmuring, and then she turned and stepped back. "Dad, I must say you have not said much about Grace. What's she like? How does she strike you, really?"

Reinhart cocked an eye at his simmering strips of bacon. He turned to Winona. "I guess you're right. I haven't told you much about Grace—for any number of reasons. Even after ten years away from your mother I still feel funny speaking of other women in front of you. But apart from that—" The subject was important to Reinhart, but he could not fail in his responsibility to the meal: again he tossed the mushrooms in their lemon-juice bath. "In addition," he resumed, "I have all my life generally had difficulty in telling one female person anything about another. Whether that's my own foible, or—"

Reinhart cleared his throat. The possibility that he might be turning into a garrulous old bore suddenly suggested itself to him: it was not a simple matter to identify oneself with the tedious sort of old-timer one remembered from one's own youth. Consciousness, however far back it can be remembered, always seems about the same. It is an effortless thing to recall, across half a century, one's intent to become a cowboy when one grows up.

"Sorry, dear. I'll make it snappy. To begin with, Grace, while not being quite as young as you, is even further from being as old as I. That is, she is not old enough to be your biological mother, whereas I suppose I *could*, technically speaking, have been her father, if just barely: she is forty." He frowned in thought. "She's a nice-looking woman, but what really matters is she's smart. I don't mean to imply that women aren't usually, but Grace has made a success in a man's world."

He closed one eye briefly and laughed. "First time we met I took her for a housewife, and a fairly dowdy and out-of-date one at that. She was wearing a cardigan and the kind of shoes that years ago were called 'sensible.' In fact, she was generally reminiscent of an earlier era, which is why I noticed her in the first place. I've found myself doing that sort of thing more and more. I suppose it's a sign of growing senility!"

Winona suddenly excused herself and left the kitchen. But when Reinhart had finished blanching the bacon she was back. She now wore the third outfit he had seen within a quarter hour: a long, long skirt, a puffy sort of blouse, and a kind of bandanna tied around her forehead. He liked this ensemble least of all: it was rather too mannered for his taste, but of course he said something flattering.

Winona thanked him. "But you weren't finished talking about Grace."

He raised his eyebrows. "Grace, you see, is all wool, no nonsense. Fact is, it was *she* who first asked me out. And why not? There we were, in front of the Mexican packaged foods—that's where we met, in the supermarket, as I mentioned earlier. She turned to me, in that cardigan and those sensible shoes. 'Say,' she said, 'do you really buy any of this stuff?' She asked it so aggressively that I thought she might be hostile to it herself. 'Not much,' says I. 'I don't cook in any Hispanic cuisine, though mind you I've nothing against any. I've eaten a taco or two in my time, and once, in that Mexican restaurant in the Wulsin Building downtown, I ate a chicken *mole*, which was fascinating with its peppery chocolate sauce, but—'

" 'I am really interested only in the Pancho Villa line,' she said, and she pointed at the cans bearing that label, which carry a picture of a Mexican bandit or general, Villa himself I suppose, with crossed bandoleers and a saber and two guns. 'I'm one of the guys who distribute that,' she said, 'and what I'm listening for is public reaction. The opinion-testers are more scientific, but I like to get the street-reaction on my own. Now, you look like a normal member of the public. Do you think this picture of a bloodthirsty-looking greaser would encourage you to buy, uh'—she chose a can at random and read the label—'uh, refried beans?'

"That's Grace's style, I'm afraid," said Reinhart. "She'll never get the mealymouthed award." He laughed heartily, though in truth he found that quality the least of Grace's attractions. "It turned out that she was an executive with this food-distributing firm, a vice-president no less. When she found out I did the cooking at my house she wouldn't let me go until I had given her a complete rundown on my choices of brands, the types of food I buy, the type of meal my family prefers, and the rest of it." Reinhart gestured with his wooden spoon. "And that would have been that, I'm sure, had I not mentioned that I had a daughter who happened to be the foremost model in town."

Winona blushed. "Oh, Dad, come on."

Reinhart chuckled happily. "No, I'm afraid I was just a statistic until then. But I didn't mind, dear. I like nothing better than bragging about you. Well, as I told you, that's how it began. That was just two days back. We found ourselves having lunch in that restaurant in the shopping center that used to be Gino's." Reinhart winced at a series of unpleasant memories under the old management. "It's a better place now, with a more expansive though somewhat hokey menu sometimes: pineapple with baked fish, and ginger with anything. Grace had the New York steak, hold the potato, and helped herself only modestly at the salad bar. I ordered the *escalope de veau*—we don't have it here very often because the price of veal is really insane"—not to mention that Winona wouldn't eat it—" and when the orders arrived, the waiter needless to say put the cutlets in front of her. . . . They were by the way more Wiener schnitzel than *escalopes*, breaded, for gosh sakes, but not badly, with grated Gruyère and what tasted like a little real Parmesan in the breading . . ."

Winona was wearing a sweetly bored look by now.

"Anyway, we also had a drink before eating: I had the vermouth cassis, and Grace, the Jim Beam and water, and the bartender remembered which was which and kidded us about it. Grace is not so big, you know, in body."

At that point the doorbell sounded. Winona gasped and scampered back to her room. Reinhart had never seen her in such consternation over a visitor: she was not above greeting a gentleman caller in an old wrapper and curlers—in which, needless to say, she still enchanted him.

Reinhart opened the door. This was but the third time he had seen Grace and the first occasion on which he might have called her almost pretty. Something had been done to her hair, and her eyes had been skillfully made up. Though she was wearing a suit, as she had on their second meeting, a dinner date, it now seemed more subtly feminine, somehow: lace blouse underneath, a bit of jewelry, and so on.

Grace was not, as Reinhart had mentioned, a large woman. To shake hands with Reinhart, her forearm was put at a steep angle.

"Welcome to the humble abode, Grace," said her host, with an expansive left wrist.

Grace controlled the shake, irrespective of the remarkable difference in fists, and peering around, she penetrated the living room. "It's hardly humble, Carl," she said in her brisk voice. "But then why should it be?" She suddenly looked vulnerable, an unprecedented and, Reinhart would have said, a most unlikely phase for Grace Greenwood. She continued to walk about in a military stride.

"Won't you sit down?" he asked. "May I give you a drink?"

She produced an abrupt, barking laugh. "Anything that's wet!"

She strode to the windows and laughed again. "There's the river, huh?" But the view was not sufficiently riveting to keep her there for a third second, and she turned and marched to the middle of the room, where presumably she could not be jumped by surprise—so it might have looked to someone who was not aware of Grace's credentials. Reinhart had never known anyone so confident at the core of her being; there was no bluster about Grace, none of the self-doubt usually apparent in some form in the boldest of women, and not one iota of vanity.

Despite her apparent indifference to the choice of potation he remembered how precise Grace had been about her preprandial drinks at their other two social engagements. (At dinner she had specified Johnnie Walker Red, diluted only by a sparkling mineral water called Minnehaha, of which, it turned out, her firm was the local distributor.)

He now poured her what she had drunk at their shopping-center lunch, a Jim Beam with tap water and ice, and was on his way to deliver it when Grace seemed all at once a frozen image in one of those cinematic stop-actions which had become a cliché in recent years, from an actress fixed toothily in mid-laugh to a car forever hurtling from a bluff into the ocean. Grace was arrested in a slight hunch of body and an enigmatic moue.

The fact was that Winona had slunk almost silently into the

room, but if Grace had seen her, it was through the back of her own head, for she, Grace, was still facing Reinhart.

"Aha!" he cried, perhaps too stridently, but he wanted to get beyond this purposelessly awkward moment. "Grace Greenwood, this is my daughter Winona."

But Grace remained in her stasis, facing him. Was she deaf? Or had she actually suffered an attack of paralysis?

Meanwhile Winona continued her sneaky approach, which seemed literally on tiptoe, but this was not the least of her eccentricities. She had changed her attire for the fourth time. She now wore black slacks, a tight black turtleneck shirt, and black shoes with high heels—it was her manner of walking in this awkward footgear that Reinhart saw as tiptoeing. Finally, her hair was pulled severely around the back of her head, where it was presumably gathered into a knot. Her eyes had a suggestion of the mysterious East: they had been slightly almondized by the tension on her skin at the temples.

Reinhart knew he would never understand the mysteries of women's styles of dress. Winona of course would have looked perfect in anything, but why for a spring luncheon she had finally settled on a costume suggestive of a Hollywood gunfighter's, sans only the pancake Stetson, was inexplicable.

At last she, as it were, rounded Grace's corner, for Grace had still not moved, and in a special low voice, one Reinhart had never suspected she could produce, she uttered only one word, "Hello," but put a good deal of force into that word, and having said it, she stepped back one pace, put her hands on her sleek black hips, and stared severely at the other woman.

"Winona," said Reinhart, "this is my new friend, Grace Greenwood."

Grace now emerged from her absolute fixity, but only so far as slow motion would take her. It seemed as though she might actually curtsy, but if so she changed her mind. Instead she glared at Reinhart and then abruptly seized the drink from him, almost spilling some in the swirl.

"Here," she said, in a kind of screech as unprecedented as Winona's baritone, and she thrust the whiskey at Reinhart's daughter.

This was the most remarkable display of something or other that he had ever witnessed, and he was so unsettled by it that he took a largish draft of the bourbon and water, a drink that he would ordinarily have put at the bottom of his list, owing to the cloying, almost confectionary effect it produced on his palate. However, though he winced at the earliest taste, the warm aftereffect now was comforting. He realized that he found Winona's performance to be lacking in graciousness: this was not like her at all.

Alas, it was obvious that she and Grace made a poor mix. He would of course stop seeing Grace, but meanwhile she was his guest and he would feed her.

"Winona," he said with a certain asperity, "I have to go now and work on the meal. Please be hospitable. Oh, Grace, if you don't want the Beam, there's Johnnie Walker Red. I've also got your favorite Minnehaha mineral water."

But Grace seemed not to hear him. As for his daughter, she said obediently, sweetly, returning to the old Winona, "Oh, I sure will, Dad. Grace, won't you sit down, please."

"Where?" asked Grace. She seemed bewildered.

Whatever the state of the world outside, everything made sense when Reinhart was with his pots and pans. With his big chef's knife he minced an onion and then a clove of garlic, and put them in a deep skillet with the blanched bits of bacon: all of these were sautéed together until they turned golden. At that point the half-cup of chicken stock was introduced, and two cups of red wine (a vintage Cabernet Sauvignon from California—not dirt-cheap, but the resulting liquid would become the sauce and must be edible), then salt, pepper, and sugar to taste (lest the reduced wine be too acid), and finally a *bouquet garni:* bay leaf, thyme, parsley, and two cloves, bundled in cheesecloth. He put this concoction on to simmer, and he trimmed the crusts from three square slices of a firm white bread, divided each slice in two, and sautéed the six little rectangles in butter.

Ten minutes had been consumed by these labors. The fragrant, simmering liquid would profit by ten more. He now had a moment in which to check on his guest.

The women were silent when he came into the living room, and they sat as far from each other as the arrangement of furniture would permit.

Grace held a glass full of ice cubes and colorless fluid.

"Um," Reinhart asked of her, "vodka or gin?"

She hastily, even guiltily, took a sip, then elevated the glass in a kind of triumph. "Diet Seven-Up!" she cried. "Delicious!"

"Good God," said Reinhart. "Is that your work, Winona? Here, Grace, let me get you something to *drink.* Winona, how could you?" He went across the room with outstretched hand.

But Grace fended him off, and from his left Winona wailed, "That's what she wanted, Daddy! You just ask her."

Grace shouted desperately, "I *love* it!"

Reinhart decided to give up his mission, whatever the truth of her averment: emotions, even if politely hypocritical, should be discouraged before any kind of meal (with the possible exception of high glee at a ball game, followed by a mustard-drenched hot dog and a paper-cupful of warm beer).

"As long as you're happy," he said, halting. "Winona has a professional reason for her diet, but even so I often don't approve of it. I can't get her to accept the fact that she first began to lose weight on my cuisine, but in a sensible way, and with no loss of nourishment or flavor."

"Please, Carl, say no more on that subject," Grace said. It was almost a command. Good, she was coming back to normal. But no sooner had Reinhart made that observation when Winona spoke up in obvious irritation.

"Daddy has a *very* good point, Grace, and you should listen to him."

Reinhart was amazed by his daughter: where had this forceful style come from?

"Sorry, Carl," said Grace, "I didn't mean to be rude."

"You weren't," Reinhart said firmly. This still wasn't going well, he was sorry to see, despite Grace's heroic efforts to get on with her hostess, absolutely the reverse of what the situation should have been. He was really getting very cross with Winona, and had it not been she who paid the rent, he might have considered sending her to bed! This thought came to him as only in part a jest. Though his daughter supported him in money, he provided her security in every other respect, and he was aware that Winona expected him to wield the domestic authority.

She got his implication now. "You see," she said to Grace in a

more decent tone, "what Dad says about food is right, but my
trouble is that all I have to do to gain weight is to smell something
delicious, I'm sorry to say. Until not too many years ago I was a
baby elephant. My brother used to call me that, and 'whale,' and
other lovely names."

Grace looked as though she might weep. In twenty minutes
Winona had evoked from her a display of feelings that Reinhart
had not suspected she had, and not once since the appearance of
his daughter had Grace shown that part of her personality that had
been salient in his previous meetings with her.

"That was because of the high-carbohydrate junk food you used
to gorge on," he now told Winona. He addressed Grace: "And so
did I! At the worst point I was almost fifty pounds heavier than I
am now, at ten years younger." He expected Grace to show some
amazement at this, as people could usually be relied on to do, but
she merely smiled vaguely into the middle distance. "Well." He
made a gesture. "I'd better get back to my eggs."

No one offered to stop him, and he returned to the kitchen. He
tasted the liquid, which had reduced somewhat in the simmering.
Despite the sugar it was still slightly tinged with acidity, but this
condition would surely be corrected when the cooked mushrooms
were added, even though they had themselves been sprinkled
with lemon juice: you learned such things with experience. He
heated butter and oil in a skillet and quickly sautéed the mushrooms. When that was done, it was time to poach the eggs in the
perfumed bath of wine and stock and bacon and onions and garlic.

The *oeufs en meurette* when done were pinkish gray, not in
themselves a ravishing display, but they were masked in the
velvety, rich brown sauce made from the poaching liquid, thick-
ened and augmented by the mushrooms, and they were mounted
on the croutons fried golden in hot butter.

Reinhart had opened a fresh bottle of the same wine that had
been used for the poaching, and he had made a simple salad of
washed and dried watercress without dressing. To follow was only
a sorbet of fresh pears, made of the puréed poached fruit and egg
white. Some light sugar wafers. And no more to the brunch but
Mocha-Java, with heavy cream: too early in the day for the inky-
black infusion of "espresso."

This meal represented Reinhart's ideal of great flavor and no
bulk. He was pleased with himself as he carried the *plat de résist-
ance* into the dining ell off the living room. The plates were heat-
ing on a Salton hot-tray on the sideboard. He put them in place
on the table and poured the wine. There was a dramatic moment
at the outset of any meal, just before anyone took the first bite,
when the napery was spotless, the cutlery unsullied, the wine
gleamed behind crystal, the dishes were at their visual perfection
—a good moment, but not the best to Reinhart, who was a cook
and not a maître d'hôtel.

No, the best time of all was when the persons for whom he had
provided the meal began to eat it! He went around the corner to
fetch Winona and Grace.

The door to the hall was open, and the living room was empty.

Before he reached the doorway Winona came through it from
the corridor, scowling inscrutably. When she saw her father she
lowered her head for an instant, then raised it and said wretch-
edly, "I guess you're ready to shoot me."

Reinhart did nothing for a moment, and then, sighing, he embraced his daughter and led her to the sofa.

"We're going to have a man-to-girl talk," he said to Winona, who
was displaying her old schoolchild sheepishness, her head inclin-
ing towards his shoulder. "The fact is, Winona: you've spoiled me
rotten!"

From the side of his eye he could detect her flinching smirk. "I
mean it! I'm the spoiled one, and I'm responsible for this awful
waste of your youth." She made some childish murmur of content-
ment. God, how hard it was to say this! What dad did not want to
keep his daughter home forever?

Reinhart rose and stood before her. "It's simply not right that
we each be the only member of the opposite sex that the other has
as a friend! I'm not suggesting it's perverted or anything of that
sort, but it simply isn't balanced. You know, that's one criterion of
a meal: whether it's balanced. Cream soup, stewed chicken,
mashed potatoes, cauliflower, and blancmange, however well prepared each by each, would be a white horror in the ensemble!"

"Dad—" Winona began.

"No, Winona, we must face the fact that you're not sixteen any more. You're almost twenty-six. You're not in school. You have a profession, and a very lucrative one, in this town. If you went to New York, or even Chicago, you could be positively rich, I'm sure, modeling for Cover Girl or Clairol Herbal Essence or something on TV for hair or skin or whatnot."

"Daddy—"

"I realize that you felt Grace would alienate my affections towards you." Reinhart took long strides to the windows and back. In the river below were two barges in tandem. He had mostly stayed home for some years: the world outside, especially from the height of this apartment, was more and more a mere picture. Often he even ordered food from a high-priced store with delivery service: Winona could afford it. He had not had a lady friend in time out of mind. And now this!

"Don't think I'm criticizing you, dear," he said, coming back to a position before the couch. He laughed for effect, but the irony was real enough. "How could I, when you pay the rent?"

Winona made an unhappy expression: she hated him to mention that. She disliked his making reference to anything that could be interpreted as being personally negative. In that attitude she was unique in all the family, at least since the passing of his own father years before, and in truth Reinhart had always considered his dad a bit simple-minded. He had always believed that his mother's predominant feeling towards him was contempt, and a final proof was provided from the grave: her will had ignored both himself and his favorite child in favor of his son, Blaine, a fellow with whom Reinhart had seldom seen eye to eye in whichever era.

"Daddy," Winona began once more, "you don't—"

"No," said Reinhart, "of course I'm not angry. But I'm afraid that I feel responsible for what had to be an unpleasant experience for poor Grace. I'm going to have to call her up and apologize, Winona." He smiled at her. "I won't bring any more ladies home from now on, I promise. But I wish you would think about what I said. We both, but you in particular, young as you are, need *some other friends.* And listen here—don't forget that I'll be jealous of your young men! That's only natural, close as we are. Now, shall we eat, before my lovely eggs are completely cold?" He clapped his hands. "Something new for you. I know you don't care much for poached eggs, Winona, but these are pretty special—poached in wine, with mushrooms! I know you'll adore them!"

In truth he was fairly certain she wouldn't like them at all, and had really prepared the dish to impress Grace Greenwood, who would probably not have liked it either, judging from what she had ordered on their two dates at restaurants.

Winona had hung her head during all his comments, raising it only to protest feebly from time to time. But finally she made a great gasp and spoke as loudly as she could in the soft voice in which she had never failed to address him.

"Daddy! You're just going to have to listen to me!"

"O.K.," said Reinhart. "I'm sorry, Winona. I didn't realize—uh, go ahead, please."

She stared at him for a while. Had he not known better, he might have believed her emotion to be self-righteousness: something he had never detected in Winona in all her life.

"Dad, I did not first meet Grace Greenwood in this apartment."

"You didn't?" Reinhart cocked his head. "Huh." Suddenly he had a premonition that he should be seated. He chose a low, overstuffed chair across the coffee table from his daughter, the kind of chair from which, in his heavy days, he would not have been able to rise without heroic effort.

"In fact we've known each other for a while," said Winona.

"Then why," Reinhart asked, pointing, "why then did you ask about her favorite color?" It struck him that his own question was silly.

"Oh, I don't know," Winona answered. "It's the kind of thing you say. The fact is, I know her pretty well, you see."

"I see," said Reinhart.

His daughter grimaced. "But I don't think you do, really. . . . Anyway, that's why we acted so funny."

"Why couldn't you have just admitted that you knew each other? Is there some law against that? Why wouldn't I have been pleased to know it?"

She grinned wildly. "I guess it *was* dumb, but once these things begin, well, you know how it goes, one expects the other will say it, and then neither one does."

Suddenly he thought: Well, what does it matter? He slapped his knees. "Sure you don't want to eat my special eggs? It's a classic dish, you know. I really made an effort."

"God," Winona groaned, "don't make me feel worse." She put her flawless face into her cupped hands.

"I didn't mean that, dear. Everything's got snarled up today! What I meant was, it's O.K. with me that you and Grace already knew each other."

"Oh, Dad . . ." Winona took her hands away from her damask cheeks. It had more than once occurred to Reinhart, looking at her, that his daughter might single-handedly evoke all the clichés that were applied to beauty: peaches & cream, silken, velvet, and so on. "Daddy, it's *how* we've known each other."

Reinhart looked towards the windows and enjoyed the glistening floor between the shag rugs: he had himself put that shine on the parquet with real wax and a rented buffer from the True Value hardware store.

"We've been close friends for a while," Winona went on, biting her underlip. "I didn't quite know how to approach the subject with you, so she had the bright idea of the meeting-you-as-if-by-accident. It seemed a good idea when I heard it, I don't know why now. It was stupid and, worse, dishonest. Not that I'm criticizing her, though: I was a full partner."

"Not that I'm criticizing *you*," said Reinhart, "but what was all the skulduggery about? Why should I object to your being friends with a bright, successful, and prosperous woman like Grace?"

"Well," said Winona, "there was an idea, you see, of sharing an apartment."

"With Grace?" Reinhart almost shouted. "My gosh. That is some idea. You little matchmaker, you. Were you anticipating that Grace and I would get married, or would it be some up-to-date living in sin?" He was pretending to be in robust good humor while all the time feeling a looseness at the core.

Winona was softly weeping. Reinhart went across to the sofa and held her. "Daddy," she said, "how could I ever leave you?"

"Darling, you won't ever have to."

"Well, that was the reason, anyway."

"The reason for what, darling?" Reinhart's own eyes were moist.

You could not call a life a failure when you had produced a child like this.

"The reason why we broke up, Daddy. Grace says she can't go on unless we live together."

Reinhart nodded. For an instant he held Winona as tightly as before, and then he relaxed his grasp. After a moment he stood up.

He spoke as lovingly as ever. "You wanted me to see that Grace was a fine person. You're certainly right about that, dear. I think the idea was a pretty good one on the part of two very decent women. And listen here, Winona, when you get a good friend in life, you want to hang on to her."

Winona's fine eyes began to widen. "Dad, I hope you're not thinking exclusively of my welfare. You always do that, you know, and I won't put up with any kind of sacrifice on your part. I love you, and I won't have it!"

"Oh, I'm not being excessively noble," said Reinhart. "I think you are so fond of Grace that maybe you'd hate me, without even realizing it, if I came between you."

Her expression was anguished. "Don't say anything like that, ever! Didn't I just send her away?"

"Take my word for it, Winona. I'm a veteran in the contradictory forces of the heart."

Winona began to weep again. "You know, I was telling Grace— it will be much harder with him than if he were the usual bigot. Damn it, Daddy, can't you make it easier by being even a *little* nasty?" She was now grinning slightly through her tears.

"Don't talk like that," Reinhart said furiously. "Talk about not making it easy on somebody!" He cracked his fingers. "Do you know why I'm such a tolerant fellow, Winona? Because I'm too chauvinist, that's why! I come from a generation of men who weren't concerned that much with women. When I was young I was obsessed with whether *I* was *virile* enough. We young men were all like that: it was the constant preoccupation in the Army, for example. Even our humor dealt with it incessantly: *fruit, fairy, swish, pansy, fag,* the words themselves were enough to provoke a guffaw. Then I'll tell you something else: if we did hear of a girl who preferred her own kind, we assumed she was some poor little bitch who had simply never met the right man."

Winona, who had never looked more beautiful, uttered one flat, mirthless sound: "Ha."

"And then," said Reinhart, "when I lived long enough to be absolutely certain of myself, I had become the father of a son, and my great worry in the late Sixties was that your brother might turn qu— gay."

"Blaine?" Winona asked in derisive disbelief.

"Well, he's grown pretty square by now, but in those days he dabbled in all the trendy things, radicalism, et cetera." Reinhart flung up his hands. "But look, you don't want to hear all this patronizing stuff. You stick to your friend, Winona. That's my advice."

She was shaking her head at him. "But, Daddy, what will become of you?"

Smiling with all the saintliness he could contrive, Reinhart did not hear the question. He was wondering how long he could conceal from this precious person, whom he loved with all his heart, that she would be the death of him.

CHAPTER
2

Of course Reinhart soon admitted to himself that he was exaggerating in his inner sense of high tragedy. For one, nobody had expired of shame in a good century. Then, sexual deviation had not been regarded by the enlightened as a disgrace since at least the fifth century B.C. and in our time even the *mobile vulgus* had succumbed to a tolerance of variants. Nowadays Gay Pride spectacles were commonplace in our major cities. (Good heavens, must he someday salute as Winona and Grace Greenwood marched by?) That it would always be a joke with respect to Nature might be considered as certain, but then so too was flying when you weren't born with wings, and eating cooked food and reading by electric light, and in fact, simply reading: no other animals did any of these things. If *Homo sapiens* in general was a pervert under the aspect of eternity, then why jib at a subspecies?

As to Winona in particular (and what did he really care about anyone else?), now at least no man would befoul her! No *other* man, that is, for one *had* used her when she was sixteen, in her most extreme moment of obesity, in fact, when she could not have got a proper date—for some men are beasts, and no female person, baby, cripple, or crone, is exempt from their detestable advances! Winona had been illegally invaded only in the statutory sense: the honey-voiced fiend had appealed to her generosity, had not used force. Yet had that experience polluted heterosex for her till the end of time? It was not a question that could be or should be asked of the principal.

The fact remained that Grace Greenwood was in love with his daughter, who, whether or not she reciprocated the emotion, at least was not offended by being the target of the other's passion. So Reinhart would put it with scientific and perhaps legalistic precision. Grace was the elder, a forceful and successful business-woman in what must be a game for high stakes, the competitive, even dog-eat-dog strife of American trade. Whereas Winona was a beautiful object whom others dressed and put in place and com-manded to turn and took pictures of. But then, whether exquisite or obese, Winona had been, since birth, the gentle, passive spirit on whom the dominant imposed their will. Bullied by her brother and habitually disregarded by her mother, Winona only came into her own when under her father's protection.

Reinhart was brooding on these matters as he cleaned up the dining room after the brunch that had never been consummated. Winona had offered to help, but her father advised her to go make peace with Grace.

She winced and hung her head.

A certain faint hope made itself known to him. "You *are* going to make your peace?"

"The problem is how," said his daughter, looking up with a different expression from any he had seen. He might have called it slyness had he not known her so well.

"Well, far be it from me . . . but can't you just give her a call?"

"No," Winona said through a firm set of mouth, "no, I can't."

"I mean when she gets home."

"Take my word for it, Daddy." She wore a strained smirk. "I think I'll go out for a while. I really would insist on helping you with the cleanup if I didn't know you were serious about wanting to do it alone."

This was true enough. Reinhart always felt a need to defend his dining room and kitchen against Winona's fecklessness. Though never meaning less than well, she tended to break plates and glasses, and it was her habit to scrape into the garbage can the contents, however abundant, of any serving bowl or platter: no doubt this suggested an attitude towards the leftovers of a meal of which she had tasted all too little of the original! But she had paid for all of this, china, glassware, and provender, while making little use of any. It seemed only right for Reinhart to continue to the end that which had been exclusively his effort from the outset.

Before she left, Winona of course again changed clothes, now to some apparently routine corduroy jeans (which were however a "designer" pair from which, in the ultimate chic, she had removed the label), a fancy blouse, and high-heeled half-boots. Reinhart was aware that this to him incongruous ensemble was actually a high style of the moment. It was not his business to ask her where she was going, but he now thought of Winona's social life in a new way. Would she sit on some bar stool until picked up by a bull dyke in crew cut and vested suit, chewing on a cigar?

It was a luxury to conjure up such bigoted images in private. He had himself, for a few days, thought of Grace Greenwood as his own girl friend. Of course his criteria for a female companion had altered greatly over the years. That sex no longer took priority among the various possible uses of a lady friend was due partly to his own time of life and partly to that of the culture. A sensitive man nowadays, even if young, did well to hang back—for example, had it not turned out that he was right to do so in this case? But not only because inversion was rife. Women in general had grown assertive, had their own magazines displaying naked men and relating filthy fantasies, took out loans from banks, tried murderers, and performed brain surgery. For ever so long now it would have been simple bad taste to buy a broad a rum-and-Coke, kid her along for a moment or two, and then expect to pry her legs apart immediately thereafter in the back seat of a gas-guzzler. Not that this sequence had been characteristic of his experience even when he was young and lusty. Oh, he might well have bought the drinks, but it was typical of the girls he frequented not to keep their part of the implied bargain. In truth, the one time that he did succeed, his companion had been Genevieve, for whom the parked car was a means to ensnare him for marriage—that being in the remote day when girls had a virtue that could be lost.

Reinhart had had nothing to fear from female "liberation": under the old system women had either disregarded him or run him ragged.

But lesbians were something else again. But what? Not "masculine," really, except for the cigar-sucking character alluded to in his bitter joke, who probably existed only in the imagination. He had seen more than one TV discussion show that dealt with these matters when the subject had come into vogue some years earlier, and while the "gay" men never seemed altogether credible when on such display, the homosexual women were seemingly well balanced and in fact often quite attractive to his eye—though in view of what had happened with Grace, should he not suppose his vision to be faulty, or even corrupt? Was there a name for the kind of pervert who preferred members of the *opposite* sex who were themselves inverts?

By the time he had finished the kitchen cleanup Grace had surely reached home, if indeed that had been her destination. He went to his bedroom, sat down on the bed, and lifted the phone from the adjacent table. He was amazed to discover that without trying he had learned Grace's number by heart. He must have had high hopes of some sort. Imagine being cut out, with a woman, by your own daughter!

He fingered the dial. Before any electronic sound was heard at the other end of the line, Grace answered. The surprise made Reinhart mute for an instant: he could have sworn the bell had not rung. This was not the sort of situation in which he was ever glib. The result was that having impatiently cried "Hello" twice, Grace gasped dramatically and began a monologue in a high, fluttery voice that sounded for all the world as though she were giving a malicious imitation of an adolescent chatterbox.

"I've been naughty! A quart of Pralines 'n' Cream! You called just in time, but I knew you would. You always come riding to the rescue like the U.S. Cavalry, flags flying, swords clinking. Oh, I was joking, you know that. I never mean these things. I just get so *flustered!* Well, I mean, I didn't really know how he'd take it, regardless of what you said. No, I didn't doubt your word, but sometimes the closest person to another doesn't see a certain side. And after all it could be pretty devastating. But he's so *sweet* I could just hug him, but of course I see so much of you in him, though I must say you're not always as good-humored—now don't take offense, you know I'm just teasing. Are you on your way? I lied: I haven't touched the ice cream. I've been waiting for you, but unless you come soon, I can't be held responsible."

Up to this point Reinhart had been paralyzed with embarrassment. He could not of course reveal his identity at this late date,
and he doubted that silently hanging up the instrument would be
more satisfactory: Grace might believe it was the work of a sullen
Winona. He was trying here to put himself vicariously in these
roles. As he had told his daughter, he was not a tyro in emotional
entanglements, but he had two barriers to cross here: plain sex, of
which they belonged to the opposite one, and then the deviation
from that. Would it have been easier if *he* were gay as well?

Fortunately Grace gave no indication that she would soon stop
talking—she who had always been so terse when knowingly addressing him. But are we not all of us different folks from usual
when in the grip of passion? Trying to be fair, Reinhart dredged
up some of his own memories, most of them necessarily ancient,
but a strange fact was that the more recent events seemed even
more remote, e.g., he had had a funny sort of fling in the Sappy
Sixties with a freaked-out young girl named Eunice Munsing. He
thought he had spotted her at the wheel of a cab the week before,
fat face like a red balloon, but that might have been a mirage: for
romantic purposes he liked to think of her as deceased. The point
was that aesthetics always called for the drawing of the curtain
across what other people called love, and perhaps one's own as
well, which is why the audience for hard-core pornography must
always be a relatively tiny cluster of stoics.

Grace suddenly arrested her breathless rush of nonsense about
ice cream and asked: "Should I call your dad and apologize?"

Reinhart thrilled with horror, and then at once, magically, his
problem solved itself. Grace answered her own question, and
added obsequiously: "Shall I do it now?"

He considered making a falsetto grunt or murmur, but thought
better of it and merely lowered the receiver to the bedside table
to simulate the sound Winona might have produced in putting
down the phone to fetch him.

He walked around the room and stared, for once not vacantly,
at a little framed snapshot of himself in uniform, taken next to a
pile of rubble in Occupation-era Berlin. He now liked the looks he
had had then, though he had not at the time: these transformations
in taste occur after one has passed fifty.

He returned to the phone, into which, unconsciously imitating Grace as *he* had known her, he barked: "Yes?"

"Oh, Carl," Grace replied, "Grace Greenwood. I wanted to just say I'm sorry I had to run like that, but I guess Win has explained. It was unavoidable, I assure you, just one of those things, and shouldn't be taken as a reflection on yourself. You're a fine fellow."

Reinhart marveled at her change of tone. Once again she was in total command, without a weakness or a doubt. On the other hand, his own situation, if judged according to relative degrees of power, had changed.

"Well, Grace, I might say the same for you! I just regret that you went without a meal." And he couldn't forbear from adding: "I wanted to introduce you to something you have probably never eaten. A classic, but not too much to take if your tastes are for simpler food. Not *aïoli* or eel with green sauce."

Grace grunted almost rudely. He suspected the regrets were all his own. But she spoke in a bright voice: "Listen, Carl, not even Winnie knows about this. I'm bifurcated like all of us: I really *am* interested in you."

For an instant Reinhart did not attend to her meaning: he was stuck on that "Winnie." If there was one thing that Winona had deplored as a child (along with being hungry) it was hearing a diminutive of her name; not even her brother at his most malicious had easily resorted to this usage.

But then he became aware of a new and even more beastly element in the woman! She was baldly confessing to be *bisexual?* She wanted to take on both father and daughter? Was he expected to be tolerant of this as well?

Fortunately he had lived long enough to know that the best defense against any moral outrage is patience; wait a moment and something will change: the outrage, he who committed it, or, most often, oneself.

Grace laughed curtly. "Head and heart!" she said. "I'm always the businesswoman."

Reinhart chuckled in relief: so that was the bifurcation.

Grace said: "Mind giving me your credentials?"

He cleared his throat. "I'm not sure what you're talking about, Grace."

"This cooking of yours. Where were you trained?"

Could he have heard her correctly? No one *ever* wanted to hear him on his favorite subject!

"Well," said he, swinging himself from a seat to a luxurious full-length stretch on the bed, "I have never taken a lesson in cookery. Years ago, when I was first married and my wife would be under the weather, I'd do a turn in the kitchen and maybe take one of those recipes off a can of something. You know, like the tuna casserole that is sometimes on a noodle box, or vice versa. Then—"

"Carl," Grace interrupted, "my idea was not to take you from grilled cheese to gourmet grub with all the steps between. The point is, you seem pretty knowledgeable about the subject. How?"

"Diligence," said Reinhart, "and caring."

"Come on, Carl," Grace said impatiently, "I'm in earnest: I'll tell you why in a minute, but first I want your story, as precise as you can make it."

Reinhart might have taken umbrage at her manner (where'd she get off, being so high and mighty, *now?*) had the subject not been that which was, after Winona, the dearest to him.

"One improves through trial and error," said he, "but the techniques can be learned easily enough, some of them on the TV cooking shows and others from books, those that take you through a recipe detail by detail, allowing for the pitfalls, like Julia Child's, who is a genius as a teacher, and Michael Field's, and *Gourmet* and other periodicals, including the ladies' magazines that once recommended only the tuna casseroles. Now they'll tell you how to make bouillabaisse and quiche and moussaka."

"Uh-huh," said Grace. "And you've only worked at home? You haven't cooked in a restaurant?"

"Never. I've never even thought of doing any professional work. I really cook for the love of it—and I use the word advisedly. Winona"—for a moment he had forgotten the situation; now he felt strange about pronouncing the name to her *friend*—"my daughter hardly touches her meals." Though apparently she gorged on high-calorie ice cream with her *friend.*

"Carl, none of that serves my point," Grace said rudely. "I'm not interested in the personal here, but rather in the public. You know

Epicon, my firm. We're expanding in the gourmet area. It's my theory that we're missing some big bucks unless we reach the people who eat fancy food. This is no small market. One way to escape the label of 'just a housewife,' which is about as popular nowadays as yellow fever, is to be at least a gourmet cook. Not to mention the growing number of guys like yourself who stay home and fix meals for the breadwinner. Isn't it true that though men were traditionally supposed to be meat-and-potato eaters exclusively, still, when they cook, they often make Cordon Bleu dishes?" She answered herself: "You know they do."

"So I've heard," said Reinhart, "but I'm no authority: I don't get around much any more, frankly."

"And that's another thing, Carl. I think you *should* get out of that apartment more often." Grace became positively avuncular. He could imagine her winking and digging him with her elbow, were he near enough. "Be better for Winnie, take my word for it."

What Reinhart found most outrageous here was that she would use his interest in cooking to promote her selfish plans to lure away his daughter.

"Grace," he nevertheless said with control, "you might be interested to know that I'm not standing in the way of your friendship with Winona. I gave her that assurance, and I believe she's now working on her decision."

Grace breathed quickly. "That's just the point, Carl. Let's talk turkey: if Win moves in with me, where does that leave you? You told me you haven't had a business in some years, or a job."

It was really majestic of him still not to lose his balance: perhaps the years had seasoned him. Apparently he *had* made these confessions to Grace on their two dates, and why not? He had trusted her to make the right interpretation: that only now, at long last, could he claim to be successful in life, now that he had withdrawn from the hurly-burly to make a home for his daughter. Was he not indeed an exemplification of the new kind of man made possible by the liberation of women? He had told his story in pride!

"By your account I sound suspiciously like a bum," he said, with more wryness than reproach. "There are still some women who call themselves housewives, or rather the more honorific-sounding 'homemaker,' and I'm sure they would insist that what we do is self-respecting, gratifying, and all the rest. True, it's not the construction of the Golden Gate Bridge or a part of the aerospace program, but—"

"Come on, Carl," said Grace, jollying him in a coarse fashion, "self-pity's not your game, old boy!"

What a grating woman! Why could not Winona have chosen. . . ? But at fifty-four he should be done with asking questions of Fate, whose answers were always implicit in the status quo.

"The fact is that for many years it was my only game," said he, "but you're right about the 'old boy.' "

Grace said: "You're jumping the gun by a long shot in this day and age. But I didn't want to talk about dreary matters, believe me! Everything's going to work out beautifully. Now here's my proposition." In a supreme effort towards charm, which with men anyway would not seem to be easily available to her, Grace said: "And if you don't take it, I'll spit in your eye." Trouble was, she sounded as if she well might.

"You may fire when ready, Gridley," said Reinhart, reverting to a time even before his own for this quotation, a favorite of his father's, who however always corrupted it in one way or another and sometimes combined it with "the whites of their eyes."

"I don't know whether you've noticed," said Grace, "the existing gourmet shelves in your typical supermarket don't get much traffic, and in fact in some stores are downright seedy-looking. Also they're usually poked away in some remote corner, where they're an easy prey to shoplifters. Products not swiped are there for months. And this in the face of the greater-than-ever interest in the aforementioned gourmet cooking. Why?"

At this talk of food Reinhart forgot his resentment. In fact he had something ardent by way of an answer. "Yes, I have noticed that, Grace. And I'll tell you why that department is usually neglected by the public: it usually offers an eccentric choice of products, which are furthermore, some of them, not at all serious: things like cocktail franks and those dreary Japanese smoked oysters."

"No," Grace stated firmly, "you're wrong, Carl. The reason these things don't move—and they are fine products, don't knock them!—the simple reason is that the public is not aware of their use."

"That's not true at all," said Reinhart. With anyone else he would have felt he was being rude, but obviously Grace was immune. "A lot of that stuff is absolute crap! Why buy ready-made sauces, like hollandaise and béarnaise, when they're inferior yet expensive as hell, and when furthermore they're quite easy to prepare from fresh materials? And don't tell me nobody knows about the gourmet shelf, with its lousy liver pâté and orange caviar and dip-mixes, because throughout my married years, which ended more than ten years ago, I was served them whenever we went to any neighborhood party."

"You're showing strong feelings, Carl," Grace pointed out. "Do you realize that you're coming alive?"

"Of course," said Reinhart, "but it's nothing new. You know I'm interested in food and cooking."

"O.K.!" she cried merrily. "I'm not debating with you, pal. I want to hire you."

"Hire me?"

"You heard it!" said Grace. "Let me sketch it out. I'm convinced that all it would take to get some real action with the gourmet products would be to highlight them with personal demonstrations. Picture this, Carl: you're in professional apron and big white hat, stainless-steel table on wheels, with whatever implements, gadgets, you need, hot plates, et cetera, preparing dishes that would make use of the products we distribute. Huh?"

"You're not joking, are you, Grace?"

She spoke in brisk reproach: "Carl, I wouldn't have time."

"But, Grace, couldn't it be that the gourmet line is doing badly because of the recession and inflation?" It had been ever so long since Reinhart had had to think about business, and considering his own lack of success at what in a more gracious time was called "trade," he did not miss it. Yet an archaic sense of what was quintessentially patriotic in his place and time—he had been one year old when Cal Coolidge said "The business of America is business"—impelled him to put this question.

But Grace had no sentimental reluctance to put him in his place. "Carl," she said, "don't worry your little head about such matters. They're *my* responsibility. Just stick to your cooking."

Reinhart supposed wryly that he should feel as insulted as women of yore had felt when so disposed of by men—or, to be precise, as militant female publicists insisted that women had felt (his own mild-mannered father had habitually done this to Reinhart's iron-fisted Maw, and she was wont publicly to applaud him for it)—but at his age it was simpler to admit the truth than to uphold principles for which one had no genuine instinct. And truly, Reinhart had always hated and feared the process of buying and selling. When he was young he told himself that this dread was due to his being a poet, but by early middle age he had had to recognize that his collected verse had yet to be written, whereas he had tried several business ventures (gas station bypassed by a new superhighway, movie house when TV came in strong, etc., not to mention involvements in various schemes with arrant charlatans) all of which had failed: in balance he could have been called, and certainly was by his wife and mother, a complete flop. At which point he came to keep house for Winona and was saved!

He was now talking to the woman who threatened his sole achievement. Why was he not more resentful? Because he had always known it would come. The irony was that he had assumed he would be deposed eventually by a conventional figure like a husband.

"This is so sudden," he said now. "I really do have to think it over. . . . I say this without animosity to you, Grace: Winona and I have had a nice life together. I suppose having just me as an intimate hasn't been sufficient for her, and that's understandable. I'm after all in my mid-fifties. I want you to know that I have always urged her to get out and circulate—and when she told me, a while ago, about you, I was taken by surprise, I'll admit. But I'm proud to say I was consistent: I told her one should stick with a good friend."

"That would be like you," Grace said, and he was touched.

"Thanks. But as to my going back into the world, that'll take some deliberation."

Grace spoke in the tone of a football coach: tough-but-for-the-players'-good: "Dammit, Carl, you're not an old man. As President you'd be a youngster. There's more than time enough to make your mark. This could be but the first step! How's anyone to know of your culinary prowess if you hide your light under a casserole?" She made a flat chuckle.

He laughed for another reason. "Do you realize that you have never even as yet *looked* at anything I've cooked? Let alone tasted it?"

Grace grew solemn. Obviously she was here enunciating one of the tenets of her faith. "I know real quality when I see a person, Carl. After all, did I not pick Winona?"

Assuming that her question had a sexual reference, he was repelled. Yet how could he protest without supplying an implication that would be unfavorable to his daughter?

In fact he had again misjudged Grace, who proceeded to reveal that her meaning had been exclusively professional. "Did I not see her in the ads for Herk's knitted ensembles and know she'd be perfect for our instant-cocktail mixes?"

Herkimer's was the big downtown department store. Winona modeled for their newspaper ads and for the special sales that were hawked on television. Indeed her married suitor was a Herkimer executive.

"She's worked for you?" Immediately he felt better. The image of Winona's being picked up in a lesbian bar (if, to be sure, there was such a thing: his fantasies were necessarily based on what he knew about male homosexuals, nor was that much) had been persistent and repulsive.

"You didn't see the ads?" Grace asked with synthetic incredulity. "The concept was an innovation of mine. That sort of product is ordinarily only advertised nationally, with everything handled in New York, of course. There's not a big market in instant mixes and never could be. So why then, you ask, do I throw away our good money on local newspaper ads? I even wanted to do TV spots, but on that I was voted down by my colleagues, who are all *male*, by the way."

Reinhart refused to feel guilty about that. "I gather you are preparing to announce a sudden burst of sales, a big run on instant cocktails."

"No sirree!" Grace cried in triumph. "During that campaign sales were no higher than ever. There's no reason to believe a single extra can was sold by those ads, featuring your exquisite daughter against the background of the best local country clubs, Wynhurst and Checkhaven, and the Silver Huntsman Restaurant in Stricksville. Carl, are you telling me you didn't see those ads?"

"For some reason Winona didn't show them to me. And I seldom see the papers of my own volition: I had been pretty well burned out so far as news goes when Vietnam and Watergate were done. But I'll say this, Grace, if I do happen to come across a newspaper, I give most of my attention to the food advertisements, you'll be pleased to hear."

"Be that as it may," said she, "you haven't asked me why I am so pleased at losing a fair amount of money on an apparently useless project. Here's why: because it put Epicon on the map." She made a sound that effectively constituted a verbal wink. "That it did the same for me is just between us." Again that sound: a kind of *chock*.

"Grace, am I correct in assuming that your company name is made up of the first two syllables of 'epicure' and the first of 'connoisseur'?"

"Carl, are you following my story?" Grace asked disapprovingly. "You're really not picking up on my points. That's hardly encouraging if we're going to work together."

"I don't think we *are* going to, Grace, with all respect." He had suddenly arrived at that decision: her world, perhaps as much in its business phase as in its private character, was utterly alien to him. "But look here, I'm grateful to you for thinking of me!" He thanked her again and hung up. He would not go so far as to say anything about seeing her around with Winona.

He switched on the television set that had its home on his dresser top and identified the intense green image of the typical Sunday-afternoon golf tournament. The competitors in this one were female, all of them with exceptionally sturdy calves, thighs, and behinds. Reinhart found most of them vaguely attractive, however. They looked like good sports and seemed feminine enough all the same, and he was comforted by the sight of their solid upholstery and, on the average, seasoned age, as opposed to the sinewy striplings of swimming competitions and gymnastics.

. . . Ah, Mildred Donleavy, her pleasant plump face shadowed by the bill of her white cap, was plotting the likely route of her putt. Her sandy hair was gathered into a neat bun; just above her waist bulged a roll, a little bolster, of flesh.

A telephone rang and, startled by the jangle, Mildred missed her putt. There should be a rule against phones on golf courses! But when the second ring came, Reinhart identified it as issuing from the instrument at his elbow.

"Dad, I trust I haven't woken you up."

It was his son. As usual Reinhart believed he detected an implicit criticism. But for many years now he had held his own against Blaine, who had undergone a total transformation since the late 1960s, in which era he had been an exceptionally obnoxious member of the "youth movement" or "counterculture" so beloved and encouraged by journalists and other rabble-rousers. Within a decade Blaine had become precisely what in his early twenties he had professed to despise most. He was now a stockbroker, with wife, two children, expensive suburban house with swimming pool, more than one gas-gluttonous car, and all the rest. He was also a regular churchgoer. His wife, first-named Mercer, came from a "good" local family.

"What's your pleasure?" he now asked Blaine.

"Listen, Dad," Blaine began angrily, and then he blurted: "Damn it all. I can't talk about this on the telephone!" Suddenly he seemed on the point of tears.

Reinhart had never liked Blaine, but if called upon he was capable of loving him, and almost everyone in distress evokes sympathy at the outset.

"Well, then, why not come over here?" he asked his son. "If it's confidential we'll have total privacy. Your sister's out for the afternoon."

"Damn her," said Blaine.

For a moment Reinhart was not sure he meant Winona, whom Blaine had habitually ignored all his life except to jeer at in her time of obesity. But the doubt was soon dispelled.

"She's just been here," Blaine said, his voice contorted with loathing. "I threw her out. I don't want my children contaminated. Dirty little bitch. Goddamned filthy little pervert."

It took all of Reinhart's strength to keep control at this point. He said sharply: "Don't speak like that about your sister, Blaine. I won't tolerate it, I warn you. But if you'd like to talk rationally—"

"I won't come there," Blaine said. He seemed to choke back a sob, but whether it was genuine or merely for effect Reinhart could not say. Blaine had a histrionic streak, derived undoubtedly from the maternal side.

"I could come to you," Reinhart told him, but with a hint of doubt. Blaine had never shown him an excess of hospitality. There were scorching days on which a dip in the pool might have been refreshing: his son had yet to issue an invitation however informal. Indeed in the several years Blaine had occupied the house, Reinhart had penetrated the front hallway but once. The holiday get-togethers had taken place at Winona's apartment and in fact were confined to the lesser, secular fetes such as Lincoln's Birthday and Labor Day. On the religious holidays Blaine consorted with his in-laws, the Seatons, to whom he had always been careful to deny his father access.

And even at this apparent extremity Blaine was none too hospitable.

"When you get here, pull down the road a little way, will you? Past the driveway, please?"

"Shall I wear a disguise?"

Blaine said: "Try to understand for once in your life, please."

Perhaps he had a point. Reinhart did have a certain guilt about his part in Blaine's upbringing. Nor did he believe that an association with the "better" people of a town was necessarily contemptible. Blaine had already, at the tender age of thirty-two, made a conspicuous success, and it would have been difficult to prove that his father had helped him in any way.

And finally Reinhart had to admit that Blaine's outburst against Winona had enunciated a feeling he had himself secretly entertained but lacked the courage to reveal even to the mirror.

"O.K., son," he said. "But the only thing is, your sister's taken her car. I'll be coming by bus. What's the nearest stop to you?"

Blaine returned to his old character. "You don't even have an automobile of your own?" He sighed in contempt. "Look, stay there. I'll drive over. I'll be grateful to you if you'll wait in the lobby."

"I'll teeter on the curb," said Reinhart, "and try not to fall into the gutter."

CHAPTER
3

Reinhart had forgotten to ask Blaine for sufficient time in which to brood over his costume. If he took it now, he ran the risk of making his son indignantly wait at the curb. On the other hand, Blaine was easily offended by his father's attire. Perfectly decent trousers and a sports shirt should be acceptable for a Sunday in late March unless one expected to call upon the royal couple at Monaco, one would think, but Blaine had austere standards. For one, he deplored an open shirt collar on a man older than, say, forty. He had a point, of course: the neck begins early to deteriorate aesthetically and is at best not one of the glories of the human physique. But as it happened Reinhart's Adam's-apple was as yet not a pendulous eyesore, and anyway he had the illusion of being strangled unless the pulse at the base of his throat had unobstructed access to the air.

His trousers were gray, his shirt a subdued plaid in shades of red. Surely a navy blazer would do on a Sunday afternoon: that was the point that should be remembered.

But when the cream-colored Lincoln glided to the curb and the power window effortlessly lowered itself and his son's face was seen, Reinhart could read immediately in the language of corner-of-eye, texture-of-lip, and angle-of-chin the message that once again he had failed to measure up.

But this expression was the work of an instant. Once it had been registered by its target, Blaine exchanged it for the mask of tragedy, a set of feature which did not well accord with his physiognomy, which was by nature of a peevish cast and more appropriate to one of Molière's disagreeable characters than to a Sophoclean hero.

Reinhart hopped in. "What kind of mileage do you get from this heap?"

"Whatever," Blaine impatiently responded, tramping the accelerator while his father was still sinking through the deep-padded leather of the seat. Blaine had once been obsessed with world affairs—in his own warped fashion, of course, holding Amerika responsible for all the horrors of history—but nowadays it was almost impossible to catch him in any reference, however subtle, to the kinds of things that were international preoccupations. The oil shortage, for example.

To confirm his sense of his son, Reinhart now asked: "Think there'll be a fuel crisis by summer?"

"How convenient that you don't have a car," said Blaine, swinging his own around the corner.

"Of course, what I wanted there was your opinion."

"Dad, I'm afraid that to make ends meet nowadays I have to charge a client for that service. It's all I have to sell, you know, and I have two children to support."

Sometimes it seemed to Reinhart that Blaine felt obliged to prove he was literally a son of a bitch. Apropos of which Blaine now said: "What this would do to Mother, I almost can't bear to think about!"

"That I don't have a car?"

"Oh, for God's sake," Blaine cried. "At such times I know what she went through." He flashed a hateful glance at his father. "I'm talking about that degenerate sister of mine! How can you be so tolerant? That filthy little scum, to think I grew up alongside her!"

Reinhart spoke in an even tone. "I told you I won't listen to that kind of abuse. Winona's your own flesh and blood, and furthermore she's a fine woman."

Blaine's features suggested that they would have been coloring with anger under normal circumstances, but he still retained a good deal of the tan he had got in the Caribbean in the early part of the month, and therefore the effect of rising blood was lost.

"Of course *you* would defend her," he said, steering the car up the ramp of an expressway. "I expected that."

And for Reinhart's part he had expected Blaine to have that very expectation. Next Blaine would graciously point out that his father was his sister's helpless dependent. But why then had he come now to seek him out?

"I have the unmistakable feeling," said Reinhart, "that this discussion is only going to make things worse." They were in the high-speed lane at the moment, else he would have asked to be let out at the nearest corner. He wondered at Blaine's choice of a place to talk. The normal thing would have been to find a back street in some quiet district, not to join a clamorous rush of vehicles heading upstate. But any thought of Blaine's characteristics inevitably reminded Reinhart of the boy's childhood: they had never been pals.

But his son now surprised him. "I knew you'd defend her," he repeated, keeping his eyes on the road. He drove as efficiently as he did everything else. "Not because you think it's a great thing that she's queer—I haven't forgotten your diatribes in the Sixties when, naturally, you used to accuse *me!* And not even because she's your sole support, so far as I know—*that* would make sense. I wouldn't fault you for that."

Reinhart realized from the last statement that Blaine was speaking the truth here, from the heart: his son condemned nothing done for a financial advantage, nor did Blaine recognize as serious any motive that did not have monetary gain as its goal. For example, he would have taken an altogether different approach to the matter at hand had Grace been *paying* Winona to be her friend: his concern then would have been only whether the fee was generous enough. . . . So much for Reinhart's cynical exaggerations: the solemn fact here was that Blaine was really not talking about Winona at all, and neither was he speaking about money.

"The truth is," he said, his mouth set, his hands clenched on the steering wheel, "that you have simply always hated me since the time I was born."

Reinhart made no immediate answer. He looked away from Blaine and watched the blacktop rush beneath them.

"Among my other naïveties," he said at last, "was the idea that one's paternal job is over when the children reach their majority, that from that point on things are equal for a couple of decades, and then with old age the father becomes the child. When the circle is complete, the curtain is lowered, if you'll permit the mixed figures of speech."

"That's it, Dad," said Blaine, "play with words. I wouldn't recognize you as my father if you didn't do that sooner or later. I'd think you were an impostor."

Now Reinhart looked at him. "But what you don't seem to realize is that real feelings exist all the same. Words really do stand for something, after all, but maybe it's not always what you expect. . . . I'm embarrassed now, Blaine, if you want a confession. You've hit me dead-center. You're not quite correct, but you're not altogether wrong, and that's what defies my powers at the moment." He had the bizarre sense that he might burst out here, not in a sob but, terribly, in a guffaw—but with the significance of a sob: somehow even in projection he could not play it straight with Blaine.

"Since at the moment I can't really deal with it, let's go back a bit to what led to this moment," he said finally. "Winona came to see you a while ago?"

Blaine grimaced and hit the wheel with his palm. "It's rich, isn't it? We've never been close in all our lives. She's certainly the last person on earth I'd confide in, and as for her, I imagine she makes a good income from that posing, but what does she do with it? Has she ever come to me? You'd think, having her only brother in the field, she might want some help with investments . . . ah, well, the devil with that. . . . So she shows up at my house on a Sunday afternoon. We have people coming for a buffet later on. The caterers are there—" He broke off in disgust, as if his sister's arrival in itself constituted a shameful spectacle for which he would be despised by his temporary servants.

Whenever Reinhart was on the verge of feeling some sympathy for Blaine, his son immediately relieved him of that obligation.

Blaine resumed: "Luckily the children were upstairs—"

Now Reinhart could not keep silent. "What does that mean, 'luckily'?"

Blaine shot his jaw towards the windshield. "I could just puke! The vicious little . . ." He nobly raised his chin. "So she asks to speak to me privately, and we go into the den, and she tells me she is thinking of moving in with some roommate, which would leave Daddy all alone in the present apartment, and she would continue paying the rent, of course, but wouldn't he be lonely? What was my opinion?"

Blaine flashed his lights to notify the economy car just ahead that he required the road just beyond it, and it obediently moved to the right.

"Well," said he, "I told her straightaway that she could forget about trying to foist the problems onto me, that she might think we had lots of extra room, but we most assuredly do not. We have hardly enough for our own household as it is, and then of course we must entertain people, and we have family responsibilities. Mercer's family is accustomed to having a number of houses at their disposal, if, say, the Boston branch comes for a Midwestern visit in force, and then—"

"Blaine, old chap," Reinhart said, "perish the thought! I wouldn't think of imposing upon you." He could have made it a bitter statement, but he did not: the emotion would have been squandered. And of course it was quite fervently true that he would have moved to Skid Row in preference to living once again in proximity to his son, this time with Blaine as head of household.

"At which," said Blaine, ignoring Reinhart's contribution, "the little hypocrite denied that she had meant that at all, that as the other child I was being merely asked for my advice, et cetera, et cetera." He glanced indignantly at Reinhart. "I realize now that my dear sister has always been the most sinister sneak imaginable. I'll tell you frankly that what I said to her was that I have my own responsibilities in life, that I can't assume any more, but I do think the apartment would be a ridiculous burden on her: I'm sure a smaller place somewhere would suit you fine. Even a nice bright room. Why throw all the money away on anything bigger? You can't use it."

Reinhart made what once was called a happy-go-lucky shrug. "Makes sense," he said blithely.

"I'm happy you agree," said Blaine, nodding at the rushing road ahead. "Well, then, I suddenly got suspicious and I said, 'Winona, I hope that what you're contemplating is not living with a man.

I know that's popular nowadays with certain trashy sorts, but the best people still prefer the traditional ways, and my profession, for one, is very sensitive to such matters. Do you think a man would be very keen to let me invest his money if he knew my sister was living with someone who had no legal attachment to her? Suppose she got pregnant, and her roommate ran off in the classic way? Who would be expected to pay the bills? Forgive me for saying, 'Not her father.' "

"Certainly not!" Reinhart agreed with an enthusiasm that even Blaine took brief, frowning notice of before he went on.

" 'Oh,' said she, goddamn her! 'Oh, you've got no worry about that.' And, ass that I was, I fell right into the trap."

Reinhart could now see the essential cause of Blaine's fury: *he* had always been the clever child, Winona the dope and dupe.

"I insisted on my point, you see," said Blaine, spitting his words now. " 'Don't be too arrogant,' I said. 'No means is foolproof. We weren't ready for our second child when Mercer somehow conceived in spite of never having failed to take measures, and I doubt very much whether you, with your woolly mind, dear sister, could be relied on to'—well, so forth and on and on, and of course, malicious as she is, she gave me enough rope." Here Blaine again showed the tragic mask he had worn on his arrival. "When I was finally ready for the kill, she did it!

" 'Don't worry, Blainey,' said she." He spoke in a falsetto impression of his sister's voice: " 'As it happens, my lover is a woman.' "

Reinhart put his hands over his mouth. For him it had been greatly preferable to hear this information from Winona herself. To have it repeated now by another (and by such another) was excessively dispiriting. He came out to swallow some air.

"It *is* unfortunate," he said, "if you want my opinion. I can't deny that. I doubt whether any person of the standard persuasion really thinks it's *preferable* that someone is homosexual—still less a member of his own family. We can accept it, think it's O.K., anybody's right, not a hanging offense, and all that, and even applaud geniuses like Sappho and Michelangelo and Proust, but would you want your sister to be one? Not in the best of all worlds, probably.

"Then if you're a parent, you wonder about your own contribution, by commission or omission." He winced at his son. "But finally you recognize that whatever else it might be, it is a fact. And most things of a sexual nature have developed naturally, however unnatural they might seem to some. That is, people don't just up and decide to deviate from the norm and against their own will, even in our decadent place and time. They would seem to be impelled by some force or another."

"Hah!" savagely cried Blaine. "So are murderers!"

Reinhart smiled at him. "What keeps striking me as ironic is a memory of ten years ago. As usual we were on the wrong side of the fence from each other, but in a decade we seem to have changed sides. More importantly, and with all respect, your position has always been extreme. If I recall, in those days any person who defied the generally accepted standards of conduct, political, moral, or sexual, was a hero to you, whereas you were ready to shoot anyone identified as conventional. Now sexual inversion is criminally loathsome?"

One thing that was perhaps to be admired about Blaine: despite his emotion his control of the car was flawless. By now, by virtue of the expressway, they were clearing the outermost suburbs of the city, where there had still been fields when Reinhart came home from the War—more than thirty years before. Certain events seemed to remain in an eternal only-yesterday. To wear the clothes of a bygone era was to be in historic costume: pegged pants and padded shoulders were quaintly incredible, but it was still very real to remember the girl who broke one's heart when one was so dressed.

Blaine answered loftily: "I think my gradual change of opinion has made sense. 'Show me a man who's not a radical at twenty, and I'll show you a man with no heart. Show me a man who's still one at forty, and I'll show you a man with no brain.' Or however it goes. I'm not forty, but I am a husband, a father, and I have had a certain success in my profession. I don't want to hit below the belt, but perhaps if I had had—well, no matter."

"I'll go on for you," said Reinhart. "If you had had a father who was like you yourself are now? Well, you did get shortchanged in that way. But consider this: maybe in that event you wouldn't have had the burning desire to make something of yourself; maybe my bad example was as effective as a good one might have been. Think of this: if I were you, *then perhaps you'd be me.* Repulsive thought, eh?" Reinhart was joking bitterly, but speaking for himself, he thought he had got off lucky: there had been a brief period in his life when his goal was to be very like what Blaine was now.

"Look here," Blaine suddenly said in a mercantile sort of voice, "I've come up with a proposition that should put us all in a situation we can live with. Queers are notoriously unreliable. She may assure you that she'll continue to look out for you financially—and sticking up for her as you have, you do have some claim on her good will—but next she'll fall in love with some other female, maybe even a little child. My God, think of that, my sister trailing a Camp Fire Girl into the park!" He made a loathing face. "It's just unthinkable, that dirty, detestable—"

"Hell," said Reinhart, "I wish you wouldn't put me in the position where I have to repeat all that tedious rhetoric of the homosexual apologists: 'alternate life-styles,' et cetera. But I really don't think it's inevitable that a 'gay' person is necessarily an uncontrollable sex fiend merely because he or she prefers his or her own kind."

Blaine showed an odd expression. "I take it you have had a sheltered life in that respect."

Ah, thought Reinhart, you have not, is that it? But he had no wish to explore the subject of Blaine's experience with his fellow man. Reinhart himself had felt the hand of Time upon his shoulder when, some twenty years before, he had sensed that he was at last beyond the range of homosexual solicitation.

"To get back to my proposition," Blaine said. "We've had our differences, you and I, but I have not forgotten that I have an obligation—limited, true enough, but it's there. Also, I'm sure you believe, whether justifiably or not, that you have gotten a dirty deal in life, and maybe you even blame it on me, for all I know."

To this incredible statement Reinhart could only respond: "You?"

"Well, I'm as convenient a scapegoat as any, am I not?" Blaine asked, going into a kind of bass whisper.

There was no reason to take this kind of thing seriously. "I suppose you are, at that," said Reinhart.

The technique proved an effective one for dealing with the most offensive of Blaine's poses. Reinhart must remember that: it frightened Blaine to hear a confirmation of his own exaggerated expression of self-pity.

Blaine hastily said: "I'm willing to let bygones be." He slipped into the righthand lane of the expressway, and Reinhart could see the turn signal blink on the dashboard. Good, they were about to turn around and head back, having accomplished what they usually did with each other: pure and simple nought.

But when Blaine took the next exit and at ramp's end made a choice, he went not south in the direction of urbanity, but rather towards the pastoral north.

"Say," said Reinhart, "aren't we getting pretty far from home for no great purpose?"

"If you'd ever let me explain," Blaine peevishly replied. "I've been trying for the last half-hour to get a word in edgewise. There's a thing our church sponsors—and before you begin to shout me down with atheist opinions, hear me out, please: there are no religious requirements made of anyone."

"When did you ever hear me say a word about atheism?" Reinhart asked in wonderment. His mother used to make such irrelevant charges as a rhetorical device to throw him vis-à-vis off balance.

"So be it," said Blaine. "But knowing how you operate, I'm trying to dispose of all capricious objections beforehand."

"You're taking me to some kind of religious service? I can't say I'm fascinated by the prospect, if that's what you mean. Is this necessary?" A devilish impulse claimed him. "Shall we pray for the salvation of sex deviates?"

Blaine shrank into himself. "Why you fil—" He caught control at the last moment it could still be captured, and coughed violently. "I'm not always prepared for what you call humor, dear Dad," he said in a voice made guttural by resentment, "but *will you let me explain?*"

Reinhart exposed his two palms.

"It's a little Christian community," Blaine said, assuming an expression that suggested sanctity, "on what used to be a farm, what still is a farm, on good, rich Ohio farmland." He showed the kind of smile that is obviously more eloquent to him who produced it than to the innocent bystander. "Clean air, fertile soil, honest labor."

"Are you serious?" Reinhart had never seen his son in this mood, which seemed perilously near the rhapsodic.

"For God's sake, haven't you the remotest shred of decency?" cried Blaine. "Can't you see this isn't easy for me?"

"Sorry," said Reinhart. He tried to contribute to a polite conversation. "It takes a certain kind of person to be a farmer, though, I'm sure. It has never seemed attractive to me."

Blaine suddenly looked too bland to be true. "But have you given it a try? How would you know?" He produced a sly smile. "I thought you always prided yourself on a liberal approach to things."

Reinhart shrugged. "I know enough about my basic tastes. But listen, I'll be glad to buy some home-grown vegetables, if you want to drop in for a minute or two. I just don't want to stay too long, because I have a feeling Winona might get home meanwhile and want to talk." He frowned. "But wait a minute: they wouldn't have fresh produce yet at this time of year. We're just getting into spring." He put the rest of it together, and peered at Blaine. "You're not proposing that I be installed at this farm, are you? Put out to pasture with the other old fogies? . . . Your point is that if Winona ceases to support me, as you fear she might, if as expected she abandons herself utterly to unnatural pursuits, I can't count on you. But I have already accepted that fact. Why elaborate on it?"

Blaine pulled the car onto the shoulder of the road, adjacent to a wire fence. In the middle distance was a group of cows, an animal of which Reinhart could not remember having seen an example at close range since he was a child. In college he had read a passage in Nietzsche casting doubt on the possibility that the beast of the field could ever explain its serenity to a human being. "Tell me why you're happy," says the man. The animal would like to answer, "Because I forget," but the creature forgets even this before it can reply, and the would-be dialogue comes to nothing.

"What concerns me, *Dad,* is that at fifty-four years of age you have no profession, no occupation, no means of support, and no property, and if you would ever have to go it alone, I can't see how you could survive without going on welfare."

Reinhart stretched his long frame. "These land-cruisers really are more comfortable than cars that make sense," said he. "You simply can't get away from that truth. . . . That's not beside the point, Blainey: long before it was fashionable, I hated big cars, probably because I couldn't afford one. But the funny thing now is that, without benefit of a movement, I am liberated from all sorts of restraints, including those I have imposed on myself. It was ridiculous that I lived almost half a century trying to measure up to the principles of other people." He smiled with genuine good feeling. "The fact is that I love to cook, and I am really good at it. I know you don't agree, but the reason for that is, gastronomically speaking, you're naïve. Not wrong, but childish. Your diet consists of essentially one kind of meat and three or four vegetables, whereas almost everything that lives can be eaten by a human being, and in fact *is* eaten somewhere in the world."

Blaine was sneering at the dashboard. "You could be kidding yourself. What does *she* eat of that gourmet stuff? And what else do you do? Mop the floors? Do the laundry?"

"Whatever has to be done. But the cooking is the center of it. I don't suppose I can ever explain to someone like you what that means: you who spurn Bordelaise sauce and drench your steak with A•1."

Blaine said levelly: "But you'll admit that whatever I eat, I buy myself." He sighed, and then pulled the car onto the road and accelerated. "You're not in an independent position. I want you to take a look at this place."

Reinhart could see that Blaine was determined, and he really didn't want to get into a downright quarrel with his son. Therefore he submitted quietly to being driven some few miles farther on and eventually up a dirt road, to a cluster of farmhouse and out-buildings, the former a shabby white and the barn and sheds the traditional faded red. The vehicles in view were routine automobiles, two of them the worse for wear, with dents and rust and jagged antenna-stems. Farm machines and/or beasts of burden were presumably behind closed doors, as was the local humanity. Reinhart remembered it was Sunday, the most inopportune time (for all concerned) to traffic with persons of sincere religious conviction, Christians anyway.

"Perhaps we're intruding."

"Nonsense," said Blaine. He parked his opulent car alongside the rusting heaps and stepped out. The parking place would have been an extravagance of mud if any rain had fallen lately. Fortunately the moment was windless and the dust lay passive. The buildings seen from closer up looked none too sturdy, but the paint was not flaking badly, and the windows of the house were clean, and the roof was still there.

"Your church sponsors this?" Reinhart asked. Obviously they spared great expense. Blaine belonged to a prosperous Episcopalian flock at which the lesser breeds might sneer, with the encouragement of the needle's-eye metaphor, but there seemed no actual law that would forbid a rich man from being devout.

Blaine stepped up to his father and stared defiantly at him. "These folks *are* very religious. *I* don't make fun of them, though I might not agree in all respects."

Reinhart glanced at the farmhouse. No one stirred there. "You're an odd one, Blaine. I'd say this would be one of the last places to find you."

Changes in those close to you are generally phases in a long and slow process, so that at any point the other person seems routine enough. But in his later adolescence Blaine had without warning, almost within a day, become what for simplicity's sake was known, to anyone who was himself not one, as a "hippie." It was hard to remember that when one looked at him today. Even on a Sunday afternoon in early spring he wore an orthodox shirt and a foulard necktie, a gray suit, and black shoes in the old-fashioned wing-tipped style. Like his father he had fair hair, but Reinhart's now was actually longer and lighter, though at one time Blaine had bleached his hair and worn it shoulder-length. Once Reinhart had vengefully crept into his son's room when Blaine was asleep and sheared away his golden locks just below the ears. They had both changed since those days.

"I know you think me the young fogy," Blaine said now, "but you might be surprised to learn that my values have been more or less the same all my life."

"Uh-huh."

"For example," Blaine went on, "I have always had the greatest respect for those with faith."

"You have?" Reinhart asked incredulously.

"Mock me if you will," said his son, staring in defiance, "but that was really what I was groping for in the Sixties, with so little help from you: faith in the essential goodness of humanity. Perhaps we were naïve, but at least we were searching."

Reinhart indicated the porch of the farmhouse, which only now he noticed was sagging ever so slightly. "Shouldn't we proceed with whatever we've come here for?"

Blaine shook his head. "I'm trying to prepare you. These people may have something of merit if you'll just be patient."

"O.K., O.K! Though it does nothing for my patience to stand here in this bleak parking lot." Reinhart walked to the porch and mounted the steps.

Blaine hastened to overtake his father, who perhaps he feared might disgrace him even among down-at-the-heels religious zealots.

While they were still approaching the door it was opened from within by a small woman of indeterminate age, i.e., she might have been anywhere from prematurely seasoned forties to well-preserved sixties. She wore a workman's outfit of blue-denim trousers and jacket and a shirt of chambray.

"High-dee-ho," she said cheerily. "I'm Sister Muriel."

Blaine quickly said: "This is my father, Carl Reinhart."

"God loves you, Carl," said Sister Muriel, but in a lackluster monotone that contrasted with the first phase of her greeting.

Reinhart nodded in neutral courtesy. Time was, he responded to everybody with classic Midwestern amiability, but somewhere along the line he recognized this as either hypocrisy or folly, an invitation to either bores or crooks, and he adopted his current style.

"If you'd like to make your contribution now," said Sister Muriel, "then there won't be any awkwardness inside."

Blaine formed his lips in an *O* even before he patted his pockets.

Again, in the old days Reinhart would guiltily have whipped out his wallet, but now he showed more patience. "Contribution?" he asked. "For what?"

Sister Muriel sighed and looked at the ceiling of the porch. Meanwhile Blaine slipped inside the door. Reinhart then splayed his right hand.

"After you," he said to Sister Muriel.

"Not without a contribution, brother!" she said with force.

But he could no longer so easily be lured into a cul-de-sac. "Heavens above!" he murmured, raising and lowering his hands and eyes, until he had dizzied her. Then he followed his son indoors.

The interior of the house was for some reason darker than it should have been in daytime—and with hardly any furniture, rugs, or curtains to absorb light. Reinhart followed Blaine through several small, dark, empty rooms until they reached the kitchen, which in old-farmhouse style was of a generous size. It was also, uniquely, furnished: a large wooden table and chairs occupied the center of the room, and along the walls were stove and fridge, sink and cabinets.

A few living souls, representing either sex and dressed much like Sister Muriel (who had remained behind as front-door Cerberus), were either in the kitchen proper or on the screened-in porch just beyond. The youngest seemed in late middle age and none was moving with purpose. They ignored the Reinharts.

Blaine went onto the porch, his father following. The old folks there were also oblivious to them, in the usual passive manner and not necessarily as a positive statement of scorn: they ignored one another in the same fashion.

Reinhart opened the screen door that led to the yard, and he and Blaine went out. The yard was a desolate place, as dusty as where they had parked the car, though, according to the indoor precedent, neat by reason of being devoid of objects.

Suddenly a door in the earth was flung open—half of a double-paneled entrance to a cellar, set almost horizontally against the house wall—and a tall, solemn person mounted deliberately to the upper world on the unseen, sunken steps. Whether or not he was being intentionally mythological—Pluto visiting the surface of the earth—it was a dramatic entrance, or, looking at it in another way, exit. That he was of the race called, according to the era, colored, Negro, or black was as always worthy of note as well as being conspicuous.

Not to mention that Reinhart thought he recognized him as the son of his old friend, now deceased, Splendor Mainwaring. When last seen, a decade earlier, Raymond had been involved with a militant group called the Black Assassins and had himself answered to the name Captain Storm. In ten years (if indeed it was he) he had got a bit thinner and his expression was no longer a fixed scowl. He too was dressed in blue denims.

"High-dee-ho," he said to Blaine.

Once again Blaine introduced his father. "Dad, this is Brother Valentine."

"God loves you, Carl," said the black man, and he showed Reinhart a pious smirk. He was not quite so burnished-handsome as he had been when displaying ritualistic malevolence towards those deficient in melanin, but perhaps that was only an effect of age.

Reinhart asked: "Aren't you Raymond Mainwaring?"

"I was once many things," said Brother Valentine, his eyes disappearing behind his upper lids, "rapist, addict, hooligan, blasphemer, traitor, mocker of the right, defamer of the good." His voice swelled with feeling, and for a moment it sounded as if he might produce an outright yodel. But suddenly he spoke in a quiet, level voice: "Praise *Gee*-zuz."

"Well," said Reinhart, at something of a loss for a response (whether to congratulate or commiserate). He decided to ignore the whole business. Instead he said: "I suppose you don't remember me? I was a close friend of your father's."

Brother Valentine had not yet looked directly at Reinhart, and he did not do so at this moment: he stared between the white men, towards the empty yard, beyond which was an empty field. "I hope," he said at last, "you are still a friend of your Father. For He is a friend to you." He managed very clearly to represent the capital letters.

"I hope so," said Reinhart, who had no wish to mock anyone's faith, but "friendship" was hardly the word to characterize adequately his own association with divinity.

"Brother Valentine," Blaine said, "I hope this was a convenient time to come. My father insisted." Alas, Reinhart was too far away to kick him.

Valentine's style seemed by now pretty well confirmed as being one that took as little note of others as it could get away with. Thus he made no answer, direct or implied, to Blaine's false statement, which of course was no less than Blaine deserved.

"I was a fiend incarnate," he cried, his voice swelling again, "a minion of Satan. I even befouled Old Glory. No vileness did I spurn."

Reinhart nodded and walked near Blaine. "Why did you bring me here?"

"Brother Valentine," Blaine said, leaving Reinhart's vicinity, "is it not true that newcomers are welcome to your little flock?"

Valentine narrowed his eyes and dropped the subject of his own evil past. "We erect no artificial barriers. On the other hand, no one has a special privilege. Each must contribute what he can, in the spirit of Christian America. God bless you, brother."

Ten years back, Raymond had been of the "burn, baby, burn" school, but then we all change from time to time according to our challenges and opportunities, and Reinhart did not find him ipso facto a rogue.

"Thank you for your hospitality," he said. "This has been very interesting." He was about to walk away, irrespective of Blaine, when Valentine at last displayed a squint of recognition.

"Brother Reinhart!" cried the black man. "Forgive me. Oh, God love you." He spoke to Blaine: "I used to call this dear man Uncle Carl."

This was utter fantasy. In truth Reinhart had seen nothing of Raymond's father during those years when the boy would have been small enough to attract the avuncular. He had known Splendor just after World War II, and then not again until the man lay dying, twenty years later. At that time Raymond had been altogether hostile to any white man.

Blaine looked sharply at his wristwatch and then gave a too casual glance at his father. "I can see you've lots of old times to exchange. Why don't I just run a couple of errands meanwhile and pick you up on the way back?"

But Reinhart blocked his route of escape. "I wouldn't think of letting you work on the day of rest! Am I right, Brother Valentine?"

The latter gave him a look that was both knowing and wary.

"Quite so, brother, quite so."

Blaine whined sotto voce: "We've got people coming . . ."

Reinhart said to Valentine: "We can't stay long, but since we're here, would you like to give us the tour?"

"No," surprisingly said Splendor's son, "because if you've come through the house, you've seen as much as there is to see. Upstairs are the dormitories, and underneath is a cellar. We haven't been here long enough to do much but clean the living quarters."

"You have me at a disadvantage," said Reinhart. "I don't quite grasp what it is you're doing here."

"This," said Brother Valentine, "is Paradise Farm." He spoke as if the name were familiar to all: if not, it would be the worst of taste to admit one's ignorance of it.

Reinhart offered: "An experiment in communal living?"

Valentine gestured grandly towards the fields. He had a style that rose above the blue denims: ten years of age had given him more force of presence than he had displayed in the SS type of uniform favored by the Black Assassins.

"Waves of purple grain," said he, "soon enough. God will provide an abundant harvest for His chosen people."

Reinhart sucked a tooth. "You're Jews?"

"Metaphorically," said Brother Valentine, "in the sense of the Judaism that is the basis of judiciousness, which leads to good judgment."

"Judge not, lest ye, and so on," said Reinhart, giving back as good as he was being given: Raymond was mocking him now.

Brother Valentine suddenly understood this. "People of weak imagination and feeble drive must be given a mystique," said he, "rather than a rationale that they are incapable of entertaining. Therefore we have certain slogans and *façons de parler*. You will despise them, but be tolerant: they are needed, I assure you."

"Raymond—uh, Brother Valentine," Reinhart said, "you'll forgive me, I'm sure, but needed for what?"

"For God's work," said the black man. "We shall restore and revitalize this fallow farm, and in so doing bring some human souls back from the dead."

Reinhart put his hands in the pockets of his blazer and kicked idly at the dust. "Those souls inside the house?"

"Oh, don't they look like much?" Valentine asked this with sufficient self-righteousness to shame Reinhart.

"No, of course I don't mean that. But aren't they a bit too old to do heavy farm labor? I hasten to say that I would consider myself over the hill for something like that."

"Brother Reinhart," said Valentine, "the people you see in the kitchen at the moment are not my entire flock. The younger folk are out in the fields, at work. Your earlier concern for the day of rest was well voiced, insofar as it concerned the world of routine commerce and excess consumption. But here, at Paradise, we toil only for our daily bread."

Reinhart still could not decide whether the man was sincere or a charlatan, but most enterprises since the Renaissance have necessarily partaken of both the honest and the bogus in equal amounts to preserve the balance known as modern civilization, and a project that managed to do no more than sway, without tipping, could survive at least for a while.

A certain void in the corner of the eye told Reinhart that his son had taken French leave. He excused himself. Trotting around the corner of the house, he saw that Blaine indeed was already behind the wheel of the Continental.

"No, you don't!" He moved himself to block the projected backing-up. At length Blaine climbed out in disgruntlement.

"Stop pretending that I am trying to dump you here. Honestly, Dad."

"Don't worry about it, Blaine. You won't succeed."

Valentine appeared. "Might I urge you to stay for supper?"

"I'm afraid not," said Reinhart, who regretted having to turn the invitation down: the food was certain to be interesting. "My son has an engagement." He looked around. "I assume you have more sleeping accommodations in the barn?"

Brother Valentine inclined his head ever so slightly, perhaps in assent. "I was really hoping you could stay for a meal. We could dine a bit earlier than usual if that's the problem."

Reinhart remembered he had eaten nothing all day since his coffee and toast on arising. The thought of the poached eggs, now chilled, was attractive: he might even take the time to inundate them in aspic, postponing the meal until the shimmering amber jelly was firm, then plunging through it to pierce and release the yolks, a rich, cool, golden cream; this on a bed of Boston lettuce. Followed by what? A chop or cutlet? Hmm . . . Meanwhile he answered Valentine.

"I'm afraid we just can't, but thank you for the invitation. Perhaps another time. I'll be back later on to see how you're doing here. Maybe you'll have some extra garden vegetables to sell?"

Brother Valentine threw back his head. "We'll have fresh eggs," said he, "and frying chickens. Milk warm from the teat, if that's your pleasure, and farm-made cheese, butter from the churn. Bread from our own wheat, ground in our own mill, baked in our ovens. Country hams from our hogs, steaks from our steers, legs of lambs from our own flock, scallopini from our calves. We'll have a lake yonder, stocked with fish. A peach orchard and a vineyard. We'll make beer, cider, and wines. We'll grind and stuff our own sausages, flavored with our own herbs and spices. We'll put up vegetables and make jams, relishes, and chutneys."

Blaine was wrinkling his nose in boredom. Reinhart realized suddenly that his son had probably never really liked food: there were people like that. For himself he could listen for hours to lists of provender. He reluctantly put out his hand.

"It's been a great pleasure to see you again, Raymond. Yours is a wonderful vision. I hope you're able to realize it." He decided to produce a piece of wisdom. "That's the only thing that seems to make sense by now: to *make* something, or anyway try to. I wish you well."

Brother Valentine's face was working in a strange way. Finally he burst out in desperation: "The thing is, I haven't eaten since yesterday. I was wondering whether you might be good for a Big Mac."

"There's a McDonald's close by?" Reinhart could think of no other prompt response: he had been taken utterly by surprise.

"Look," Valentine said, shrugging, "anything'd be O.K. Burger King, Colonel Sanders, Arthur Treacher's Fish and Chips, Dairy Queen . . . they're all within a mile."

"O.K., Blaine?" Reinhart asked. "Can you spare a few minutes for this errand of mercy?" He turned back to Valentine. "I'm sure he can. Come on."

But Raymond né Mainwaring shook his head. "It would make a bad impression if I were seen leaving at this moment, when there's a certain *crise de nerfs* around here. If you could just drop the burgers off on your way back, with perhaps some fries and Cokes and—"

"You don't mean—"

"Well, now, I can't very well eat in front of all this hungry folk, can I?" Raymond asked indignantly.

"So that's food for how many?"

"The young field workers are due back soon." Raymond closed his eyes for calculations. "Say a couple dozen portions of everything, whatever you get."

"I've got about seven dollars," said Reinhart. "About seventy would be required. Blaine, what are you carrying?"

His son snorted. "A dirty handkerchief," he cried, plunged back into the Continental, and started the engine. Reinhart feared that his own body and Valentine's would no longer prove a deterrent to Blaine's callous getaway, and lest they disappear under the wide trunk of the enormous car, which was already vibrating with power under slim restraint, he drew the black man aside. "This is one of those crazy things," he said. "Because we can't afford to feed you all, you all will go hungry. There's some basic flaw in all communal efforts. I wish I had the answer."

Brother Valentine stared at him for a moment. Reinhart would have been at a loss to say what emotion was being felt by the man.

"All right," Splendor's son said finally, turning away. "You'll see: we'll have something fine here."

CHAPTER
4

"Grace? Carl Reinhart."

"Yes, Carl?"

"I'll accept your offer."

"Eight A.M. tomorrow, my office," said Grace. "Know how to get there?" Obviously she wouldn't waste time telling him if he knew already.

"Glenwood, in the industrial park, isn't it? I can find it."

"See you there," said Grace. She seemed especially abrupt even for her. He wondered unhappily if he had called her away from some intimate moment with Winona.

He hung up the pay phone and returned to the car in which Blaine sat impatiently revving the engine.

"I don't regret having gone to the farm," said Reinhart. "Raymond—Brother Valentine—is an enterprising fellow. Seeing him reminded me that I really did consider his father a good friend. I do want to keep in touch. The results will no doubt be disappointing, but I like the idea he is trying to do something on that order."

Blaine said: "Look, if worst comes to worst, I may be able to find something for you at the office. Speaking of blacks, they nowadays won't do custodial work."

"Have I translated that correctly?" Reinhart asked. "You'll put me on as janitor?"

"Dad," Blaine said slowly, turning back to stare briefly into the hub of the steering wheel, "you can't *do* anything. You have no skills." He threw his head back. "God, that's the kind of thing one should be saying to some high-school dropout and not to a man of fifty-four."

"Look, old boy, I have a confession to make," Reinhart said, clapping his son on the shoulder, a blow from which Blaine recoiled slightly, in an instinctive pretense that it was given with malicious intent. This was too quick to be studied. Their basic enmity, at least from Blaine's point of view, was profound. "I've got a job. You don't have to worry about me."

Blaine pulled away from the curb. They were more than halfway home, already in the outskirts of the city, when his father had asked him to stop at the outdoor telephone. "Please," he said, "don't bother to spin fantasies for my sake. Don't waste the effort."

Foolishly, Reinhart was stung by the implication that he was lying. "All right," said he, "you just ask Grace Greenwood. I start tomorrow. I'm going to demonstrate food products."

"You're going to work for Winona's *girl friend?*" Blaine asked incredulously. "You're trading your daughter to an old dyke *for a job?*"

"Remember ten years or so ago, when you were always able to get a rise out of me?" Reinhart asked calmly. "That was the era for that sort of thing, the baiting of the older by the younger. It was especially offensive because people of my generation had always believed they held nothing more sacred than the welfare of their children. To find that the children disagreed with this conviction was devastating. Now we have come to a time when a son can accuse his father of being a pimp for his homosexual daughter—and the father, shameless as he is, fails even to be insulted by the accusation." Reinhart shook his head and spoke really to himself: "Now you can see why I have submerged myself in cooking—food is really kinder than people."

Blaine drove the remaining blocks in silence, chewing his thin underlip. In profile he somewhat resembled his maternal grandfather, Blaine Raven, a penniless snob, a disbarred lawyer, and a man who had never been sober for the last twenty years of life; the day finally came when once too often he fell into bed, lighted cigar in clenched teeth, and burned himself alive. Reinhart's son was not so good-looking as his grandfather. Neither, in all fairness, could he be said to resemble him in much else but snobbery.

Blaine Reinhart, his father had to admit, was far from being all bad. Notwithstanding his "radical" youth he had got good grades in college and had remained to take his degree, which was more than could be said for Reinhart, who had dropped out of school to support his wife, who was pregnant with—Blaine. How strange could be the most banal of life's sequences.

When Blaine pulled up before the apartment house he had obviously come to a decision. Not unkindly in manner, he looked at his father.

"I'm sure you won't believe this, but for years I've actually been your defender against a Certain Person."

"Your mother," Reinhart said.

Blaine blinked gravely. "No sarcasm, please! The point is that in recent years I've got some sense of what a male human being is faced with."

This philosophical temper was a new one for Blaine—at least in his father's experience. He seemed to expect something. Reinhart therefore shrugged inscrutably.

But Blaine made an unpleasant expression and turned his head. "What's the use?"

Reinhart said: "Blaine, will you please go ahead with your statement? I'm not resisting you, believe me."

Blaine peered at his father and said slowly, suspiciously: "Women can't always understand the pressures on us."

"Good heavens," Reinhart said, "you're becoming a chip off the old block—if you'll forgive the insult. But the irony is that times seem to have changed in that regard, too, and I suppose so have I. The female propaganda, like the black and all the others, has got really tedious, and like them all it is at least half lie, but one useful thing to have learned from it, maybe, is that *no one* understands the pressures on *anyone* else, irrespective of sex. Beyond that, I don't want to think again in this lifetime about those psychosocial bromides. Surely this is the most boring era in the history of the race!" He moved to open his side of the car, then turned back. "I couldn't interest you in an exquisite dish of eggs-in-aspic, could I?"

Though distracted, Blaine managed to reject this invitation with a hideous grimace before going on to prove that he would disregard his father's statement as well: "What do they know?"

"Son," said Reinhart, "are you trying to tell me something?"

Blaine instantly drew back, asking coldly: "What does that mean?"

"I don't have a clue," said Reinhart, almost guiltily. "Forgive me. I thought maybe you wanted to talk about something personal."

"If I did," Blaine answered, "I would hardly—"

"To hell with you." Reinhart opened the door. "I'm not going to listen to another insult."

Blaine set a precedent here. He slid to the passenger's side and caught the door as Reinhart flung it to. "Wait a minute, Dad," he cried. "I didn't mean it the way you thought."

Reinhart turned back, but Blaine simply stared at him through the window of the Lincoln as he slowly closed its door.

"Do you have anything more to say at this time, Blaine?" He wondered whether anyone else ever had such a son.

"Why haven't I *ever* been able to talk to you?" This was wailed with no apparent bitterness, simply in helpless incomprehension.

"The answer to that, son," said Reinhart, "was supplied by a Roman named Virgil, if I remember my Comparative Lit: 'There are tears in things.' "

As he expected, the response got them both over a bad moment. Blaine, who in whatever phase despised literature, leaped back to the driver's seat and positively sped away.

Reinhart felt rotten about this, but probably less so than if they had continued to talk. It seemed likely that Blaine had a problem with his wife, but how to deal with him when whatever one said was taken as an attack?

The doorman on this shift was a large middle-aged Negro of a vanishing breed regardless of race: the competent professional servitor. But he had either misidentified Reinhart early on or mocked him, for some reason, in an honorific style.

"Good afternoon, Colonel." The doorman opened one panel of the double glass portal.

"Hi, Andrew. It's a lovely day, isn't it?"

"Clement, Colonel, very clement." Except for the use of the undeserved title, Andrew was a specialist in the *mot juste*, another earmark of the now rare specimen. Brother Valentine's father had been that sort of guy. Reinhart was suddenly the prisoner of an exquisitely painful nostalgia as he traversed the gleaming, arid lobby and entered the stainless-steel cubicle, which presently lifted him to the fourth floor.

He turned his key in the lock and opened the door of the apartment. Ah, Winona was home. Her keys and change purse lay on the little foyer table, and he could smell a flowery scent. Another thing done by cooking was, so to speak, to hone the nose. His daughter stuck to no special perfume for long: she had access to many.

He called her name.

After a long moment her closed bedroom door opened a crack. "Daddy?"

"The very man," said Reinhart. "May I fix us a bite of supper?"

"Gee, I don't think I can eat anything more today." Winona opened the door sufficiently wide to display her head. No doubt she was changing clothes for the nth time. In answer to Reinhart's cluck-cluck of dismay she quickly added: "I ate a while ago. Honestly!"

"O.K. Want to talk?"

Winona let her head sink. "I'm dog-tired at the moment, Dad. Do you mind?"

"Of course not! But I do think you'll be interested: I took the job with Grace."

Something came and went in her eyes. "Oh."

"So everything's O.K. now, dear."

But Winona was not responding in an appropriate way. Reinhart amplified his statement: "I'll have an income, you see." He realized that he had not even asked Grace about the salary. "I'm going back into the world. You don't have to take care of me any more."

Winona looked at him with feeling. She quickly made some manipulations behind the door and emerged, wearing a white terry-cloth bathrobe.

Reinhart said: "Nothing lasts forever, darling. We've had many good years." This was beginning to sound like the divorce-of-still-good-friends, which one heard about from time to time but which was always allegedly corrupted by the greed of the respective lawyers. Reinhart's proper marriage had been sundered under conditions of maximum hatred between the principals.

Winona came to him. "If that means you're leaving, then all right." Her eyes glistened. "But I'm not going anywhere."

Reinhart backed away two steps. "You're not going to be Grace's roommate?" He had a bizarre feeling that he could not identify: a kind of dread, intermixed with pleasure, whereas of course he should simply have been overjoyed.

"That's the last place I'd go!"

"This is none of my business. But do I gather you two have had a disagreement?"

Winona produced a negative expression that, for the first time in Reinhart's experience, suggested her blood-tie to her brother, whom ordinarily she resembled not at all. But then her own basic nature reasserted itself. She smiled the old generous Winona smile.

"It's just personal," she said blithely, and hugged herself with crossed arms. "I'm sure the job offer still stands. She's very reliable in her profession. I'll say that for her."

Reinhart had no experience with quarrels between lovers of the same sex. It was a widespread assumption that male homophiles could be violent in their intramural disagreements, but who had ever known a certified les— That word had not grown easier to use throughout the day, and in fact he could not understand why the persons to whom it applied did not denounce it as abusive.

"Look—" he began, but Winona suddenly flounced past him.

"Maybe I *will* have something to eat!" she cried, and went towards the kitchen.

He suspected that her energy was false, but Winona's deceptions were invariably of kind intent.

They went in tandem as far as the dining room, which, he had forgotten, was still set for the brunch that never took place. He had put away the food, but from the unrewarding task of dealing in cold china and cutlery he had been distracted by the claims of life.

When he saw the table now, he enjoyed a momentary fantasy in which time was reversed and the entire afternoon lay virginally before him: Winona and Grace had never met, the latter was still his "date," his eggs were hot from the simmer.

Winona obviously had her own emotion on seeing three place-settings. She could no longer dissimulate.

"So after making my decision, I called her up," she said, in a voice so raspy with emotion that Reinhart would not have recognized it on the telephone. "And who answered?" She balled her fists. "Someone else was there already! So much for her friendship! I waited a little too long to come around, obviously, so she made other arrangements!" Winona's face, contorted as it was, had returned to childhood. She had looked like that when given the slip by her friends at the movies: only yesterday to Reinhart. He had supposed the current era an improvement until now.

She would have run from the room had he not seized her.

"Do you know how many reasonable explanations there could be for that?" He pressed her hands in his. "Wrong number, for one."

But for the first time in her life Winona rejected his consoling. "Oh, Daddy," she said, pulling away, "how could you possibly understand? The things are all so different. You've got to keep always ahead. You can't be reasonable and find excuses: you can't even just simply accept apologies. You either run things or are run by them. You can't *ever* be in the wrong."

"And you think that's different? You think you're unique?" He dropped her hands. "Isn't that the way everything works, for everybody?"

"I don't know."

"Yes, you do," Reinhart said. "Every living thing already knows everything it needs to know: how to succeed, how to fail, how to survive, and how to perish. Sometimes we pretend we don't know, but we know all right. The older I get, the more I realize that nothing is a genuine surprise." He squinted at her. "And what was the decision you had made about Grace? Were you going to move in with her or not?"

"Not," Winona said defiantly.

"Well, there you are. Perhaps she anticipated that."

She raised her chin. "Oh, no. Nobody does that to me. They wait, you see. *I* decide what's what."

Reinhart had done his best to postpone the recognition of a much more shocking discovery than that which merely pertained to Winona's sexual character. But he could no longer cope in this situation without admitting that his gentle, sweet, and yielding daughter, the very model of passivity, could be a tyrant to others. It was of course she who had dominated Grace Greenwood, not the reverse. And why not? *She* was the beauty. He could even feel a fatherly pride! *My daughter leads a powerful executive around by the nose—in fact, the same person's my boss. Does it matter that she too is a woman?*

"Of course there's no question now that I'll take the job," he said.

She looked carefully at him. "Dad, I hope you know I wouldn't say this if I thought it wouldn't be good for you: I really want you to take it. And if you think she got the idea to please me or something, you're wrong. She was already looking for somebody who would fill the bill. When she heard about you she was interested, but she was really sold by meeting you and seeing for herself that you have a marvelous personality. You're just the kind of person who can charm the pants off those housewives."

Reinhart felt himself blush. The image was almost indecent for a man of his years—and also exciting, of course. But that his daughter should conjure it up was unsettling, even though she. . . . He asked himself a wretched question: Was she now exempt from the usual rules that governed the association of daughter and father?

"Yes," he said sardonically, "I'm notorious for driving women wild. Your mother could tell you that."

"Oh," said Winona, "by the way, Mother's back in town." She ran her fingers along the lapels of her terry-cloth robe, as if this were information which he could accept casually.

There were days on which one was hit with everything at once. "Has she got in touch with you?"

"Blaine told me."

"That's more than he told *me*. I spent some of the afternoon with him. I understand you saw him earlier." At her look he said quickly: "I think it's great that you two have got closer!"

"Huh?" The comment seemed to startle her. "Oh, yeah. Well, anyway, I thought I should warn you."

"Thanks," Reinhart said, "it *is* helpful. But you know I can't decently discuss your mother with either you or Blaine. . . ." He went into the kitchen, but turned in the doorway. "If she's 'back in town,' then it's more than a visit?"

"I don't know. That's all he said. We were talking about other subjects."

Reinhart said: "I really shouldn't say much about your brother, either, Winona, but I hope you're not too hurt if he isn't always as sympathetic as he should be."

"Funny you say that now. He's nicer these days than he has ever been in all my life! I don't like to be cynical, but I do wonder if that's because of his trouble."

" 'Trouble'?"

She raised her hands. "I shouldn't have said that. He asked me not to. Gee."

"Better go the rest of the way, dear, as long as I know there's something I'm not supposed to know." Funny the way that sometimes works out: the precise details are often anticlimactic.

"Mercer has left him."

Reinhart repeated this, again with a purpose to get past the worst moment. How much of life passes in this fashion!

"So that's what he meant, poor devil," he said mostly to himself, with reference to Blaine's cryptic remarks about women. "God, how rotten for him." He pulled a chair from the dining-room table and sat down. "Did she take the children?"

"No. She simply took off." Winona shook her head. "He'd die if he thought I told you."

"Yes, and isn't *that* awful?" Reinhart made a doleful sound. "I wish I knew some way to earn his trust, but this has been a lifelong thing. . . . Your mother has come to look after the kids, then? I hope they get fed properly." He was as scrupulous as he could be when speaking of Genevieve in front of Winona; therefore two truths went unuttered. One, Genevieve was responsible for Blaine's distrust of him in the first place; the situation had no hope of being improved if she was nearby to feed her son more poison. Two, Genevieve was an even viler cook, when she deigned to prepare food at all, than his late mother, whose only culinary technique had been frying-to-ash. Indeed, it had been the combination of these two women, between whom he had spent more than four decades, that drove him into the kitchen. "So you saw her then?"

"Mother—or Mercer?"

"The former," said Reinhart. "Had she already arrived at Blaine's house?"

"She was upstairs, I think. She didn't come down. Maybe she didn't know I was there."

"And you didn't go up?"

"No."

Winona had never enunciated her precise feeling towards her mother, but it was unlikely to have been excessively warm: ten years before, she had readily chosen to live with Reinhart.

"I wonder how the shop will run without her." Genevieve was manager of a dress shop in Chicago. Blaine kept him apprised of her career. She had started out, in the late Sixties, in a local boutique. She and Reinhart, Blaine and Winona, had all lived as a family at that time, and it was Genevieve who supported them, Reinhart having lately suffered the last of his failures in business. He also slept alone: Gen's favors went to her boss, one Harlan Flan, a boutique-chain tycoon in his early thirties. When she divorced Reinhart, however, Flan not only failed to marry her: he coldly dumped her altogether. Reinhart had fitted this story together from various bits and surmises, but the pity was that he got no comfort from it—unless indeed the consolation was that he had thereby been proved to be not a spiteful man.

Genevieve had subsequently emigrated to Chicago, where according to Blaine she had made a new and successful life for herself. Unfortunately, the last five years of their life together had been so bitter as to color Reinhart's memory of that earlier time when he at least had been happily married.

But "normal" life was long gone for him; Blaine's was the case at hand.

"You know," he said to Winona, "for him Mercer has always been more than a wife: she's the proof he has bettered himself socially. It gives him a lot of private satisfaction. And no doubt he is helped professionally. His in-laws are all in the financial world."

"I feel sorry for him," Winona said. "When he gets to feeling bad enough to call me for sympathy—"

"It was he who called you?"

"This morning when you were showering, I guess—but as I say, he doesn't want you to know anyhow."

It really was disgusting of Blaine, despite his anguish, to pretend that Winona had sought *him* out to reveal her sexual orientation.

Reinhart decided to be candid about this. "He did say you had been to see him. I was wondering, Winona, why you decided at this time to tell him about your personal life."

She smiled. "I thought it might make him feel better about himself."

Reinhart rubbed his chin. "Better?"

"I've known my brother all my life. It always makes him feel great to think he's got something on you. Besides, what other help could I give him?"

She really was one in a million. "Have I told you lately," said Reinhart, "how much I love you?"

She made a pshawing sort of wave and left the room.

He was about to remove Grace Greenwood's place-setting, at long last, when the telephone rang. There was a wall-mounted apparatus just inside the kitchen door. When Winona was home he never touched the phone unless she was bathing; all calls were for her.

The bell now continued its spasmodic jangle. He came around the corner of the dining ell and shouted her name. No answer. Either she had slipped out or she was distracted in some fashion. He seized the instrument that was on the table near the front door.

For a moment there was no response to his hello. Then the connection was broken without a word. That sort of thing always gave him the willies.

He went to look for Winona. The door to her room was closed again.

He spoke in the hallway. "I think I'll make some fresh tomato soup, dear. Remember how you used to love Campbell's when you were a child?" He had always made the canned version with milk. Winona's practice had been heavily to butter a handful of saltines and press them one by one into the liquid, crushing them with the back of her spoon, until her bowl contained a thick pink mush.

There had been more calories in that dish than she consumed in an entire day now.

She made no answer to his announcement. She had probably gone to bed. It was not a simple matter for him to accept the simple explanation: that she had been unlucky in love.

CHAPTER
5

Reinhart had been outfitted with a long two-tiered white enamel table on wheels. On one level or another were implements of the *batterie de cuisine:* copper chafing dish, virgin pots and pans in bright chrome, a two-ring hot plate, a food processor, a portable mixer, and various smaller tools including that manually operated essential, the long-handled wooden spoon, invented no doubt by the original cave-chef for the stirring of aurochs-tail soup.

This unit was placed in the far northeast corner of the Top Shop supermarket in the Glenwood Mall, in a situation routinely occupied by the rack for day-old bakery products and the bin for damaged canned and boxed goods. The corner was the most remote in the store, the checkouts being diametrically in the ultimate southwest. But the manager, an elongated, even stringy sort of man with a chin that suggested inherent aggrievement, insisted that no other position was available: i.e., the cable that brought power to the electrical devices could here be deployed with least danger to the customers.

But it was obvious that Mr. DePau cared little for the project, which he tolerated only because of Grace Greenwood's arrangements with the higher authority in the headquarters of the Top Shop chain.

"Frankly," he said to Reinhart on the latter's arrival that morning, before the store was open to the public, "the gourmet shelf does not move, and it is my contention that it won't."

"That's why Epicon is trying this angle," said Reinhart. "There *is* a big interest in this country for fine cooking, and—"

"Look here," DePau said impatiently. He led Reinhart to the "gourmet" area, which happened to be nowhere near where the demonstration table was installed, but rather tucked away, all two short shelves of it, in the middle of a duke's-mixture aisle displaying shoe polish, moth balls, clothesline, replacement mopheads, and beer-can openers of the type outmoded by the pull-ring.

DePau pointed at the shelves. "So what do we have here that's edible? Between you and me?" He pointed to a vial of spices. " 'Crab Boil'? And look at what we have to charge for this little can of patty doo faw: the markup's not that much."

Reinhart had to assent. "Nor does that stuff contain any goose liver, though it's called 'Strasbourg.' It's pork liver, as you can read on the can, and it tastes mostly of tin, for my money. You know you can make a marvelous pork-liver *pâté* at home. The labor takes two minutes or so with a food processor or blender, and it's dirt cheap."

DePau's nostrils arched ever higher above his lip. "Sounds really awful!" It could have been predicted that he was one of those people. He was about to stride away, but checked himself. "You're not going to make a bad smell, are you?"

Reinhart gestured. "This is supposed to be 'gourmet' food."

"That's why I asked the question," said DePau. "I'll tell you frankly."

Reinhart smiled. "I think I know what you mean, and you're not wrong. For that matter, nobody's ever *wrong* when it comes to speaking of their tastes in food. That's private business if there ever was any. But life really can be enhanced if one expands one's palate, and then there's always the question of nourishment."

"Can't be much of that in garlic salt," said DePau. He was anxious to get away, and food was not the sort of subject that could be argued about. It was not simply that any strife, however mild, had a negative effect on the appetite. Food was a great positive, yea-saying force, the ultimate source of vitality—until a phase of the cycle was completed and oneself became food for the worms. It is only through food that we survive, and we die when we are fed on too heartily by microbes, or by the crab named cancer who

eats us alive. In the emotional realm there is no more eloquent
metaphor: lovers feed on one another, and passion is devouring.
A philosopher lives on food for thought. One is what one eats, and
eats what one is. Jews and Muslims, old adversaries, are old comrades in abstaining from pork, and Christians are exhorted to eat
the flesh and blood of their god. Everybody eats to live, but not
everyone who lives to eat is a glutton or, still less, overweight. The
world's foremost gastronome, M. Robert Courtine, of Paris,
France, who eats two multi-course meals per day, with the appropriate wines, is of a modest weight for his height and furthermore
has not exceeded it in twenty years.

DePau loped to the end of the aisle and disappeared. Reinhart
had no great expectation of making an epicure of the man, but he
would have liked to disabuse him of the opinion that the miserable
products on these "gourmet" shelves were in any degree whatever gourmet sans inverted commas. But the word itself had long
since become flabby and useless for any service: a hot dog became
"gourmet" if treated with anything other than mustard, e.g., tar-
tar sauce, and in fact the term was applied in general to the use
of any condiment beyond salt, pepper, and the standard American
ketchup. On the lowest levels of gastronomic journalism, that
printed on the sides of boxes and cans, the addition of Worcester-
shire sauce was usually sufficient to gourmetize any dish.

Reinhart returned to his portable kitchen. He had yet to don his
apron and the billowing chef's hat which Grace Greenwood had
insisted he wear. In France a cook worked for years to earn the
toque blanche. But Reinhart had not forgotten that the members
of the American Expeditionary Force were qualified, by the mere
fact of their arrival in Europe, to display more decorations than
any of their allies who had been fighting for four years. Furthermore the white bonnet had been Grace's only prima facie require-
ment. He had been on his own as to which of the "gourmet"
products distributed by Epicon he would choose for demonstration, and he was not limited to the selection currently offered at
the Glenwood Top Shop. There was a much more generous inventory from which he could choose, and supplies of the appropriate
products were available from a local warehouse.

After some deliberation Reinhart had chosen crepes Suzette: a

name known to all as the quintessence of Gourmetism, a dish that
was simplicity itself to prepare, and a demonstration that could be
given a dramatic character, for attracting an audience was the
purpose of his job. The particular stimulus for his choice was an
Epicon-distributed product called Mon Paris Instant Crepe Suzette Mix: a package containing two envelopes, the larger of which
held sufficient powder, when added to a cup of milk, to make a
dozen six-inch dessert crepes; the orange-colored dust in the
smaller envelope when mashed into softened butter became the
sauce in which the crepes were to be bathed.

When tested by Reinhart in his home kitchen, the mixture had
yielded rubbery pancakes on the one hand, and on the other, a
sauce the predominant flavor of which was markedly chemical,
though it was obviously intended to be orange. He prepared several batches of crepes and a number of bowls of sauce, each with
another variation of the recipe as given—more or less milk, sometimes thinned with water; a greater or lesser proportion of butter
in the sauce—but no effort could alter the truth that the product
was simply inferior as food and at $4.75 a swindle as an item of
trade, since aside from the chemicals the packages contained re-
spectively only flour and sugar.

At an earlier time of life Reinhart would probably have presented these bald facts to the appropriate authority, but he was by
now sufficiently seasoned to understand that a person like Grace
Greenwood had not attained her success in the food business by
a devotion to the principles of either nutrition or serious gas-
tronomy. What he determined to do then was to make his own
mixture, from the authentic materials, of course, the juice and peel
of fresh oranges, orange liqueur, and cognac.

But was this not as unscrupulous as what he would replace? For
the only point of the demonstrations was to sell Epicon products,
and in fact he was not to be alone in the public phase of the
project, but rather to be accompanied by a pitchwoman named
Helen Clayton, who while he cooked would give the spiel and
then, after the audience had tasted the product, then and there
sell packages of Instant Crepe Suzette Mix from an adjoining table.

The answer to the foregoing question was surely Yes, if having
tasted one of Reinhart's authentic crepes, some naïve housewife

bought the wretched powdered product and assumed that from it she could reproduce the model. But there was still another way to look at this situation: wasn't it quite as likely that, incensed by the difference between the real and the bogus, she would, in this era of the aggressive consumer, return the mix with a complaint? And could not the result of enough of such incidents be that Epicon would cease to distribute the offending product?

. . . Actually, Reinhart had no serious hope that the right thing would be done by anybody else but himself—which was the real reason why he must prepare good crepes Suzette.

Getting the equipment and supplies together had taken a good week despite Grace's efficiency and authority. The project was the least among her many, Epicon's major business being in popular junk foods with no claim to being gourmet: various sliced or minced-and-reconstituted deep-fried substances, potato, banana, corn, etc.; powdered soups, puddings, dips; aerosol-canned cheese; tinned meat spreads, stuffed olives, pretzels, relishes, crackers, all manner of munchies, yummies, and tummy-stuffers, comprising most of the joke-provender extant in the Western world, made available, presumably, for the people who lived to eat, rather than those who ate to live, for it did not pretend to offer nourishment.

But a more obvious cause of delay was a general disinclination on the part of all male employees beneath the executive level to work with more than a fraction of the dispatch of the typical practitioner, in whichever job, of a decade earlier, the last time Reinhart had exposed himself to anything that could be called business. Furthermore, this persistent delay as practiced by all functionaries was apparently so firmly established by now as to rouse no ire from the victim, evoke no regret from the perpetrator, and indeed not even stir any wonderment. A kind of half-paralysis, with no political significance, seemed to have claimed the American work force. But he had himself been a downright dropout for more than ten years, and it certainly was easier to get back into a system that was forgiving.

Now back at his demonstration-kitchen, Reinhart assembled the raw materials for a batch of crepes sucrées: flour, eggs, butter, sugar. His colleague, Helen Clayton, was once again rearranging her pitchwoman's table. She was a robust woman in what might be as late as her early forties or as early as the late thirties, with sandy-red hair, pale skin, and a self-possessed, even slightly hostile manner.

Earlier in his life this was the type of woman who would have caused him most discomfiture, and perhaps he would naïvely have believed her seemingly otherwise unmotivated resentment to be caused by a lesbian leaning. But now it seemed likely that matters of relative power, not sex, were in question. Which of them was to be boss? It would be difficult for him to reassure her without being despised for his pains.

When Helen had restacked her little boxes of Instant Crepe Suzette Mix he asked: "How should we go about this?"

She raised her eyes but not her face. "Huh?"

"You're the professional at demonstrations, aren't you? I'm a raw recruit." He spoke with a certain breeziness of voice: obsequiousness would not be the note to strike.

She was no warmer as yet. "How long will it take you to make those things?"

"A few minutes, once the batter's ready and the skillet's hot. I mean the crepes themselves. Then to sauce them, only a minute or so more."

Helen winced. "You don't have a stack already made?"

"I thought of doing that," said Reinhart. "But the Suzetting isn't all that much, just swishing them around in the sauce a moment or two and then folding them in quarters. Of course the flaming adds drama. But I thought the demonstration would have more interest if I started from scratch, more or less. Crepe batter has to rest awhile under refrigeration to be at its best: what I will mix here I won't use immediately. What I *will* use I prepared last night at home: it's in the portable fridge there." The latter was the standard plastic-walled device for picnics. Its interior held two gallons of the batter, surrounded by ice cubes. This was enough for two hundred crepes, surely a sufficient number to get them through a routine morning. By the afternoon the batter he had mixed in the demonstration would have rested sufficiently to be used.

"The thing to remember," Helen said, "is that we're here to move the product, not to give free cooking lessons or free food. Be careful about kids: they're a pain in the ass. They'll want sample after sample, and some of the smaller ones might try to help themselves to things they're not supposed to have, and for God's sake don't let anything dangerous get out of your close vicinity: knives and hot things. Keep 'em away from those burners! That's the bad news. But the good news is that if they like a product, kids will make their parents buy it, so you've got to remember that and put up with them. This time of day you'll have the very little tots who pull things off the shelves and screech incessantly. But they like sweet stuff, so make those crepes as sweet as possible, with extra-heavy fillings of jam." Naturally she pronounced the essential word to rhyme with "grape."

He answered in good humor: "These are crepes Suzette, and they aren't made with jam. Most of their flavor comes from the hot sauce that they will be inundated in. It's quite sweet and rich, with lots of sugar, though, and butter and orange juice—"

Helen peered at his work-table, and then at him. "You're not going to use the packaged sauce mix?"

"Uh, no."

Her eyes were fixed on his mouth. Her own lips were threatening to—yes, definitely, to smile. "You've got a lot of nerve."

Now he smiled in return. "You disapprove?"

She laughed outright. "It's not my affair, is it?"

But why was it so funny? Finally he asked.

"I don't know," said Helen. She lifted one of the little boxes of instant mix and snorted. "Have you tried these?"

"Yes."

She protruded her lips and pronounced, silently: *Sh-it?*

He nodded. "I suppose I'm being dishonest—?"

"Not unless we *say* you're using the mix," Helen said quickly. "But look, this can be to our advantage. You show the real way to make the sauce. The crepes will be terrific, and those are the ones they'll taste samples of, right? Then I'll say something like, 'Well, that's the long way. If you want to do it the short way, here's the instant mix!' "

She had lost her coolness. They were co-conspirators now. She was really quite a nice-looking woman, tall and full-bosomed, and not wearing, he was happy to note, a pungent scent which could be deleterious to good cuisine, distracting or confusing the olfactory sense.

"Yes, I guess that's fair enough," said he. "Makes me feel better anyway. I hate to be dishonest about food, but on the other hand I don't like the idea of cooking anything that's lousy, merely so as to be honest."

Helen shrugged and said, with a pout: "I'll tell you, I myself don't care. I like simple food. Anything fancy makes me sick to the stomach."

He raised his hands at the wrists, signifying that he would not have her shot, though privately he believed the statement insensitive in view of his profession; but then it was humanity's way to suspend the rules of courtesy when speaking of food or art.

The big clock over the fresh produce department was not so large that it could be seen across the vast distance that separated him from it, and he wore no watch. Helen, when applied to, told him it was a minute or so to nine. He took the white bonnet from the bottom shelf of his work-table. It was in a collapsed state. He shook it, inflating its flatness. He put on an apron, the strings of which crossed in back and came around to be tied in front.

Helen was looking at him in what appeared to be approval. "Gee," she said. "Remind me to get some recipes from you." Obviously the costume had transformed him in her eyes. He realized that Grace had been right to insist upon his wearing it.

"Do you like to cook?"

"Hate it," said Helen. "That's why I wanted you to show me some shortcuts."

"First one," he replied in good humor, "is to get yourself some Instant Crepe Suzette Mix."

Helen, who was proving an amiable sort, assured him she was earnest about acquiring "kitchen tips."

"Of course we eat a lot of take-out. I can't do this all day and then come home and cook much at night."

"Who's 'we'? You and your husband?"

"Well . . ." Helen leaned towards him as if to share a confidence; he sensed that she might have dug him in the ribs had he been close enough. "You didn't think I was one of *them,* did you?"

"Them?" The question was altogether honest.

Once again she made her lips prominent and silently mouthed a word. It was *lesbian.*

Reinhart averted his face. "No," he said, "certainly not." He had not yet had time to think of this third phase of coping with the problem of Winona: he had first to deal with it himself, then to witness Blaine's reaction, and now finally to deal with the rest of the world.

With unwitting cruelty Helen persisted. "Did you know *she* was? Grace, I mean."

He mumbled: "I guess so. But I don't much care." He tried to keep from sounding the defiant note.

"I've always kept away from them. They make me feel creepy. But Grace is all right to work for. I've done a number of jobs for Epicon, usually through her, and she's always been a perfect lady with me." Helen laughed coarsely. "But, then, I doubt I'm her type. She likes them skinny, and she likes them young."

"Well," Reinhart said, "here come our customers." God had mercifully steered a young mother and a small child to the head of their aisle.

But Helen Clayton still had time for another innocent thrust: "You should see her present *friend.* My God, she's positively beautiful. I've seen her call for Grace after work in her car. I've seen—"

"Madam," Reinhart desperately called to the young woman, though she was still remote and was at the very moment bending low to poke into a frozen-food compartment, "would you like a crepe Suzette?"

Futile as this was practically—the woman could not hear him—it did serve to distract Helen from her previous theme.

She said in an undertone: "That's supposed to be *my* job."

"Sorry," said Reinhart. "I've got beginner's nerves."

"Aw, you'll be just fine." She considered him a buddy now.

The young mother had not heard him, but it could be seen that her little son was attracted by the promise of a novelty, down there in the corner, a man in a marshmallow hat and a red-haired lady, and he trotted their way.

"Hi, little kid," said Helen, when he came near. "Do you like real sweet things like candy and ice cream?"

The child silently thrust his open hand at her.

Reinhart said: "I haven't even sauced any crepes yet!"

Helen ignored him and continued to smile at the little boy. When the mother came along, the child turned to her and made demands. The young woman sighed and groaned. Reaching past a stack of the crepe-mix boxes on Helen's table, she found a jar that Reinhart could not have seen from his angle, unscrewed the top, chose a bright green pellet, and gave it to her child. He was pacified for the moment. His mother shrugged for Helen's benefit, put the jar on her wheeled cart, and pushed on.

"What have you got over there?" Reinhart asked. "Are you selling other things?"

"I took the precaution to get a jar or two of Gourmet Fruit Drops off the gourmet shelf," said Helen. "You always want to have something to use on the real little kids."

Reinhart was impressed by her acumen. "I'm going to take your suggestion and make some finished crepes, in sauce and all ready to eat, so that the customers can taste them right away. Then maybe they'll stay and watch me cook some more from scratch." He looked at Helen, expecting approval.

But she frowned. "Thing is, you'll be giving them the pay before they do the work. That's never a good principle. Think of it. If you got your money in advance, do you think you'd work as hard? Human nature."

"But will they have the patience to stand and watch a demonstration? That young woman just now didn't even glance at my setup."

"Thing is," said Helen, "you've just got to get the feel of the crowd: some will do one thing, some another. I mean, as crowds. Individuals within the crowd are something else: they can usually be ignored, but not always. There might be a troublemaker, for example. But there might also be somebody there you want to play to, like maybe, for you, a good-looking girl. If you can hold her, you get the feeling you can hold anybody, and that's good for the self-confidence. Or maybe you like a different kind of challenge, some sour-looking individual who will be against you by nature, skeptical, you know? That might put you on your best behavior."

No other customers were yet in sight, and in the preceding hour Reinhart had seen hardly any of the supermarket personnel but the manager, DePau. As yet it was an inappropriate place, this isolated corner, to speak of the psychology of crowds.

"I don't think I'm so good at handling people," Reinhart said. "If I have any gift in life whatever, it's for *making* something. I discovered that late enough. I wish I had known it when I was young, but in those days I never showed any inclination to work with my hands. In manual training at school, for example, I couldn't saw a straight line. I never had any talent at art, and with mechanical things I'm at a loss. When I got out of the Army, I just sort of fell into real estate, and from then on it was a series of jobs of different types that dealt with the public. I don't mind admitting I never did well at any of them. Then I took up cooking, just as a practical thing at home: I had to bring up and feed a daughter."

"Listen," said Helen Clayton, speaking with solemn conviction, "being really able to make something is the greatest ability there is, because you've always got that regardless. People come and go, but what do you care? You've always got what you do. You could be alone on the moon."

Again Reinhart wryly scanned the deserted aisle. "There's a somewhat different character to working with food than, say, with wood or precious metals. Cooking is a craft, or perhaps a performing art, but the product that is created is made to be consumed in a unique way: it is taken internally and, if digested, becomes part of the flesh of a living creature. In a sense then, cookery is the *only* truly creative art. But you do need people to eat the resulting product."

But the point seemed lost on Helen, who was very intelligent but whose philosophy was of another character, being tactical rather than strategic, and in fact Reinhart's favorite people had been her sort during what in retrospect now were established as the most happy times of his life, viz., his days in the wartime Army.

Suddenly customers appeared in bulk. A plausible reason for this might be that the crowd had been waiting for the doors to open: admitted together, they had toured the aisles in ensemble and had only now reached the last. But subsequent events of the same sort, at arbitrary times, disqualified the argument. People appeared by ones or en masse, crowds formed or failed to collect, according to some law that could not easily be identified. Reinhart discovered that though the action could be hectic when people appeared in number, it was more satisfying than when persons came by sporadically. Although his private code had always exalted the individual and, as the case might be, dreaded or despised the mob, in a public situation such tastes are a weakness and not a strength.

But the principal difference between this role and all the previous jobs that had pitted him against his fellow man was that for the first time he had a genuine skill to display, and his being in this situation was not still another example of Fate's inclination towards the arbitrary.

As he mixed his batter and poured his crepes one by one and turned them, stacked them when finished between precut squares of waxed paper, meanwhile bathing others in the hot sauce in the chafing dish (a luscious amalgam of sugar, butter, and orange juice, flamed with Grand Marnier and cognac), folding them into triangles, and serving them to the members of his audience on paper plates, with forks of plastic, as he went through this sequence as smoothly as his batter flowed, Reinhart was conscious of a feeling that was unique in his more than half a century of life: for the first time he did not feel as if he were either charlatan or buffoon. Thus, late, but presumably not too, was proved the wisdom of what in his boyhood had been conventional advice but which, alas, he had long ignored: *Learn a trade.*

But when suddenly, as usual for no reason, their corner was devoid of humanity except for Helen and himself, and he had a moment in which to turn to his associate, intending to show an expression in which gratification and exhaustion were compounded (that old face of the happy worker, none too familiar nowadays except on amateurs at charity functions), he saw that Helen did not share in his pleasure.

"Something wrong?"

She indicated the stacks of boxes. "Four sales, Carl."

"Well, it's early yet. Give it time. We seem to be attracting the audience."

Helen came to the kitchen table and spoke earnestly: "For freebies, Carl."

Reinhart looked at her. "I'm doing something wrong again?"

"Will you forgive me for speaking frankly?" asked Helen. But the question was a genuine courtesy, and she did not offensively wait for an answer. "This isn't a lunch counter. The customers aren't paying for their food. You don't have any obligation to feed as many as you can within a certain time."

"I'm sorry," said he. "I guess I did forget. Stupid of me, but I was just mindlessly having fun. I realize that's not the point."

Helen had expressive eyes within those pale lashes. "There's no law against that," said she. "I enjoy what I do, too, most of the time. Please don't think I'm criticizing."

He realized guiltily that, distracted by his own performance, he had not even been conscious of what she had done when the crowd was there, had not so much as heard her spiel.

He scowled now. "Don't be so damned nice, Helen! I told you I'm a raw beginner at this sort of thing. I really want your suggestions." He scanned the empty aisle, and then lowered the Grand Marnier bottle to the second shelf of the work-table, where he tipped its mouth towards a plastic measuring cup and poured out a drinkable quantity of the orange liqueur. He passed the cup to Helen, below the level of the table top.

She lifted it to her mouth and threw down its contents as though they were bar stock, then lowered the glass and said: "I thought you'd never ask."

Reinhart suppressed a wince. He liked delicacy in a woman. And Grand Marnier was not appropriately drunk in a rush, as if it were what his father called a "cordial" and sometimes furtively tossed off behind the tree on Xmas Eve with other male relatives whose wives were teetotallers. He now recorked the bottle without having had one himself.

But Helen was pushing the glass across his counter and leering significantly. He had no choice but to open the bottle and pour another. She drank.

"It's a hustle," she said, "like everything else." She held the glass just beneath her full breasts. "If you don't mind my saying so, you seem a little too anxious to please the public. In business you have to remember *they are the enemy.*"

Reinhart changed his mind about having a drink, but he chose the cognac and poured himself a tot. He postponed drinking it, however, and left it on the lower shelf.

"Huh," he said in response to Helen. "That isn't an easy theory to reconcile with the serving of food. It seems like a contradiction. Can you feed people you hate?"

"Hate?" asked Helen. "Who said hate? I'm not talking about anything nasty. What I mean is that they are what we feed on, like one animal eats another. Does a tiger hate its prey? Maybe 'enemy' is not the right word exactly. It's not that kind of war. I said that because I have a friend who uses the term. He's in carpets."

At that moment a parade of wheeled baskets came around the head of the aisle. "I'll try to remember," Reinhart said. "I mustn't be too eager to hand out free crepes."

"But you don't want to seem stingy either," said Helen, tossing her right earring, a large green ball, with a movement of her head. "A good thing to remember is that we get them to stop by offering something free, but soon as they receive it they don't have any further use for us. In other words, it's in their interest to get the sample as soon as possible and leave, and it's in our interest to make them stay until they hear our pitch. But once they've heard it and either bought the product or not, then it becomes our interest to get rid of them and not give them seconds."

"Did I do that?" Reinhart asked. And he had been so pleased with himself for keeping the crowd in the obscurity of the mass and not identifying individuals!

"Well," Helen said generously, and she even came to touch his forearm, "here comes a new attack. You'll do just fine."

It went without saying that the difficult aspect of any endeavor was the human.

The first basket to arrive was propelled by a very fat young woman. Neither did she have the flawless skin that sometimes accompanies obesity, whether or not as a result of it.

"Can I have another of those crepes?" she asked. "They're the most delicious darn things. . . ."

Which meant she was the kind of customer who should be discouraged. Seconds! But she was also the very sort of person who delighted a cook. She had not been able to resist coming back for more.

Reinhart managed to restrain himself from hastily meeting her wants. "Do you know," he said genially, "these are easily prepared at home." He looked over at Helen, but she was occupied with an older woman who had actually approached her of her own volition.

"You don't mean that lousy mix she's selling!" cried the fat girl, though in good humor. "I notice you don't use it."

Reinhart served her not one but two of the folded crepes and generously spooned sauce upon them. In addition to all else he could still remember his own days of obesity and the concomitant lust for sweets—which like all ardent appetites grew by its own feeding, but what could one do?

"The instant version saves a lot of time," said he, having so to speak bought her attention. "You have to allow for that. Not all that's quick is bad!"

"The trouble is," said the young woman, already putting the soiled paper plate into one of the two ex-oil-drums that served as trashbins (she had virtually inhaled the crepes), "all that makes a crape Soozette worth eating is the flavor of the expensive ingredients: with the brandy and stuff even the mix would taste good, but who can afford them?"

The approaching crowd had suddenly dispersed, or perhaps it had been not so much an actual accumulation of persons as a trick of perspective. He turned to Helen. She too was again free.

From within she pulled her face into an elongation. "All my lady wanted was the way to the toilet. She got nasty when I said they didn't have them in supermarkets." Helen laughed in her hearty style. "Say, Carl, if worse comes to worst, we'll just have to drink up the booze, so the prospects aren't all bad."

He asked her for the time and then he invited her to have lunch with him.

A certain quick transformation could be seen in her eyes. She looked at her watch and said: "Eleven twenty!"

"Can it be?" asked Reinhart. "We haven't done much business, but we've got through the morning."

"I'd like to take you up on the invitation, but I can't."

"Sure," said he. "Some other time."

"I'll make it up to you." She spoke in an intense whisper. It was a strange thing to say, and an odd style of saying it, and whatever the intended significance, Reinhart was all at once aroused. This happened seldom enough to the sedate middle-aged gentleman he had become.

He turned quickly back to his work. The cooked-crepe supply was not especially low—the stack held at least a dozen—but you could never tell when they might get another crowd. He put the iron skillet on a burner of the hot plate and turned up the heat. In his right peripheral field of vision he saw a lone, cartless shopper approach from the top of the aisle.

What precisely did Helen mean? Or did she herself know? He was shocked to find that where women were concerned he had regressed in recent years to the moral condition of his adolescence. Though today's youth, according to certain authorities, reached adulthood with the sophistication of a procurer, in Reinhart's day and place it had been routine enough to arrive at one's full growth without any experience but the autoerotic, and dealing in fantasies was ineffective preparation for so much as conversing with a live female.

"Carl?"

He was being addressed by the person who had come down the aisle without a cart. He had actually recognized her at the instant she had come into sight, and he furthermore had done so from the corner of his eye. But when you had lived with a woman for twenty-two years—that portion of life generally known as the prime, when all the emotions whether loving or hateful were high, and there was a peculiar vitality even to the worst despair, and when at the end she had discarded you brutally—it was no great feat, even a decade later, to see her through the back of your head.

His ex-wife stood across the work-table from him.

He caught himself just as he was about to burn his hand, instead moving it deftly to take a paper plate to the chafing dish and there choosing a hot crepe. He spooned extra sauce upon it and presented it, with plastic fork, to the mother of his children.

"Free sample," he said. *"Bon appétit,* Genevieve."

CHAPTER
6

When Reinhart told himself that he had recognized Genevieve on
her first entering the top of the aisle, he was speaking with the
habitual lack of precision that characterizes the internal dialogue.
Undoubtedly there had been something about the figure and its
movements that suggested an unpleasant memory, but it was a
severe shock to be actually confronted by his spouse of twenty-two
years, his ex of a decade. The presentation of the crepe was an act
of the bravado that Genevieve had so often evoked from him in
the last catastrophic years of their association.

It was typical of her to ignore the outthrust plate.

"Carl," she said again, and neither time was it a greeting, "we
have to talk."

Reinhart continued to hold the crepe towards her. He began
again, in the proper style. "Hello, Genevieve. It's been a while.
How have you been?"

At least some of his shock was due to her altered appearance.
When last encountered—she in her early forties, he in the middle
of his fourth decade—Genevieve had been the sort of woman who
could be termed "handsome": her features were well cut, with no
ragged edges; her eye was clear, her skin uncreased, her hair of
a uniform color, her figure as fit as if she were ten years younger.
And if one loved her there was no reason to be this objective: she
was a damned good-looking woman by any standard and miraculously so as the mother of two children, the elder of whom was in
college. Reinhart himself, on the other hand, had been a sorry

specimen, more than halfway through his third hundred pounds, spongy-faced, habitually flushed, short of breath, and loose of bridgework in time of crisis (which came with the rising of each sun).

But by now he had no visible paunch, despite the lowering of the chest which is nature's fee for gaining the age of fifty; and if the hue of his hair was no longer youthful, its growth was, miraculously, as dense as it had ever been. He could still, unspectacled, read a menu at less than arm's length, and he had needed no dental work since early in his forties. He believed that he looked his age but could reasonably be termed a healthy specimen of it. He might turn no female heads, but neither would he cause the aversion of faces. In truth, his current appearance might be pretty close to achieving second place on a personal list of his own lifetime images (first being always himself at twenty-one, or at any rate the representation thereof on a snapshot taken at a ruined German monument in Occupation Berlin, among other GIs and Russian soldiers, buddies for then and forever, conquerors of all the evil in the world—for the rest of that week, anyway).

But Genevieve was not simply a faded snapshot of herself of a decade past: she was the worn and cracked photograph of someone else entirely. Reinhart found he could recognize her better from the corner of his eye than straight-on. It would have defied his powers to say in precisely which respect she had *not* changed, e.g., the cartilage in her nose seemed to have undergone a softening; her eyes flickered behind what looked like peepholes cut through inorganic material rather than living skin; her hair was arranged significantly to lower her once high brow; the joints at the under-ear angles of her jaw were almost as evident, and stark as those on the skeleton that had dangled in the biology lab at high school, forty years before. Not to mention that she was very thin in body—and not in Winona's sense, the willed emaciation of chic. Genevieve looked as though she simply had not had enough to eat in recent weeks: her complexion was a mixture of yellow and gray, her posture was none too steady, her clothes were too large.

Reinhart now found himself urging the crepe on her as emergency nourishment, as one would extend warm soup to the starving. And he was joined by an ally.

"Go ahead, ma'am," Helen Clayton said encouragingly, coming towards them. "It's free!"

"Get rid of her," Genevieve told her ex-husband, without so much as a glance at the other woman. "I told you I wanted to talk."

Despite her current disguise, which could have inspired pity, Genevieve's stark spirit was all too familiar.

Reinhart retracted the crepe. He also became conscious of the pan on the hot plate, in which the butter had blackened, but he was not so distracted as to burn himself on its handle. He gathered up a wad of apron and lifted the skillet away.

Helen shrugged in good-natured indifference and turned away. Reinhart saw that she was that salubrious sort of person whom one need not worry about: she did not seek situations in which to find offense. He saw no utility in chiding Genevieve in front of her.

His ex-wife continued to stare at him.

At last he said: "I can't deal with personal matters until I'm off duty."

"What's that supposed to mean?" Genevieve asked, for all the world as if she genuinely did not understand.

"I'm working here. This is a job, to promote the sale of a crepe mix." She frowned. Had she turned mentally incompetent in some fashion? "I'll meet you for lunch if you like."

"Lunch?" Her stare lost coherence. "Oh." She returned her eyes to his. "I'm not looking for a handout."

"You're hardly being offered one," Reinhart answered in a level tone. "I assume you've got something serious to talk about, if you bothered to look me up here. And if so, then lunchtime would seem to be the moment to talk about it, and I at least will be hungry then, having worked all morning."

As if in support of his point, a cluster of shoppers were approaching, and Helen went out to gather them in. Now, incongruously, Reinhart heard her pitch for the first time.

"Have some free crepes," she said, "and learn an easy way to make them at home. Why not? You don't have to buy anything." The words were less eloquent than the spirit in which they were spoken. Helen seemed to have a naturally persuasive manner that came into play in this function. The women rolled their baskets near. Among them was an old gent in a cap of hound's-tooth check, who put his head on the side and squinted suspiciously at Reinhart.

Genevieve became aware, almost fearfully, of the strangers who moved to surround her. "All right," she said, with a suggestion that these people were Reinhart's bullies, summoned to force her to comply with his wishes. "Noon." She filtered through the shopping carts. Reinhart was ignorant of women's fashions—as he was reminded every time he looked at Winona—yet he knew that Genevieve's attire was out of style by some years. In fact, he thought he could remember the coat from 1968.

"What you got here?" asked the old man, peering at the chafing dish. "Swedish meatballs?"

Reinhart served him a crepe Suzette. The old-timer took the entire triangle of it into the back of his mouth and swallowed it whole, as if it were an oyster. He rolled his rheumy eyes into his yellowed forehead, but said nothing. He took a paper napkin from the little stack at the edge of the table, cleansed his plastic spoon on it, and put the spoon into his pocket. "Why not?" he asked Reinhart with a shrug, and left.

But with successive waves of female shoppers Helen Clayton began to do good business. Insofar as Reinhart could spare attention to the matter, he thought he could identify the power of precedent. If one of the earliest arrivals in any cluster bought a packet of crepe mix, some others usually would follow, but if the customer waited until the group thinned out, a trend was unlikely to be set, not only for the obvious reason that fewer persons were there to be influenced, but also because the principle of like-follows-like can only seriously be applied to the mass. Thus an early purchaser could be seen as a leader and those who came next as followers, but the straggler was probably an isolated eccentric.

Of course, as Helen pointed out between sequences, "buy" was not the precise word for what a shopper did in dropping a packet of mix into her basket: she was as yet a great distance from the checkout stations and could, at any point between here and the wire rackfuls of gossip-tabloids, mounted just before the cash registers, discard any item which failed to pass the test of second thought.

Reinhart endeavored to keep himself in a state of commercial distraction, but succeeded only in part.

"I suppose," he said in that same interim, yielding to an irresistible force, "you wonder who that woman is?"

"What woman?" asked Helen.

"You're being too diplomatic." He smiled sadly. "But I appreciate it. She's my ex-wife. I haven't seen her in many years."

Helen shrugged and then smiled in return, but not in reflection of his wryness: she had a remarkably sweet temperament. "Hell, Carl," she said, "what the hell?"

"Yes."

"I mean, I wouldn't worry. If it's done, then it's done. That's the way I always feel." She continued to smile at him.

"Well," he said finally, "I've got my companion for lunch, and I'm not looking forward to the occasion." He rubbed his chin and added, on what was really an innocent impulse: "I'm sorry it won't be with you."

Helen swallowed visibly. Her reply had a certain intensity, an undue earnestness. "I should be able to make it right after work, if that's all right. I can't ever at lunchtime, you see. I'm sorry, but that's a standing arrangement."

Again he was taken by surprise, but he felt he must apologize. "Oh, I didn't mean— That is, your personal business is, uh, your business . . ."

"Listen," said Helen, "I wouldn't say it if I didn't mean it." More shoppers were coming; she turned to deal with them.

Reinhart poured and cooked more crepes, served them to smiling women. This was more attention than he had got from the female population in decades. Things were supposed to be changing in the relations between the sexes, but women still seemed to like being served by a man who specialized in a craft that was routinely their own.

But what did Helen mean? *What* would she "be able to make right after work"? But more importantly, whatever, why was he apprehensive? What a tame old fellow he had become!

Finally the batter he had brought from home was coming to an end, and he was about to ask Helen for the time when he saw Genevieve rounding the corner at the head of the aisle. He served the crepes, of which luckily there were two more to divvy up than the number of customers who awaited them, and then addressed his partner.

"I guess we can break for lunch now? Though, come to think of it, a lot of people who work might do some shopping on their lunch hour, and we'll miss them."

"No," said she. "The kind of people who shop at lunch aren't the kind who'd buy this product, generally speaking. Take my word for it."

"O.K.," said Reinhart. "I will. I always take your word."

Helen rolled her eyes and made a lump in her round cheek. "But don't turn on me when I'm wrong!" This was the kind of affectionate-joking exchange that he was comfortable with. Though he had few personal precedents for it, the movies of his youth and the early TV comedies often depicted men and women who were pals with an undertone of something warmer, which might come to fruition when the girl removed her owlish spectacles or when the man simply opened his eyes: but you, the moviegoer, even as a kid, knew the score all the while. The wit inherent in this situation was far from being inferior.

"Have a nice lunch." He was reluctant to leave her company, especially to join Genevieve. He realized that he was thinking of Helen as his protector!

Genevieve stopped about four feet from the table and waited expressionlessly—which in her current case was actually with an unpleasant expression even when she was not intentionally displaying one: her lower face was strained and pinched and overlooked by nostrils seemingly tensed in reaction to a foul smell. She showed no acknowledgment of his apron and chef's bonnet as he now removed them. In the latter years of their marriage he had assumed he could have come home in a full suit of armor or loincloth and turban without provoking her to make a response.

DePau, the manager, had assigned him a locker in the employees' coatroom at the rear of the store. There had been only one available, and Reinhart and Helen had to share it. Reinhart had felt odd about this on his arrival that morning. Now the intimacy of the narrow metal cabinet, in which his old tweed sports jacket hung against her trenchcoat, was inviting to think about.

"I've got to go back in for a minute, to get my street clothes," he told Genevieve. Her nod was curt, and it seemed bitter as well, but that may have been but the effect of her permanently disagreeable configuration of feature.

Reinhart would have liked to be bolstered by one more encounter with Helen, but when he reached their locker her coat was already gone: she lost no time in getting to her noontime date, which she had furthermore characterized as being habitual. Was she that attached to her husband, or did the brute demand punctuality? No doubt some men were still like that, or more so than ever, now that classic virility was under siege.

On the way back, passing through the storage area, beyond which the trucks were being unloaded, he ran into DePau. The manager looked careworn: he shook his head and hastened on. It was doubtful that he had recognized Reinhart. Reinhart was old enough to remember a time before the supermarket, or at any rate before it was the institution without which most citizens of the republic would presumably starve. So many basic matters had changed during his lifetime. In his boyhood it was not unusual to know people who had no telephone, and a great many persons went without gasoline-driven vehicles: among them milkmen, whose vans were pulled by horses. Patches of dung, flattened and imprinted with tire-treadmarks, were not uncommon features of the roadways. Dogs, who ran free in those days, had an addiction to public excrement ("It's their perfume," said an aged female neighbor), of which horse droppings were fortunately the least offensive.

But reminiscence did not armor him against the prospect of lunching with his ex-wife. Luckily he had permitted Winona to impose upon him a generous loan against his first paycheck and could afford to take Genevieve to one of the better of the several eating places in the mall, i.e., not to a fast-food assembly line, of which the familiar names were present, nor to the Chinese establishment, which appeared to be the standard chop-suey parlor.

On joining Genevieve, he took the initiative. "I was surprised to hear you were even in town." He began to walk up the aisle.

But for a moment she did not move. She squinted at him and asked: "Why did you say that?"

He refused to return to her, but he did slow his pace.

"Because it's what I felt."

"Why 'even'?"

"Excuse me?"

" 'Even in town'?" She scowled. "I didn't come here to be insulted."

This reminded him of his own admonition to Blaine, at the end of their Sunday drive a week earlier. It was becoming a favorite family saying.

"I trust you're not going to keep being so touchy," he told Genevieve. "I meant no insult. By 'even' I meant that I hardly realized you were in town. I didn't anticipate seeing you. It's been a good ten years, hasn't it?"

She merely shrugged. Time was apparently of no importance to her. To Reinhart it was incredible that you could be so intimately associated with someone in one era and meet as distant acquaintances in the next. Human relations remained a good deal less explicable than anything in atomic physics. Certain platitudes had not changed since Homer.

Genevieve's stride had altered since the old days. It was hard not to see it as a trudge.

They turned at the head of the aisle and went along parallel with the endless shelves of products baked from dough and packaged in cellophane.

"I didn't come to talk of old times," said she.

"No," said Reinhart.

And simple and honest as that word was, again she responded defensively. "You're saying I don't have any feelings, is that it?"

Reinhart made no answer until they had gone the entire route to the front doors, which swung open automatically when their weight reached the mats.

Outside, on the concrete ramp, he stopped and said: "Believe me, I'm not trying to needle you in any fashion. I apologize in advance for anything you interpret as a gibe. And that's the last I want to hear of it. It was your idea to look me up, remember. So far as I was concerned, we terminated our association a decade ago."

As he had suspected, this speech, which really should have been considered insulting, was favorably received by her. Mean people are usually deeply gratified when others confirm their ruthless assessment of humanity.

"All right," said Genevieve, trudging on, "that's fair enough. I don't want any special favors. I didn't come for myself."

"I didn't think you did," said Reinhart, stepping onto the black-top. Across a block of parked cars was the restaurant he thought he'd head for, a place called, merely, "Winston's." He simply liked the name. The façade was mall-banal, and he knew nothing of the cuisine, but at least it was not called by some term which evoked unpleasant gastronomical anticipations (like "Old" something, or any name in the diminutive).

Nor did the place immediately offend upon entrance. They were seated by a young woman who was civil but not falsely enthusiastic; her clothing and style of hair were unobtrusive but attractive; and she was prompt but not breathless. She led them to a table capacious enough for two more persons. The table top, though not made of wood, was at least not of mirror-gloss, and the disposable mats were not imprinted with patriotic lore, maps of the region, or little-known and useless facts intended to entertain. The cutlery was clean and of a goodly heft, and the napkins were of paper but thick and wide.

Reinhart asked Genevieve whether she wanted a drink.

She sat rigid, both forearms pinning down the prone menu. "No," she said. "In fact, I don't really want lunch. I don't want anything from you."

Having taken it all, is what he might have said at some early time, just after the divorce. But the honest fact was that a great deal of their worldly goods in the last years of the marriage had been provided by Gen's effort and not his own: he could admit that now. Not to mention that he had always disliked the house, the neighborhood, and the suburb, which was not altogether the fault of those three entities, as he could also admit now, but the truth was that he had never been unhappy to be done with them all. The further truth might be simply that he was never cut out to be a father or even a husband. But it is not an easy matter to disqualify so much of your life. Being in Genevieve's presence summoned up such basically disagreeable questions.

"And furthermore," she added, "I don't want to drink anything."

He felt a quick flash of rage at this command, but before he acted upon it a reason for restraint appeared with almost the same speed. His balance of spirit was still new enough to wonder at. There were deeply gratifying rewards for living well into middle age.

"A lot has changed, Genevieve, since we last saw each other. I'm no longer a boozer, but neither am I that other monster, the teetotaller. I just don't drink for effect any more."

"Then why drink at all?" she asked in her manner of old, in anticipation of an argument that was not only untenable but ignoble as well.

"To amuse the palate," Reinhart said. "Beyond sheer matters of nourishment, that should always be the purpose of putting anything in the mouth."

"I'll drink a cup of coffee."

"And what will you have to eat?" He opened and scanned his own copy of the menu (which was unsullied by thumbprints, grease spots, or ketchup drippings). Wonder of wonders, there were other foods than shrimp and steak and prime ribs. For example, there was fresh ham. There was meat loaf. There was Irish stew! Reinhart had a good feeling about this place, though of course the only proof would be in the eating. "It's quite an adventurous bill of fare, for this place and time," said he. "If that's real Irish stew, made of lamb, then it'll be a treat. Nor is a really good meat loaf to be dismissed. . . ." He looked at Genevieve over the bill of fare. "You really should eat something."

For the briefest instant she showed a look of vulnerability such as he had never before seen. "Coffee will be fine, Carl," she said, and perhaps it was his imagination, but he detected the hint of a softer note than he had ever known her to sound. One of the alterations in her appearance (now that he was seated across from her in a good light) was her color of hair: it was off, somehow; still brown, but without a glint of life. It occurred to him that without heavy dyeing she might be pure white: that happened to some younger than she. Suddenly, as if warm water had been poured on him from above, he felt flooded with pity.

He leaned forward and asked: "Are you O.K.?"

But she bridled at this. *"I'm* not the problem." She could not resist adding: "I never was."

The waitress came then. Genevieve would not budge from her lonely cup of coffee, but Reinhart had put in a solid morning of labor. He asked whether the stew was of lamb. It was.

"I don't suppose you have Guinness?"

But surely they did. The waitress was a mellow-voiced young woman with neat hair and a clear complexion.

"All right, Gen," he said when they were alone again. "I realize you're showing great patience. . . . You want to discuss Blaine's problem, I'm sure. I don't know what I can do. He's so touchy with me that I can hardly talk to him. He didn't even want me to know about Mercer's departure."

Genevieve pointed a finger at him. "Don't worry about Blaine," said she. "We'll work that out, he and I. That's no big deal."

The waitress arrived with the cup of coffee.

Reinhart remembered that Genevieve was wont to smoke a cigarette at table, and he dreaded the moment, no doubt imminent, when she would take the pack from her purse. But it did not yet come.

Genevieve pushed the coffee aside without tasting it. "It's your daughter," said she. "My God Almighty, to have something like that in our family. I could just imagine what you'd be saying now if *I* had raised her. But she's lived with *you* during these ten years."

"That's right," said Reinhart, "and I'm very proud of her. She has been a wonderful daughter, and I love and admire her."

Genevieve looked at him for a long time, and then she said: "Blaine told me you were completely brazen about it, and I'll tell you, despite my private opinion of you, I thought he was not being quite fair. 'She supports him,' I said. 'He's not going to openly attack her, even to you—especially to you, given all those years of bad blood.' But I know something about you, Carl, or I thought I did anyway, after more than twenty years of marriage. I know, or thought I knew, that you can't stand sexual perversion. So far as I know, that's your only sacred principle."

Reinhart stared down into the tines of his fork. What was interesting about this accusation was the tiny grain of truth amidst the inert matter. It had never quite been "sacred," nor had it been his "only," but "principle" had a certain justice. Nor was he repudiating it now.

"I'll stick to what I told Blaine. I don't intend to be a spokesman for gay liberation. What I would like most is never to consider the subject. I wish everybody would drop the matter as something to be discussed and go about their business, each in his or her own way. But I know that's hardly likely, at least not for a long time. And of course there's no getting away from the fact that one is more sympathetic—make that *less unsympathetic*—to certain things if they apply to someone close."

Genevieve's face had become ever more masklike. "I always wondered why she wanted to live with you after the divorce, leave her nice home and room and all, her mother and brother. I really resisted accepting the loathsome suspicion that you and—"

"No, Genevieve," Reinhart said with kindly firmness, "no, you don't want to pursue that line, whatever the malice you still have towards me. No, I have never had a sexual connection with my own daughter. I realize that incest is the current fashionable subject with the quacks of popular psychology and the hacks of TV, but Winona and I would never make case studies."

At that point the waitress brought him a mug of almost black liquid, surmounted by a good two inches of yellow foam: they knew how to pour Guinness here! But he could feel with his fingertips that it was much too cold; very chill stout tastes like varnish smells. He put both hands around the mug, to warm it a bit, but it was too cold to grasp for long.

"The fact is," he said to Genevieve, "Winona is doing fine. There's absolutely nothing to talk about with regard to her, unless one wants to praise her for becoming a success. But Blaine *is* in trouble. I don't mean to disparage what you're doing for him: I'm sure that's going to help. But neither would I dismiss his difficulties."

Genevieve breathed with effort and seemed to suppress a cough. "Mercer's just a bit high-strung. I've had some experience in that area. Daddy was apt to go off half-cocked occasionally." She made the kind of crooked smile reserved for lovable rascals.

At Reinhart's most benevolent hour, full of holiday fowl and spirits, he could have elevated Blaine Raven no higher than the level of dirty skunk. Another of television's recent trends, complete with new jargon-term for the actors to mouth in lieu of showing credible emotion, was the theme of the "battered" wife.

Genevieve's mother had been a forerunner in this area of domesticity, but luckily she was able to escape from time to time for a ride in the flying saucer which landed secretly in a vacant lot near her home. When, after many years of Raven's disgraces (arrest for beating up a whore who had been his client, disbarment as an attorney, bankruptcy, alleged indecent advances towards a black sailor in the men's toilet of a downtown tavern—in view of his lifelong record as a bigot this may have been a bum rap, or again a logical conclusion) and finally his self-incineration while blotto, when Reinhart's mother-in-law was free at last, she soon died, whether or not of a broken heart no one could ever know, but Reinhart thought it likely. One person may be connected to another by bonds which a third person can never understand. He was himself still attached to Genevieve, but in a fashion he could not have understood without this meeting. His old fear of her (yes, always, fear by one name or another) had been replaced by . . . God, could it only be pity?

"Yes," he said, after a sip of his still-too-cold Guinness. "Well, I know you'll do whatever you can for Blaine. You've always been his best friend in the world, and he reciprocates. I wish I had been on that kind of good terms with my own mother. . . . I wish I could be closer to Blaine."

The deft waitress brought his Irish stew. The aroma was the sort that expunges all forebodings. He sat there for a moment while the fragrant vapors warmed his face.

"Gen, why not order something to eat? If you don't feel so well, how about some soup? I suspect it'll be homemade and very good here. Or eggs in some form? Omelet?"

She pulled her black coffee to her and looked bleakly into it. "It's not healthy to eat when you don't feel hungry," she said, and added, with a new vulnerability: "Ask anybody."

"Your coffee's probably cold by now," Reinhart said.

She became the old Genevieve for an instant. "You just stuff your own face. Don't worry about me! I'm doing just fine. If I wanted to eat I could go to the finest restaurant in town. If you knew anything about Chicago, I could tell you of the famous places I dined at there all the time. I knew all the best people, was invited to the best functions. I wouldn't be back here at all but for the fact that my children need me." She suppressed another cough.

Reinhart was quite guiltlessly hungry, for the best reason in the world, and with unclouded pleasure he forked up a plump piece of meat and put it between his lips. Tender and juicy, exuding the quintessence of lamb, that unique identity which stewing reinforces even as it brings about the penetration of other flavors, the vegetables and herbs; but all the diverse fragrances are finally complementary. And the last condiment, that which made perfection, was supplied by the now cool bitterness of the swarthy stout.

"This Irish stew is really first-rate," said he. "Who would have thought that such a place could be found in a suburban mall?" It would certainly have been nicer to have had lunch with Helen Clayton, or in fact anyone else who would have eaten something, but he had survived the time when he was at the mercy of a table companion. It wasn't as much fun to eat alone as when accompanied, but he managed.

He even told Genevieve: "I doubt your main purpose in looking me up was to talk about Winona." He did not add what he believed to be the truth: that she had no interest whatever in her daughter, irrespective of Winona's sexual arrangements.

"I expected to be insulted," Genevieve said, and took him by surprise when she smiled in a saintly fashion. "And I guess you know it's not easy for me to turn the other cheek, but I'm willing to try, Carl. I understand a lot more than I used to. I got out into the world. I spread my wings."

He continued deliberately to eat the lovely stew. He was soon down to about an inch of stout. Did he dare order a refill? The risk was not that he might defy some diet, but rather that by taking too much of an attractive flavor he would corrupt the entire experience of it. Then, too, this was his first day at a job in more than a decade, and brewed liquids tended to make him sleepy. Therefore he decided to save the last hearty draft of Guinness to follow his final morsel of lamb.

Having made this decision, he turned to the task of fashioning a courteous response to Genevieve.

"Yes, Blaine has kept me informed. I know you did well in Chicago, but it was no surprise."

"What's that mean?" she asked suspiciously. "Are you making fun of me?"

Reinhart wearily shook his head. "You'll simply have to accept literally what I say nowadays. I'm not in the irony game any more, believe me. I'm too old for it. I was not surprised, because I always thought of you as being extremely good at whatever you tried."

She blinked, though whether she had really been appeased was hard to say. She rubbed her hands together. "I doubt you'd include being a wife in your list of my successes."

Reinhart had finished his stew. Now he took the last drink of stout. "I'd be the worst authority on that, considering the kind of husband I was." He thought about what else he might eat or drink. A simple green salad would be welcome.

"Aw," Genevieve said, "you weren't the world's worst."

This was a sufficiently unrepresentative utterance to distract him from his thoughts of food. "Good God, I wasn't? You could have fooled me."

"Now, now," Genevieve said coyly, waggling a finger at him, "you just said you've given up sarcasm." She touched her hair behind an ear. "The thing is, we were so *young*, Carl. So godawful young. We hadn't lived long enough. We left high school and got married, period. There was a great big world out there that we didn't even suspect existed."

How individuals assess their experiences rarely has any universal application, Reinhart had long since noticed. He could have pointed out, speaking for himself, that he had surely been young when he married, but he had also previously been halfway around the globe with the wartime Army: at least he had been made aware that a world existed from as far west as Texas, where he had trained, to as far east as Berlin, where he served on Occupation duty. However, she was right about his having been naïve in emotional matters—but that had still been true in his forties.

"I couldn't talk you into trying a dessert?" he now asked her. "Or a fresh cup of coffee anyway?"

She pushed towards him the cup that had sat neglected at her elbow. "I haven't touched this one. You might as well take it and save on ordering one for yourself."

The suggestion was so squalid that Reinhart could barely restrain himself from doing something rude: recoiling or sneering. He also realized that his revulsion was due at least in part to the thought of drinking from a vessel that had been consigned to her, even though she might not have drunk from it. The woman with whom he had lived twenty-two years, the mother of his children!

Genevieve never failed to bring out the worst in him, whatever the era. Guiltily he was about to take the cup she continued to offer and do something with it—at least knock it over as if by accident—when he was saved by the arrival of the impeccable waitress.

"We could both use hot cups of coffee," he said to the young woman, and was gratified to see the old cup carried away with his plate and glass.

"Just see they don't charge you for two," Genevieve said meanly. She went on: "This isn't much of a place. You have to eat all your meals here?"

It occurred to Reinhart that she had paid no real attention to him since arriving, had asked him nothing about his job, knew nothing of his talent in the kitchen—but then perhaps he was being just as bad in assuming she should be interested in these matters. But why had she looked him up?

"No," he replied patiently. "This is my first time here, and I think the food is very good, to my surprise."

But she continued to shake her head in what she apparently considered a show of pity. "Poor guy. You could use a home."

"I've got a home," he said, with quiet force. "Winona and I have a very nice home."

"Look," Genevieve said relentlessly, "I realize I threaten your ego with my intensity, my independence, but you may not really know yourself as well as you think. It's quite possible that, underneath it all, it's just such a challenge as I provide that you require." She was staring at him through that odd new mask of a face.

"Those years were not all bad, by any means," he said, "and when they weren't good, it was mostly my own fault. Anyway, we learned a lot, didn't we?" What an empty phrase! If life was all learning, then where did you go to put the knowledge into practice? But it was a thing to say.

The waitress came with the cups of coffee and the bill. She was

an attractive person. Time was, when in the company of Genevieve, Reinhart might have desired this young woman, might
even have imagined that her smile had a special, secret meaning
for him alone, that only his wife's presence obstructed him from
making a new friend—but if he returned alone, the girl would not
even be civil! Had he experienced that in reality or fantasy? Or did
it make any difference now?

He tasted the coffee. It was too weak. Winston's did not succeed
in rising above the norm in this case, but they did supply Half 'n'
Half in the thimble-sized container that was difficult to breach
without being splashed. Thin coffee was enriched by the adultera-
tion of cream: his was potable enough after being dosed.

Meanwhile Genevieve suggested by her inactivity that she
would not drink a drop of her current cup. He decided to take the
bull by the horns. The meal was virtually over anyway.

"Have you been getting enough to eat?"

She let a moment pass and then said in coy reproach: "I've been
waiting for a compliment on my slender figure. Don't you think
I'm pretty fantastic for a lady of my age?" She pursed her lips,
leaned forward, and added, sotto voce: "I had a little help with my
face, of course."

Reinhart made a neutral expression, presumably: he could not
have characterized it further without a mirror. He suddenly saw
the light. "You mean plastic surgery?"

"I'd only admit it to you, Carl. Nobody else knows. If I do say
so myself, it looks completely natural."

Poor devil. Reinhart realized that he could probably never be
matter-of-fact with regard to Genevieve: she could not fail, her life
long, to make him unhappy in some way, even if only in compassion.

"Oh, right," he said, "quite right. You've managed to keep your
youth, Gen, but you should be careful not to diet too much. It's not
healthy. I tell that to Winona all the time, but I feel I'm talking into
the wind. But at least she does stoke up on vitamins. I must admit
she's never sick."

This turn of subject met with little favor from his ex-wife. She
sniffed disagreeably before resuming her favorite theme. "I don't
mind saying that I've fought back against adversity and held my

ground. And yet I've never become cynical. Believe me, Carl, despite my sophistication there's still a lot about me that can still remember that young girl who conquered your heart."

For a moment he was nonplused. Had she learned about his 1968 "affair" (such as it was) with Eunice Munsing—and approved? . . . No, she was talking about herself. He should have understood that from the loving intonations.

"I'm sure there is, Genevieve." He picked up the check. The damages were not severe. Winston's was not out to punish its patrons. He was definitely pleased with this restaurant: the tables were now filled, and yet one's comfort was not reduced one whit, the noise had not increased by much, the service had not turned frenzied, the aromas remained fragrant. . . .

"Don't you get it even yet, Carl?"

He was being stared at with increasing intensity. He hated that in the best of times. He pushed his chair back and stood up. The check directed him to pay the cashier.

"Why, sure I do, Gen," he said with all the amiability at his disposal. "You wanted to show me how great you look and how well you're doing. I'm glad you did. We'll do it again some time, now that you're back in the area." He found his money and placed a tip on the table. He was aware that Genevieve had stayed where she was and was making no move to depart. Nevertheless he turned slowly in the direction of the entrance and began, as it were, to mark time.

"Carl."

"I'm afraid I've got to get back to work, if you don't mind. It's my first day on the job. It's very gratifying to me: I'm self-taught as a cook, you know. I've gone quite a ways beyond the meals I used to make when we were all together."

"We could be all together again," said Genevieve in a low, penetrating voice, a kind of stage whisper.

Standing there in a crowded restaurant, he thrilled with horror. But at last he managed to say: "We really must do this soon again."

Now she cried aloud: "You fool, you lovable fool, can't you see what I'm saying?" The polite eaters at the nearest table pretended not to hear.

Reinhart foresaw that her next speech might be at sufficient volume to command the attention of the entire room, unless he could placate her with an immediate response. She was quite capable of shaming him publicly, on his first day of work. He thought of something even worse: she might pursue him into the supermarket itself!

"Come along, Gen," he said, trying for a devil-may-care grin. "Let's take a walk."

Wondrously, this worked. At least she left the table. Now the nearby people decided to abandon their discretion and gawked rudely. Reinhart hoped no one who had seen him cooking crepes would recognize him now. That's the kind of thing you could not control once you went amongst the public. But it bolstered him to think of himself as a celebrity whom everybody was out to get the goods on.

He hastened ahead to the cashier's station, but that woman, as if in league with his ex-wife, found trivial things to occupy her until Genevieve reached his side and even put her hand through the elbow he necessarily crooked while tendering his money. Then, while the cashier was in the very act of counting out his change, her phone rang. Anticipating that he would be harassed by Genevieve while this woman engaged in a lengthy conversation, he found the energy to say impatiently: "Would you mind? I'm in a real hurry."

This was the sort of thing that he could not have succeeded at in the old days, especially when accompanied by the saboteur to whom he was married, but either the times or his style had improved.

"Oh, sure." Without a hint of annoyance the woman let the telephone ring and completed their transaction.

Once they had passed through the door, he tried discreetly to break Genevieve's hold on his forearm, but she only took a firmer purchase with her talons. This was the woman who, ten years before, had derided and demeaned him in all the classic ways and perhaps invented a new one or two. There had been a time when a moment like this could have occurred only in a desperate fantasy. She was abasing herself before him! He should see it as a triumph. But these reversals traditionally fail to happen at the right moment: when your adversary is at last at your mercy, he is no longer the proper object of revenge.

Moving decisively, Reinhart lifted Genevieve's fingers off him.

"I have to say good-bye," he said with the same firmness. "I'm due back at work."

She was leering at him. This could not have been a successful expression even when she was still pretty. Now it was ghastly.

"Hell," she said in a husky low tone, "you got time." She came close and dug at him with an elbow. "Want to go to a motel?"

"No, Gen, not really." He decided, on a whim, to add: "That won't be necessary."

She was still leering, even as he drew her aside so that an oncoming party of four could enter the restaurant—four businessmen, by their look, the kind of fellows Reinhart had in his day tried to resemble. He had exhausted a lot of life to arrive at where he was now.

Genevieve said: "I know I used to be naïve."

Reinhart was reaching the end of his string. "No, you weren't. You were O.K. Now I really *have* to go, Genevieve. But please let me know if there's anything I can do to help Blaine."

But she persisted, horribly: "I've improved, Carl. I really have. I know how to do everything now. I'm not shocked by—"

He felt a sneeze coming on, all at once, and whipped out his handkerchief. No doubt she said something vile during his nasal explosion. Fortunately he had not heard it. He put his handkerchief away.

"I'm sorry, Gen. You see, I've taken a vow of chastity. It's a religious thing."

A piece of rank cowardice, to be sure, but it was the best he could do on short notice, and if he stayed longer in her presence, he might lose all responsibility for his actions.

As he walked away she cried in a voice that sounded as though it might have come from a loudspeaker: "You pansy!"

She was really broadcasting her age: that had been an archaic term for ever so long.

CHAPTER
7

It was not to be believed. No sooner had he gone back into the world than he encountered his old nemesis. Fate always arranged it so that Genevieve was there to hamstring him at the beginning of any race.

He slowed his stride, looking unhappily across the parking lot at the supermarket. He had half a mind not to return: simply to bug off and not be seen again. It would scarcely matter that much to Grace Greenwood. He suddenly convinced himself that this employment could have no possible motive but to please Winona by giving him a sinecure. Blaine had recognized that truth. And even DePau had been quite right: it could not be imagined that the gourmet department would ever come to any good.

What a fool he had been to spend all morning cooking crepes, and in a foolish costume! The result had been that he now felt worse than at any time during the last decade. In his despair he even began to think otherwise of his lunch: had the stew really been all that good? And as to Winston's in general, what did he know after eating only one dish, not even followed by a salad?

The sequence of unhappy thoughts was interrupted when, slowly as he walked, he was almost struck by a car, a white Cadillac that rolled swiftly across the blacktop on the bias, so to speak, in defiance of the painted parking slots. Reinhart was called back to responsibility. He straightened up, looked left and right . . . and heard an ugly cry behind him. It was Genevieve. Had she been shouting all this while, unheard by him in his slough of depression?

". . . warn you, you pervert. I'll tell the world. I'll get you if it's the last thing I do!"

She was not following him. It was far worse: she remained in front of Winston's and raised her voice to a greater volume as he receded from her. Never had he suspected that her vocal cords could be so powerful.

He refused to look about and count the persons who were observing this ugly episode. No doubt there were some, but fortunately at any given time in such a place most people were contained in cars, usually with the radio playing and, according to season, heater humming or air conditioner blowing, deaf to outdoors. Not to mention that few nowadays had the stomach to interfere with a disorderly person: this was even true of policemen, who could be killed, and doctors, who could be sued.

The white Caddy which had passed him earlier on had come to an abrupt stop and was, reverse-gear lights illuminated, backing up at excess speed. This took Reinhart's attention off his old problem and gave him a new worry. But the car stopped just before running him down, and Helen Clayton got out of the passenger's side.

The Cadillac accelerated away. Helen came to Reinhart. Never had he been so glad to see anyone. He wasn't sure what effect this might have on Genevieve. It might even aggravate her problem, but at least he was no longer alone, back to the wall.

"Hi, partner," said Helen, who was a significant presence even upon a flat sweep of blacktop. The belt of her trench coat was loosely tied, and her green scarf flapped in a breeze he had not hitherto noticed. She came to Reinhart and linked her arm with his, but jovially and not in the raptorial fashion of Genevieve.

She cried: "Back to the old assembly line!"

Reinhart decided against immediately looking back to see what effect this would have on his ex-wife. It might be possible to make some distance without Helen's identifying the shouting, hysterical woman as being associated with him, though it was true that she had seen Genevieve in the supermarket.

"Well," he said bluffly, "did you have a nice lunch?"

She elbowed his ribs. "Not really." She made a snorting kind of laugh, which probably was not mirthful, but listening as he was for obstreperousness from the rear, he could not be as precise in his reactions to Helen as he would have liked.

"I see," he said, though of course he did not. He was still tensed for a shot in the back and could not believe that he was no longer under fire. But the fact remained that he heard nothing from Genevieve. "Uh, I had a good meal, or a fine dish anyway, at Winston's. Have you ever been there?"

Helen stopped and turned to him. "She didn't make a scene, I hope."

Reinhart shook his head. "I was hoping you wouldn't notice, Helen. I'm sorry."

"Gosh, Carl, it isn't *your* fault." She took his arm again. "It's just lousy you have to be embarrassed."

Now he took the nerve to look for Genevieve. . . . She was gone. Utterly. She must have parked her car over that way, unless she had gone into one of the shops. Was it beyond her to duck down behind the automobiles and stalk them? Could she have slipped behind the buildings, to circle around and arrange an ambush?

"You know," he told Helen, "this is the first time I've laid eyes on her for ten years. I thought I was done with her forever, and I'm sure that would have been true if she had been successful in Chicago—that's where she's been for some time."

"Bad penny, huh?" They resumed their walk.

"No," said Reinhart, "not really. Genevieve's a capable person. She's quite good at business. It's in her private life that she has difficulties."

"Now, Carl," said Helen, squeezing the arm she held, "let's not hear you speaking without respect for yourself."

"Was I doing that?"

"Why, sure you were!" Helen said with vigor.

He knew no serious reason why he should have found Helen so reassuring, but he did. Perhaps it was a matter of her physical solidity. From time to time, turning to speak to him, she rested her left breast on his arm. Again she was arousing him. Already they seemed not only old friends, but comfortable lovers—if there was such a thing as the latter: you wouldn't know from Reinhart's experience from at least as far back as the end of his Army days. He had not had a girl *friend* since then. He had never been interested in females whom he had not craved. And when sexual desire came into play, matters of relative power soon took precedence over feelings.

Back at work, an hour passed too swiftly to be believed. More persons than Reinhart would have thought shopped for food in the early afternoon, at least on this day. He had almost exhausted the crepe batter made during the morning session when DePau materialized at the table.

"Say," he said, "your boss wants to talk to you."

"On the phone?" Reinhart served hot, sauced, triangulated crepes to three customers. More were waiting. "Could you tell Grace I'll call back when I get a break?" He looked up the aisle. Still more carts were coming his way. "We're on a roll."

There was a spiteful note in the voice of the supermarket manager. "Fella, she wants to talk to you *right now.*" DePau turned and addressed the crowd: "I'm sorry." He waved his arms. "That's all for today. We have to close the stand down now." He moved so as to block their access to the area of the table occupied by the chafing dish.

Reinhart wiped his hands on a towel and removed his chef's bonnet. He intended to complain to Grace about DePau's officious rudeness. Surely, it was his supermarket, or anyway it was managed by him, but he had no call to be so lacking in common courtesy. Besides, another batch of batter had been made just after lunch and put to rest in the portable icebox; it would be almost ready for use now. They weren't closing up! He considered asking those who had been turned away to wait the few moments he would be on the phone. It grieves a cook to deny an eater.

Helen, selling packets of the instant mix, looked over the bent head of a customer and raised her eyebrows at Reinhart.

"All right," said DePau to Helen, and he actually snapped his fingers at her, "let's close up over here too. I'll have somebody take care of your stock."

Helen grimaced. "What?"

"You'll get credit for what you've got coming," DePau said. "Just leave now!" He was clearly in a state of great impatience.

Helen shrugged and, turning from him, tended to something at her table.

"Did you hear me?" DePau's voice rose an octave.

Reinhart had started away, but he lingered when the manager addressed Helen. At this latest piece of outrageousness he could not restrain himself.

"Listen here," he said to DePau, moving towards him. "You keep a civil tongue in your head."

The manager looked as though he might be suffocated by his internal humors. He coughed and spoke in a voice so constricted that much of what he said was unintelligible. "Police . . . publicity . . . sue . . ." Reinhart could distinguish at least these three words, which were menacing in a general way, but nonsensical as to particular application.

"Just calm down," he said, his emotion changing from outrage to a concern for the man's sanity.

But DePau seemed even more highly exercised when this had been said. Reinhart determined to get to the bottom of the matter without further delay.

"All right, let's get to the phone."

DePau twitched his index finger at Helen. "You too."

They all marched through the rear to a bleak room walled in cinder block and containing battered office furniture and a remarkable amount of papers. In one corner a thin, blade-nosed woman was punching at a large calculator.

The manager handed Reinhart a telephone handset.

"Hello," said Reinhart. "Is this Grace?"

He waited for several moments until she came onto the line.

"Carl, I think we'll wind up the Top Shop demo, O.K.? Take the rest of the day off, and I'll be in touch. Now give me Clayton."

"Grace," he asked, "has something happened?"

"Time to move on, Carl! Now just put Clayton on the line."

Grace really was hard to withstand when she spoke ex cathedra. Reinhart licked his upper lip and gave the phone to Helen.

"Uh-huh, uh-huh. . . . O.K., Grace," Helen said. "Sure." She hung up and said to Reinhart, smiling: "Not a bad deal, Carl. We got the rest of the day off with pay. C'mon, let's get lost."

DePau was hovering near the door. "You can leave by the back."

A plump young woman appeared. She was dressed in the blue smock that constituted the store's livery, and she carried what turned out to be the clothing from the locker that Helen and Reinhart shared.

"Listen here," Reinhart told DePau, "some of that kitchen equipment out there is my personal stuff. I'm going out—"

The supermarket manager put a finger into the air. "All of it," said he, "has already been packed and is on its way to the Epicon office."

They took their outer clothing from the girl, and DePau led them quickly through a dimly lit, windowless storage area, found a door, and opened it.

Reinhart and Helen emerged onto a potholed patch of blacktop on the southern side of the building. Around the corner came an enormous truck, and to avoid being splashed by it from a pool of standing water, they moved along the sheer cinder-block wall to the corner and a vista of the rest of the shopping center.

"Mind telling me the explanation of this strange episode?" Reinhart asked. "Now that we've got a minute? In fact, now that we've got all day?"

She was laughing at him. "You've still got your apron on!" He undid the strings. Helen was getting into her trench coat.

In the same good-humored way she said: "Some woman called up DePau and bad-mouthed us."

"What?" He had balled the apron and taken it in one hand while with the other he helped himself get into one sleeve of his jacket.

"Said we were drinking in public and pawing one another."

Reinhart's jaw ached. After a moment he realized the pain could be relieved by unclenching his teeth.

Helen went on: "Grace, to give her credit, said she didn't believe it, but he complained to her, so what could she do?"

With wincing hang of the head, Reinhart said: "You know who that was, don't you?"

She shrugged generously. "I've got an idea."

"And I was feeling sorry for that bitch." He finally was able to shift hands on the ball of apron and get into the other sleeve of the jacket. "Ten years! I don't see her for ten years, and the first time she shows up . . ."

"Well, hell," said his genial colleague, "look at it this way, Carl. She got us half a day off."

The extraordinary thing was that he did not feel as dispirited as he should have. That he was not utterly devastated by this experience was due only to Helen. It was difficult to feel hopeless in her presence. He smiled at her.

"And anybody but DePau would have ignored it," said she. "But he's always been a dirty creep."

"You've worked there before?"

"Sure," said Helen, "and he's never missed once in sneaking a feel back at the lockers."

"That guy? I'll be damned! And he looks like such a prude. In the old movies a man who looked like that would play a preacher or maybe a mortician." It was amazing: Reinhart couldn't get over the basic fact that he was in a good mood. As they walked slowly towards the parking lot Helen was usually touching him with hip or shoulder. They formed a unit of affection.

"I don't know whether he really thinks we're in cahoots," said she, "but he wants to get back at me. He's not my type." She bumped Reinhart for emphasis.

"*Cahoots,*" he echoed happily. He had a deep attachment to the slang that predated World War II, probably for the simple reason that he himself was of the same vintage, but there had been a geniality to that language and an ebullience, which so far as he could see had been replaced only by grunts of insolence and anxiety: *get it on, hang in there, that's a turn-off.*

"Should we take both cars?" Helen asked. "Probably simpler to leave one here and pick it up on the way back."

"I don't have a car," said Reinhart. "So that's even simpler. But where are we supposed to be going?"

She swung in against him. "When will we have a better opportunity?"

An erotic interpretation could be made of this, but Reinhart was not yet so old that he had forgotten the frustrated expectations of his youth. In those days, anyway, women conventionally implied much more than they meant to do, and he had been marked for life by such experiences.

Therefore he said, modestly: "We might have a drink." They were now walking among the ranked cars.

"Thing to do," said Helen, letting his arm go and plucking into her strap-hung purse, "is to pick up a bottle." She found some keys and went purposefully to a large, battered, dirty blue automobile parked between two sensible, neat, economical vehicles manufactured by former enemies of the United States. Reinhart had not owned a car in a decade, and he could by now identify few makes. Helen's chariot looked as though it had been designed for the sheer purpose of squandering fuel.

She entered the front seat on her knees and slid over to lift the peg on the passenger's door. The interior of the car was in somewhat better shape than the coachwork. It had a homey feeling, though probably only because it was Helen's. Funny how machines are like that.

Reinhart slipped in. The plastic seat was warm, no doubt from the sun that had penetrated the windshield, though at the moment it was in seclusion behind a barrier of cloud. Helen started the car, making a noise like that of a dishwasher within which a glass has broken, and having driven no more than a hundred yards across the asphalt, she stopped at a liquor store.

Reinhart understood that he was expected to make a purchase. He asked Helen for her choice of beverage, though he was puzzled as to where they were going to drink it: from the bottle, in the car?

"Gee," said Helen, "I'm partial to Scotch, but it's pretty expensive—"

Reinhart raised his hand. "Say no more, my lady. Your needs will be answered." After what should have been a degenerative experience—perhaps his job was gone for good, and would Genevieve stop at that?—he had moved ever closer to exuberance.

He dropped his balled apron on the seat and went into the store and examined the appropriate shelves.

The bulbous man behind the counter said: "Can I help?"

"Just choosing a Scotch," said Reinhart, "for my friend. She thinks it's a good way to kill an afternoon."

"If she's somebody you're out to impress," said the liquor dealer, "may I suggest Chivas?" He turned to the shelves behind him and found a boxed bottle.

"By George," said Reinhart, playing a role for his own delectation, "I think we ought to spare no expense to please the little lady." He withdrew his wallet and paid the bill. He assumed that

Helen would give him a lift home after their drink: he now no longer had bus fare.

"Where do we give this a belt?" he asked her when he regained the car. "We really ought to have glasses and ice." He brandished the bag and could not forbear from gloating: "This is the *crème de la crème.*"

Helen frowned as she started up. "Uh, that's not like cream dee menth, is it? I don't go much for cordials, in general."

He allayed her fears by unbagging, unboxing, and displaying the bottle. "The fact is that I'm not much of a whiskey drinker," he said. "Not nowadays, anyhow. In view of that, I thought only the best would do."

She gave the Scotch a loving smile. "Now you're talkin'." She gunned the car off the blacktop onto the highway. This was a suburban shopping area in which one mall abutted another for what a local promotional effort sought to have called the Miracle Mile, but it consumed even more space than the name asserted. Beyond the malls began a sequence of motels: the notable names were represented, Ramada, Holiday, Best Western, and a far cry they were from the bleak "tourist courts" Reinhart could remember from childhood trips with his parents, when in fact Dad usually decided he could not afford such luxurious accommodations and instead checked them into that even quainter facility of those times, the "tourist home," viz., someone's private house, where Grandma or Sister Sue had to vacate her little bedroom, second floor rear, for the lodging of strangers at one dollar the party, and you had to queue up for a toilet of which the seat never cooled.

But in among the local examples of the famous chains, with the conspicuous landscaping of genuine shrubbery which doggedly persisted in looking like synthetic, the palatial parody of their reception areas, the high marquees celebrating the current gathering of men dressed in polyester—tucked into an interstice, as it were, between two of the gaudies was a simple, almost austere rank of discrete little huts, called, remarkably for this day, Al's Motel.

It was into the forecourt of Al's that Helen easily swung her car. Reinhart honestly believed, by at least 75 percent, that she was stopping there in the performance of some errand.

Helen slowed to a crawl in the approach to the square little building where respects, and a fee, must be paid before access was gained to the cottages behind, but she now said, with evidence of concern: "This is real private, Carl," and pressed her foot down. The car gained speed. They descended a slight elevation and turned in back of the little office building. Helen stopped there. "You can check in through the back door if you want."

Now Reinhart was suddenly soaked to the skin, as it were, with embarrassment, as if God had peeled away the roof of the automobile and poured a bucketful on his head. He sat there grinning as moist heat went everywhere except into his cold toes. As it happened, he had never his life long checked into any public hostelry with a woman who was not his legal spouse, in fact, who was not Genevieve, his only wife. And indeed seldom since their honeymoon had he stayed overnight with her except at their own dwelling. They had rarely traveled in their two decades together. There had never been a sufficiency of money for routine existence, for the two children had arrived in the earliest years (Blaine indeed so soon that Reinhart still might all too easily wonder about the boy's paternity). His extramarital experiences, most of them with professionals, had been in private places, their own apartments or the hotel bedroom which was his first temporary home after the break with Gen.

"Helen," he said, "can't we just be friends for a while? Maybe when we know each other a little better, things will work themselves out."

"Gee, Carl," she said, smiling an insinuation, "I guess I misinterpreted. . . . Uh, well, you're a special kind of guy, you know. It's not easy to figure you out at first."

Reinhart rubbed his chin. "Do you think I'm gay? Is that what you're saying?"

Helen raised her hands. "Listen . . ."

"Well, I'm not." He wondered whether he might have been too defensive.

"It's O.K. by me, whatever," she assured him. No doubt she meant it: generosity seemed a basic trait with her. But it was evident that her disappointment was still greater than her tolerance. She smiled wryly and put her car into reverse.

"Wait a minute." Reinhart had said this on an impulse, surprising himself. "It *would* be a shame to waste a perfectly good afternoon."

But perhaps it was in the interest of pride that Helen continued to back out of the slot down behind the motel office.

"I think the moment has passed, Carl," said she, though in as friendly a manner as ever.

"The idea was terrific. I'm sorry I didn't understand it at first."

Helen was now driving up the ascending slope, towards the highway, the old engine laboring. "I think you were kind of shocked, that's what I think."

"I may have been," Reinhart confessed. "I guess time has caught up, maybe even passed me in some respects, Helen. It's funny when you realize that has happened."

The car had reached the entrance to the highway by now, but Helen stayed where she was even after a gap appeared in the traffic.

"Is that your trouble?" she asked. "Is *that* all?"

Reinhart was actually a bit annoyed by her scoffing, kind as he knew she meant to be. "It's a real thing," he said, "feeling your age. You can't say that time suddenly pulls a trick on you. You've had plenty of warning, God knows, but it seems as if you are suddenly in a different category. I'm actually in better condition now, in every way but chronologically, than I was ten years back. I'm even healthier! I'm not overweight, and I drink very little. My blood pressure's lower, and so on. But I've got *ten years less.*"

"Gosh," Helen said, "I hope *I* didn't make you so morbid. Heck, I've got at least one friend who's older than you, and he still has a lot of fun." She looked at him in what he took to be compassion, and his pride was affected once more.

He said seriously, but with a smile: "Sorry, I really didn't intend to throw myself on your mercy." A thought came to him. He looked back at Al's and saw what he wanted: an outdoor telephone at the corner of the office. "I'm going to use that phone. You want to stay here or back up?"

She did the latter, and he got out and went to the booth.

He dialed his home number and waited until it rang uselessly a dozen times. He remembered that Winona had a modeling assignment which would occupy her all day. Furthermore, the job was about thirty miles from town, at the warehouse of a furniture firm. No doubt she would be depicted sitting at the foot of one of the beds currently on sale. Reinhart suddenly wondered whether there were men who might find this an erotic image.

He returned to Helen's old car.

She immediately asked: "Is the coast clear?"

"Huh?"

"Didn't you just call home to see if anybody was there?"

Reinhart laughed in admiration and a certain embarrassment. "Woman, you scare me! Can you always read minds?"

Helen joined in the laughter. She started the engine.

Reinhart said: "I've never done this before, but I don't see any real reason why it wouldn't be O.K." In truth, he could see several reasons, foremost among them being that he had always considered the apartment as Winona's, where he was essentially a guest. "See, I live with my daughter. But she'll be working for several hours yet."

"If she's a good girl," said Helen, driving forcefully along the highway, "she won't begrudge her dad doing what comes naturally, I don't think." She operated the car in what not too many years before had been thought a style peculiar to men: wheel in a firm but easy grasp, body comfortably slumped. "Gosh, my dad used to like the girls well enough, the son of a gun. Not that that made me happy when I was a kid! I caught him once kissing some floozy in the garage when we lived over on Elm. They were probably going to do more, but I just blundered in. I was ten or eleven, went to put my bike away . . ." Helen rambled on in this wise. Reinhart found her presence to be very soothing. This was hardly the mood in which he had gone to any other tryst in all his life. But, once again, you change with age. One of the first things to go is the sense of sex as suspenseful.

He gave her directions from time to time, but said little beyond that. She related another anecdote about her father's lighthearted lechery, her mother appearing as only a pale, inconsequential shadow. Still another symptom of Reinhart's growing older, to his own mind, was his recognition of the miracle of descent. It was common enough not to see how X, a beauty, could have been born of ugly Y, or how the genius Bill could be the sire of Bill Jr., the imbecile, or why the Fates would bring a saint from the loins of a criminal. But the fact was that no sons or daughters, spitting images though they might seem to be, resembled their parents in any way but the superficial! This was quite a radical theory, but it was firmly founded on Reinhart's own experience as son and father. Really, the more he thought about the matter, the more he saw that his immediate relatives had always been utter strangers.

When they reached the apartment building he directed Helen to enter the underground garage and find the parking slot that was assigned to Winona.

The elevator could be boarded at the level of the garage, but only after its door was unlocked. Reinhart found the proper key on his ring.

"They've got it all worked out, haven't they?" asked Helen. "The way to do things right, how to lock a place and so on. I'll bet this is an expensive building."

"Do you like that?"

"Are you serious?" she asked, and pulled his face to hers and kissed him.

The experience was unprecedented for Reinhart, so far as he could remember; and try to remember is what he did now, lest he lose his bearings utterly. Men of his age and situation were not routinely embraced in elevators. In emotional moments he took comfort in the crafting of general rules, while knowing, all the while, that the only truth is particular.

The door slid away, and they deboarded at the fourth floor. Reinhart was in an equilibrium between wanting vainly to encounter a recognizable neighbor and hoping to sneak in and out undetected. That is, he had a perfect right to bring a woman home, on the one hand, while on the other furtiveness made for more excitement. Yet Helen was the married one. She seemed to move boldly enough around town. He thought of asking her about this, but decided that it would be bad taste until they knew each other better. Which in turn caused him to reflect that he had never gone this far with any nonprostitute of whom he knew less.

But they were alone in the hallway as he unlocked the apartment door.

"This is real nice," said Helen in the foyer.

"There's a river view," said Reinhart. He helped her out of the trench coat, which he hung over a straightbacked chair. Whenever the need came to dispose of a guest's outer clothing, he was reminded of a deficiency in the apartment: there was no closet near the front door. He and Winona were in their third year of residence and had yet to provide a halltree or row of hooks or whatever. Yet he forgot about the problem as soon as the guest went away. In his uncertainty now he spoke of this banal matter to Helen.

Suddenly he saw that she was now as uneasy as he was, rather, as he had been, for this state is oftentimes relieved when it is seen as shared.

He put his hands around her from the rear and lowered his face into her neck. How long had it been since he had last done that sort of thing? This was much too simple an embrace to try on a whore, and too immodest. The complicated ecstasies can easily be purchased, but nobody sells an honestly warm caress.

She took away his hands, but only to pull him by one of them into the short hallway that obviously led to the bedrooms. Her taking the initiative, in his domicile, excited him. He had always been aroused by sexual rudeness or arrogance on the part of a woman, though in early life he had never understood this.

Until this moment his bedroom had been a monastic cell. He went to the buttons of Helen's blouse, she to his belt buckle. He would have lingered at the task, but she was impatient, and they were both undressed in no time at all.

He thought of something. There was an outside chance that Winona might come home early; accidental events were always possible. He stepped across his bedside rug and began to close the door. He could hear Helen draw the sheets over herself. Her body was as opulent as he had supposed: he was worried about doing justice to it.

Something hard to identify either by outline or movement entered the hallway. A shadow is exceptionally fearsome when one is naked, and for an instant Reinhart shrank back. But then he remembered Helen, whom he was obliged to protect as guest and as woman, and he projected his head through the doorway.

The figure had reached him. It was identifiably human by now, and smaller than he, but bent as he was he looked into its face. It was Mercer, his missing daughter-in-law.

She supported herself with two hands on the doorframe and made a strenuous attempt to speak coherently, but succeeded only in breathing on Reinhart. That such exhaust fumes were not colored blue was a wonder.

"Mercer," said her father-in-law quietly. "You've given us all quite a scare."

"Wwww . . ." said she, and spun suddenly about and staggered back up the hall, turned the corner, and by the sound of it, soon fell.

"I'm sorry," Reinhart said to Helen's face on his pillow. "That's my son's wife. I'll have to do something about her." He opened the closet and took his robe from the hook behind the door.

"Some days," Helen said cheerily, "are like that." She made no move to leave bed.

Reinhart closed the door behind him and went in search of Mercer. He came back immediately.

"Say, Helen," he said, "I'm going to be occupied for quite a while. I guess you're right about it's not being our day."

She climbed out of bed. Helen was really something to see, and she lacked absolutely in false, or perhaps even real, modesty.

"Can't I help?"

"I don't think so," said he. "But thanks."

"Is this an old story?" She began deftly to dress.

"I don't really know. Until now I've been on only the most polite terms with the lady. My son and I aren't the closest of pals. . . . Listen, I really am sorry."

Helen for the first time turned inscrutable. "Better get out there," she said. "Don't worry about me."

It occurred to Reinhart that some member of his family, small as it was, had been available to ruin every effort he had made during the last fortnight.

CHAPTER
8

Mercer had the thin, fine-angled sort of face that was once thought to be aristocratic, especially by those who had been filmgoers in the pre-War era. Whether cut of bone was still a criterion for good birth, or whether indeed there was still something, anywhere in creation, that deserved the designation of high-class, was one of the many matters on which Reinhart lacked authority.

His daughter-in-law was a slender, comely young woman, with good long legs, a flat chest, and skin that seemed always somewhat roughened by the weather. She had exceptionally fine hands, of which Reinhart was aware because in the six years of her marriage to his son his association with her had amounted to little more than a handshake on arrivals and departures. And all too few were even those occasions, owing no doubt to Blaine's disinclination to frequent his father. But though Mercer might not be to blame for a negative situation, neither could she be commended for making the least effort towards the positive. Reinhart would not have been astounded had she failed to recognize him on a public sidewalk.

And even now, as he clasped her naked body to him, they were no more intimate except in the most superficial sense. Mercer in fact was unconscious.

Here he was, alone in a bathroom with an unclad young woman, himself quite stark beneath the terry-cloth robe, of which even the knotted belt had worked loose in his struggles to move her person, which could change in an instant from altogether inert to woodenly rigid, to rubbery elastic, to pluckingly prehensile. . . . He had not performed such a job since delivering his father-in-law from the parking lot of a roadhouse bar many years before. At that time brute force was an available, even a gratifying technique. But you couldn't handle a young wife and mother with the same means that were appropriate to a husky drunk you furthermore detested. Moreover, you weren't getting any younger.

He had stripped and hauled her showerwards because she had vomited all over herself and, alas, not only down her bosom and through her lap and onto her shoes—no, she had also puked onto the predominantly pale-blue couch and the altogether beige rug and rolled over the one and tracked through the other. Even more regrettably, she had been drinking not gin or vodka or Italian vermouth or even dry sherry, but rather a fluid that was, at least when regurgitated, maroon.

He propped her now in the shower stall in his tubless bathroom, and because her knees threatened to buckle, he briefly held the knobby patella of the left one, so discouraging the incipient slump. Her sleek thigh rose above his wrist, her flat belly pressed against his shoulder cap. He could not help noticing when undressing her that her chest was not so flat as when she was clothed. She had indeed a remarkably shapely figure for a mother of two. These observations were not erotic, but rather in the service of a moral inquiry: why would such a young healthy body have nothing better to do on a standard weekday afternoon than fill itself with red wine?

When it seemed as though she might lean there in the tiled corner and not slide away, at least not until he quickly got the water flowing, Reinhart released Mercer's kneecap (surely one of the most discreet below-the-waist points of contact, if contact had to be made, and it did), rose smartly from his bend, and seized the glass knobs that controlled the flow of water to the shower. The mix could be a tricky matter when one sought a compromise between melting iceberg and searing steam. In the strait compartment of tile, the characteristic stench of vomit could not be eluded. His own children had been great pukers when small, and in fact Winona, as might have been expected, was notable at the art or craft, performing it often, at a certain age, in public places: restaurants, movies, and of course on parents' night at school.

"Throwing up" had its endearing side for Reinhart, and washing the puker was to some degree an exercise in nostalgia, for it had usually been he, and not Genevieve, who had handled such emergencies as might soil the handler.

In mixing the waters to achieve a comfortable balance, one could not, when sharing a narrow cubicle with another body, avoid getting soaked. Almost immediately his terry-cloth robe absorbed several pounds of water. He had avoided looking at Mercer's face, because though she had been consistent in keeping her eyes closed thus far, she might at any moment open them up, and her subsequent embarrassment would be a horror to him, for he would have no means of relieving it at this moment. Whereas if he could just get her cleansed, put into a pair of Winona's pajamas, and tucked into bed, the worst of it would be in the past when eventually she came to consciousness.

But to clean her effectively he could hardly keep his face averted. God, there was puke on her fine chin and snot running from her delicate nose. This was, he had to admit, less repulsive on a handsome face than it would have been on someone ugly or old: yet another example of life's inequity. Furthermore, one quick shot from the shower-head and her face was impeccable once more. He seized her, by shoulder and waist, and turned her under the spray of water.

He would have preferred to disregard the matter of soap, in applying which there could be no modesty, but when undressing her he could hardly have ignored certain olfactory suggestions that she had not lately had a good wash.

He lifted her over the curb of the shower stall. She had not yet come to, and he gently toweled her dry. Only a few more yards of thin ice to cross. He dropped the dampened towel and draped her trunk with a dry one. Obviously Winona should not be inconvenienced; he would sleep on the couch tonight. He lifted Mercer again and carried her to his own room. This was a more taxing job than any he had yet performed. He had to swing her this way and that to negotiate two doorways, and even slender young women are much heavier than they look. In the hallway the towel that had covered her slithered to the floor.

Reinhart was now carrying an unconscious, naked woman while

himself wearing a soaking wet bathrobe that gaped open almost
to the crotch. What a perfect moment for someone to burst in
unannounced. Blaine, for example. Or, far worse, Genevieve! He
actually listened in bravado-dread for such an intrusion. *Come on,
it's all I need!* But how could they get in? Well, how had Mercer
penetrated the locked door? It might well be the kind of day when
such things were arranged by the Fates, to whom it meant no
more to spring a lock than to whip ex-wives into frenzies of hatred.

So goaded by resentment and self-pity, Reinhart managed to
carry the leadenly limp burden to his bed. He covered Mercer
with the spare blanket from the closet and then went to Winona's
room to fetch night clothes. His daughter's chamber was scarcely
uncharted territory. Winona would have hired a maid, but why
squander money when he was home all day? He ran the vacuum
twice a week, changed linens, and whatnot: little enough.

Winona had been none too neat as a fat girl, but as she turned
sleek she became tidier in all respects. Of course, her appearance
was her fortune. She could not be seen in clothes that had spent
the night on the floor. Her walk-in closet was a rustling, ghostly
forest of dry-cleaner's plastic bags. Reinhart had no cause to in-
spect her more intimate apparel, but when by chance he was
present as she opened a drawer, the contents thereof always
looked so immaculate that he was once moved to ask whether she
wore anything twice. "Oh, gosh, Dad, a few more times than that,"
she had said solemnly. But not many more, he realized: which
explained why when emptying her wastebasket, he always saw
tumble forth so many of those little tags and labels, straight pins,
and clear plastic.

And yet, and yet . . . you could share a home with somebody,
somebody of your own blood, you could sleep in the next room,
you could vacuum their quarters and empty their waste can, and
yet be utterly ignorant of an essential feature of their life.

Reinhart chose the effective dresser drawer on his first try,
merely by application of reason: it was on the last level before the
floor. He kept his own nightgear in a similar situation. As he expected, along with several sets of pajamas that had perhaps been
laundered once or twice, there were even more pairs yet in their
original packages. These were invariably of a hard, flat fabric and

in a single and simple color: beige, pale yellow, powder blue, or light green. Winona stayed with the matter-of-fact when it came to bedwear.

Reinhart chose a new pair of blue pajamas for Mercer, shut the drawer, and straightened up, feeling a twinge in the small of his back: that kind of thing was routine when you were older, and often happened for no good reason, i.e., you made no real exertion, whereas you might lift a heavy weight with impunity. One wondered whether Nature was really on the ball at all times.

He walked deliberately to his own room. Now that his daughter-in-law had been washed, it would be even more embarrassing to deal with her bare body.

... The aforementioned problem was shown to be an idle worry by his glance towards the bed. The blanket was obviously empty, yet in disbelief he wasted a moment by probing into its rumple. Mercer had gone!

He ran into the hallway, but stopped and turned and came back to explore his small bathroom. He then sprinted into the living room, made the righthand turn, passed the dining table, looked into the kitchen, wheeled about, and dashed back.

It was not out of the question that she could have hidden in a closet and emerged after he had gone by. Therefore he once again searched his own quarters, and because by now she might have gained Winona's suite, he looked into his daughter's bedroom and bath.

It was not until his second trip through the front of the apartment that he noticed the door was ajar. No, it was simply not possible that she had gone out. For one, he had not heard a sound. For another, her wretched, reeking clothes were still on the floor of his bathroom. Persons whom one knows do not go into public stark naked, no matter how drunk. Still, searching the place again would clearly be useless. He would not find her within its walls. Reason must insist that she had gone elsewhere.

There was one hope, not by any means farfetched: perhaps she had attired herself in garments from his closet or dresser.

He opened the front door just enough to allow the thrusting of his head into the corridor. At the very outset of any emergency there is often a moment or two in which to admit doubt that there *is* an impending disaster. Suppose that Mercer, wearing, say, his raincoat, was waiting for the elevator out there. Or, at worst, was so occupied, though jaybird-naked, but no one had seen her yet. On this side of the building most of the tenants were employed persons who did not return until evening. Reinhart was the only live-in housekeeper of the fourth floor East, and though some of his neighbors had visiting maids, these women usually came towards the end of the week. The chances were excellent for evading a scandal.

The only trouble was that Mercer could not be seen. He left the apartment and explored the length of the hallway, turning all corners and going through West after finishing with East. He had of course straightaway checked the indicator lights on the elevators. Neither car had been in use since he left the apartment. Again he had to consider what was left after all the eliminations: in this case, stairways. Hardly anybody used the stairs. If you had to choose an area in which to be disgraceful, there was none more inconspicuous. Despite the twenty-four-hour presence of a doorman and the locking of all exterior entrances, the stairways suggested, by their very nature, crimes against the person. If Mercer had gone by that route, she would be unlikely to meet anyone respectable, and all might still be well—unless of course she had been raped or killed.

Reinhart chose the stairway on his own, east side. There was another on the west, but he must assume that even distraught drunks took the line of least resistance. He descended to the third level. Would she have gone on down directly to the ground, or might she have stopped off at one of the intervening floors? If he examined each floor uselessly, and she meanwhile headed for the bottom, there would be no reaching her before it was too late.

He quickened his stride, but he touched every step, not daring to evoke from the distant past the reckless schoolboy style which consumed two at a time. The possibility of being crippled is something to be taken seriously after a certain age—whichever age one is in when the thought occurs.

At the ground level he went through the door to the lobby. A bald man, carrying an oblong case, was just boarding one of the elevators. No one else was in evidence but the stately black door-man, who was gazing serenely, hands clasped in the small of his back, through his portal of plate glass.

"Andrew," asked Reinhart, and though no one else was present he discreetly lowered his voice, "have you seen a lady pass this way?"

"A lady, Colonel?"

"Young," said Reinhart, "and perhaps—just a moment! You must have been on duty when she arrived, else how did she get in? Did a young woman ask for our apartment earlier today? Second, did the same young woman leave only a few moments ago?"

"Well, sir," said Andrew, "I saw no such young woman on her entrance. She might have arrived while I was on my lunch, at which time Joe DiLassi from the custodial staff watched the door for me. Or she could have come in through the garage. But not too many moments ago I did open the door to let out a young woman not known to me to be a tenant in this house." Andrew had a rich bass voice. Reinhart wondered whether the man might have been a professional singer at one time, but never asked for fear that the speculation might be true and the career had ended thus.

"Could she have been dressed in what might be men's attire? Though of course it isn't always easy to make that distinction nowadays."

"No, Colonel, not this lady."

"I see," said Reinhart, putting his hands in the pockets of the terry-cloth bathrobe, which no doubt had dripped down four flights of stairs and across the lobby but had lost scarcely any of the water it had absorbed in the shower. However, one had been distracted. *He was barefoot and, under the robe, naked.*

"You must be wondering," he said bluffly to the impassive Andrew, "why I am dressed the way I am."

"No, sir. That's not my proper concern."

Suddenly the correct question occurred to Reinhart: "How was the woman, the young woman you saw, dressed?"

"She was not really dressed, sir," Andrew replied. "She was wrapped in a towel."

"And you let her out?"

"Sir," Andrew said, manifestly taken aback, "I don't think I have the right to restrain a citizen if she is going about her business, clothed or not."

"God," grunted Reinhart. Closing his wet robe a bit more snugly (it had worked itself almost open), he strode out to the walk, abrading his soles, and scanned the world in both the directions that Mercer could have taken. Persons in passing cars gaped at him, which was not odd, but some did not, and that was. He saw no daughter-in-law.

He returned, really outraged, now that he thought about Andrew's failure.

"Do you have an outside phone here?" he demanded. "Or do I have to go back to the apartment?"

But at that moment a police car stopped outside, and two officers came from it into the lobby.

"You put in the call?" the first of them asked Reinhart. "Which way'd she go?"

"No, Officer, I put the call in," Andrew said. "She went to the right. You might take a look down by the river. You can get there by going around that way: there's a path."

"Oh, my God," said Reinhart. "The river?"

"You always have to consider that possibility with a demented person," Andrew said.

"He's right about that," said the second officer. The policemen ran out and disappeared down the gentle declivity to the right.

"Thanks, Andrew," said Reinhart, recognizing the doorman as not only an ally, but one possessing authority: a very rare item these days.

"Sir." Andrew touched the brim of his cap.

"This is really terrible," said Reinhart, who suddenly felt the cold of the tiles on which he stood barefoot, despite the worry that should have diverted all his attention. He stepped from one foot to another, several times, as if he rather were treading on embers. "I guess I'd better go back upstairs and get dressed."

"Yes, sir."

"I can't do much good here, in a wet bathrobe." There was every reason for haste, but some inscrutable power of anxiety restrained him. He realized what it was, and he explained to Andrew: "The young woman was not in my apartment for immoral purposes."

"No, sir."

"She's my daughter-in-law. She was ill, sick to her stomach, you see. I was washing her . . ." It wasn't easy to make the situation clear.

"You need not give me any idea of it at all," said Andrew, who was as tall as Reinhart and heavier at the chin and around the waist. An imposing figure of a man; had his gray-green uniform not been unadorned, he might have been taken for some contemporary tyrant of the Third World.

"I know I'm not, but—"

"But thank you, Colonel," said Andrew, who had the kind of voice that invariably sang "Ol' Man River" in Reinhart's boyhood. Such Mohicans were dwindling. "I don't think she would have had time to drown as yet," the kindly doorman added, "if she did go into the river, and very likely she did not."

Reinhart took the elevator and returned to the apartment. He gathered up the clothing that he had doffed in the intention of going to bed with Helen: an eternity of fifteen minutes ago. While dressing, he went through the living room, carefully evading the vomit, and looked out the picture window that gave onto the river. He could see no one that fitted into his disaster: not even the cops.

He had got into his shoes and was headed for the door when Winona entered.

"Good God, Winona, something awful . . ." But she was waving both hands at him.

"They have her," she said. "The ambulance came and took her to Willowdale. I wanted to go along, but she was violently opposed to that, so what could I do?"

He sat down on the straightbacked chair usually employed for the holding of coats.

"Poor Daddy," said Winona, patting his shoulder. "How did you know?" She started into the living room.

"Don't go in there! I haven't had a chance—"

But she had already seen the mess on the couch and rug. She came back. "Poor Daddy, you'd better get to bed."

Reinhart got up. "*I* didn't do that, Winona. That was Mercer. I was cleaning her up and turned my back for a second, and out she ran."

"Mercer?"

"Of course," said Reinhart. "That's how she happened to be down there with her clothes off. They're in my bathroom."

"Oh, God," Winona wailed. "As if Mother's not enough!"

Reinhart squinted at her. "You weren't talking about Mercer just now? You were talking about your mother? Your mother has been taken to Willowdale Hospital?"

"I didn't know about Mercer," said Winona, hanging her head in a way that summoned up memory of her adolescent despair.

"She was so drunk she was out on her feet. She was here when I got home—I suppose you know your mother had me thrown out of the supermarket. When I arrived here, Mercer had already vomited all over. I cleaned her up and put her to bed, but while I was getting out a pair of your PJs to put her into, she sneaked out of the apartment, naked except for a bath towel. She got all the way downstairs and out of the building, but Andrew quite sensibly called the police. They are still looking for her, I guess. I couldn't help because I was soaking wet." He did not find his own story at all credible. "It's my fault, I'm afraid, all of it. I should have kept a closer eye on her."

Winona came and clung to him. "Don't say that, Dad. You did everything right. It's me who's at fault. *I* gave Mercer my car and the apartment key." She was on the verge of tears. "I've really been ruining your life lately, haven't I?"

Reinhart said: "Don't be silly. . . . I'd better go down and help the police look for the poor thing." Actually he was somewhat out of patience with Winona by now.

She was resisting his effort to go out the door. "See," she said, "Mercer left a call for me at the agency. Because of some equipment trouble we got back from the shoot a lot sooner than expected. I picked her up at a drugstore where she was waiting. She didn't seem drunk at that time, but maybe she was on something. Tranquillizers, maybe?"

"Better get the story later," Reinhart said, firmly detaching his daughter from him. "The poor thing's out there someplace. Why don't you come along and help search?"

The intercom buzzed.

It was Andrew. "Mr. Reinhart?" He had never before used that mode of address, and Reinhart believed, terribly, that it was now the introduction to disaster.

"Yes, Andrew."

"She can't be found in the neighborhood," the doorman said softly. "But the police don't think she came to grief in the river. There are some workmen down there who would have seen her. Perhaps she got into her car. A UPS driver told the officers he saw a naked lady driving a green automobile."

"That's probably it," said Reinhart. "She *had* borrowed my daughter's Cougar, and that's green. Thanks, Andrew." He hung up and told Winona. "In a way we're lucky, I guess, unless she cracks up somewhere. Better in a car than running along the street."

"For Blaine," said Winona. "For us all. But hardly for her."

She had called him back to reason. "You're right, of course. What am I saying? God, when she was in the apartment she was out on her feet. Driving a car! And we don't have any way to look for her now if she took your Cougar. I suppose we should go down to the garage and see whether she *did* take it. But she must have. She arrived in it."

Winona looked up a number in the telephone directory and then dialed it. In a moment she spoke into the instrument: "Listen, I need your car right now.... Well, postpone it.... Yes, right now." She hung up.

"Who was that?" Reinhart asked. Somehow he did not believe it was Grace.

Winona was moving towards the rear of the apartment. Her answer was curt and given without looking back: "An acquaintance." She went into her bathroom and closed the door.

Reinhart consciously avoided thinking about Genevieve, with whom he had had no connection, domestic or legal, in a decade. Consequently, he had no responsibility towards her. Moreover, she had reappeared in his life only to do him harm. It could be proved, to a neutral observer, that she had always been more enemy than friend. She *belonged* in the bughouse.

He waited until Winona came back from the bathroom. "Listen, dear, when your friend comes with the car, maybe you could go look for Mercer? I'd better go see your mother. After all . . ."

Winona showed a peevish expression. She looked at her watch. "Isn't she here yet?"

"It hasn't been five minutes. Where does she live?" But Winona sniffed at the wall. "Dear," he resumed, with a slight edge, "did you hear me say I think I'd better go to Willowdale and see your mother while you look for Mercer? If you have any idea where to look. And I suppose we'd better tell Blaine. By now it's gone too far."

"Oh, sure, Dad." Winona was a bit sheepish now. But the doorbell sounded at that point and she visibly hardened. These transformations amazed her father.

She marched to the door and opened it. There stood a person almost as tall as Reinhart, dressed in a gray sweatsuit and sneakers.

"You took your time."

"Oh, Winona—"

"Let's have those keys," said Winona.

But Reinhart came forward. He saw no reason why he should play his daughter's game (of which he could not understand even the rules) to the neglect of common courtesy.

"Hello. I'm Carl Reinhart, Winona's father. Darned nice of you to come so quickly. We have some family problems."

Winona sullenly backed up and the large young woman (for such she was) entered and, thrusting forth a fist comparable to his own, squeezed Reinhart's hand.

"Edie Mulhouse," said she. "I'm a neighbor."

"Oh, yes." But in point of fact he had never seen or heard of her. Edie had short, pale hair, pale eyelashes, and a scattering of pale freckles. Her build seemed of the sort called rangy, though it was hard to tell precisely in the baggy sweatsuit. But her shoulders were broad, and she looked almost six feet tall.

"I'm on Five West," she said.

"Ah." In a moment Reinhart would be uncomfortable. He was too weary to make polite conversation, and Edie looked as though she wanted to linger.

But Winona stepped into the breach. In a falsely sweet manner, which Reinhart identified as being put on for him and not the recipient, she said: "Gee, Edie, it's very nice of you to do this." She reached towards the visitor, who in an almost agonizingly exquisite fashion unfolded her left hand to reveal two car keys on a plastic tab bearing a heraldic device. Winona snatched the keys in a style that suggested anything but mercy.

Edie smiled at Reinhart.

"Yes, indeed," he said. "You're very generous."

Edie looked as though she might cry out in glee, but Winona virtually pushed her towards the door, if not by actual physical power, then certainly by the brute force of the will.

Edie said: "Garage slot 516W. Keep the car as long as you w—" At that point the door was closed in her face.

In the current emergency Reinhart did not believe it sensible to chide anyone for rudeness. "What do you think?" he asked. "I'm always on shaky ground with Blaine, but shouldn't we give him a call?"

Winona ran her tongue inside her upper lip. "I guess we don't have a choice."

Reinhart grasped the phone. "You or me? . . . I'm not trying to dodge the job, but don't you think it wouldn't be quite as bad if you . . ."

"Sure, Daddy. Sure." She looked in the little leatherbound private directory for the phone number, then dialed it.

Almost immediately she cried: *"Mercer?"*

Reinhart reached for his chin.

Winona spoke with the faint smile of incredulity. "It's Winona, Mercer. Are you O.K.? . . . Uh-huh. . . . Uh-huh. Oh, I'm sure. Yeah, the vase. . . . Yeah, if you want." She covered the mouthpiece and said to Reinhart: "She says she left the car keys in the blue vase." He went into the living room to the shelf-and-bar complex and upturned the vase: a pair of keys joined by a beaded chain fell into his left palm. He dangled them at Winona as if the whole thing made perfect sense, but he felt worse in a certain way than when Mercer had been at large. Perhaps *he* was the lunatic?

He made gestures at his daughter. He feared that she might simply hang up after exchanging these polite commonplaces.

Winona chuckled into the telephone. "I just thought of something, Mercer. How'd you get home if you left the car keys

here? . . . Oh. . . . Well, I'm glad to hear you're feeling better. . . . Listen, any time!" Despite more violent gestures from her
father she did now ring off.

"So that's it?" He looked at the ceiling.

Winona was shaking her head. "She claims she took a cab
home."

"Jesus Christ." He strode back and forth. "I don't know what to
think. If it weren't for Andrew, I might believe I had a hallucina-
tion. How did she sound? She was first sick as hell and then unconscious. That should have some effect on anybody."

"She *sounded* O.K.," said Winona, shrugging and speaking in an
adolescent style, which was often characteristic of her response to
any questions from her father. "That's what's so *funny.*" Then she
peeped at Reinhart in a fashion that could have suggested dubiety.

"You think I imagined all of it?" He was annoyed. "Then look
at what I'm going to have to clean up!"

"No, Daddy, of course not."

"You didn't know whether Blaine was there, I guess. I keep
thinking of that poor guy."

"He may not be back yet from Willowdale."

"He went along with your mother? Aw, hell . . ." He felt he
should sit down; the strain was known. But the couch, and in fact
the living room as a whole, was unusable. "Let's go to my room and
talk. I've been on my feet a lot today."

In his bedroom he made an ushering gesture at the overstuffed
chair in the corner, where, under an old-fashioned bridge lamp (an
heirloom from his childhood home, having indeed faithfully provided light since the Depression), he had, ever since moving in,
intended to settle down with a good book, but in practice he
invariably flopped on the bed and watched television.

The blanket with which he had covered Mercer was in a reassuring heap. Had it been folded and put away, he would have been
in trouble. He flipped it aside now and sat on the bed's edge.
Winona accepted the chair, but hardly had she sat down in it when
she rose, went to the foot of the bed, and found something on the
floor.

"Huh." She held up a beige, waferlike object.

"What's that?"

"Pad from a shoe. I guess Mercer's heel was being chafed."

But he hadn't undressed Mercer here: her shoes were in the bathroom, with the rest of her stained attire. Suddenly he remembered Helen, as if from many years before.

"There's a wastebasket over there," he told Winona. "Now we'd better work out a strategy. First, let me tell you about the earlier part of the day." He omitted any mention of Helen except as a vague personage who assisted him in the demonstration. Nor did he chide Winona for telling her mother where to find him—as she undoubtedly had told her. He spoke only of Genevieve's obviously disturbed state at lunch. "I assume the causes had to do with her career in Chicago. When things go well, a person generally doesn't suffer a breakdown." He realized that he sounded insufferably smug. "I'm sorry. I don't know what else to say. In a way I don't want to analyze my precise feelings towards her, and if I did, frankly, I wouldn't want to do it in front of you. A man in my situation has many responsibilities. Some of them even apply to her. I have an obligation to myself. On the other hand, I can't be too critical, if half *your* blood is hers."

Winona was shaking her head. "Mercer can't stand her. That's what set her off."

"Who?"

"I mean, Mother didn't show up because Mercer walked out— like Blaine said. The fact is that Mother came down from Chicago about a week ago and announced she was going to live with them. That's what caused Mercer's trouble."

Reinhart was grinding his teeth. "Still, it was a bizarre response, no? Mercer didn't just leave, period. She must have troubles of her own."

"I don't know much of anything about her," said Winona. "Today was the first time I've ever seen her alone. You know how she's always been at the family get-togethers."

Reinhart felt like getting into bed and pulling the blankets over his head, but he forced himself to stand up now. "What I meant about working out a strategy was how to deal with her after this, and also what we can do about Blaine, with both his women in trouble. Think about that, will you? I'd better get to work on the living room before the stain is permanent."

"I'll help, Dad," said Winona, nobly, and got up. "Tell me what to do."

"Go about your business. This is my affair." He waved a finger at her. "I mean it. I'm a veteran in such matters. A great deal of my Army service was spent on latrine duty. You go and take your bath. By the time you're finished, I'll have cleared the decks." Which would be true, given even his dirty work. Winona's sessions in the bathroom were lengthy, and until she left next morning, she would be seen only in bathrobe and turbaned towel.

But now she said neutrally: "You don't want to hear the details about Mother, I guess."

"If you want to tell them."

"I met Mercer at this drugstore, in some mall over at Elmhurst. I hardly knew what to say, never having exchanged more than ordinary greetings with her. But it turned out O.K. I didn't have to talk. She just wanted someone to listen to her troubles."

"That's often the way, Winona," said her father. "And you make a very sympathetic listener."

"You trained me, Daddy, if so. Remember all the times . . ."

As a young teenager she had often come to Reinhart with her problems. The tenderness of this reminiscence was somewhat limited now by his acceptance of the truth that such confidences were things of the past.

"So Mother shows up there a couple of weeks ago, walking in unannounced so far as Mercer was concerned. But of course it turned out that Blaine simply hadn't told her Mother was coming! Now, Mother needless to say began right away to take over, and to keep the peace Mercer—who's anyway a polite sort of person —wouldn't resist. But Mother simply takes that kind of thing as surrender—"

"Yes, yes," Reinhart said quickly, a sour taste in the back of his throat. No wonder at Mercer's performance in the living room. "We don't have to dwell on that subject." But he couldn't forbear from adding: "I'm the world's foremost authority on it."

"Well, Mercer and Blaine aren't any too intimate on things of this sort, apparently." Here Winona sniffed disdainfully, reminding Reinhart of her immunity to heterosexual failures.

"She made a mistake in letting herself be run out of her own house," he said. "You might say I did the same, ten years ago, but it was mostly your mother's house at the time, and she had lots of justification for her dim view of me in those days."

"Well," said Winona, "I'll tell you what she *says* you're going to do now: get married to her again."

So he was not the only person to whom Genevieve had spoken on that subject: he had not even been the first.

He stood up, leaving the springy side-of-bed without the aid of hands: his legs were not yet finished. "Listen, how about going out to dinner with your old dad? This would seem the night to get out of this place for a change. And I'll even pick up the tab —if you'll lend it to me." He was no longer so sensitive about taking money from his daughter, now that he had worked at least half a day.

"Daddy, *are* you going to remarry Mother?"

"I see the question bothers you. Do you mean you'd like to see us back together after all these years?"

"Oh, God, no," Winona said on one intake of breath.

"Good," said Reinhart. "Because it's not going to happen."

But Winona had more to say, more than she had said or so much as implied on this subject in all her life, but obviously she had been storing up her thoughts. "I hate her, Daddy." She struck both arms of the chair, but the movement was not that of a little girl in tantrum. Nor did Winona, an old addict of tears, look even close to weeping now. Indeed there was a glint of metal in her eye, the like of which Reinhart had seen only in—Genevieve's. It had taken him a quarter of a century to find this lone resemblance between mother and daughter.

"That's your business, Winona. I acknowledge your feeling. If I said anything further it would be offensive to the gods. Now, let's get to our respective tasks and then go out to dinner in what—an hour?"

Winona got up. "Gee, Dad, I wish I had known . . ." She mumbled something.

"You're saying you're engaged."

She blurted: "I have to see Grace."

"Oh. Well, good. Give her my—" Reinhart had started to leave the room, but he stopped now and turned and said to Winona, walking just behind him: "You might ask her whether I've still got my job—and where I should go tomorrow morning, if so."

"Oh," Winona said smugly. "You've got it—if you want it."

"No," Reinhart said. "I don't want it on that basis, Winona."

She almost wailed: "I didn't *mean* anything! I mean, what I meant was, why wouldn't you have the job? Grace is not going to be impressed by what some crazy woman told her. . . . I'm sorry. But you should have seen her."

"Your mother? You were at Blaine's?"

"After what Mercer told me, I really thought I had to speak to him. While I was over there Mother came back from lunch with you. To show you how far gone she is, Daddy—she was raving that you hired some Mafia hit man to murder her."

"Christ Almighty."

"What choice did I have but to call for help?"

"It was you?"

"Do you think Blaine would have had the guts?"

Reinhart shook his head. "Me neither. To have someone committed . . ."

"If someone is being violent? She threw a heavy vase against the wall."

"So they came and put her in a straitjacket or something?"

"No." Winona laughed coarsely. "I called the police. They came and talked to her and to us for a while, and then they called an ambulance. When it came, the attendants gave her a shot of tranquillizer, I guess."

"So the cops were called twice in the same afternoon for members of our family?" Reinhart shrugged. "We're getting to be like the Jukes and the Kallikaks."

"Who?"

"It doesn't matter." He finally left the room, clearing the doorway so that Winona too could emerge.

"Some gangster in a white Cadillac!" she howled.

Reinhart marveled at how a diseased mind could put quotidian phenomena to its own use. Genevieve had seen the car from which Helen Clayton had emerged to join him in the parking lot. He had not really thought much about that episode, but he realized now that he had assumed the driver thereof not to be Helen's husband. She had said she was never free for lunch, and she was hardly a newlywed. Ergo, she met a lover every day at noon and not a spouse. And yet she had enlisted Reinhart as still another alternative!

"But wait a minute," he said now to Winona. "Your mother says both that I am going to remarry her *and* have her killed?"

"She's nuts, isn't she?"

He went to the kitchen to fetch the materials and equipment needed to clean up the living room. For a good many years of his life not only the starring roles, but even all the interesting subsidiary parts, had been played by women.

CHAPTER
9

Blaine called his father on the morning after his mother had been taken to the hospital and his wife had returned home from her escapade.

"We have to talk," were his first words on the telephone, and this morning Reinhart found it easy to forgive his failure, habitual, to offer any kind of greeting.

"Come over here if you want privacy," Reinhart said. "Your sister has gone off to work, and I'm alone. I had a job myself for a day, but already I'm on vacation." He said that as a lightener-of-the-moment, but no sooner was it out when he regretted having given Blaine the opportunity to remember, from back in the bad old days, how often his occupational matters had come to grief.

"That's how it *usually* goes, doesn't it?" Blaine asked. "You haven't changed, and now it's happened, hasn't it? You've finally driven Mother beyond the point of no return."

In another time Reinhart would surely have risen to this bait, but now he maintained self-control. "No, if that were true, you wouldn't be calling me now. I'm not, ten years after the fact, the cause of her troubles, and you know it, Blaine. So let's please have a minimum of horseshit."

The admonition had the desired effect. Blaine was silent for a moment, and then he said, somewhat sullenly but without the accusatory note: "They'll be examining her for a day or so, I guess. But what happens then? Will she be kept in the hospital? What will that cost? But if she comes out, where will she go?"

"That could be a problem. Has she really closed out in Chicago?"

"What's that supposed to mean?"

"Only that she lived there nine–ten years. She must have made friendships, associations, had some kind of home. She wasn't back much to visit here, if ever: am I right?"

"We were always in close touch," said Blaine. "I saw her frequently."

"In Chicago, though, right? What I'm getting at is—"

"I know what you're getting at," said Blaine. "You're telling her to go back to Chicago. You're saying you're washing your hands—"

"No, I'm not saying that, Blaine. Not at all. I'll do what I can to help. But what I *am* saying is that I *shall not live with her again.*"

"Then how *could* you help?" Blaine replied contemptuously.

Perhaps in involuntary resentment, Reinhart asked: "How is Mercer?"

"*Mercer?*" said Blaine. "Why would you ask about *Mercer?*"

"She's my daughter-in-law, I think."

Blaine said loftily: "I try to keep my own family matters from her, frankly. She was raised among a different kind of people."

"And the boys?"

"Don't worry about them. They're being fed."

This struck Reinhart as a bizarre thing to say, but he passed over it. "Look, Blaine, I'd go to see your mother at the hospital, but I suspect it wouldn't help her to recover. I don't intend to give her a home, and I could scarcely contribute financially if I wanted to. And, frankly, I don't think I'd want to. When I was younger I wouldn't have had the nerve to say such a thing, or when even younger, even to think it, but with age one gets morally braver."

"Brave? You call it brave?" Blaine snorted. Reinhart was prepared to hear a vicious attack on himself, and was wondering how much of it he must tolerate. The boy had certainly been under pressure. Perhaps his father could do him some service by sustaining an assault, rolling with the punches.

But Blaine all at once changed his tune. "O.K.," he said explosively, but without apparent rancor. "What I'm really calling for is to invite you and my sister to dinner tonight."

"You're joking," Reinhart said quickly, and then apologized with the same speed. "I didn't mean that. What I do mean is that I accept, thank you. I don't know about Winona, but I'll leave a message with her agency and get back to you when she calls." He added prudently: "If she turns out to be busy, am I still invited?"

"No," said Blaine.

Reinhart found it possible to laugh at this. "We'll be there unless you hear otherwise. What time would that be?"

"Seven," said Blaine. "It shouldn't take long, tell her. Tell her I very much want her to make it."

"Yeah," Reinhart said and hung up. Some invitation! He dialed the agency and left the message. And then he called Grace Greenwood's number, but her secretary told him she was out.

"Will you ask her to give Carl Reinhart a ring?" He still didn't know about the future of his job. Winona had apparently come home the night before, after he was asleep, and then left for work this morning before he got up. She sometimes did this, with the energy of youth. Reinhart lacked in one symptom of age: he was not an early riser.

Before hanging up, he asked and received Helen Clayton's home number.

When Helen answered he said: "Hi. This is—"

"Carl!" said she. "How'd it come out, Carl? I was thinking of calling you, but I didn't want to jeopardize anything."

He told her about Mercer's adventures.

"Well," she said finally, "let's hope that's the last we hear of the problem. It might have been a one-shot, and from now on she'll keep her nose clean. You know, they talk about menopause, but a lot of women have their real trouble when they're younger. Especially nowadays."

"Is that right?" Reinhart continued to find new depths in Helen's sense of things.

"Expectations are greater. That always leads to trouble. Just because people expect more doesn't mean they've got it in them to deliver more."

"I should tell you, Helen," said Reinhart, "I get a lot of comfort in talking with you."

But now she showed her limitation, interpreting his speech in another way.

"Gee, Carl, I wish I could, but I can't today."

For a moment he was utterly perplexed. "Can't what?"

"Meet you anyplace. I told you it's tough for me."

"Sure, Helen. That's O.K. I really enjoy talking to you: that's what I meant."

Helen ignored this sincere statement. "I haven't been able to get through to Grace. We're on her shit list, Carl. You know how dykes are: let them hear about anybody with normal urges and they look down on you."

There had been a time when Reinhart himself would not have found this assertion altogether irresponsible. Perhaps even now he might have his doubts that it could be easily refuted, but . . .

"I think she's just busy," said he. "Grace is a real professional at her job. . . . The thing that hurts is that in attacking me, my ex-wife got you as well. By the way, she didn't settle down. They finally had to commit her."

"Aw," said Helen. "Aw, hell. I'm really sorry, Carl."

"Yeah," Reinhart said. "My own feelings are pretty complex. I hate her guts in one way, and then in another I—well, just in a human way you've got to have some pity. She has this paranoid idea of being persecuted." He snorted. "For example, you know that Cadillac you got out of? She claims that the driver was a Mafioso and that he threatened to kill her."

There was a long silence on Helen's end of the wire. At last she said: "Well, she's out of harm's way now, Carl. She belongs there, I bet. Anyway, the doctors have the problem, not you. You're not still paying her anything, are you?"

"At the time of the divorce I didn't *have* anything. She had previously put the house in her name."

Helen spoke softly through the telephone: "You're a real nice, gentlemanly person, Carl."

"Oh, I guess we're even all in all. I'm not speaking in self-pity."

"I hope I see you again," Helen said, "whether or not we work together."

"Oh, we will!"

"I don't know," said Helen, her voice drifting away.

"Well, I do," he said sharply. "You know, the Top Shop demo wasn't my idea. Grace came to me."

"Uh-huh," Helen said.

"You don't believe me, do you?" he asked, almost aggressively. "I'll tell you this: Grace wants to keep on my good side." He was taken aback by his own recklessness, but was not entirely displeased. It was, after all, a symptom of vigor.

"Gee, Carl," said Helen, "don't go away mad!" She said this with mock petulance and a throaty chuckle. "You've got something on her? It wouldn't be hard to get! Except I don't believe she'd be ashamed. There's a new attitude around, you know. How about having gay teachers in the schools? Would you want a daughter of yours in Grace's clutches?"

Funny how the worst could happen before one knew it—and turn out not to be the worst, after all.

Reinhart was even able to make a joke: "Or vice versa!" And before she could react to this, he said: "I always thought that if I were king, I'd let my subjects be whatever they wanted to be, sexually. But to punish by execution anyone who mentioned *what* he or she was." He cleared his throat. "What I meant was that Grace and I are old acquaintances. She enlisted me for the job because she knows I like to cook and she needed somebody to do that. Don't ask me why she didn't hire a professional chef. But she had to talk me into it. She's not going to deny me now, when I want to continue. I really do enjoy working with you."

An intake of breath was audible from her end of the wire. "Gee, Carl . . . I'll *try* to make it this afternoon. Can I call you someplace?"

"Here, I guess," said Reinhart.

Helen laughed gutturally. Oddly enough, she reminded him of certain guys he had known in the Army, for whom everything had an immediate sexual connotation. It wasn't easy to get on to that style again, more than thirty years later and from a woman—though no doubt it was better.

Towards noon Winona returned his call. He told her of Blaine's invitation.

"Can you make it?"

"Oh, sure."

"He wanted you especially. Frankly, Winona, I must warn you that whenever your brother gets that earnest he undoubtedly wants something. So be prepared. I think it has to do with your mother."

Winona seemed lighthearted enough. "O.K."

"Seven, Blaine said. That'll be all right? You won't be on some overtime assignment?" It occurred to Reinhart for the first time that, in the standard style of the wandering husband (that stock character), Winona might sometimes have pursued romance of a kind while claiming to be held overlong at work. If so, was it not absurd of her? Why should she have needed an excuse?

"I'm taking the day off," she said, "so there's no problem."

"Glad to hear it, dear! You could really use a little vacation."

"The agency's not that understanding," said Winona, "but the heck with them. They can just tell the client I'm sick for a change."

"Damn right," Reinhart agreed. "You have a nice time."

"Wait," said Winona. "Here, Grace wants to speak to you."

Grace came on the wire: "Carl, sorry I haven't been able to get back till now. Everything's cool. We'll have something for you in a day or so. Meanwhile you're on salary, of course. Take care!" She hung up.

Reinhart remained for a while with the receiver in his hand, looking into the vulvalike thicket of lines in the etching that hung over the telephone table. Winona had brought that home one day.

He was chagrined to have so quick an answer to the question he had asked himself. *Q.* Why had Winona needed to pretend she was working late when in truth she was having fun with her friends? *A.* Look at her friends!

Hardly had he hung up when the telephone rang again.

"Mr. Reinhart? Edie Mulhouse."

"Oh . . ."

"Remember last night? Winona borrowed my car."

"Oh, sure, Edie. That was very nice of you."

"Uh, was there anything wrong with it, do you know? I noticed it is still in its slot in the garage."

"As a matter of fact," said Reinhart, "as it turned out, Winona didn't have to use it. But you were very kind to lend it, and on such short notice."

"It isn't a very fancy car," said Edie. "She probably didn't want to be seen in it."

"Why," he protested politely, "that isn't so." Large as she was, Edie seemed overfragile of soul. "It's a lovely car, I'm sure, and you're a very generous neighbor. I know that Winona was very grateful. I hope she made that clear."

"She doesn't owe me anything," said Edie. "I admire her a lot."

"She's not all bad," Reinhart said modestly, "if I do say so myself." And then he added soberly: "It's nice to know you, Edie. The only other neighbors I've met in the almost four years we've lived here are just at the end of this floor. You know, I never lived in an apartment till I was middle-aged. I spent all my earlier life in houses in suburban communities where you necessarily were acquainted with everybody else. But there are things to be said for privacy."

"I hope I haven't intruded on yours," said Edie.

Something suddenly occurred to Reinhart. "Winona *did* return the car keys, didn't she? Did you look in your mailbox?" She was silent too long. "Just a moment, please, Edie. Hang on." He put the phone down and went back to Winona's room, where he saw the alien keys as soon as he entered, on her dressing table.

Back at the phone he asked: "The tab is blue plastic, and it has a Chevy crest?"

Edie said in a kind of horror: "I used to have a Vega, but this is a Gremlin. But I kept the same key thing. I guess I should get another. Is that why Winona didn't use the car? Maybe she couldn't find it? She was looking for a Vega? How stupid I am!"

Reinhart was annoyed with Winona, but there was also something regrettable about Edie's self-abasement.

"No, no," he said with a certain harshness. "You're too generous. We somehow slipped up on returning the keys: each thought the other was going to do it, I guess. What's your apartment number? I'll bring them to you right now." He suddenly got a better idea. "What are you doing for lunch?"

"Oh."

"Are you calling from your apartment?" It always took him a

while to remember that most people, even women, worked somewhere outside during the day. But Edie said she was at home. She
stayed noncommittal on the luncheon invitation: Reinhart found
her frustrating, but in a challenging sort of way. He decided simply
to bully her into being his guest, so as to expunge Winona's bad
treatment of her, which seemed to bother him more than it troubled her, to be sure, but that was no excuse.

Edie met him in the garage. She wore jeans and a sweater today
and over them a tweed coat. She was not a bad-looking girl, with
pleasant clean features and very good skin. Something probably
should have been done with her fair hair, which was cut short but,
so far as Reinhart could see, according to no plan. And her expression tended towards the lackluster, though her blue eyes were,
physically speaking, bright enough.

"I didn't realize," Reinhart said by way of greeting, "that when
I got up this morning I'd have a luncheon date with an attractive
young woman." He surrendered the keys.

Edie flinched in response to the compliment. It would not seem
by her manner that she had many such dates. She opened the
passenger's door of the Gremlin for him, held it, closed it. He was
made uncomfortable by this courtesy—as he would not have been,
had not indeed been, when it was done by Grace.

When Edie climbed behind the wheel he said: "Do you know
the Glenwood Mall? There's a nice restaurant there." He realized
that his basic motive for this expedition was actually not to pay
Edie back for her generosity (which gesture thus far seemed only
to make her uncomfortable), but rather to eat another meal at
Winston's—and with, this time, a placid companion.

In contrast to Edie's social manner her style of driving was as
forceful as a trucker's. She was a notable tail-gater, light-jumper,
and a bluffer in turning left at high-traffic intersections, blocking
with her little yellow Gremlin any opposing vehicle, be it city bus
or tractor-trailer. In no time they swung into a parking lot near
Winston's, in fact just facing the place where Genevieve had stood
the day before to abuse him.

Remembering that sorry event caused him to be less quick
about hopping out than was Edie, though true enough they diff-
ered in age and spring of reflex. Whatever his excuse, she had time

to sprint around the rear bumper and to get to his door before he
had more than opened its catch.

For quite a few years now he had been the occasional recipient
of gallantry from young women, but the irony was evident for both
parties when the smaller human being assisted the larger in a
physical passage. However, Edie was sufficiently large and sinewy
to give Reinhart's spirit a shock as she not only seized and took the
door as far away as it would go—for a moment he believed she
might tear it off its hinges—but also slipped a large hand under his
elbow and exerted enough lift so that if he had not quickly projected himself into the parking lot, he might have gone through
the roof.

On the approach to the restaurant, in anticipation of her proba-
ble intent to perform another manhandling maneuver at the
entrance, Reinhart determined to forestall her: he was after all
essentially the weight-lifter he had been as recently as 1941. He
slid a hand up her near forearm, hooking elbows. But soon she
ripped herself away and positively loped, with great, long, high-
arched strides, to the large ornamental bronze opener, a bracket
and not a knob, on Winston's portal and pulled it and the door
attached, and Reinhart was, or anyway felt as if he were being,
scraped into the restaurant on the spatula of her left hand.

The place was jammed today, though the time was pretty much
as it had been the day before, when just after twelve a third of the
tables had still been vacant. There was a good-sized, more or less
unorganized queue at the moment, gathered before a sallow-
faced man in his forties. This fellow was being conspicuously incompetent at the job. No doubt the regular hostess was not at hand
for some reason, illness or vacation, and the man was on loan, so
to speak, from a superior situation: perhaps he was the manager.
Therefore he was doing a rotten job so that nobody would take
him as naturally a functionary who merely directed diners to tables.

Actually Reinhart and Edie, tall as they stood, were in a com-
manding position in the crowd, whose mean height was several
inches lower, and the temporary maître d' proved to be a snob in
such matters.

"Two?" he cried at them, up and over several intervening persons who had been waiting there since before Edie had parked the car. Reinhart considered making some public note of this, for justice's sake, but was soon pleased he had not, for the man's cry proved but the prelude to what was not the extension of a privilege but rather a virtual command. "Wait in the bar!"

Reinhart was none too pleased to obey, but decided that any objection might upset his guest. "Well," he said in a jolly tone, "shall we wet our whistles, Edie?"

She giggled shrilly and made a shivering agitation of her large frame. He had not noticed the bar the day before, but there it was now, in a wing off to the left. He took a deep breath and tensed his ligaments before touching Edie's forearm again, should she take retaliatory action, but he believed, even so, that she could more easily be led by contact than by speech at this point. As it happened she proved docile and almost weightless.

The bar was empty, as Reinhart saw once they got inside it and his eyes made the adjustment to the gloom.

"Have a seat, Edie," he had to say. "What would you like? A glass of white wine?"

The bartender came along. He was a young man with a supply of tawny hair and a brushy mustache that were "styled." He looked silently, gravely at Edie.

Reinhart grew impatient. "I'll have a dry sherry, imported, if you've got one."

The bartender went away.

Reinhart asked her: "Have you ordered?"

She shrugged and said hopelessly: "I'll try." When the bartender returned with the sherry, she leaned towards him: "Got any juice?"

"Tomato," said he. "Orange."

"I guess it's not fresh?"

"No," said the bartender, "that's too much to expect."

"Uh-huh."

Reinhart supposed he should have assumed she would be a teetotaller. "We should have our table before long," he said. "I'm sorry about the delay."

"Oh, that's all right," Edie said expansively. The bartender slid away, giving the illusion he moved on rollers.

"Well," said Reinhart, "so we're neighbors. What do you think of your apartment? Have you lived there long? Which direction do your windows face?"

Edie gave him a long and earnest look. Her eyes were delicate in this attitude, and of a color that might have been seen as pale blue or again as a rich gray.

"You're just doing this to be nice, aren't you?"

He waited a decent moment before responding. Then he said: "If you really believe what you're saying, you're being rude."

"I guess you're right, at that." She began to smile.

"Why don't you have a glass of wine?" he asked. "It's the natural product of the grape, you know. A wonderful food, and an aid to digestion. Would God have made fermentation if He didn't want people to taste its products?"

Edie was now simpering in good spirits. "Oh, Mr. Reinhart," she said, "you certainly enjoy life."

This was a novel observation, but he was flattered. He signaled the barman, who came up with a skating kind of movement. Reinhart understood belatedly that the young man considered himself something of a comedian.

"A glass of white wine for the lady, please."

The bartender said: "I'll go squeeze some white grapes."

"Did you know this?" Reinhart asked Edie when the glass had been brought and put before her. "That most white wine is made from red grapes?"

"I certainly did not." She looked back and forth between her glass and him.

"If they leave the skins in long enough after the juice has been pressed from the fruit, the color goes into the liquid. If they take out the skins right away, the liquid remains clear."

"Gee."

"Enough of that," said Reinhart. "Tell me about yourself."

Edie rolled her eyes. "Oh, gee. I'm twenty-four."

Reinhart said: "A human being changes drastically every couple of years. The earlier in life, the shorter the time span, so that a baby's alterations come with weeks, even days. Then you get past thirty, and while time is of course as inexorable as ever, it is very difficult to measure in a credible way. You don't make higher marks on the doorjamb each birthday." She brought out the teacher in him.

Edie still had not tasted the wine. She put the glass down now to say: "I was relieved when I stopped growing, I'll tell you."

The bartender had scooted up expectantly. Reinhart was low on wine, but he would not reorder if their table was ready. He had to rise and go to the doorway to see what was happening with the queue. There was none at the moment: everybody else had been seated, apparently, for no one but Edie and himself had come to wait in the bar.

Furthermore, yesterday's hostess was back at her post, and her male replacement was nowhere in evidence. The couple sent to the bar had been forgotten. Winston's was falling in Reinhart's estimation.

He went over to the hostess and entered a complaint. The young woman was in a different character from that of yesterday, when she had been so quietly amiable.

"But I've been here all the while," she said coldly. "There isn't any man who ever does this job."

Reinhart slapped his hands together. "Then I guess it was a practical joke." He smiled at the hostess, who did not return the favor. "You were probably seating someone, and while you were gone this guy pretended to take over. I fell for it. Sorry." He felt himself begin to smile. "Actually it was pretty funny, now that I think about it." This was the kind of trick that ten years ago would have made him furious: to be able to laugh freely at it now was to enjoy a luxury.

"Well, I don't think it's humorous," said the hostess. She looked very pale. "I'm going to have to ask you to leave."

Now Reinhart laughed in amazement. "Leave? Because I was duped?"

The young woman trembled. He realized that she was afraid of something. She reached towards the phone on the kind of pulpit that held her equipment. "I'll call the police."

"No, don't do that. I'll leave peacefully, if you want. But first will you please tell me what I'm supposed to have done?"

The hostess kept her hand on the telephone. "The lady with you at lunch yesterday—you don't know that she came back in here later and threatened me?"

"God." He moved towards her, but then caught himself and retreated: it might seem as an attack. "Believe me, I knew nothing about it. How lousy for you! If it's any relief to know, she's in the hospital now. She cracked up suddenly, I guess. It was nothing personal."

The young woman made a silly grimace. "Now I feel worse," said she. "The poor thing. . . . But I tell you, it was pretty scary. And I don't know you at all, do I, sir? She accused me of carrying on with you."

"You smiled as you took us to the table," said Reinhart. "No doubt that's what she was thinking of. It's too bad. I'm very sorry, miss." He shook his head and in so doing caught sight of the impostor who had directed him to wait in the bar. It was with relief that he saw the man jollily eating lunch with three companions: he had considered the possibility that the guy was another deranged soul, with delusions of grandeur.

"I hope she gets better," said the hostess. "I really do. Was that her doctor who picked her up in the white car?"

"When was that?"

"Right after she left here," the young woman said, with raised brow. "The second time. You and she had left, and then she came back to make that threat, and I said I'd have to call the manager if she didn't go away, and then she went outside and this white Cadillac pulled up and she got in."

Reinhart apologized again and walked out the door into the parking lot. He would certainly have some questions for Helen. . . . But he had momentarily forgotten about Edie!

He returned to the bar. "Sorry. I was checking on some private matter." He noticed that she had not yet drunk any of her wine. "Well, shall we have lunch?"

"You'll want to kill me, Mr. Reinhart," Edie said sheepishly, holding up her wrist as if in defense, but she was actually displaying her watch. "But I've got a dentist's appointment in fifteen minutes, and I want to run you home first."

"What a rotten host I've been," said Reinhart. "I'll make it up to you, Edie."

She stood up. "Actually, I've had a wonderful time."

They went out to the car. Edie went to the passenger's door, but Reinhart stopped her.

"I'm not going to need a ride home. I'm going to stay here for a while. I have to get something for my grandsons, whom I am going to see tonight."

"How will you get back?"

"Oh, there's a bus that's near enough." He touched her forearm. "Thanks again for offering to lend us the car last night. I'm afraid we Reinharts haven't done much for you in return, but—"

"That's what you think," said Edie with uncharacteristic pertness. She got into her little yellow car and drove rapidly away.

CHAPTER
10

Parker Raven, age four, Blaine's younger son, opened the door on Reinhart's ring of the bell, but he blocked the entrance with his small body so that his grandfather and aunt could not proceed.

Winona pleaded: "Come on, Parker . . ."

Parker extended his hand. "Let's have your money," said he.

Reinhart gently moved Winona out of his way, and then he lifted Parker from the threshold and, carrying him, entered.

The boy did not resist this action. Instead he chortled and asked: "What you got for me?"

"A punch in the nose," said his grandfather, holding him, as usual marveling silently at what tough stuff a child's body is made of: not only sinew but the flesh is so *hard.*

Winona was digging anxiously into her purse. Reinhart said to her: "Huh-uh. I'll take care of this."

"And what else?" asked Parker. "Come on, Grandpa."

Reinhart had always believed that both boys favored his son in appearance, but in his new awareness of their mother he realized that Parker anyway bore a strong resemblance to Mercer.

"I've got a terrific story for you," he told Parker. "If I told it to you now, then you wouldn't have it for later."

Parker struggled in his grasp, and Reinhart put him down.

"I mean a *thing,*" said the boy, "not talk. Come on."

"Well," said Reinhart, "I tried. I don't like to see you being so grasping, but I can remember when I was little I too was a materialist." He took a folded paper bag from the pocket of his raincoat, unfolded it deliberately, and removed from it a blue bandanna. "See this? Every cowboy wears this around his neck at all times. It keeps dust from blowing down his shirt. He can wipe his face with it when he's hot. He can put it across his nose and mouth when he's in a sandstorm." Reinhart demonstrated this use, knotting the bandanna's ends, and then he handed the blue-and-white figured cloth to his grandson. "Oh, this thing's got a hundred and one uses. A bandage if you're hurt. Or you can put your money and other valuable possessions in the middle of it, tie it in a bundle, and hide it—or whatever you want."

Blaine appeared in the entrance hall. He was wearing a cardigan. It had been years now since Reinhart had seen his son in anything but a business suit and tie. In informal garb, with an open-necked shirt, Blaine looked somewhat vulnerable.

"Well, I don't like that," he said peevishly. "Teaching him to be a holdup man."

Reinhart saw that Parker had put the knotted bandanna across his mouth and nose to protect himself from the imaginary sandstorm. The aperture was too generous for his small head, however, and the cloth fell around his neck.

Reinhart's explanation was not received sympathetically by Blaine, who made an even more disagreeable face and then scowled at his sister.

"You know where to put the coats, I hope."

Winona went to help Reinhart take off his outer garment. It was amazing: her brother's ability to make an instant servant of her.

But one guest should not so serve another, and her father fended her off. He removed his outer garment without assistance.

Blaine asked: "When's it supposed to rain?"

"Oh, come on," said Reinhart, "it's perfectly sensible to wear a raincoat as a light topcoat, and you know it." He gave the article in reference to Winona, who took it, along with her own, and went down the hall and opened a closet.

"Do you have to go to the toilet?" asked Blaine.

Parker, pulling at his bandanna, was galloping into the doorway of the living room. But he stopped now to laugh and say: *"Toilet."*

Reinhart could remember from the childhoods of his own offspring as well as his own the special interest invariably evoked by that word. And he remembered another, which he now shouted at his grandson: "Underpants!" Parker naturally was rendered hilarious by this bon mot.

Blaine found nothing amusing in the exchange. "You know," he said bitterly, "you have to finish your first childhood before going into the second."

He marched through the door on the right. He had not invited his father to accompany him, so Reinhart waited until Winona came back. She was dressed in an exceedingly conservative style, by his judgment: dark dress, pearls, little earrings.

He asked her: "Where do we go now?"

She shrugged. "Living room, I guess." She preceded Reinhart through the door on the right.

Parker meanwhile had disappeared, but his shrill voice came from somewhere in hiding: "Hey, Grandpa! *Poopoo* and *doo-doo.*"

"No, Parker," said Reinhart, "we've changed the subject." The human animal, from pup to patriarch, was such a bizarre creature. What other breed found its wastes so comic?

They entered a large room full of ponderous, men's-club kind of furniture: at least so it seemed to Reinhart, who had seen that sort of place only in movies and on TV. It seemed incomplete without a bald or white head here and there amidst the dark-green leather chairs, and the mantel cried out for a moose's head, though equipped with the next best decoration, viz., a mountain-ous landscape within a dark frame inner-edged in gold and il-luminated from a tube lamp below. It was indeed the latter which provided the only light in the room at the moment.

Reinhart squinted. He asked Winona: "Do you see your brother anyplace?"

"Not really," said she. "He's probably in the den."

They steered towards the lighted doorway across the room. The den, when reached, proved to be an appropriate neighbor to the living room. Though much narrower, it was furnished with similar leather-covered overstuffs, and the table lamps here, as next door, were four feet high, with husky shafts in old gold. Along one wall were built-in bookshelves.

Reinhart's son sat at the end of the rectangular enclosure, behind the sort of desk that looked as if it were not made for use, being of carved leg and high-polished finish, its flat top a glossy expanse of tooled leather.

"Nice den, Blaine," said his father.

"It's the *library*," said Blaine. As could have been expected, he did not invite them to take seats.

Reinhart looked at the row of titles on the bookshelf near his elbow. They were so uniform and lifeless in gold-stamped leather that for a moment he took them for a Potemkin collection, an unbroken façade of book-spines only, cemented to a solid board, in front of no texts. But he poked the *Iliad,* and it receded.

"I see you've got some good yarns here," he told Blaine. "Did you have these specially bound?"

"Or something," said his son, who reached into a desk drawer and brought out a pad of yellow so-called legal paper. "Now I've made a few preliminary notes . . ." He probed at the pad with a closed silver pen or pencil.

Reinhart plucked a book off the shelf. You didn't often come across volumes bound in real leather nowadays. This one proved to be *The Last Days of Pompeii* and belonged, with the rest—the *Aeneid, Black Beauty,* and so on—to a series entitled The World's Greatest Masterpieces.

"Dad," said Blaine, looking up. "Put that back and pay attention."

"I thought I'd make a pile of books for us to sit on," Reinhart answered. "Here, Winona, lend a hand."

"For God's sake," Blaine said, throwing down his pencil. "Is this the way it's going to go? Winona, get some chairs from the main sitting room."

"No," said Reinhart to his daughter, "I'll get them." He found a couple of straightbacked chairs just inside the big room, one on either side of the door, where presumably the footmen used to sit in the house of Bulwer-Lytton, author of *The Last Days of Pompeii:* Reinhart had some vague recollection of his being a lord.

"Here's the point," Blaine said when his father and sister were seated across the desk from him. "We're going to have to come to some kind of terms about Mother." He sucked his body in slightly and opened the center drawer of the desk and found a pair of eyeglasses within. He unfolded the temple pieces and put on the spectacles. The lenses were undersized. The little glasses looked like something he had retained from his countercultural days, but when he wore them now Blaine seemed to have a foot in middle age.

"Now," he went on, squinting through the small spectacles at the pad before him, "I have sketched out what really seems to me a really fair arrangement, because this is not the kind of thing a family really ought to squabble over." He tapped his silver implement on the pad. "A three-way split is what I've come up with." He looked between Reinhart and Winona and smiled. For a moment his father believed that someone had entered the room behind them, but then his attention was claimed by the import of what Blaine had so easily said.

"A split of what?"

"Why," said Blaine, smiling pseudo-warmly now, but at Winona and not his father, "the expense of treatment and care."

Reinhart was reminded once again of life's tendency regularly to face one with the choice of folly or swinishness. On an impulse he decided not to choose; that is, to say nothing at all—and then he was shamed anyway, because what Blaine proceeded to say was quite true.

Blaine addressed Winona. "Of course you'll want to take Dad's share."

"Oh, sure," she replied immediately.

Reinhart sat forward on his chair. "Now just a minute," he said. "First, *Dad has no share.* Blaine, you'll just have to face the truth: I am not related to your mother. I haven't been for ten years, and I absolutely refuse to accept any obligation with regard to her. True, that's academic in my current situation, but it should certainly apply to Winona's assuming a burden that is supposed to be mine."

"Oh, Daddy," his daughter said in sweet reproach, "you know you don't owe me anything."

Blaine was still smiling, but now with a venomous quality. "I don't see it's your affair, then, *Daddy.* Winona and I agree."

Reinhart put his hands on his knees. "So you pay one third, and she pays two thirds." He looked at his daughter. "I'm not going to let you do it." He pointed his finger at her. "Do you hear me, Winona? I won't stand for it."

Her eyes began to fill with tears.

Now Blaine showed himself enough of a diplomat as to toss his chin in apparent indifference and say: "Well, we've got lots of time to make up our minds. . . . Let's enjoy our get-together!" He started to make a toothy smile but obviously decided that his talent was not up to such an imposture at this moment, and his face returned to its habitual pale length and the expressionless character, presumably a professional tool, that he showed to the world, except when, disdainful of his relatives, he wore a pronounced sneer.

"How's about a glass of sherry, Winona?"

At his sister's refusal Blaine smirked in what seemed, for him, good humor, and Reinhart could not help reflecting that the guest who would most please his son was the stubborn abstainer from everything.

"But she's got one coming," he told Blaine. "So I'll take it."

Blaine now produced a dirty grin, and it occurred to Reinhart that perhaps they could, father and son, someday create a kind of friendship based on cynicism alone.

"O.K., Dad," Blaine said. "Fair enough." He rose, went to one of the doored cabinets beneath the open bookshelves, and brought back a faceted decanter half-full of an amber fluid, and a stemmed receptacle of small capacity: in fact, a liqueur glass. Either the wine was an Olympian elixir, too rich for earthlings to take except by the thimble, or Blaine was being consistent in his meanness.

When Reinhart was a boy, before World War II, the local drugstores had sold pints of fluids called sherry and port, and highschoolers on New Year's Eve would contrive to get a bottle and drink it empty and puke on the sidewalk by midnight. Domestic fortified wines had improved greatly since that era, but Blaine seemed to have acquired, no doubt at great expense for such a rare antique, a store of that peculiar decoction of rubbing alcohol and caramel coloring.

"Mmm," Reinhart murmured after wetting his tongue and grimacing in an effort not to celebrate a nostalgic New Year's on the library rug. But to save face he had to go through with it. "Where's Winona's? I've got another coming, remember?"

"Ah," Blaine answered, actually enjoying this badinage, "you've got hers. I didn't ask *you* to have one, if you'll recall."

"By Godfrey," said Reinhart, "you didn't, for a fact. You son of a gun!" He saw that Blaine was seriously gloating, and realized that they had each won a victory. What was incongruous, however, was that the horrible "sherry" had been served in a glass made of exquisite crystal. He held it to the light of the brass lamp on Blaine's desk and turned it so that the facets could do their work. He saw no reason why he could not occasionally be civil: "This is a fine thing, Blaine."

But Blaine's return broke the mood. "Be careful, for God's sake. Those glasses are very expensive."

He took another glass and poured himself a minimeasure. He went behind his desk.

Winona, sitting on her father's left and slightly behind, had been silent. Reinhart now turned and looked at her.

She thereupon, as though they were in league and this was her cue, asked Blaine: "How's Mercer?"

His answer was bland. "No reason why she need be bothered with this. She doesn't know about Mother, and so far as I'm concerned that's all to the good."

Reinhart had wondered all his life which made the more sense: *Ignorance is bliss,* or *The truth will make you free.* There was something to be said for both. In this case the former was probably to be recommended for all the principals: if Mercer was unaware of Genevieve's current situation, Blaine presumably was still ignorant of Mercer's adventure. At the moment only Reinhart seemed to know everything about everybody. But he was old enough to know as well that the person who occupies such a situation is likely to be the greatest dupe of all, serving as mere audience for all performances.

He now asked: "Where's my other grandson?"

"In his room, I would think," Blaine said impatiently. He sniffed and finished his wine. "Now, if we could just wrap up this matter." He tapped his pad of yellow paper. "Maybe the most practical thing would be to get down to details, the actual dollars and cents involved."

His sister spoke humbly: "Whatever you think, Blainey."

Reinhart said: "Tell me this, Blaine: has any determination been made of your mother's problem? Has there been a diagnosis of any kind?"

Blaine passed a hand across his eyes. "Please," said he, "I'm trying to be understanding, believe me. But how can I see these questions as more than hypocrisy? When any question of money comes up, you say you have no obligation. Then how can you really care? Forget it! I'll carry on as best I can alone."

Winona said: "Well, you know I won't let you do that."

"No, no," Blaine cried, throwing his hand on a diagonal rise. "I've made my mind up now. I apologize for introducing the subject. You're here for pleasure. Let's finish up our wine and then go to the billiards room."

"You have a pool table?" asked Reinhart.

"Doesn't everybody?" Blaine obviously did not enjoy being taken literally in his self-righteous irony.

"All right, Blaine," his father said. "I don't want to be callous. And believe me, I don't wish your mother bad luck of any kind. Furthermore, I do think Winona is right to feel a duty. But I don't want her taken advantage of."

Winona spoke with quiet force. "Daddy, I think this is really my affair, if you don't mind."

And all at once Reinhart was struck by a sense that beyond this point he would be out of order; perhaps he had already crossed the line. In his earlier life he had so often been the fool that in compensation nowadays he was capable of erring in overcaution, excessive shrewdness.

"You're right," he said to his daughter. To Blaine he said: "So, probably, are you. I'll go shoot some pool by myself, if you'll show me where."

"Go out to the entrance hall," said Blaine, "and turn right. The billiards room is downstairs. The door's next to the closet where Winona put the coats."

Reinhart followed these instructions and descended to what persons of a lower social order would probably have called the game room, though, true enough, it contained only a pool table. The multicolored balls were nicely collected into the classic vee on the vibrant green felt, which looked very new. Reinhart had

not had a cue in his hands since the Army, and never in his life had
he had access to such a glowingly virgin table.

He was choosing a stick from the rack on the wall when a
juvenile voice said: "Are you allowed to be down here?"

"Yes," he answered without turning. "I was sent here."

"I don't believe that."

Reinhart turned, stick in hand. It was his elder grandson, age six.
"You know, Toby," he said to the boy, who was squinting suspiciously at him, "it would be nice if you greeted a guest in a hospitable way."

"Why?"

"It would be classier. Hospitality is an old tradition in all soci-
eties, I think even among cannibals."

"Put that stick back!"

Reinhart took a leaf from Toby's book and asked: "Why?"

"Because it's not yours."

The easiest thing would have been simply to see the child as a
monster, and admittedly Reinhart had sometimes given in to that
natural identification. But with a little extra effort one could extend the leeway of a six-year-old. He winked at the boy and bent
over the pool table again.

"Damn you," said Toby. "I told you to put that stick down."

"Now you're getting nasty," said Reinhart, sighting on the cue
ball. "There's a thing you should know about being nasty. You
should be big enough or smart enough to get away with it without
being treated even more nastily in return. Otherwise you're a
fool." He slammed the cue ball, characterless bald eunuch that it
was, into the rack of brightly colored spheres. That first impact
always made a marvelous sound, and then came the blunt, subsidiary sounds as the balls struck the rubber banks and angled away
to collide with one another, and then, in a kind of slow motion, two
of them fell into as many pockets. This last seemed a gain, though
he could no longer remember how to score any of the various pool
games.

"You're in big trouble now," said Toby.

"No, I'm not." Reinhart sank an easy ball: the One, as it happened, which had already been hovering on the very lip of a
pocket. "Get yourself a stick, and we'll have a game."

"That's just the point," said the child. "That's *my* stick that you stole."

Reinhart had his doubts about the claim, but he sighed and handed the stick to Toby, who marched across the room and placed it in its slot against the wall.

"You're not going to play?" asked his grandfather.

"And neither are you," Toby said decisively, and he came to the table and leaned across it, with an aim to reach the switch of the big round lamp that hung above. But lacking an inch or so in length of arm, he threw a knee onto the edge of the table and tried to climb up. Reinhart inhibited this effort with a single finger on Toby's shoulder. The boy then turned and punched and kicked at his grandfather but was maintained firmly at arm's length.

Toby eventually exhausted himself, dropped his arms, and stood in silent sullenness.

"Come on," said Reinhart, "why don't we have a game?"

"I don't want any presents from you anyway."

Damn! Reinhart had of course brought a bandanna for Toby as well, but having dealt with Parker alone and gone through the little instruction speech on the uses of the cotton square, he had satisfied his own needs and forgotten the other grandchild.

But it would never do to reveal that to Toby.

"I'll tell you," he said. "I was waiting for you to greet me politely before I gave you what I brought."

"Don't tell me that Parker greeted you politely!"

"I don't know that he did," said Reinhart. "But your brother is a little boy, hardly more than a baby. Whereas you should act like the young gentleman you are. Don't you go to school and everything?" He reached into the pocket of his jacket in which he carried the other bandanna.

Toby scowled at the blue square when it appeared. "Is that your *own* handkerchief? Is it full of snot?"

"Certainly not. Here. It's brand new, you can see that for yourself. I threw the sales slip away, never suspecting I'd need it." He handed the bandanna to Toby and wondered whether he should repeat the how-to-use advice given Parker. You never knew what omissions would be resented by children.

So he began: "A bandanna will save your life in a sandstorm, and—"

"Oh, I know all that junk."

But Reinhart nevertheless suspected that he had been right to give the boy an opportunity to reject him in this wise. "O.K. And you should also know how to say thank you."

"Oh," said Toby, "I don't have to say it to you! My father says he owes you no thanks."

To hear devastating truths from children is both better and worse than to hear them from larger persons. Better, because what can a child really do in the way of damage? Worse, in that one's conscience seems to have taken an exterior form, appearing as a derisive midget.

He laughed loudly while thinking up an effective response. It was not a bad tactic. Toby looked with astonishment at the man who found funny what should be negative news. "He's certainly right about that," Reinhart said at last, laughing more. "He owes me no thanks, because I didn't bring *him* a bandanna!"

It was not yet possible to tell whether Toby bought this. The boy looked confused at the moment. "Well, he says you don't have any money anyhow. Aunt Winona has all the money, and if he wants some, he will have to get it from her."

It would serve no cause to let Toby see his anger. Reinhart coughed, at which the boy shrank away and said: "Don't give me your germs!"

Reinhart said, smiling: "Oh, your dad is a great one for getting money out of people. My gosh, he's quite a guy! Who'd he say that to, your mother?"

"No!" Toby spoke with a child's impatience. "To Grandma."

"That's what I thought."

"Grandma's been taking care of us," said Toby.

"Yes. I know your mother hasn't been feeling well."

"She goes away a lot. I think she drinks."

Reinhart's response was involuntary. "Oh, that happens with a lot of people. It doesn't mean they don't like you." If he had thought about it, the sentiment would never have been voiced, but sometimes the preposterous is just the right note to strike, that

which agrees with life's preference for burlesque to the deprivation of melodrama, not to speak of tragedy.

"O.K.," sprightly said Toby, who anyway had not been down-
cast. Like his brother, he resembled Blaine in configuration of jaw
and the spacing of his eyes, but unlike Parker he showed little
physical suggestion of his mother, except in coloring. Reinhart saw
nothing of himself in either grandchild.

"Do you like your grandmother?"

Toby said: "I'll say this: she certainly knows her own mind."

Reinhart frowned. "What does that mean?"

"I dunno. I heard it on TV." Toby squeezed his bandanna into
a ball and put it into the back pocket of his jeans. "Do you think
television is a bad influence on children?"

This was the longest conversation Reinhart had ever held with
either grandson. Blaine would never have tolerated it had he been
present. In a sense the privilege was being bought at Winona's
expense.

He answered: "Probably, but if you think about it, what isn't?"
He leaned over the table and switched off the lamp that Toby
couldn't reach, and they both left the room by the light from the
stairway. "I have to go see your father and your aunt now," he said.
"But maybe we can do something together sometime and take
Parker too. Like going to the circus or the rodeo when it comes
to town?" But he had no real hopes of getting Blaine's permission.

Toby asked: "Do you go to bars and take dope and have sex with
hookers?"

"Not much," Reinhart answered soberly. "I'm pretty old for that
kind of thing."

"Uh-huh," said Toby. "Well, I'll see you, Grandpa." He dashed
on ahead, taking the steps in a series of leaps, and soon his lithe
body vanished through the doorway to the ground floor.

CHAPTER
11

Reinhart knocked on the doorjamb at the entrance to the library, and entered boldly. He expected some resistance from Blaine, but in point of fact his son smiled at him.

Blaine asked: "How's your game?"

"Huh?" For a moment Reinhart was at a loss with this reference. "Oh. Gosh, I haven't held a cue in years."

"That's a championship slate table," Blaine said genially. "You won't see many of those."

Reinhart looked at Winona with some concern. "How are you, dear?"

She shrugged. "Fine, Daddy."

"We'll have to play sometime," said Blaine, rising from behind his desk. "Unfortunately I don't get much opportunity to use that table myself. No sooner do I pick up the stick when the phone rings." He grinned at the carpet and threw his arm in a sweep at the bookcase. "And those pricelessly bound volumes are waiting for me when I get a moment to relax—if it ever comes."

Reinhart's spirit fell. Blaine seemed in an ebullient mood, which could only mean that he had taken savage advantage of his sister.

"You've got an impressive place here, Blaine," he said. "Young as you are, you've done so well. You're to be congratulated. I'm proud of you."

His son peered suspiciously at him for a moment and then said: "That's true. But I'm not made of money. We all have our responsibilities."

For a moment the two men looked at each other, and then Blaine turned to Winona, who had just risen from her chair, and said: "We must get together more often. Living in the same town, really, why . . ." His voice fell away as he slid towards the door.

It seemed that they were being led out to dinner. Reinhart wondered who had cooked the food. But when they reached the front hall Blaine went to the closet and brought back their coats. Winona got into hers in the same stoical fashion in which she did everything at her brother's house.

Reinhart accepted his raincoat in one hand and asked: "Are we going out to dinner at a restaurant?"

Blaine smiled bleakly. "That's generous of you, Dad, but I'll have to take a raincheck. I'm going out of town in an hour. You see—" He broke off to open the front door and in fact never resumed, but simply showed them out.

"Do you realize," Reinhart asked Winona, in a delayed reaction that had waited until they crunched together through the gravel of the driveway and climbed into her car, "do you understand that we were not given anything to eat?"

"I'm not hungry," she said, turning the key in the ignition.

"Neither am I, but that's not the point." He peered from his window at the house as they passed it, going around the crescent drive. Blaine had turned off the front light before they had reached the driveway, and little illumination came from within. "I'm afraid Blaine has become really an eccentric miser."

Winona braked at the exit onto the road. "His expenses are staggering," she said.

Reinhart thought about this for a while. "I gather that he drove a hard bargain," he said at last.

In silence she turned a corner laboriously. As in so many mundane matters, she was the old-fashioned girl: awkward driver, light eater, self-effacing with her brother, obedient to Dad. "Medical care costs a fortune."

"Maybe your mother just has a temporary problem, what used to be called a nervous breakdown. Years ago those were common, and almost everybody had one at one time or another, and then they'd recover, and nobody thought the worse of them for it, either. On the other hand, real maniacs were confined in institutions and never let out if they were dangerous. Nowadays perfectly normal people are hospitalized and madmen often roam free, murdering people. But what I'm wondering is where was Mercer tonight? Did Blaine have her locked upstairs someplace? He is beginning to live like someone in a gothic novel."

"Oh," Winona said quickly, "she was probably just taking a nap." Suddenly she seemed to have an interest in regarding her brother and his household as routine in all respects.

When they reached their apartment house she turned carefully into the entrance of the underground garage, rolling across the strip of front sidewalk. At the bottom of the descent she stopped before the locked door, and Reinhart claimed the key from her, got out, and unlocked the big portal to the garage, which proceeded to lift itself electrically. The security was efficiently managed in this building, but you could never be too careful: he locked his car door again for the short drive to Winona's slot, and when they came to rest, he surveyed the concrete place through the window. Because of the endless energy crisis, it was lighted none too brightly.

Then he climbed out and pushed down the peg to relock his side of the car. In so doing he happened to glance into the rear of the two-door Cougar. There on the seat, in her green dressing gown, lay Mercer Reinhart. She appeared to be unconscious again.

Winona had closed her own door and started for the elevator. She had been distracted since leaving Blaine.

"Uh, Winona," Reinhart said, in one of those voices in which you hope to be heard by the right person without disturbing the wrong one.

But in her state she failed to hear it, and in fact did not notice that her father had been detained until she almost reached the elevator.

He signaled her to come back. She had the car keys. When she reached him he pointed at the back seat.

"Oh, no!" She unlocked the door. "She's not dead?"

"Not likely," said Reinhart. He drew Winona from the slot and leaned in, pulling the seat-back down. "Mercer?" He was reaching towards her when her eyes glinted in the weak light. "Mercer, are you awake?"

She replied in a murmur: "No, thank you." And turned over on the seat, her face to its back. Folded up as she was, she again reminded him of a child, indeed of Winona, who as a little girl was wont to snooze on the backseat in this fashion and then without warning sit up and be carsick—unless her brother sat alongside, in which case she proved the perfect traveler.

"God," said the grownup Winona, quailing. "I guess I'll get the blame again."

"We've got to get her upstairs," Reinhart said, hoping it would not be necessary for him to do much manhandling, the backseat of a two-door being a bastard of a place from which to take anything the shape of a limp human being. Brooding about that, he suddenly became fed up, and leaned in and shouted: "All right, Mercer, rise and shine! Haul your butt out of there, on the double."

The effect was immediate. His daughter-in-law rolled over, put a foot down, and projected herself out the door as he stepped aside. Her eyes looked perhaps wild, certainly bloodshot, but she stood as if at attention, and retied her sash and smoothed the gown.

"Now, Mercer," Reinhart said firmly, though without the hectoring note, "we're going up to the apartment. Can you walk O.K.?" At least she was shod in thin slippers.

She nodded, making big eyes.

"You're not sick, are you?"

She shook her head.

"All right, Mercer, we're heading for the elevator over there. Let's go. *Hut,* two, three, four . . ."

She seemed a bit rigid but otherwise in serviceable condition. The elevator was coming down when they reached it. In a moment its doors slid away and a brisk young couple emerged. Reinhart did not recognize them, nor apparently did Winona. And anyway they greeted only Mercer, in her dressing gown, and went on into the garage.

Reinhart's little party boarded the elevator. He asked Mercer, "Do you know those people?"

She smiled noncommittally and said: "Aren't they nice?"

Winona stared warily at her sister-in-law from behind the barrier of her father, and when they reached the fourth floor she hastened ahead to unlock the door of the apartment.

"Now, Mercer," said Reinhart when they were inside, "you go and lie down."

He told Winona, "Take her to my room. And listen: please shut the door when you come back."

While the girls were so occupied he went to his bathroom, where the clothing left behind by his daughter-in-law on the previous day now hung along the shower-curtain rod. Reinhart had hand-laundered these garments, including the wash-and-wear slacks, and they were now all dry. He collected them and took them discreetly down the hall to Winona's room, passing the door to his own quarters, where Mercer was in the act of lying down. Did she remember having been there before?

Winona shut the door and joined him. "Here," said he, handing her the clothes. "It all comes out even. She left these behind yesterday."

"What a break," Winona said with quiet emotion. "We can get her fully dressed, anyway. That'll be an improvement." She spoke even more softly: "It won't make *him* think it's so crazy."

Reinhart pulled her into her own room and sat her down on the bed. "You've got some idea of concealing this episode from Blaine?" He turned so that he could keep an eye on the closed door of his bedroom. One did not leave Mercer alone with impunity.

"He doesn't know that she has recently been coming to *me,*" Winona said, assuming a hunted look. "Or he'd have mentioned it, you can be sure of that."

Reinhart paced the bedside rug. "Are you referring to the meeting you just had with your brother?" She nodded gloomily. Reinhart brought his two sets of fingers together. The situation was both gross and very delicate. "Let me, uh . . . This may not be any of my business, uh, Winona, but did he talk you out of a sizable sum of money for your mother's medical expenses?"

She raised her head. Despite the sheepish expression she said: "It really isn't any of your business, Daddy."

A rebuff from Winona was so unusual that Reinhart's astonished response took the form of a grin.

"You're quite right when it comes to the figure," he said, looking towards his bedroom door, "but I'm certainly involved in everything else."

"It won't affect the way we live." Her smile was very tender.

Reinhart had not considered that subject in the light of her reconcilation with Grace Greenwood: who would live with whom and where? For so long he and his daughter had lived in eventless serenity—or at any rate, so it had seemed to him. But Winona very likely had had crises and recoveries of which he had known nothing. In the first few months after coming back from the War he had lived at his parents' house: no matter what extravagance he had been involved in when at large, at home he maintained a bland façade; it was no more than good taste.

"Well, look," he said now, "I'm going to have to call Blaine. I'll take the responsibility here, if it must be taken, but I won't put up with any of his nonsense. After all, I knew him before he could go to the toilet unassisted."

This was supposed to be a joke, but Winona was not as amused as she might have been.

She winced. "It's different with you, but then, *you're a man.*"

He went to pat the crown of her lowered head, but refrained: that was model's hair. What he really felt like doing was to give Blaine a brutal hiding. Alas, the boy had regularly inspired such feelings in his father from birth onward. That was the pity, and nobody was at fault. It is much easier to understand how the wrong people get married to one another than to recognize that Nature too makes mistakes. That is, it was his emotional error to have married Genevieve, but his connection to Blaine was through the most basic of physical elements, the chromosomes, etc.: this was a dirty trick of God's.

He began: "All my life I've been trying to decide whether spelling things out, telling the whole truth, and so on, really helps, and I have never succeeded."

But Winona looked up at him and said: "You know my brother's style. Mother's gone crazy because of *my* private life."

"He actually said that?"

"What do you think?"

"I think I'd strike him if he were near enough," said Reinhart.

He thought for a moment. "First, I hope you know there's nothing in the accusation. Nobody does anything of that sort because of somebody's, as you say, private life. . . . You know you have always been the most forgiving of women with the menfolk of your family, Winona. I have noticed that you are quite different when among your female friends. And that fascinates me."

He wanted to say more; perhaps he was at last even ready to consider that Winona's generosity towards himself and Blaine might be condescension on her part, a radical idea if seriously entertained by a father. But at this moment the door to his bedroom opened, and Mercer emerged.

When he moved quickly into the hall she smiled and said: "I've had a very nice time. I'm sorry I have to leave so early."

"So am I, Mercer," said Reinhart. "Won't you come back here? Winona wants a word with you." He stepped into his daughter's bedroom. "Get her into the clothes, huh? I'm going to phone Blaine."

Mercer continued to smile in her genteel fashion as she slipped by him in an almost Oriental glide. Reinhart went to the telephone extension in the kitchen and dialed his son's number. There was no response to several rings, and he was about to hang up, assuming that Blaine had gone out to search for Mercer, when the instrument was lifted at the other end.

"Hello," he said. "Blaine?"

"No."

"Parker? Grandpa. I want to speak to your father."

"Give me a dollar," Parker said.

"You get him right now."

"I don't know where he is."

"Parker, I want you to promise me something."

"Huh?"

"When your father comes back, tell him to call me. Can you do that?"

"It would be nice if you tell me what you're going to bring me next time."

"Did you hear me, Parker?"

Someone else came on the line, lifting an extension in silence. Reinhart said: "Blaine. Is that you?"

"No, I *told you* it was Parker."

This was getting nowhere. Reinhart repeated his instructions and hung up.

He left the kitchen and was passing the front door when the nearby phone rang. He shouted to the back bedroom that he would get it, and picked up the instrument.

"Carl, believe it or not, I can make it now if you can."

"Excuse me?" The female voice was familiar, but for the life of him he couldn't immediately identify it.

"I'll explain when I get there."

He suddenly remembered: Helen Clayton. Huh. "Helen, I'm really tied up at the moment."

"Well . . ."

"Really. I've got family problems. You remember yesterday afternoon?"

"Oh. Is she—"

"More or less. But listen, there was something I wanted to ask you about." He cupped his hand around his mouth and both lowered the volume of his voice and increased its intensity, so as to be audible to her but not to the back bedroom. "You know your friend with the white Cadillac?"

"Who?" asked Helen.

"You know, the white car you got out of yesterday after lunch."

"Carl, I told you I wasn't free. Now, you've got no right to be jealous."

"I'm not snooping, believe me, Helen. But a funny thing happened in connection with Genevieve, my ex-wife, you know. It seems she was seen getting into that same car that your friend drives."

Helen was silent for a while. Then she said: "We were trying to help, Carl."

"Help?"

"I saw her there screaming at you in the parking lot, so I mentioned it to my friend. He said he'd have a word with her, and I guess he did. Why? Didn't it work?"

Reinhart was shaking his head. By chance he saw the etching on the wall above the phone but now could not find the configuration of the female sexual part or indeed any other. He asked: "Is your friend in the Mafia?"

Helen chuckled. "Naw, he's Jewish."

"Uh-huh. Well, she seems to have taken him for a gangster."

"I could see that, yeah," said Helen. "Well, O.K.. Does that answer your question?"

"I wonder why she'd get into the car with a strange man, though. Your friend, he wouldn't actually threaten her, would he?"

"What do you mean?"

"Pull a gun or anything?"

Helen thought for a while. "Gee, Carl, I don't know why he would. I couldn't see any reason for it. He's in business, you know."

"Uh-huh."

"Floor coverings."

"Is that right?" She heard the girls coming up the hall. "Well, thanks, Helen. I've got to go now. I'll get back to you."

"I'll try, Carl, but I don't know . . ."

"Sure, Helen."

Mercer came out of the hallway as he hung up, Winona behind her. Blaine's wife wore her clothes of yesterday and carried the folded dressing gown over one arm.

To Reinhart she said: "Winona was just showing me her room. The colors are lovely, and I especially like her choice of fabric for the curtains."

"Uh-huh," said Reinhart, as if he were still speaking with Helen. "How are you feeling, Mercer?"

"Very well, thank you. And you?"

"In the pink," he said.

Winona seemed more hangdog by the moment. Reinhart addressed her with fake verve: "Shall we get the show on the road?"

She handed him the car keys. "Do you mind, Dad?"

"Taking Mercer home?" he cried bluffly. "Is it likely I'd complain about being in the company of a good-looking girl?"

Each of them made some show of mirth. Mercer actually produced a whinnying sound: it was even possible she was genuinely amused.

"Oh, that would be very kind. I'm sorry to put you to this trouble, but . . ."

Reinhart bit his lip. On an impulse he decided to ask, flatly: "How'd you get here, Mercer?"

"It wasn't far."

"You walked from your house?"

"No, just from where my car broke down. . . . Will you excuse me, please?" She pointed down the hall and proceeded in that direction. She went into the nearer bathroom, his own, perhaps familiar to her unconscious memory.

Reinhart shrugged at his daughter and spoke in a low voice. "God Almighty, that's more than drunk. Her mind is gone."

Winona peered down the hall. "She's on something."

"Can that be all, though? Can you get that demented on pills?"

His daughter nodded. "You can get anything."

Perhaps Winona was right. Suddenly he wondered whether her own sexuality had been, was being, warped by some chemical means. Was Grace Greenwood slipping something into the Fresca? What a wild hope to have, but perhaps less preposterous than a great many phenomena that were now seen as commonplace. At almost hourly intervals he was reminded of how harmless had been the time of his own youth: the most vicious types of that era would today qualify as the most wholesome of citizens. The young toughs of high-school days freaked out on drugstore wine. Someone's second cousin knew a swing musician who sometimes smoked reefers. The love that dared not speak its name was named only in jest.

"I guess one should hope it's only drugs," said he.

"You know, I was thinking," said Winona, looking down the hall. "Grace has a good friend who's a lady shrink."

No matter how good your intentions, you immediately ask yourself: another one of them? Reinhart cleared his throat, expunging the thought. "You may be right," he said. "It would be up to Blaine, or really, to Mercer herself, if she's capable of making such a decision."

"Some of the worst junkies in this country are young married women with children," Winona said, with a TV reporter's note that deepened her voice at the end of the sentence. She was probably repeating some news item verbatim. Reinhart had heard many to the same effect. "I know you've never cared much for psychiatrists, Dad."

Reinhart felt a surge of affection for her. This was one of the times when, without warning, he thought of her as good old Winona—despite her current chic.

"But then, what do I know?" he asked in good humor. "Aw, it's just that I crossed paths with one or two throughout the years, and of all people I have ever met they seemed to know the least about human beings. But, then, perhaps that's the right idea."

He could see that Winona paid little attention to his speech, for he knew her so well. Then she proceeded to prove again that he knew nothing.

"Dad," she said, coming to stand in front of him and lowering her eyes, as if in a proper form of confession. "She's really good, this doctor. She's not a phony."

He nodded. "I'll take your word for it, dear. You went to her yourself, is that what you're saying?"

"For a while. . . . You're not angry?"

"Winona," said he, "I think I've been a jerk. I never meant to imply that you needed my approval to go to a psychiatrist—or to do anything else. I have seldom been able to remember what a good daughter you've always been—an amiable child, as I believe the term went in a more graceful era. You don't have to share my tastes and opinions, nor apologize when you differ." It was true that he meant this earnestly and that he was being hypocritical as well. What he really wanted was that she naturally and voluntarily agreed with him on all matters. "I take it you were helped."

"Oh, yes." Winona said this fervently. "A lot."

He very much did not want her to spell out how. "That's impressive testimony. You might talk the idea over with Blaine and Mercer—and by the way, isn't she taking a long while?" Luckily there was only a ventilation duct and not a window in Reinhart's bathroom.

He and Winona were at the head of the hall when the door swung open and Mercer emerged. She had freshened her make-up and brushed her hair. She was an authentically good-looking young woman, not beautiful nor pretty, but simply damned well made. When Reinhart saw her in this way he sometimes thought of horses: she might appropriately be holding one by the bridle. Again, there was in her own neck a suggestion of the equine. He could easily be envious of Blaine: this was the kind of girl who would never have been aware of his own existence when he was young. And only yesterday he had stripped her nude and washed off the puke! Today she was revealed as being demented, whether permanently or for the drugged nonce. But there was no getting away from it: she still had genuine class.

"Ready to go?" he asked, jiggling the car keys.

"Oh, if you don't mind," said Mercer, with a dazzling grin that seemed to have no emotion behind it. "I really am in the mood to have some fun. I've been home all day." She turned her smile on Winona. "Want to do a disco?"

Taken by surprise, her sister-in-law opened and closed her mouth in silence.

Reinhart said: "We'd better get you home, Mercer."

"*He* won't let me out."

"You understand, we can't operate in that fashion. We'll help you, but we won't do anything behind Blaine's back. . . . By the way, I just remembered he said he was going somewhere. When will he be back?"

"Who knows?"

"Are you serious?"

Mercer gave him a solemn look. "I think I'll just lie down for a while."

Reinhart said to Winona: "Help her to bed in my room. I'd better go over and bring the boys back here."

CHAPTER
12

"Carl, you're booked tomorrow on the *Eye Opener Show,* Channel Five, to go on right after the seven forty-five headlines. Know the show?"

Grace Greenwood was on the telephone. Reinhart seldom watched TV before late afternoon at the earliest, but he was aware in a general way of the programs offered.

"That's the local one, isn't it?" Then he was belatedly struck by the meaning of the announcement that had preceded her question. "What do you mean, I'm booked?"

"I've got you a three-minute spot. What can you cook in that time? It should be something highly visual."

He repeated his question. "I don't understand."

Grace chuckled with the sound of crumpling paper. She was in a capital mood, for some reason. "It all started with the cathode-ray tube, I think. Get the rest of the explanation at the public library!"

"I'm sorry, Grace. I don't know whether Winona mentioned that we have some difficulty et cetera in the family. It takes all my attention at the moment."

"Carl, I'm *trying* to help," cried Grace. "This might well lead to something, and it's only three minutes. My God, do a Hamburg Hawaiian or something."

In spite of himself he asked with horrified fascination: "Is that with pineapple and coconut?"

"Who knows?" said Grace. "I just made it up. But that's the idea:

something colorful, inventive. Lots of people watch that show, and everybody's interested in unusual cooking nowadays."

In fact, Reinhart knew nobody at the moment who was even interested much in plain eating, but it was true that he got no further than his troubled family these days.

"Tomorrow? God, Grace, I wish you'd asked me first." Still, he could feel the faint stirrings of a vanity that had been so long quiescent, as was only appropriate in a man of his years and history. "Television! I don't know that I'd have the nerve."

"Well, just watch some of it and you'll get plenty!" said Grace. "Wear your big white hat and apron, and half the battle's won. I promised you'd be there at five thirty for make-up." She gave him the address of the studios.

"I don't want to be crude, Grace, but is this for free?"

"Certainly not, Carl. Epicon gets a plug for providing you and the products you use. You're still working for us. Bye."

He hung up, nodding wryly to himself. He still didn't know what his fee or salary amounted to, and he was embarrassed to reflect that he could never bring himself to ask.

It was eleven A.M., and he wore the clothes of yesterday, for the reason that Mercer was still in his bedroom, presumably asleep. And presumably Blaine had not yet got home to find Reinhart's note on the whereabouts of his wife and children. The boys had been put in Winona's room. Reinhart had slept on the living-room couch (which was *still* not quite dry from the scrubbing), and his daughter had gone to—where else?—Grace Greenwood's.

In the midst of all this he was supposed to go on television and cook something in a hundred eighty seconds?

He heard stirrings behind the door of his bedroom. He had talked with Grace on the extension near the front door.

Mercer opened the door and came out, rubbing her eyes. She wore a pair of Winona's pajamas, though not in the blue that Reinhart had chosen for her the day before, but in pink, and a borrowed robe.

"Good morning," said he, out by the phone, and she turned her head towards him as if in fright.

"Oh. Hi."

"Winona came and took the boys off to their respective schools,"

Reinhart said. "We saw no reason to wake you up. Was that O.K.?" Toby went to a private academy of some sort, and Parker to a "play school." Winona had arranged the night before to collect them next morning, and so she had done.

"That was a good idea," Mercer said dully.

But nobody should be kept standing in front of a bathroom when they first arise! Reinhart waved at her. "Go ahead. I'll fix breakfast. Do you have any preferences? Or phobias, for that matter?" If Winona ate anything at all before leaving in the morning, it was likely to be something bleak, like wheat germ and skim milk. Of course she had a horror of eggs. "How does French toast strike you?"

"Oh," said Mercer, smiling vacantly, "anything, anything at all."

Reinhart was sorry to hear that unreliable phrase, but he went to the kitchen and broke an egg into a shallow bowl and agitated it with a whisk. For the boys he had made one-eyed sailors, i.e., slices of bread in each of which, in a central hole, an egg was fried. These had even made a hit with Blaine when he was little: Reinhart could number such successes on one hand without exhausting the supply of fingers.

His version of French toast called for a topping of sautéed apples. He had a few red Delicious in a wire basket: they were in decline, but after the peeling and reaming and trimming of discolorations they yielded enough slices to cover two pieces of toast. He cooked them in butter until they were translucent, and then, turning up the heat, and keeping the apples in motion with a spatula, made them golden.

He could still hear the shower, which was just behind the kitchen wall, and was beginning to feel some apprehension—given the fact that the bather was his daughter-in-law—when at last the water was turned off. He stepped into the dining area, which was glowing and warm from the bright sunshine this morning, and had just pulled one of the chairs from the table, expecting something of a wait if Mercer was finishing up in the bathroom only now—when that person came around the corner.

Her hair was wrapped in a damp towel, and she wore his own terry-cloth robe, which he had left that morning, after his own shower, on the back of the bathroom door. She was barefoot and dripping. Apparently she had not dried herself before simply climbing into the robe.

The whole procedure seemed to have its feckless side, but she was a guest.

He held the chair for her. "Here you go, Mercer! The sun's so nice here, I'll set a place at the table." He himself generally breakfasted off the kitchen counter, perched on a stool of appropriate height.

It occurred to him that she might want to lend a hand in the place-setting, but she made no such offer. He got out one of the better, gold-edged plates from the low cabinet against the wall and the requisite cutlery from the set of silver purchased by Winona in an extravagant moment and rarely used since. And a good napkin, of the snowy kind.

"Now," said he, as she leaned aside so that he could arrange these things before her, "what's lacking is a single rose, in a crystal bud vase."

Her face was as handsome as ever under the towel, but Reinhart really didn't like to see a wet towel at table, not to mention his bathrobe, which had never dried from yesterday's soaking and was furthermore too large for her in an unattractive way: absent was the charm of the spunky but modest girl, a standard role in pre-War films, who, overtaken by rain and darkness, ended up, in all innocence, wearing the hero's oversized nightclothes, though he would not kiss her until they were engaged.

Mercer said: "Oh, don't go to any trouble. I just have black coffee in the morning. You wouldn't have any cigarettes around? I ran out."

"No. Neither of us smokes." He went into the kitchen.

She persisted. "There's not a machine down in the lobby?"

He came to the door. "Not that I know of." Actually, there was such a device, he now remembered, in the rear of the basement, outside the laundry room, but he had no intention of revealing its existence until breakfast was over. He turned up the heat under the teakettle, which was already full and warm, and took the canister of coffee beans from the refrigerator. For his standard lone breakfasts he was not wont to fresh-grind Mocha-Java, but this was an occasion.

The kettle, warmer than one had thought, was already beginning its whistle. Before he had switched off the burner Mercer was in the doorway, china cup, sans saucer, dangling from a hooked finger.

"Got to have my coffee quick as I can!" she said, with smirking affection for her own foible. "Where's the jar? I'll fix it myself."

"I was just about to grind some coffee." He showed her the open canister.

She scowled into it. "Is that coffee?"

"That's how it starts," said Reinhart. "Then it's ground." He poured beans into the blender. "This is one way to do it, but there are hand-turned grinders and also little electric ones." He pushed the button that caused the blades to whirl. "That should do it." He took the top off the blender jar and displayed the contents.

Mercer shook her head dubiously.

"You see," Reinhart said, "when you buy coffee in a can, the grinding has already been done."

"I've never made it except with powder," said she. "I guess I never have thought about anything but instant."

"Well, why don't you go out and sit at the table? It'll take just a moment for the coffee to drip through. Meanwhile I've got half a grapefruit here." He opened the fridge. "I'll just put some honey on it."

"What I generally do is take a cup of coffee with me to the bathroom while I dry and brush my hair."

Reinhart patted her damp shoulder. "I want you to eat this breakfast, Mercer. It'll do you a world of good, believe me."

He heated the milk and made *café au lait* for her. The slices of apple were arranged in orderly overlap atop the French toast, dusted with cinnamon and anointed with maple syrup. In accompaniment were three slices of bacon, cut from the chunk by Reinhart's own keen knife and thus not quite regular but thick enough to proclaim their substance, of a robust but natural hue and rendered absolutely of fat.

Mercer ate a respectable amount from this plate, to her own announced surprise. Reinhart was enormously pleased to have cooked something that someone ate, and for the second time this morning, the boys having polished off their own breakfasts.

After tidying things up, he poured himself a cup of coffee and went out to join her. But she was leaving the table as he arrived.

"That was terrific," she said, not looking at him and his coffee. "I'm going to get dressed." And away, around the corner, she strode.

Of course he felt let down. There was now no sense in sitting there to drink his coffee, with no company but her dirty implements of eating. He cleared the table and went back to the kitchen.

An hour later Mercer was still shuttling regularly between his bedroom and his bath, effectively continuing to deny him access to either: which meant not only that he couldn't brush his teeth, a function he was psychologically unable to perform until he had been up for several hours, but also that he had not had a change of clothing for more than a day. The older he got, the nicer his ways: even as late as the War years he might still display a teenager's indifference to the freshness of his underwear, but nowadays, in an essentially sedentary existence, day-old drawers and T-shirt seemed lined with grit, and the thought of his feet in yesterday's socks was loathsome to him.

It occurred to him that he might take this opportunity to clean Winona's room, which no doubt would need some attention after the night spent there by the boys. But here again he was obstructed: this time because of modesty. Just as he arrived at the head of the hall on his first attempt, Mercer passed from bedroom to bathroom, still wearing the robe, but the belt had been unfastened and the garment swung open. Of course he had seen her in the altogether the day before, but now she was conscious—if you could call it that: she was oblivious to him.

He turned and went back to the other end of the apartment. The sun continued to show itself genially, after a procession of gray days had crawled through the no-man's-land between winter and spring. Reinhart was often indifferent to nonextreme weather, but a walk in the warm light, going down towards the river, might be just the ticket this morning, and he believed he should take Mercer along. She seemed all right thus far, even boringly so, occupied with the routine of getting into the day, but he did not like the idea of leaving her alone.

After allowing more than enough time for her to clothe herself, he tried again to penetrate the hallway, but again he was obstructed, at least theoretically, by his daughter-in-law, who was in the act of going from bathroom to bedroom. Now the robe was missing, and though she was not in the altogether, she was hardly overdressed, wearing, as she did, only two pieces of flimsy underwear. For Reinhart this was no more erotic than his cleaning her of vomit the day before, but much more embarrassing. And this time she not only noticed him, but spoke, though did not, thank God, stop.

"You didn't find any cigarettes, by chance?"

She was inside the bedroom by the time he answered. "I'll tell you, I'll go down and see if I can find a machine. Maybe there's one in the rear of the building." He had not forgotten the risk in leaving her alone, but had begun to feel a desperate need to escape until she was clothed. What bothered him, as always, was not really Mercer, nor himself, but his son. The classical theories of the emotions were usually fixed on the guilt felt by the child towards the father. Reinhart had felt little of this that had not been artificially stimulated by the trend of the times, but absolutely genuine was the wretchedness evoked in his soul by any thought of Blaine. He assumed that were Blaine to come here now and find Mercer in a state of undress, his son would believe him a degenerate—and perhaps be justified in so doing.

He took the elevator to the ground floor and went through the corridor that led to the laundry room. He found the machine, had the right combination of coins with which to feed it, worked the appropriate button, and received the package of cigarettes: a brand chosen solely for its silver wrapper. This took no time at all, and he returned hastily to the apartment. Mercer had the capacity to make him anxious by either her presence or the threat of her absence.

But she was there when he got back, and, thank God, fully covered at last—if only in the dressing gown she had worn when lying on the backseat of Winona's car the evening before.

"Say, Mercer," Reinhart said. "It's a nice morning. How about us taking a walk down to the river?"

She was standing in the doorway of his bedroom. "Oh, I think I'm just going to stay here and watch television."

Of course this meant the set atop his dresser. His private quarters were apparently to remain off-limits to him so long as she stayed in the apartment.

He shrugged. "Then do you mind if I get some things of mine from the closet?"

She gave him a vague look which he interpreted as acquiescence, but preceded him into the room. He had hoped for some privacy as he rooted through his supply of clean underwear.

The room itself was in remarkable disorder. How one slender young woman alone could have so twisted the bedclothes, distributed the pillows so widely (one under the chair, the other on the floor beneath the window), and have been so profligate with towels (one underneath the bed, another on the window sill, and still another draped over the little wastebasket), was beyond him.

He opened a dresser drawer and took what he had come for. Mercer stood in front of his closet, and did not move away when he approached. It dawned upon him that she seemed lacking utterly in a sense of existence other than her own, either had no natural radar or disregarded it. Another oddity was that, having made so much of her need for a cigarette, when presented with a supply, she failed to extract one and light it up. In fact, she had dropped the unopened pack into the frozen maelstrom of bedding.

"Excuse me," Reinhart said at last, and sharply. "I want to get into the closet."

She moued and moved aside. He opened the door and took out a pair of trousers and a clean shirt, both on hangers.

He remembered that she was more to be pitied, etc., and said, "Go ahead, put on the TV. But I don't know that at this time of day there's much but reruns of comedies from the early Sixties."

"I like the game shows," said Mercer. She acted on his suggestion, and when an image appeared on the screen she increased the volume of the sound, even though a strident commercial was being broadcast at the moment, with a jangling musical accompaniment. That the product being hawked was a deodorant spray for the private parts of women was so preposterous and ugly a state of affairs as to be answered only with a jolly chuckle from Reinhart. But despite the noise, or perhaps because of it, Mercer seemed oblivious.

He tried once more and now had to shout: "You might keep it in mind, taking a walk. I'd like one, myself. It really is a fine sunny day. . . . I just got a bright idea: we might have a picnic on the riverbank. Not baloney sandwiches, either. I'll make something more serious, a quiche or salade Niçoise. An iced bottle of, uh"—he caught himself—"mineral water."

Mercer smiled sweetly and nodded at him, though he believed it doubtful that she had listened. Without straightening the tangle of bedclothes, she flopped herself down upon them, shoulders against the headboard, and stared dully at the television screen.

Jesus Christ. He left with his change of clothes and went across to his bathroom—compared to which the bedroom had been neat. More discarded towels, it went without saying. Unfortunately, though smaller than Winona's, his was the one with the linen closet, from which Mercer had helped herself as if it were a giant box of Kleenex.

He gave himself an electric shave and washed his face in his hands—the supply of washcloths, too, had vanished—and let the air dry his cheeks. In fresh attire he gathered up the bathroom laundry and added it to that from the built-in hamper, filling a pillowcase and a half. The sound of the TV across the hall was especially oppressive when the musical commercials came on.

He had intended, while gathering up the towels Mercer had strewn around the bedroom, firmly to turn down the volume, but while crossing the hall had second thoughts about such rudeness. The poor thing . . .

"Say, Mercer, do you mind—" he began as he entered the room. But he addressed an empty bed. She was gone again.

Looking on the bright side, at least she was respectably covered. Her dressing gown lay in the overstuffed chair, and her street clothes were gone. Reinhart decided not to pursue her. Were he to admit to the truth, he might even allow himself to be relieved by her departure. His first move was to shut off the television. The room stank of smoke: she had finally opened the pack and, the ashtray told him, already had smoked about a third of each of three cigarettes. He opened the window and carried the trayful of butts across to the toilet.

After putting the room in order, he dreaded what he might find in Winona's suite, used by the sons of such a mother, but the marvelous surprise, in both bedroom and bath, was the general neatness. The boys had even pulled the bedclothes into shape (a bit crudely, but good God!) and hung up their washcloths and towels (after using them!) in a splendid try at military precision. Their toothbrushes were not in a perfect arrangement on the curb of the washstand, nor had the cap been replaced on the tube, but their grandfather himself was wont often to commit these very misdemeanors.

Indeed, this evidence that the boys were already, and untypically at their tender ages, responsible beings somehow made Reinhart feel better about Blaine's family, wretched as were its adult prospects.

CHAPTER
13

At the television studio everyone encountered by Reinhart was young, slender, dressed in jeans, and quick-moving. They were also, all of them, unfailingly civil. When he realized that he was actually going to appear on TV that morning, he had dosed his coffee with brandy, but he remained anxious. The studio people needed him two hours before he was scheduled to face the cameras, which meant he had had to arise at four-thirty, after getting almost no sleep. The fact was that Mercer had, perhaps unfortunately, not gone on another binge, but rather had returned to her own house by cab and come back to the apartment in her own car, filled with suitcases containing clothing for herself and the boys. Reinhart had therefore spent another night on the living-room couch, and by the looks of things he could expect to remain there until Blaine turned up.

He had not been able even to close his eyes before three A.M. For one, his daughter-in-law seemed to be making a heroic effort to stay on the wagon. This was certainly laudable, but resulted, inconveniently, in her drinking vast quantities of noninebriating liquids such as coffee, tea, milk, and the root beer which Reinhart had provided for his grandchildren: in fact, anything but water, which she could have obtained from the nearby bathroom. All else was to be found only in the kitchen, to reach which the living room must be crossed.

For another, she habitually operated the TV set at too high a volume for anyone of his age to sleep under the same roof, even though the bedroom door was closed. And when he finally registered a gentle complaint, she was too contrite and turned off the set altogether—to put it on again half an hour later, when she no doubt assumed he would be asleep at last. But of course it took that long to get used to the silence, and no sooner had he done so than the noise began once more.

At the studio he was seated in a corridor through which many people walked briskly. Finally one of them, a young woman of characterless brunette good looks, stopped and introduced herself as Jane.

She consulted a piece of paper affixed to a clipboard. "You're the chef, O.K.? We'll get you into make-up in a few minutes, O.K.? You want to check your pots 'n' pans 'n' stuff?"

He followed her, around little clusters of people and lights and cameras and cables, onto what was obviously a corner of the set.

"You've got a whole kitchen here." It looked like a permanent installation and had everything one would need, within two walls without a ceiling.

"We do a cooking segment of some kind every day," said Jane. "Sometimes we just dye Easter eggs or make Play-Doh from flour and salt."

Reinhart opened the copper-colored refrigerator. Just inside, on gleaming chromium-wire shelves, was a large glass bowl filled with eggs and a generous chunk of butter on a plate of glass. A glass canister bore a solid white label, imprinted in large black letters: GRATED CHEESE.

"Everything there?" asked Jane. He had ordered these omelet-making materials the day before.

"Except salt and pepper," said Reinhart. "I gather they'll be over here." He turned to the free-standing counter that would face the camera. He had not seen much of this show, but he had watched other programs on which cooking was done. Ah, yes: electric burners were built into the top of the counter, and a ceramic jug stood nearby, holding spatulas, big forks, etc., and salt and pepper were alongside in large white shakers, again labeled in black.

"Oh, and the skillet. I was going to bring mine, which is seasoned, but my boss insisted on one that her company is apparently thinking of putting on the market, in a new line of cooking utensils."

"Grace Greenwood," said Jane. "Yeah, she sent over some special stuff." She poked amongst the open shelves below the countertop, on the left of the burners. "Take a look. It should all be here."

Reinhart bent and found a skillet, a lightweight stainless-steel job with a thin wash of copper on the outside bottom. "This is it?" He winced. "I'm going to have to be very careful to keep from burning the omelet. This is trash."

Jane put one finger on the nosepiece of her glasses—which until now Reinhart had not noticed. "If it does burn, then just don't turn it over on camera, O.K.?" She sniffed. "Don't panic: this is the magic of video, remember."

Some young man shouted her name, and she went away. Reinhart looked about: everything seemed a good deal smaller than anything he had ever seen on the screen. For some reason he thought he might have been more at ease had things been larger. He was suddenly jumping with nerves.

Jane returned and took him into a room where he sat in a kind of barber's chair and was made up by a deft, laconic young man. When the job was finished, he ducked into a booth in the men's room and drank some cognac from the half-pint in his pocket.

The well-known movie star Jack Buxton was urinating in one of the stalls as Reinhart emerged. Apparently they were to be fellow guests on the show.

Jane came from nowhere when Reinhart left the lavatory and led him back to a chair in the corridor.

"Sorry we don't have a real Green Room," she said.

"Wasn't that Jack Buxton I saw in the men's room?"

"He's plugging his show." Jane consulted her clipboard. "You go on the air at seven forty-seven, but we'll do a run-through in about five minutes from now, so you'll have your moves down pat. This is live, you know. We can't do retakes." She left the area.

And here came Jack Buxton. Reinhart seldom went to the movies nowadays, and he hadn't seen a performance of Buxton's in— God, could it be that long?

"Hi," said the actor, flopping his large, heavy body into the chair next to Reinhart's.

"Hi," said Reinhart. "This is quite a pleasure for me. I've always enjoyed your pictures."

Buxton's face, perhaps owing to its familiarity, seemed enormous. He grinned at Reinhart. "Thanks, pal, I needed that. Listen"—he dug into an inside pocket of his Glen-plaid jacket and withdrew a leather-covered notepad—"I'll send an autographed picture to your kids, if you give me the names and address."

"My kids are grown up," said Reinhart. Buxton's long lip drooped. It was true he looked a good deal older than when Reinhart had last seen him. "But I'd like one for myself." This lie failed to cheer up the actor by much, but he pretended to take the name and address.

Reinhart asked: "Are you in a new picture?"

Buxton inhaled. "I'm considering some scripts," said he. "But I'm in town here to do *Song of Norway.*" He put his notebook away and adjusted his jacket. Like Reinhart he was wearing face make-up that made the skin look beige. The heavy pouches under his eyes and the deep lines flanking his mouth could be seen all too clearly at close range but probably would be diminished on their voyage through the camera.

"Oh," said Reinhart, "I'll have to see it." If memory served, the vehicle was a musical: he hadn't been aware that Buxton sang. The actor was best known for his war films.

"It'll be my pleasure," Buxton said, cheering up now, and he reached into his pocket and withdrew a pair of tickets. "These are for the show only. Dinner's separate, I'm afraid, but . . ."

Reinhart accepted the tickets with thanks. He joked: "I wouldn't expect you to pay for the food I ate before going to the show!"

Buxton frowned. "It's the dinner theater. That's what I meant. It's no comedown either. That's the latest thing. I don't mind it at all."

But clearly he felt humiliated at the thought of people digesting their steaks while he performed. For his own part Reinhart was only now remembering that he had never really liked Buxton as an actor—or at any rate, he had not found Buxton's roles sympathetic: there was always a resentful streak in the character, of whom one expected the worst, owing to the cocky, smart-ass personality he displayed at the outset. But then he came though courageously in the pinch, kept the plane aloft though badly wounded, or fell on the grenade, saving his comrades.

Buxton was still worrying. "I started out on the Broadway stage," said he. "I was trained for musical comedy, long before I went to Tinsel Town."

So they really said that. "I'll bet you're good," said Reinhart. "I look forward to the show."

Buxton leaned over. He had maintained his familiar widow's peak of yore, and the scalp looked genuine, but why a professional would have his hair dyed matte black, leaving sparkling white sideburns, was not self-evident.

"Say," he said, "you wouldn't know where a man could get a drink?" His breath smelled of mint Life Saver.

"Well, now . . ." Reinhart reached into his pocket for the half-pint of brandy.

But Buxton said: "Not here."

They got up and were heading for the men's room when Jane came along and carried Reinhart away.

"We'll do the omelet run-through," said she, and when they had left Buxton behind she said: "It's Has-Been City around here lots of mornings. Watch yourself with that one: he'll hit you up for a loan."

Reinhart felt he owed Buxton some loyalty, the actor having embodied the old-fashioned virtues until both he and they went out of fashion, to be replaced by nothing and nobody worth mentioning. "I always liked him in the movies."

"He was through before my time," said Jane in her brisk way.

Time was all. Twenty years earlier some Jane might have seen Buxton as a rung on her own climb to success.

They were in the kitchen now. Reinhart practiced the movements he would make on camera. Taking the eggs and butter from the refrigerator to the counter consumed too much of his allotted three minutes. On the other hand, as Jane pointed out, too much premeditation would diminish the dramatic effect. The eggs, for example, should remain whole, to be broken on camera.

"Debbie will ad lib something about making the perfect omelet," said Jane. "O.K., that's your cue to answer. You say, 'Well, Debbie, first you break the eggs.' Don't, for God's sake, tell the old

Hungarian-omelet joke—you know, 'First you steal two eggs'—
we'll get too much bad mail. Everybody takes everything personally."

Debbie was the "co-host" of the program, with a man named
Shep Cunningham. Meeting her backstage apparently violated
some show-biz rule, and having rarely tuned in to Channel Five
at this hour, Reinhart had little sense of the woman. Cunningham,
however, had formerly been anchorman on the *Six O'Clock News:*
his amiable, insensitive face above a wide-bladed tie and even
wider lapels was remembered. But Reinhart was to have no direct
connection with him whatever this morning.

"For all the woman's movement," said Jane, "anything in the
kitchen this time of day is always played to the ladies." She looked
up at one of the clocks that were mounted overhead at frequent
intervals throughout the studio. Monitor TV sets were everywhere, as well. Someone was speaking through a public-address
system: it was like the voice of God, and hence quite startling
when it uttered foul language.

Jane said: "You'd better put on the chef's hat and apron."

Reinhart was getting into the spirit of the place. "Oh, God," he
said, with real despair, "I forgot to bring them!"

Jane shook her head. "Your office sent them over." She led
Reinhart to a little dressing room, where he found the cook's
costume and donned it. The *toque* was pristine, but the apron was
imprinted, over the region of the heart, with the logo of Grace
Greenwood's firm: the name EPICON printed in the form of a
croissant. This was something new.

Jane came along just as he emerged: she apparently had a sixth
sense about these matters, for he was certain she had not been
lingering there. Again she took him to the chairs in the corridor.
Buxton was missing.

Jane said: "O.K., it's just waiting now. You can watch the monitor." She pointed to one high on the wall across from him. "I'll
have somebody bring you coffee, O.K.?"

A young man brought the coffee. As discreetly as he could,
Reinhart dosed it with brandy. He had had the sense to buy expensive cognac: cheaper stuff was hardly drinkable in the best of
times, but with morning coffee it would erode the stomach.

The monitor was showing a rerun of an ancient situation comedy, in which the adult male characters all wore crew cuts and suits a size too small, and all the children were well behaved and everybody did absurd but decent things. The sound was turned down to a murmur, and when the old show gave way to the seven o'clock news report, the volume came up to a level of command and the backstage noise died away.

International crises were routine this morning and given little more than noncommittal platitudes by the newscaster, an attractive fair-haired woman who used the intonations of a man. Locally a citizen had handcuffed himself to a light-pole at a downtown intersection as a protest, but against what had not yet been established, and opening the cuffs had thus far been beyond the powers of the police, who believed them of foreign origin.

Then, to the strains of a lilting musical theme, the *Eye Opener Show* came on. There was Shep Cunningham, between his desk and a photomural of the cityscape. Reinhart saw and heard him on the monitor screen, though presumably the man himself was just a partition away.

After a greeting and an observation on the rainy weather, Shep said: "But enough of this nonsense. Let's get to the beauty part. Here's Debbie Howland." The camera panned to his left, the curtains there parted, and out came a very winsome young woman with dark red hair and a jersey dress in lime green. She had an ebullient stride.

"Good morning, Shep," said Debbie, taking a seat next to her partner.

Shep winked at the camera and said: "Notice *I* don't get to walk across the set. Maybe if I lost ten pounds?" He grinned and shrugged and said: "Tell us who we'll meet today, Deb—or should that be 'whom'?"

Debbie smiled into the camera. "Shep, when you think of that classic quality known as Hollywood there are a few names that embody it in themselves alone: personalities like the Duke and the never-to-be-forgotten Bogie, and likewise with our guest this morning, Mister Hollywood himself, Jack Buxton."

"Oh, wow," said Shep. "I want to ask him how he feels about our new pals the Chinese Communists—after fighting them so many times in Korean War films."

Reinhart suspected this reference was not authentic: in his own memories Buxton was always involved cinematically with World War II Germans. Indeed, if memory served, at least once he had played a Nazi.

Debbie went on: "And then our own Bobby Allen, Man in the Street, live out there in the pouring rain, will get an answer to today's question—hey, Shep, it's not about sex for a change—"

Shep groaned. "That's bad news."

"C'mon, now, this is important: 'Nuclear Power—Love It or Leave It?' "

"That *is* important," said Shep. "I was kidding."

"And then," Debbie said, "a French chef will show us how to make the perfect omelet in a minute. Sound good?"

"Mouth's watering already," said Shep. "My beautiful wife Judy's on a diet kick. I don't know, maybe I'm weird, but alfalfa sprouts on low-fat cottage cheese is not my idea of breakfast."

"Come *on,*" said Debbie.

"Washed down with herb tea."

"Come *on.* You're kidding."

"Yes, I am," said Shep. "Incidentally, that's the same thing my wife said the last time I tried to get friendly with her."

Debbie rolled her eyes. "Oh-oh. I think it's time to hear from our first sponsor."

Under his apron Reinhart tipped the cognac bottle into the now empty Styrofoam cup. It was just as well that Buxton had not reappeared: the cook would not have been keen on sharing his supply of Dutch courage. He was himself no professional performer, and the nearer he got to going on camera, the more he realized how crazy he had been to let Grace do this to him. For God's sake, he wasn't even a professional chef.

Anxiety makes the time fly. Suddenly Jane came and led him onto the TV kitchen, holding a finger to her lips, so that he couldn't ask questions. But he looked up and saw a clock, and already it registered 7:35—and then without warning was at a quarter to eight and a voice was reading brief headlines from the news, and then, in an instant, a red light glowed from the darkness before him and Reinhart was on the air! Or so the sequence seemed.

Across the room, though actually very close to him, Shep Cunningham sat at the desk, and Debbie was just entering the kitchen. Reinhart had been deaf to the preliminary comments, and for a moment he had the terrified feeling that she might be coming to expose him as a fraud.

But she was smiling. *"Is* there a secret to omelet-making, Chef?"

Reinhart was amazed to hear a deep, mellow baritone voice emerge from his chest, as if he were lip-synching to a record made by someone else. "I suppose it could be called that, Debbie, but it's not the kind of secret that would interest a Russian spy."

Debbie giggled dutifully here. Luckily he overcame an impulse to build a large comic structure on the feeble piling of this witticism.

Quite soberly he said: "It's simply speed. The egg, once out of its shell—which has been called nature's perfect container incidentally—the naked egg is a very sensitive substance." He was aware that persons out there, off camera, were gesturing at him, and now Debbie stepped lightly on his foot. Of course, he must begin to break eggs!

Amazingly enough, everything he needed was at hand—and his hand was sure, in fact even defter than when he was alone in his own kitchen. In one movement he seemed simultaneously to have not only cracked two shells but opened them and drained them of their contents. His flying fork whipped the yolks and whites into a uniform cream. Meanwhile the butter was melting in the skillet.

He was speaking authoritatively. "Speed's the secret, but we don't break the fifty-five-mile limit: we let the butter reach the frothing point. Meanwhile, we've got our filling ready. In this case it's Swiss cheese, for that simplest of dishes, a plain cheese omelet. But if it's properly made, there's nothing better, and nothing more elegant."

"Or more nutritious," said Debbie, nodding vigorously. "Gee, Chef, I can't wait."

"Just about time . . . We've got our cheese all grated already—and may I strongly recommend that you always grate your own cheese from a fresh piece: you can do that in a blender or a food processor, if it's too much work for you by hand. In this case the cheese is simple Swiss, but an even more delicious filling would be Swiss mixed with a bit of Parmesan." A moment earlier he had put two tablespoonfuls of the cheese from the canister into a shallow bowl. "Ah, there we go, just as the frothing begins to subside and before it turns color, the eggs go in quickly, quickly, and you keep stirring them, stir, stir, as they begin to thicken and curds appear . . . and *now* the cheese goes in, all at once!"

He emptied the contents of the bowl onto the mass of eggs, lifted the skillet from the burner, inserted the fork under the near edge of what was already an omelet, folded one half across the other, and slid the finished product onto a china plate.

"My goodness," said Debbie, "you don't even cook the top side? That must be my trouble, why my omelets are so dry. I always turn 'em over." She accepted the dish from him, and holding it high, raised a fork in her other hand.

"Yes, the top becomes the inside of the omelet, and you want that moist," Reinhart said. "And you must remember that whenever uncooked eggs are around heat, something's going on. The hot omelet continues to cook for a while after you take it from the pan. That's happening right now, in fact, Debbie."

"Mmm, oh, golly," said she, making rapid eyeball movements as she tasted a modicum of egg from the end of her fork. "Hey. Say. Oh-oh, Shep, we've got a winner, and don't think you're getting any of it." Shep in fact was not behind his desk or anywhere in sight, so far as Reinhart could see. Debbie waved her fork and looked into the camera. "Well, now you know how to do it like an expert." She turned back to Reinhart. "Thank you, Chef—who appeared here courtesy of the Epicon Company. Back to you, Shep."

And just like that, Reinhart was off and Shep, back at the desk, was on, and reading a list of local announcements: fund-raising charity dinners, Shriner circus, and the like. Debbie put down her plate and disappeared behind the set. For a moment Reinhart was desolated: not only was his performance over, but functionaries kept hauling equipment past him as if he did not exist and he stood in what seemed evening, for the glare of the lights was gone.

But then the estimable Jane was at his elbow, steering him out. When they reached the outer corridor she said: "You were dynamite, Carl. Thanks a lot."

"Thank *you*, Jane. Do I go back to Make-up to get cleaned up?"

The light had gone from her eye with her thank-you. Already she looked at him as if he were a stranger. "You can take it off with soap and water." She pointed to the men's room and went away.

So much for show business. Reinhart shrugged and laughed for his own benefit. He went through the door into the lavatory, which was deserted. He had always assumed the performers had a private washroom of some kind, but perhaps that was true only at the big network studios in New York and Chicago. This place was clean enough, with dispenser of liquid soap and a wall-hung paper-towel device. He began to run a bowlful of warm water, but turned the faucet off abruptly.

He had heard a muffled sound: it had been barely audible, but there was sufficient of it to raise the hair on the back of the neck, though he could not have said precisely why: something instinctively dreadful.

He went back to the toilet booths. In one of them a human being was obviously sagging in a terrible way: trousered knees could be seen on the tiles below the door. Nothing else was visible. Again the gasping sound.

The stall was locked from within, and furthermore it would open the wrong way, given the interior obstruction. Reinhart climbed on the seat of the toilet next door and leaned over the partition.

Jack Buxton was kneeling on the floor, clawing the bleak metal wall. He had gone bald in back, just down from the crown of his head: a large hairpiece had become dislodged in his writhings. Trousers and underpants were halfway down his thighs. He had apparently been sitting on the can when the attack came.

His large torso filled the short space between the bowl and the door. There would be no sense in Reinhart's trying to climb down to join him.

Reinhart ran out into the corridor and stopped a young man wearing outsized eyeglasses.

"Jack Buxton is dying in there!"

"Who?"

"There's a man in the toilet, having a heart attack, by the looks of it," said Reinhart. "Show me where to call an ambulance."

For an instant the young man resisted the thought, suggesting by his set of nose that he might respond sardonically, but then he took a chance and said: "There's a house doctor. I'll get him." He went rapidly down the corridor.

Reinhart was trying to decide whether to go back inside. Would his presence, though practically useless, be of some remote human comfort to Buxton? He decided to guard the door until the doctor arrived. Those who might come to use the facilities should be warned.

Of course the waiting seemed endless. Considerable traffic passed him, but none brought the physician. He kept reminding himself that in such a state a second's duration was tenfold, and avoided watching the clock. But when he could no longer forbear, he looked at the dial and saw that he had indeed waited a good ten minutes.

At that point Jane came walking rapidly by, studying her clipboard. She would not have seen him had he not called out.

She stared without expression, perhaps without recognition.

"Goddammit," he cried, "Jack Buxton is having a heart attack in there! Get a doctor!"

His alarm caused some visible consternation among the backstage studio folk. Persons passing in the vicinity looked at him in fear and repugnance, and a young man came running to scowl at Jane and say: "Get him *out* of here. You can *hear* that on the set." He resembled the guy who had gone, presumably, to fetch the doctor, but Reinhart couldn't be sure—else he'd have hit him in the mouth.

Jane was staring at Reinhart. "Buxton's supposed to go on at eight nineteen."

Reinhart put his face into hers. This time he spoke almost softly: "You fucking idiot: *I said he's dying in the toilet.* Go get help!"

Her immediate reaction was odd: a wide, even warm smile, and for a moment he considered putting his hands towards her throat, but then she whirled and moved smartly away, and now it was no time before a bushy-haired youth in jeans and denim jacket, but carrying the familiar black bag, arrived and identified himself as Dr. Tytell.

Buxton was still living when, with the help of a skinny, nimble member of the staff, the door was unlatched and the actor was examined, there on the tile floor. And he was yet alive, if barely, when the ambulance took him away.

Jane came along as Reinhart stood watching the attendants wheel the stretcher down the hall, and seeing her, he said: "Sorry I had to be nasty before. It was nothing personal."

She made no acknowledgment of the apology, but stared intently at him and said: "Carl, can you fill another ten minutes? All we've got is still only eggs and butter, but there must be lots of tricks you can show with those."

It was Reinhart's turn to smile nonsensically, but even as he did it he understood that, as with Jane on learning of Buxton's heart attack, it was momentary fear. And yet not half an hour ago he had wanted only to continue performing forever!

"Let me think," he said, doing anything but. The effect of the cognac had been dissipated by now.

Jane looked at him for an instant and then left quickly. He sat down on the chair in the corridor. The threat of another performance was warring with the reverberations of the experience with poor Buxton: perhaps it would be resolved by his own heart attack.

But suddenly before him, in all the radiance of her bright hair, dress, and make-up, was Debbie Howland.

She took the chair previously occupied briefly by Buxton, leaned over to touch Reinhart's forearm, and said: "Carl, poor Jack's accident has left us with a great big hole from eight thirty-three till the quarter-of-nine headlines. We've got a couple of commercial breaks and a public-service announcement during that period, so call it eight and a half minutes for you to fill. Can you do it? I know you can. Got a cookbook you want to plug? It doesn't have to be new. Or restaurant or whatever?"

Jane had been wise to fetch Debbie. This appeal was as from one professional performer to another, and Reinhart took heart from it.

"Sure," said he, with confidence, "sure, Debbie. Glad to help out."

She flung her head back, but not one strand of hair seemed to stir. "Oh, godamighty, what a superloverly sweetheart you are!" She leaped up and strode presumably towards the set.

Another repetition of the uneventful news came at eight thirty,

and then, after a commercial or two and an exhortation from the
Coast Guard, Shep returned to say: "Debbie's hungry again. She
can eat all day long, and her waistline just keeps getting smaller.
Me, I chew a leaf of lettuce and gain ten pounds. It ain't fair. Let's
see what's happening in the kitchen this time."

And Reinhart was on again!

"We're back again with Chef Carl Reinhart," Debbie said into
the camera, "for more with eggs. I guess they're one of the most
versatile foods around, wouldn't you say, Chef?"

This was actually true enough. "Yes, Debbie," Reinhart smil-
ingly replied in his on-camera voice and manner, which though
not studied was markedly different from his style in real life. "You
will never run out of ways to cook eggs, and then if you think of
all the dishes of which eggs form a part you have a whole menu,
because eggs can be the star, as in a big beautiful golden puffy
soufflé, or a co-star, as with ham or bacon, a supporting player, as
in crepes, and finally, a modest bit performer or even an extra,
when, say, a raw egg is mixed with ground beef to make a delicious
hamburger."

"Well," said Debbie, "is the trick with eggs always speed, as it
was with that scrumptious omelet you made earlier?"

"Not always. With a soufflé of course you might say it's patience!"

Debbie chuckled. "I know we don't have time to make a soufflé
this morning, but the next time you come back I wish you'd show
us that trick. I guess that's one of the toughest dishes for the home
cook to learn, isn't it?"

Reinhart smiled with mixed authority and sympathy. "You
know, Debbie, a lot of people believe that, but it isn't at all true.
It's just one of the many things in life that are mostly bluff."

"Like early-morning television," cried Debbie. Giggling and
addressing the again-empty desk, she added: "Right, Shep?"

"I can't believe that," graciously said the cook, "but with a
soufflé all you have to understand is the basic principle: air. Somebody way back in history discovered that if you take the white of
an egg from the yolk you can whip it so full of air that it becomes
a kind of solid matter, while remaining feather-light. What a wonderful discovery! And a whipped white is pretty strong, too. It will

hold in suspension any number of fillings and flavorings: shrimp, asparagus tips, and even eggs themselves, whole poached eggs. That makes a fabulous soufflé, incidentally. You dig down through the fluffy stuff and suddenly come upon a gem of a poached egg. It's like a treasure hunt."

Debbie laughed happily. "I can see you love your work—and by the way, that's essential in cooking, isn't it? Love, I mean."

"It doesn't hurt," said Reinhart. "But I wouldn't want to discourage the people who don't have a natural inclination. You *don't* have to be passionately interested in cuisine to do a commendable job at the stove. I say that because I think there are a lot of people, women especially, who have found it necessary to cook for others and think they have no talent. Even if you can't cook well, even if you hate the idea, you may be in a position where you have to do it—and I assure you that there are scores and scores of wonderful dishes you can make easily."

"Easy for you, anyway," said Debbie. She was looking into the camera. "We'll be back, but now this."

Reinhart waited until the red light went off the camera pointed at them and then saw by the monitor of the wall that a commercial had come onto the screen.

Debbie asked: "What should I say you're going to cook now, or are you?"

"Poached eggs." He took a pot from the shelf below the counter and went to the sink behind him. "Does this work?" He turned the cold-water faucet, and, by George, it did, but he got a better idea and ran the hot water. The commercials were still on the screen when he came back with the water. He sprinkled a bit of salt into the pot before closing it with the lid and placing it on a lighted burner of the electric stove.

Debbie said vivaciously: "Do you know, something I enjoy eating but never have been able to cook right is a poached egg. Can you help me out with that problem, Carl?"

They were of course on the air again. He had to fill some moments before the water came to a boil.

"There are various kinds of gadgets that will do the job," he said. "Have you seen the little pots that have a metal insert with depressions, little wells that take one egg each? You boil water underneath them, and the steam comes up to cook the eggs. But in this case the eggs are steamed and not poached. There is a difference. The classic poached egg is cooked directly in the water and is lovely and tender and always better than anything prepared with a gadget." He reached into the jug which held the variety of tools for cooking, and removed a soup ladle.

"But *how,*" Debbie asked in a tone of mock despair, *"how* can we keep the egg from just busting all over the place when you take its shell off and drop it in boiling water?" She mugged at the camera.

Speaking of boiling, his potful of water had begun already to show wisps of steam around its lid.

"Well, first, you don't want a violent boil: just kind of firm and medium, a little higher than a simmer, but not a storm. Next you take your soup ladle and rub or melt a bit of butter in its bowl." He demonstrated this piece of business. "Now, when the bottom of the ladle-bowl is covered with a thin layer of butter, you break an egg into it. . . . This is easy to do if you can break a shell with one hand. If you can't do that, simply prop the ladle up inside an empty pot."

"Gee, you think of everything," said Debbie. "That's how you can tell a Cordon Bloo cook."

"The egg's in the buttered ladle," said Reinhart, speaking of the self-evident, but then perhaps there were TV sets with murky pictures and elsewhere busy housewives were listening as they worked, backs to their sets. "You lower the ladle into the boiling water . . ."

Debbie gasped in enlightenment.

"A white film of coagulation forms around the egg, where it touches the ladle. Now, you gently and smoothly tip up the ladle so that the egg slides free into the water."

"Ooo, but look—"

"That's O.K.," said Reinhart. "Don't worry about the ragged streamers of white that blow around in the water. Also, a bit of the coagulated film remains in the dipper." He grinned. "You rise above such things. Seriously, you see that within a second or two the egg is shaping firmly up. Later we'll trim off the ragged edges —which you always get, no matter the method, unless of course you use a gadget. Meanwhile you quickly add another egg in the same fashion, and so on. If you have more than three or four, you might keep an eye on the order of insertion: the earlier will be done sooner than the later. But for the first few the difference in time will be so little as to be meaningless."

"Well, you could knock me over with a basting brush," said Debby, leering into the pot, then at Reinhart, and finally at the unseen audience. "This man is a marvel. By gosh, if those eggs aren't forming beautifully. I always end up with strings of scrambled *boiled* eggs. That ain't to be recommended, friends. . . . We're going away for a few moments. When we come back, Chef Reinhart will tell us what to do with the eggs now we know how to poach them to perfection."

When they were off Debbie leaned into Reinhart and whispered: "Just terrific, Carl. You're saving our asses."

He wondered briefly what had happened to poor old Buxton—who himself would understand, in the tradition of show business, why any more concern must wait until the performance was over.

He asked his partner: "How much more time do we have to fill?"

"Forty-five seconds."

Could that be true? He confirmed it by the wall clock. Where had the time gone? He could continue for hours!

When they, or the audience, had "returned" (from wherever whoever had been, and whatever was real) Debbie said: "O.K., Chef Reinhart. You were going to tell us how to use our poached eggs."

"I should say first, Debbie, that *I* cook them by instinct, but I'd really advise the use of a timer: about four minutes should do the trick. Ours here haven't been on quite that long yet. But to answer your question: a poached egg goes with almost anything: on top of asparagus or puréed spinach. Or cold, in aspic, as an hors d'oeuvre. Covered with caviar—lumpfish, not the expensive kind. And above all in the ever-popular eggs Benedict: a toasted round of bread or muffin, a slice of ham, a poached egg, and over it all a thick, creamy, lemony hollandaise sauce—which by the way is childishly easy to make—"

"You're killing me!" wailed Debbie. "You know that. Because we're out of time, and I'm dying of hungerrrr! But can you come back sometime soon?" She gestured at him. "Chef Carl Reinhart, courtesy of the Epicon Company, distributors of gourmet foods and their new line of copper-clad cookware. Thanks, Chef. Now back to Shep."

When they were "off," Debbie squeezed his forearm. "Thanks, pal." She walked briskly away, behind the set.

On camera Shep was reading the news headlines. Jane came to conduct Reinhart off.

When they had reached the corridor she said: "You were fabulous, Carl. We're grateful a whole bunch."

Reinhart asked: "Have you checked with the hospital?"

"Huh-uh."

"I'm thinking of Jack Buxton," he said. "It was pretty shocking to find him like that, in the men's room. I wonder whether he pulled through."

Jane looked at him with solemn eyes. "Carl, I'll call right now."

"That'd be nice of you."

"We owe you one."

When she was gone it occurred to him that he could himself have placed the call to the hospital: in other words, his self-righteousness should be restrained.

For the first time since he had put them on, he remembered that he was wearing the apron and chef's bonnet—had indeed been wearing them when finding Buxton in the toilet—and now took them off at last. Once he was out of costume he was more resigned to being off the set. But, God, he enjoyed performing!

When Jane returned she was carrying the jacket to his suit and his raincoat. She helped him into these and then said: "He bought the farm."

"Huh?"

"Buxton. He didn't make it. He died in the ambulance."

"Aw," said Reinhart. "Aw, the poor bastard."

Jane nodded in a noncommittal fashion.

"See," Reinhart said defiantly, "I remember him when he was Hollywood's most notorious ladies' man. The fact is—it just comes back to me—he was in court from time to time for sexual things: paternity suits and charges of statutory rape. He had a taste for sixteen-year-olds. My God, that was before World War Two. It's a good forty years ago. He must have been about seventy now."

"Well," said Jane, "I've got to get back to work. Bye, Carl. Hope you're on again soon."

"Uh," said he, "you know what I forgot? To turn off those poached eggs."

"They're in the garbage long since," said Jane. "Don't worry."

Reinhart left the studio reflecting on mortality, but when he reached the parking lot where he had left Winona's borrowed car, the attendant, a young black man with a marked limp, said: "You're that cook I just saw on TV."

Reinhart could see the little set, through the open door of the shack where the attendant sat between arrivals and departures. Debbie was back on the screen. It was hard to believe he had just left her company. He realized that he had never got around to washing off his make-up.

"I knew you right away," said the attendant. "That's what TV gives you: a high recognition potential." He went, with a jouncing stride that defied his limp, to fetch the car.

Reinhart suddenly understood that as a celebrity he would be expected to tip generously.

CHAPTER
14

Reinhart wanted to watch the *Six O'Clock News,* though he would have to disturb Helen Clayton to reach the set: she was lying heavily against him. Which was by no means unpleasant, but he believed he owed it to the memory of Jack Buxton to see the actor's videobituary.

When he was younger he would have probably succeeded both in missing the news and offending his partner. But for every year past fifty, perhaps in compensation for the weakening of the physical powers, one has more emotional self-reliance.

"Helen," he said, patting her bare shoulder, "I want to turn on the TV."

She groaned. "That's flattering." But she grinned then and rolled away.

Reaching from the bed, Reinhart found his boxer shorts amidst the clothing on a nearby chair, and he got into them while in the act of leaving the horizontal position. He was still deft at that trick, though he was practicing it for the first time in a while. He did not like to climb from bed with a woman and walk across the room, displaying his bare behind to her: it was his foible.

"No," he said to Helen, "I just want to see what they have to say about Jack Buxton's death."

"Jack Buxton died?" she asked, with what appeared to be deep feeling.

"You remember him?"

"I was wild about him as a kid."

"He was older than that," said Reinhart. "His era was during and even before the War."

"He was still plenty big, late Forties, early Fifties. Hey, you just trying to find out my age?"

Reinhart snorted and said: "I trust Al's TV set works."

They had finally made it to Al's Motel. Reinhart had told her about his television appearance but had said nothing about Buxton's death: the two experiences had nothing in common, were actually at odds.

The picture came on, big, beautiful, and in vibrant color. Actually the set looked brand new. But the plumbing seemed to date from the pre-Buxton age: the toilet had an incessant hiss, and the rusty stall shower was surely Navy surplus (perhaps ex-dreadnought, conflict of 1917–18).

The news was already under way. The story from the early-morning report had since reached what probably would be its conclusion: the man who had manacled himself to the lamppost at a downtown intersection had been freed by a young boy who owned a similar set of toy handcuffs and thus was privy to the secret of their springing. The episode was revealed to have had no ideological reference: two friends had bet on the outcome of a basketball game; he who lost must so exhibit himself.

"Honestly," Helen said from bed, holding the sheet up across half her large bosom, "some people are so childish."

Reinhart felt a draft on his bare back. He returned to bed and pulled his part of the sheet up. It was quite warm under there, no doubt because of the heat exuded by Helen's substantial body.

"Here." Helen handed him a motel tumbler that clinked with ice.

He smelled carefully at its brim to determine whether it was the one with plain soda. Helen had brought along the Chivas purchased the day before. She had mixed her own with Sprite.

On the screen at the moment was the two-man team that held down the desk on the news: one of them a lively fop and the other a kindly, folksy sort.

It was the former who said: "And now for today's Short Takes. *Bread:* local bakery drivers on strike. *Lead:* it's in the paint that flakes off public-school walls, says PTA leader. *Fed:* -up, says Oak

Hills bus driver, who lets off passengers, then sends vehicle into the river. *Dead:* former Hollywood great Jack Buxton, at the age of seventy-two." Without prelude a commercial began to unfold.

"Jesus," Reinhart said, swallowing Scotch-and-soda, "that's all?"

"I guess he wasn't that big any more," said Helen.

Affectionate soul, she had moved over to touch him again with the entire length of her body, and he could not remember when whiskey had tasted so delicious. Reinhart had an unalloyed sense of well-being. He was alive and Buxton was dead. Well, *he* was guiltless, had done what he could to save the actor's life. Still, it made a man wonder.

"Honey," Helen said, stirring. "Put down the drink."

"I'd better turn off the TV." He would have got out of bed had she permitted.

"Why? Let 'em watch!" She had a laugh that he was always pleased to hear. She also had a capacity that could not be believed, considering that she also had a husband and a regular lover.

"Today's Feature Close-Up," said the less dapper of the two newsmen on the screen, "by Field Reporter Molly Moffitt."

"That noise really does distract me," Reinhart said. "I better switch it off." He started to get up. He had to feel whether he was still wearing his underpants.

A beautiful young black woman came onto the television screen. Behind her was a familiar-looking farmhouse, beyond which stood a recognizable barn.

"We're here at Paradise Farm," said the young woman into her little club of a microphone. "What's Paradise Farm? That's what we asked its founder and spiritual leader, Brother Valentine."

Raymond Mainwaring appeared in close-up. "Paradise Farm is first of all an idea," said he. "On the surface it might be perceived as an experiment in communal living, and to be sure, it *is* that, but—"

"Carl," Helen said.

"Excuse me, Helen, I know that fellow."

"You know everybody on the news tonight." She spoke with some annoyance.

Raymond had continued: ". . . combining in one effort all the various needs: clean living, nourishing food, brotherhood, security, and a relationship with the Higher Power, whatever you choose to call Him or It: God, Allah, the Great Spirit, or the vision of pantheism."

"Could God be a woman?" asked Molly Moffitt, in close-up. She had a flawless face, the color of coffee heavily creamed.

"I don't see why not," said Brother Valentine.

"And how would you describe your own posture?" Molly asked, in her accentless voice. "Are you priest, preacher, rabbi, monk—?"

"I'm but a servant," said Raymond. "I'm the least of the least."

Molly interrupted him by merely moving the mike to her own lips. She seemed never for an instant to forget that she possessed that power. "You're not saying you're an Uncle Tom?"

Raymond scowled at her. "I don't dignify such terms by even acknowledging that they exist. I've got important things to do, missions to carry out . . ." He was getting the wind up, in a quiet, intense way.

"Carl," said Helen to Reinhart's back: he was sitting on the edge of the bed.

Raymond was continuing: ". . . better to do than *talk about pigment!*"

Molly Moffitt was absolutely unfazed by his passion. She said: "But were you not a militant in the Sixties? A leader of a group called the Black Assassins? Did you not advocate the use of force and violence against the white power-structure? Did you not come pretty close to asking for a racial war?"

Raymond closed his eyes as the microphone came back to him. "All memory of the past was expunged as of that moment at which I was reborn: ten twenty-seven A.M., on April third, nineteen seventy-five."

Molly Moffitt reclaimed the mike. "But just what is it you do here, Brother Valentine? Is this really a farm? I mean, do you grow things? Do you raise livestock?"

Raymond nodded gravely. "Indeed it is a farm, and we are farmers. We are dairymen too, and carpenters, painters, roofers, whatever we need to be. We shall, with God's help, be self-sustaining."

"Utopian, is that it?" asked Molly. "What kind of people are

here?" She addressed this question to the television audience.
"What manner of person seeks this refuge? Let's go inside the
house."

The scene changed. Reinhart saw the empty ground-floor rooms
he had himself walked through ten days before.

An unseen Molly demanded: "Why is there no furniture here?
Is that because of some religious belief?"

The camera came around in front of Raymond for his answer:
"At the moment we do not possess any furniture for these rooms.
We're rich only in faith."

Behind Reinhart, Helen groaned. "Come on, Carl, that's one of
those stupid documentaries. What do you want to watch that for?"

"I told you, I know that guy. In fact, I visited that farm recently."

"Looks like one of those cults," said Helen. "I don't know what
a man like you would want with that kind of thing."

"*I* wouldn't," said he. "My son was curious and—"

Molly, Raymond, and the camera now reached the big old farmhouse kitchen, where it looked as if the same people seen by
Reinhart were still in place along the counters or at the table.

Helen said to Reinhart's spine: "Your friend is pretty stuck on
himself, isn't he? That's no criticism, but . . ."

"He's stuck on something," said Reinhart. "I'm not sure what.
He interests me. I knew his father, who was a great idealist and
would have liked Jack Buxton's films, for example."

The camera had followed Molly and Raymond out the back
door. They proceeded towards the barn.

"What are the criteria for acceptance here?" Molly was asking,
and before Brother Valentine could answer she amplified her
question: "I guess what I'm trying to do is find out what makes this
community tick in an overall way. In other words, have you collected together for a religious purpose, primarily, or is it ecology,
or are you, Brother Valentine, AKA Captain Storm, AKA Raymond Mainwaring still, underneath it all, a political animal?"

Molly stopped at the door of the barn. "Or," she asked blandly,
"or are you, as some have charged, in it just for the bucks?" She
looked into the camera. "A provocative question, a provocative
man! Brother Valentine, the spokesman for the communal project
called Paradise Farm. Watch tomorrow evening for his answer to

this question and for the conclusion of our report. This is Molly Moffitt for the Channel Five news team."

The picture switched back to the pair at the desk in the studio.

"She's part white, don't you think?" asked Helen.

Reinhart said: "Um. I suspect from her remarks that Paradise Farm has been the subject of a muckraking investigation of the kind that has become fashionable in recent years. Probably one of the newspapers, with nothing better to do. Poor Raymond. Though of course for all I know he *is* a crook." He realized he was talking to himself. He extinguished the TV set and went to do his best to answer Helen's remarkable need, unprecedented in his memory. She really deserved a stripling, not a graybeard.

When they had concluded their commerce, she abruptly hopped from bed, plunged in and out of the quaint rusty cubicle that stood for a shower, toweled, dressed, and picked up her purse from the rickety table near the door.

Reinhart was both relieved and slightly hurt to have witnessed the foregoing sequence. "You're on your way now, I take it?"

"Got to," said Helen. "It's almost suppertime."

"Gee, past it! You'd better have a good excuse."

"Don't have to go far," said she, putting the bottle of Scotch into the pocket of her trench coat, where it bulged conspicuously. "Everything's O.K." She went to the door. "So I'll call you, Carl, huh?"

"I'm certainly glad you did today," Reinhart said, stretching down to his toes. He still lay supine in bed, under the sheet. "Your call came at just the right time. I was feeling a letdown after my TV appearance. It's really an odd experience: there you are, before thousands of people one moment, and the next you're all alone. I thought I did a pretty fair job, if I do say so myself, and Debbie and the studio people seemed to also, but then you go home to complete silence." But once again he was thinking of himself. "Thanks, Helen, you're really a nice person. . . . Say, don't I get a good-bye kiss?"

Helen kissed him and while so doing ran her hand down his body. It did not escape his notice that until only recently her performance would have been seen as infringing on the masculine, whereas his own . . . After she left, he rose and before the mirror performed various body-builder's poses: face overlooking distended biceps, forearm, wrist, and hand in the swan's-neck formation; then the full-front wedge, with prominent deltoids; then the hands joined at the crotch, trapezius muscles sloping between shoulder and neck. By God, he still was far from being a wreck. In high school and the early time in college, pre-Army, Reinhart had religiously used the products of the York Barbell Co., York, Pa., and for several years his principal heroes had been not of the tribe of Jack Buxton, but rather the extraordinarily swollen men depicted in the York weight-lifting magazine, *Strength and Health*, fellows who had to turn sideways to penetrate the standard doorway. His fifty-four-year-old body had not altogether forgotten this period of its history, and one already had had, after all, a few years in which to practice stoicism with regard to the relentless degeneration in muscle tone. And Helen had commended him as lover. No doubt she was merely being polite, but what the hell, it was anyhow nice to hear.

He unflexed as he felt the first suspicions of a crick-in-the-neck. The fact was that no middle-aged body, not even one well maintained, could do better than just get by. There *were* laws that could not be abrogated by state of mind.

Checking out formally at Al's was not done. One merely walked away, leaving the key in the door. Nor had Reinhart himself checked in. Helen had performed that task for him. That she was obviously a habitué of the motel did not bother him any more than, presumably, it bothered Al, if indeed there was one. Helen was a fine figure of a woman: he was not required to assess her beyond that point.

After taking an inordinately lengthy shower for such wretched facilities—indeed, the hot water ran out before long, and finally even the cold dwindled to a staccato drip—Reinhart drove home in Winona's Cougar, which had been his all day, and which in fact would be his so long as she stayed with Grace, who had an extra vehicle. It occurred to her father that it had been Blaine, really, who managed things in such a fashion that Winona had finally been *obliged* to move in with her lover, an action which until now she had been reluctant either to take or to forget about.

Where *was* Blaine? And what of Mercer and the boys? How long

could they continue to live at the apartment—by which question
Reinhart actually meant: how long could *he* stand it? Because, by
all appearances, *they* were coping very well. . . . Yet he had been
on TV for almost ten minutes that morning, and later on Helen
Clayton, his junior by a dozen or fifteen years, had praised his
performance in bed!

Therefore it was in a hearty, Elizabethan mood that he drove
home, and with ebullience that he opened the apartment door to
join his grandfamily, whom he had by no means neglected to go
and roll in lust with a doxy. Far from it! He had that afternoon
roasted a lovely plump chicken, with butter and thyme in its
cavity and bastings on the quarter-hours, and made a potato salad
with a vinaigrette of olive oil and shallots. Remembering his own
childhood, he believed that what had pleased him most when
eating elsewhere than at his own home had not merely been the
dessert as simple sweet course, but rather as an entertaining, even
surprising event, e.g., when the ice cream was dosed for once not
with Hershey's chocolate syrup but with jam made from green-
gage plums or pulverized hard candy, or the Jell-O came to the
table as turned out of a ring mold, the central well filled with
high-peaked whipped cream and surmounted by a maraschino
cherry. (These events had never taken place at his own home: his
mother disapproved of such caprices.)

Therefore he had applied thought to the dessert he would leave
for the boys and of course for Mercer too, if applicable. It must be
something that, like the chicken, could be eaten cold to advantage. He decided upon a splendid *dacquoise*, in which layers of
meringue alternated with a filling compounded of butter, sugar,
and almond extract, and the whole structure was eventually
shrouded in sweetened whipped cream and dusted with powdered almonds. There was no mammal who could turn away from
such a confection until it had been devoured: one could stand on
that truth.

He prepared as well a platter of choice crudités: bright cherry
tomatoes, sticks of jade pepper, serene cucumber, stanch celery,
and romaine allowed to stay in the long whole leaf. (As a boy he
had hated salads made from iceberg lettuce, a gnarled and ugly

plant that seemed to be made solely for packaging. And what fun it would have been to choose the raw elements and eat them from the fingers.)

All these lovely things he had left in the fridge, wrapped and in fact identified by Scotch-taped label, and on the kitchen counter lay a prominent notice addressed to whom it concerned among his guests (for either of the boys might be treated as being at least as responsible as their mother): the menu was printed in capitals, for the convenience of those who could read at all, big or small, in the order in which the dishes should be attacked, which was optional, but it was required that each of them know that the chef left his best wishes for a good appetite and, it went without saying, his affection.

Now nobody was home when he got there, and when he went into the kitchen and saw that aside from the filthy coffee cup on the counter, three cigarette butts in its saucer, there were no dirty dishes in evidence, he understood, before opening the refrigerator, that his guests had not touched the supper he had provided, for not only was Mercer incapable of washing a plate, she could not manage even to scrape one, still less insert it into the dishwasher below this very counter.

Reinhart discarded the butts in the pedal can and rinsed the heeltaps of powdered coffee from the cup. It was not until he opened the otherwise unused dishwasher that he saw the note, which was impaled on one of the little plastic-covered fence-palings around the wire tray designed to support glassware during the commotion of the wash.

Went out for burgurs.

M

The only thing that really annoyed him, he told himself, was the misspelling. How could anyone who lived in this culture make such an error? Jesus Chryst!

Cold roast chicken being one of the glories of the world, Reinhart ate his supper in good appetite. There was a virtue in dining alone. In Mercer's presence he would have felt obliged to wash down his food with the homogenized milk he had laid in for the children. As it was, he could dig out of the broom closet the crisp little Chenin Blanc and quaff it in good conscience.

"Hi," said Mercer, in the doorway of the kitchen.

"Mercer! I didn't hear you come in: I was thinking." In the grip of his old-fashioned, instinctive manners Reinhart left his stool. His daughter-in-law was both female and his guest. "May I get you anything? Coffee? Hey, where are the boys? Is it too late for them to have some of the meringue-and-whipped-cream cake I made?"

"Gee," said Mercer, "they really stuffed themselves at Burger City. You know how kids are: eating makes them sleepy. They went right to bed." She lowered her chin and up across her thick eyebrows gave him a long look of the sort that signals its maker's preoccupation with another subject than that under discussion.

Reinhart asked: "Do you want to talk to me about something, Mercer? Let me get you a chair." He did as promised, from the dining room. The kitchen was equipped only with the one stool, which, after he had seated her, he regained.

Mercer proceeded to sit there in silence. She was the sort who could persist in that sort of thing without apparent discomfort, but Reinhart was surely not. Nor did he even feel he could properly finish his wine. Unfortunately he had not got in one last swallow before she appeared, for he had had one coming for quite a while and had been prolonging the suspense: a little funny thing he had been doing with favorite foods and beverages since childhood.

Finally he rose and Saran Wrapped what was left of the chicken. The roast bird also gave him a pretext to say something pertinent as well as morally neutral: "Still a lot of chicken left, if you want a snack later. Remember it's high in protein and low in calories, especially if you don't eat the skin." He shrugged and put fowl and plate into the fridge.

"I was thinking," Mercer began at last. She vigorously rubbed an index finger beneath her nose.

Reinhart took his stool once more, but by the time he had sat down she had again established silence.

When he was certain of this, he said: "What were you thinking?"

She looked up. "Huh? . . . Oh . . . well, I don't even know if I could say it to anyone else."

"Why, sure you could, Mercer," said he. "If you wanted to, that is."

Suddenly she grinned. In such an expression her nobility of feature disappeared entirely. A grin for her was a grotesque disguise. Furthermore it was utterly mirthless. Reinhart suddenly felt like slapping her face, to bring her out of it.

But instead he said: "Or then don't tell it, if it's embarrassing." He eyed the wine bottle longingly when she turned her head away, but then plugged it with the cork and pushed it out of their lines of vision. There was still a good solid mouthful of it in the glass. What would be better, to let it sit there quietly or to empty it in the sink?

She stopped grinning at last and said: "The thing is, my parents always wanted me to have a profession. I mean, it was me who wanted to get married and have children."

"Uh-huh." She had taken him by surprise, but he thought quickly. "You mean, it was a switch, given your place and time."

"That's right!" Mercer said brightly. "Another funny thing is that I got really good grades in college, in the tough stuff like math and science. You can ask Blaine."

"I wouldn't call that funny," said Reinhart. "I'd call it impressive. Blaine, you know, was a brilliant student, but I think he did least well in math."

"I remember!" Mercer cried. She seemed happily nostalgic. "I really hated him then."

"That's right. You *did* know each other in college."

"Well, I knew who *he* was, but he never noticed me."

"He was probably too busy with his political protests and so on," said Reinhart.

"I hated all that," said Mercer.

So had Reinhart, but he was actually embarrassed to remember that period, from which nobody, of whatever stripe, emerged victorious. Suddenly defiant, he seized his wineglass and emptied it into his throat, then put it in the dishwasher.

This event had no discernible effect on Mercer. Now that he thought about it, she had been in residence for twenty-four hours and had spent at least part of that time alone in the apartment, and though he had concealed his few bottles of alcoholic beverages, she could easily have purchased her own. But he had seen no evidence of that. Nor had she acted as if drunk or drugged.

Mercer was shaking her head. She addressed the black-and-white vinyl tiles of the floor. "I should have gone into computers."

Reinhart sat down again. "Excuse me?"

"Or something," said Mercer. "But you see, it never occurred to me that you could think you were cut out for something naturally and then discover that you weren't. That doesn't seem to make sense, but actually it's true."

"That's right," said Reinhart. "It's the damnedest thing, isn't it?" For the first time he actually felt an affinity with his daughter-in-law. "I know just what you mean! For about twenty years I thought I was supposed to be a businessman. Isn't everybody? You know. That everything I tried ended in failure made no useful impression on me: I always assumed that I hadn't yet found the right business. I was in my late forties before I discovered the truth."

"But," said Mercer, "I was designed by Nature to be a mother, and if you bear young, then it's certainly your job to care for them. No matter what they say, that's obviously the way things were designed. And if you're taking care of your children, you can't go out and chop down trees and find food and do a man's work. No matter what they say."

"Mercer," said her father-in-law, "I'm going to make some coffee. I hope you'll join me in having some." He put on the water. "I take it that by 'they' you refer to the people whose profession it is to harangue the populace in the interest of various causes that will obviously benefit the haranguers but be of dubious service to those listening."

Mercer made a wry mouth. "Funny, isn't it? He was a war-protester in college. But he told me once that secretly he would have liked nothing better than to be a fighter pilot or hero at hand-to-hand combat."

"Blaine? I'll be damned." Did one's son inherit, along with certain physical traits, one's own fantasies as well?

The water was boiling. He had intended to make powdered coffee, but it was just as easy to grind some real beans and put the product into the four-cup filter pot and fill the top with water. He went to the dining-room china cabinet and brought back a pair of demitasses and the sugar bowl.

Mercer accepted the cup but spurned the sugar.

She rolled her eyes. "Let's face it, we belonged to the wrong generation."

"But then again," said Reinhart, "who hasn't?" But this was polite hypocrisy: there had been nothing wrong with his.

CHAPTER
15

Next morning after breakfast and the wait for the bathroom Reinhart eventually got himself cleaned and shaved and put together, and he left the apartment, intending to shop for food.

But while he was in the garage, unlocking the door to Winona's car, he was hailed from across the way.

"Oh . . . good morning, Edie!" For it was that tall young woman, at the door of her own automobile. He found himself pleased to see her. It had been years since he had known someone so slightly as to forget her when she was not present and yet feel a mild gratification when encountering her by chance.

He closed the Cougar's door and went towards Edie. For a moment she looked as if, in a kind of panic, she might dive into her car and flee—never had he known a shyer person—but he slowed down, grinned less broadly, and looked not directly at her but just beyond, and she was able to hold her ground.

"Well," he said, "well, well." He decided to seize her hand and shake it, being certain that once contact had been made she would lose a good deal of her nervousness. This proved true.

She showed him owlish eyes. "Well . . . how is Winona?"

"She's fine," he said. "If you haven't seen her for a day or so, it's because she's staying with a friend."

Edie nodded vigorously. She was dressed in a beige cardigan, plain white blouse, and, he noticed, not jeans but what resembled the so-called sun-tan pants that were the summertime uniform of the U.S. Army in World War II. He always imagined that he could smell soap when near her.

"She must," said Edie, "have lots of friends."

"Enough, I suppose."

Edie looked unhappy, and he immediately regretted having told her: after all, she was a defenseless creature.

"Speaking of friendships," he said quickly, "we've also got a lunch to make up for. How about today?"

In answer she heaved a great sigh. Reinhart had never seen anyone do that at such a point, but he found it strangely attractive. Or perhaps it was strange that he found it attractive, for it might be taken as merely a helpless acquiescence to fate.

"O.K." He beckoned and almost bowed. Something about Edie caused him often to come close to doing a parody of an old-fashioned gentleman. "Shall we step over to my car? Or rather Winona's, which I have the use of at the moment."

But suddenly she became defiant. "No, at least I can provide the transportation." She marched around to the passenger's door of her Gremlin, unlocked and opened it.

Reinhart didn't mind being chauffeured. Now that he operated an automobile only sporadically—Winona generally drove her own car—he found that he no longer had the old ease that had once characterized his technique of driving, and the traffic seemed heavier and more uncompromising, despite the "fuel crisis," which should in reason have had another effect. But then one's sense of anything is highly colored by one's age.

Having pulled out of the garage, up the inclined driveway, and stopped at its intersection with sidewalk and street, she turned questioningly to Reinhart.

"Take a left."

She accelerated away. He noticed that she tended to take him literally, in her need to comply, but he had lived long enough not to confuse this with obsequiousness: there are people who perform this way because of a serious outlook based inconspicuously on self-respect.

When they had reached a street important enough to have traffic lights he asked: "What kind of food would you like to eat?"

"Oh, anything, really." She was stealing little glances at him. She

shook her head at the dashboard and swallowed with apparent
difficulty. "Uh," she said, "what's it like, being on TV?"

Reinhart smiled expansively before he realized that he was
doing so. When it did occur to him, he frowned: vanity in a man
of his age was an embarrassment. "You saw me?"

"Oh, sure." She now gave him a smile that could be called
dazzling. Her teeth were slightly larger than average and absolutely perfect. "You were just terrific!"

"Thank you," said Reinhart, crossing his ankles the other way.
"Thank you very much."

"Imagine that," Edie said, "cooking like that. What a terrific
thing!"

"You're being generous."

"Oh, I think it's really great. But it's hard to understand how
Winona stays so slender, with you in the kitchen!"

"That's simple," Reinhart said. "She hardly ever eats anything
I make!" He worried that he sounded indignant, and added:
"Makes sense, of course, for a model. I'm not complaining. I cook
in the spirit of scientific inquiry. I'm fascinated by what happens
to flavors and textures when food is prepared in certain ways. But
of course I myself like to eat. What I cook never goes to waste."

"I'm certainly never going to miss that show from now on," Edie
said.

"Actually," said Reinhart, "I was just making that one appearance on the program. I gather they have all sorts of guest cooks.
I do some things for this food company, you see, to promote their
products, and they booked me on the show." He was reminded
that Grace Greenwood had yet to be heard from on the subject of
his performance. She had not even had the courtesy to return his
call.

Edie stopped the car at a red light. They were now in an old-
fashioned suburban shopping area, which, unlike the malls, had
not been constructed for the role but had simply grown into it
over the years and now was congested and somewhat down-at-
heel and gave Reinhart the familiar feelings of nostalgia and de-
spondency.

"See that delicatessen?" he asked, pointing. "My uncle took me
in there once in 1936 or 7. We were coming back from a ball game.

I had a cold roast-pork sandwich, heavily salted, on homemade bread. The proprietor was a Swiss. His wife made all the baked goods, and he made his own horseradish and sausages and of course all the cooked meats. Funny how I still remember that, though in more than forty years I've never been back."

"Do you want to try it now?" Edie asked eagerly. "We could get something there for lunch." She had a dreamy smile for the deli; she was probably sharing in his nostalgia.

"No," he said decisively. "I'll tell you why. It's unlikely that the Swiss would still be there, and I really don't want my memories polluted by the sight of what it may have become. But the idea of getting some takeout food is a great one on a day like this. We'll pick up—not here, but in the next bunch of shops we come to— some cheese and decent crusty bread, if it can be found, and wine, and have a picnic. There are various parks to choose from, or we could just drive out into the country somewhere."

He found Edie's presence much more satisfying than that of any other female person he knew at this time, which might not be saying much had he not been able to include Helen Clayton, who was enthusiastically heterosexual.

Edie made an odd shrugging movement and hunched farther forward over the steering wheel. "I think a picnic would be great."

"Hey." He pointed to the shopping mall that was coming up ahead, the signs for its principal enterprises towering on great standards which rose from the flatness of a former meadow: BOGAN'S . . . TOP SHOP . . . KIBORWORLD. "Pull in at the Top Shop, and we'll take on some provisions."

"O.K.!" Edie made her agreement an ebullient little event. She slid the Gremlin into a parking space on the asphalt plain, and they entered this branch of the Top Shop, an even larger example than the one in which Reinhart had cooked crepes Suzette.

They went through the automatic doors and once inside stopped and looked at each other with affectionate smiles. Hers was only slightly below the level of his. He had not known so large a female person since he was in the Army. But unlike Edie, Veronica Leary, his friend in the Nurse Corps, had been a great beauty. Of course he himself had been but twenty-one years of age at that time.

"Well," he said finally, breaking the deadlock of genial silence, "shall we go see whether they have any edible cheese?"

They loped in step for a while and with a purposeful air, but had no reason to suppose they were nearing the dairy section. There was here the kind of vastness on which progress had no effect, as when one drove towards a distant mountain: for every step they took, the farthermost wall receded in the same degree.

But at last they reached the long, open, refrigerated trough that held the various products which took their origins from the milch cow, and Reinhart was about to sift through the packaged cheeses in search of one that would bear being eaten, when, down at the bottom of the aisle, he saw a familiar figure.

It was Helen Clayton, at work alone. She stood before a metallic table which held paper-platefuls of cubed cheese. There were two kinds, bright orange and off-white, and in each cube was an embedded toothpick. Helen extended a plate to anyone who passed her.

Each saw the other at the same moment. Helen's greeting was to elevate her paper plate. Reinhart's wave was a kind of salute.

"Would you be offended if I talked to that woman down there?" he asked Edie. "She's a business associate."

Edie simpered at the extraordinary suggestion that anything would offend her.

"I just want to say a word to her about business," he nevertheless found himself explaining almost guiltily. "It would be boring for you. Look through these cheeses and choose something you like."

Helen greeted him breezily when he reached her table. "Hi, there!" She thrust the paper plate at two female shoppers in turn. Then there was a lull in the traffic. She put down the selection of samples and gave him a more personal grin. "Whatcha doin' in this neck of the woods? Grace send you to check up on me?"

"Pure accident," said Reinhart. "Just was passing by and dropped in to pick up a few things. Speaking of Grace, she hasn't been in touch since I did the TV thing. I thought it was successful, if I do say so myself, and the television people seemed to like it. They said something about inviting me back. But Grace hasn't even returned my call."

Helen made a slow wink. "She's having love problems, I believe.

I didn't get this assignment from her. I hear she's been out sick for a while."

Reinhart felt an involuntary wave of revulsion. He simply couldn't help it: Nature did assert itself from time to time. "Oh. Well, that's the way it happens, I guess."

"Yeah," Helen said with a wry mouth. "You can't have your cake and eat it too."

In desperation he reached for a sample of cheese: an orange-colored piece was closest. He clasped the cube behind his front teeth and slid out the toothpick.

"This has no taste at all," he wonderingly told Helen while chewing. "Why are you giving out samples of it?"

She shrugged. "It's new, I think. I haven't tasted it. I'm watching the calories, as usual." She suddenly leered at him, in a discreet but intense way that had almost the intimacy of a touch. "I'm off when the cheese is gone. That'll be any minute by the looks of it." She opened her lips and closed them silently, moistly, warmly.

"Uh," Reinhart replied, "I can't make it today. Uh . . ." For some reason he was at a loss for a feasible excuse.

"Look, honey," Helen said, changing into a pal, "I know you're with your daughter. What I meant was, only if you were going to be free a little later."

Now Reinhart moved quickly, without reflection, to consolidate this fraudulent, fortuitous gain: Helen had actually seen Winona once, calling for Grace, but didn't know she was his daughter. Let it go at that! And it was even better if she believed that he was Edie's parent. But what would happen when Helen found out? That was the kind of thing Reinhart would have found inhibiting as a very young man, but he had since learned that a good many claims in life are never put to the test, and from those that are, often enough, truth still does not issue, and finally in the rare event that it does, even rarer is to find the mortal to whom it matters.

Anyway, he and Helen, though colleagues of a kind and certainly lovers in the physical sense, would quite likely never really know each other at all well.

"Yes," he said now to his friend, "ordinarily I don't get to see that much of her at this time of day. We thought we'd get something for a picnic."

Helen looked up the aisle. "I'd know her if you weren't any-where around. She's a chip off your block, that's for sure. Doesn't look anything like the ex-wife."

Reinhart stepped out of the way so that she could offer the cheese to several women who appeared, distractedly pushing their carts. Two of them spurned the offer, but one, a jolly, fortyish person, took a cube in an excessively dainty fashion, fingers fanned. After an instant he understood that she did this in an intentional burlesque of gentility.

After taking a nibble, she asked Helen, in good humor: "Why are you giving this away? Because you can't sell it? It's *terrible.*"

"It's a cheese-industry promotion," said Helen. "To get people to eat more cheese. There were several other kinds when I started, blue and Swiss and so on, and flavored spreads, onion, mustard, port wine, but they're gone by now. There were also some bro-chures that gave various recipes for dishes made with cheese—soufflés, casseroles, and the rest—but people have taken them all by now. One thing, though, never did show up: I was supposed to have some standing posters for this table. I don't know what be-came of them! You run into that a lot these days."

"Gee," said the woman, depositing her toothpick at the end of the table. She looked quizzically at Reinhart. "You'd think they'd give out better cheese if they want you to buy some. Put the best foot forward, you know?" She rolled her cart away.

"I'll be seeing you, Helen," said Reinhart.

"I'll give you a call tomorrow," said Helen. "It can't hurt."

Edie seemed in a standing coma as he approached her, but eventually she saw him and smiled.

"Did you see any cheese you liked?"

"I wasn't sure what kind you'd want."

"What about yourself? Don't you like cheese?"

"It's just that I don't *know* what cheese to get!" Her tone was that of authentic distress.

He had been unknowingly inconsiderate. "Well, it doesn't mat-ter. Suddenly I've lost interest in cheese. Let's attack the subject from a new angle. Tell me what would be a typical lunch for you."

"A hot dog," said Edie. "Or a hamburger, unless it would be a pizza."

"Let's go to the car," he said, "and drive someplace in the country and get a hot dog. This place is depressing me."

When they reached the car, she gave the keys to him. "Please drive where you want."

Reinhart unlocked the passenger's door and held it open for her entrance. Then he went around to the driver's side. Edie was looking at him when he inserted himself behind the wheel. He did not of course need to push back the seat.

She said: "I'm sorry I couldn't choose a cheese."

"You're a real criminal," said Reinhart, winking at her.

"Are you angry?"

"You betcha." He touched the back of her near hand, and started the engine.

She did not speak again until they were on the motorway. "I've met some nice people in our building—at the mailboxes and around. I met Winona!"

"That's a pretty nice building," said Reinhart. "We've always liked it."

Edie asked anxiously: "Is your apartment satisfactory?"

"It's quite nice. It's my favorite of all the places I've ever lived in."

"Good," she said. "Because if anything's wrong I wish you'd let me know."

"With the apartment?"

"My father owns the building."

"I see," said Reinhart, speeding up to the fifty-five mark on the dial. "That's right, now that I think of it, there's that sign on the front corner of the building, isn't there? 'The Mulhouse Corporation.' That's your father?"

"I guess so," Edie said, flinching.

"Nothing wrong with that. I've seen the name on quite a few buildings around town. Your father must own a good portion of this city." Furthermore, Mr. Mulhouse was probably no older than he, perhaps even younger.

Edie said fearfully: "I just have a studio apartment. I'm not taking up any extra space that should go to couples with families."

Reinhart smiled at her. "You're too apologetic, Edie. You don't have to ask the world's permission for everything! Did anyone ask you whether you wanted to be born?"

He grinned at her. She was apparently a real-life example of the poor little rich girl, but in the course of life, he had become aware, it is routine to encounter at least one example of every legendary type.

CHAPTER
16

Reinhart had been driving for some time as it were unconsciously. An exit sign was coming up.

"Look where we are already: Brockville. We'd better get off here if we're ever going to get anything to eat."

He sent the little car down the ramp, at the bottom of which was a blacktopped county road.

Soon they were entering Brockville. Reinhart could not remember having visited this community, though it was not an uncommon name in his personal gazetteer. Now and again throughout the years "Brockville" would be pronounced by someone as being a point in space from which something else could be measured. "Worthing? Oh, that's on out north of Brockville." The town itself, into which within a moment or two they had penetrated to the heart, had a business district one block in length and occupied really less than that measurement of distance would imply, for on only one side of the street were there any establishments of "business," if a café-restaurant and a little delicatessen, both of them of the seedy if not flyblown character, could be said to have a serious association with the term.

Brockville was the kind of place in which at noon you could park at the curb directly in front of the only restaurant in town.

Reinhart shifted into neutral and switched off the ignition. "Shall we try this place? If it looks too bad inside, we can just have a cup of coffee and leave. It has been my experience to be horribly disappointed in life when I've looked for anything quaint."

He had meant that in ironic jest, but Edie said soberly: "I don't think I've ever looked for anything of that kind, unless I just don't know what it is."

They left the car. Reinhart noted with approval that the façade of the place had not yet suffered the hand of the routine renovator who applies solid siding or wooden shingles, leaving only a tiny window displaying a neon beer-sign and a framed liquor license. No, the Center Café had the big plate-glass front window of yore, though seeing clearly through it was another matter.

They entered. If the population of Brockville was at lunch, it obviously ate at home, for few representatives were currently in the only eatery. Of the three options, far-left counter, central tables, far-right booths, only the first-named was in use: three men, spaced intermittently, sat at the counter, but only one of them seemed honestly a diner: that is, only he had a plate before him. Another simply sucked at what looked to be a stark coffee cup. The third man partook of nothing at the moment, though it was possible he had already fed. He was dressed in dark-green work clothes, shirt & pants, and he talked with, or rather listened to, the proprietress, a blousy, voluble, spirited woman of about Reinhart's age.

She shouted at him and Edie: "Take a booth, kids." Reinhart waved at her, and she refined the invitation: "Take *any* booth."

"Who knows what we're in for?" Reinhart muttered as they went along the far-right aisle. There had been a time in life when he would have chosen the farthest booth, and another when the nearest would have been most attractive to him, and again there had been eras for the nearest-but-one and the next-to-the-last. No doubt a man's philosophy could be measured in hashhouse seating arrangements.

He said now to Edie: "Let's boldly take the one in the middle. We've got nothing to hide." But once again his little witticism was accepted almost dolefully by her.

By the time they had, leggy persons that they were, inserted themselves at their respective sides of the table—though there was plenty of room here, Reinhart always felt a certain emotional pressure when bending to penetrate a booth—the woman said good-bye, with a jovially rude sound, to the man in the green uniform, and crossed the room. She seemed more loose of flesh than actually fat, but it was hard to tell. She was wearing a kind of smock, in pale orange; it was clean enough. She had small and blue but warm eyes.

"Well, sir," said she, including Edie in the address, her little eyes swiveling, "what can I do for you today?"

"What's the specialty of the house?" asked Reinhart.

The woman winked at Edie, jerking an elbow in Reinhart's direction. "There's a brave man." She turned to him. "Sure you wanna know?"

Reinhart said: "I live dangerously." He winked at her. "Does a fellow have a choice in Brockville?"

"Say." The woman put her hands on her hips. "You serious? The shopping center's got 'em all: the Colonel, King of Burgers, Chinky Chow Mein . . ."

"Well, lucky for us, we missed all of that," said Reinhart. "We're from the city, and are trying to get away from all the known junk."

"O.K.," the woman said robustly. "I sure hope your will is in order! I don't have a long menu, because I don't have many customers for any meal after breakfast, and in fact I don't stay open very long for supper. But I'm here as of four thirty A.M., and I get enough business from the truckers to keep my head above water. I'll tell you what I've got all day, every day: I've got eggs any style. I've got ham and cheese sandwiches. I've got hamburger of course. I've got chili con carne. And then I always have a daily special. Today it's red-flannel hash."

"The hash sounds terrific," said Reinhart, "but I think I'll try the chili if it's homemade."

The woman shrugged. "It is."

"Edie, what do you think?"

Edie said: "Oh."

"Two chilis, then," cried the woman in her energetic way.

Reinhart liked her a lot, though he feared the worst with reference to her cuisine, suspecting her of carelessness.

"Say," he said, "I don't suppose you sell beer?"

She bent and pressed her midsection against the edge of the table. "Hon, I'm going to take a chance you're not a state inspector. I don't have a license, but I'll be glad to step over to the store and bring you back some brew. They keep it ice-cold."

"Sounds good to me," said Reinhart. The woman went away. He noticed that she wore sneakers. He spoke to Edie: "Seems to be a little place that time forgot. At least, the old part of Brockville. No doubt the shopping mall's in the new part. Did you notice those houses on the opposite side of the street? Imagine that in the middle of a business district these days, little houses with porches. At least one is equipped with a swing that hangs from chains. I can remember when those were routine on front porches, and the people who wanted to be up-to-date replaced the old swings with a sofalike thing that rested on the floor and was called a 'glider.' "

Edie gave him a long, intense, probably worshipful stare.

"Of course," he added, "that was during the Depression, and one had to have money to buy a glider. There were men, neighbors of ours, who had been out of work for years, and there was a form of welfare then called 'relief,' but some people were too proud to take it. Another word from those days was 'prosperity,' but that didn't really come until the war. A good many people had to be killed, in other words, before others had a good life in the material sense." He picked up the nearby salt shaker. Its chromium top was shining; its contents were as loose as dry sand. "This place is cleaner inside than it looks from out. Also the woman seems to be here alone, and she trusts the two guys at the counter, and of course us, not to open the cash register while she's over at the beer store. You don't see that kind of faith every day."

Whenever he looked at her Edie's eyes were fastened so intently on him that he could not bear to meet them, for fear that his own would water in sympathy.

It was with relief that he saw the woman returning with the beer. She carried a whole six-pack but went first to the counter and took two bottles from their slots in the carrier. She brought these to the booth, along with two squat water tumblers.

"Sorry I don't have any nice glasses," said she. "But the beer is cold. I brought the whole six-pack to be on the safe side, but you don't have to pay for what you don't drink. Now's the time to put the cuffs on me if you are state inspectors." She put down the bottles and thrust her wrists at Reinhart.

"Thanks for not getting cans," said he, "and in fact for getting the beer in the first place."

"I'm just trying to soften you up for the food." She laughed widely but silently. "It isn't much of a risk. My old man's the Brockville chief of police, which is more of a job than you might think if you've only seen this part of town. The new part's where the shopping center is. We live in back of it, in a new ranchhouse. The café's got sentimental value for me. My folks used to run it when I was a kid, and I grew up in the apartment upstairs. I don't make enough nowadays to hardly pay the expenses, but it's a good hobby for me." She withdrew her hand from a pocket in the apron and produced an old-fashioned bottle-opener made from one continuous piece of brass wire. Reinhart could not remember having seen one of those in forty years.

After she had poured a glass for each of them and gone to fetch the food, he raised his tumbler at Edie and took a swallow. It was a local brand and, thank God, one that chose to be yeastily flavorful rather than insipidly "light."

Edie gave him a strained smile and with a sudden effort picked up her own glass and drank deeply from it. She swallowed with a wince.

The woman arrived with two heaped plates.

"What's this?" Reinhart asked admiringly. He had expected the kind of chili that contains at least as many kidney beans by weight as beef, ground beef—but the plate before him held a lovely dark-chocolate-colored and chunky stew, with meat that looked tender enough to embrace the tines before they could pierce it, and the fragrance that rose from the sauce, which was so thick that a spoon thrust into it and raised would not have dripped, was almost of cinnamon.

"This is the real Tex-Mex McCoy, isn't it?"

"I learned how to make that down in the Panhandle," said the woman, "when my husband was in the service. That's pinto beans and rice underneath the meat."

Reinhart dug in. "By George," said he, after having chewed and swallowed a specimen forkful. "Marvelous. What all's in it? Chili powder, garlic, what else? Bay leaf? But something else. What am I missing: cinnamon, ginger?"

She rolled her small eyes and sucked the air from her cheeks. "Well, sir," said she, laughing slyly. "That's my secret weapon."

Edie spoke up: "Do you know who you're talking to? The TV Chef, that's who!"

Reinhart protested. "Come on, Edie."

"TV?" asked the woman. "You're not kidding?"

"Aw, well . . ."

"Cumin and oregano."

"Is that right?" Reinhart repeated the names of the spices, and he tasted the chili again. "You know, these pinto beans and rice, what could be a better complement to the chili? This is an excellent dish, Mrs. . . ."

"Huffman, Mrs. Gerald T., but you can call me Marge. When are you on television? I don't want to miss it."

Reinhart introduced himself and Edie. "I'm not appearing on a regular schedule at the moment. But I'll tell you something that's more important right now. I have a connection with a food company, a firm that sells specialty products. At the moment it's mostly that fake gourmet stuff: instant sauces, canned liverwurst *pâté*, et cetera. How about my selling them on your chili? What about a deal in which they make it up in bulk according to your recipe and can it?"

Marge looked as if she were in pain. She squinted as though she were about to weep.

Edie said again: "Do you realize he has the power to do this? He's on *television.*"

Reinhart reached across the booth and took Edie's wrist in his fingers. "She knows," he said.

"God Almighty," said Marge. "Who ever thought something like this would happen to me?"

"I don't want to get your hopes too high," Reinhart said quickly. He should have said that earlier. "I can't guarantee they'll want to handle it. All I can do is to take the chili to them. I'm just sort of a consultant." Or whatever you could call a man whose daughter was the lover of a female executive, a man who had been given some make-work but no money, a man who—"But listen," he said aggressively, "I'm going to tell them they had *better* take it unless they want me to go to their competition." This was more than bravado; he had a certain feeling of strength: was cumin an aphrodisiac of power?

Marge went to the refrigerator back of the counter and returned with two more bottles of beer, though Reinhart had as yet drunk only half the first bottle. However, he noted with surprise that Edie had finished her own and was now diligently applying herself to the second, though her chili had scarcely been touched.

Marge said: "Listen here. This is all on me." She raised her eyebrows without increasing the size of her eyes.

"No, certainly not," said Reinhart. "We might be confidence men who go about getting free meals. People may be trustworthy in Brockville, but you should be aware of how they are in the outside world, Marge." He raised his elbow. "If this chili idea catches on, it'll probably ruin your serenity."

Marge shrugged joyfully. "I'll take that chance."

The final coffee-drinker pushed his cup away and rose from the stool at the counter. He stepped behind the cash register, pushed a button, and made some transaction in the drawer that shot out.

"I wouldn't mind having a place like this myself," Reinhart said. "Gosh, a customer makes his own change."

Marge asked solemnly: "You serious? Are you in the market for a restaurant?"

"Probably not." He smiled rhetorically at Edie, who was finishing her second beer already. He wondered whether he should worry. "I'm an amateur cook, you see, and I guess I sometimes think of having a place where I could show off my talents."

Marge straightened up and put her hands in the pockets of her smock. "It hasn't always been so quiet here. When my folks ran it, years ago, they used to do a lot of business. One time in the Thirties a couple of fellows came in and ate a real nice lunch: breaded veal cutlet, mashed potatoes, peas 'n' carrots, stewed tomatoes, and fresh peach pie à la mode for dessert. Used to have more of a menu those days. Anyway, after they paid up and left, my dad said, 'Know who that was? That was John Dillinger and Homer Van Meter.' I wasn't there at the time. I was in school. I suppose it could have been them. Dad always insisted on it and would rattle off what they ate."

Reinhart asked Edie: "Do you recognize those names? They were famous bank robbers of those days. Real celebrities of the Midwest. Household words. When Dillinger was killed by the FBI in an alleyway next to a movie theater in Chicago, newsboys came out from the city to sell extras on the residential streets of the suburb where I lived. Do you even know what an 'extra' is?"

Edie was smiling at him. She made no verbal response.

To Marge, Reinhart said: "Could have been them. They certainly came through this part of the country. Probably was them." Dillinger had supplied to the region its only color, so far as was known: it seemed reasonable enough to claim it whenever feasible.

"About that chili recipe," Marge said. "Do you want me to give it to you now, or do you want me to make up a take-out order to bring back to the city with you?"

Reinhart drank some beer. "I think I'd rather bring somebody out here from the city to taste the product on the spot. They might get some ideas for packaging it when they see your restaurant. Does that overhead fan work? This is a great-looking place. That's a real vintage Coke sign, isn't it?" He referred to a framed rectangle of metal against the back wall, with "Coca-Cola" in bas-relief script. "You see reproductions of stuff like that on sale in shops that cater to young people."

Marge nodded. "We're rough and ready but real," said she, chuckling. "How about calling it John Dillinger's Chili?"

"With a tommy gun on the label," said Reinhart.

After more of this badinage Marge went away to let them eat their meal. When Reinhart finally poured the remainder of the first bottle of beer into his glass and reached for the second, he saw three empty bottles: four, counting the one he had just drained. Edie had her glass to her lips at the moment. She peered strangely at him over the rim. Had she drunk three bottles of beer?

Before long Marge was back. "How about more chili?"

"No, thanks," said Reinhart. "This was quite a generous portion, and it's just right. I don't want to dull my taste by eating too much. This flavor's like a rich perfume."

Edie spoke up. "He's an authority. He's a television chef." She emptied her current glass.

"I'll get the rest of the beer," said Marge, and set off.

But Reinhart called her back. "We have to be on our way, Marge. I mean it about exploring the possibility of marketing the chili. I'll be in touch soon. Write down your phone number for me, and I'll give you mine." Marge went to fetch writing materials. Reinhart said to Edie: "I wish you'd eat some of your food. If you're not used to drinking, that's too much beer on an empty stomach."

She wrinkled her nose and looked as though she might whine, but then straightened up on the seat and stoically forked up chili, pinto beans, rice.

Marge arrived with a piece of brown paper bearing her name and phone number, followed by a dash and the word "chili." Reinhart tore a strip from the bottom of the paper and wrote upon it his name and Winona's number.

"I really have to warn you again," said he, "that I can't promise anything. But we'll give it a try. And at the least I'll be back to eat your chili myself and will recommend it to others."

"On TV?" said Marge. "I guess this is certainly one of the most important days of my life."

Reinhart feared that irrespective of his warnings she would encourage her hopes to go as far as they could, and he remembered only now that on his first meeting with Grace Greenwood in the supermarket, her position on the Pancho Villa line of Mex-Tex canned goods, distributed by her own firm, had been none too enthusiastic.

Edie was undoubtedly feeling the effects of the alcohol. When they got into the car she lowered her head until her chin touched the base of her neck and said nothing as Reinhart drove back to the motorway and entered it pointing south.

Owning a restaurant! What a crazy fantasy. Nevertheless he entertained it for some miles before noticing that Edie had awakened.

He glanced at her and said: "Are you O.K.?"

"I'm just fine," she said coolly.

They exchanged no further speech during the remainder of the homeward drive. The beer had apparently extinguished such light as Edie had, and Reinhart had really never quite known what to talk to her about: his intent from the first had been merely to be kind.

CHAPTER
17

When Reinhart returned from his country outing his grandsons were home alone. They were peacefully occupied, Toby in the hallway with a fleet of miniature cars and Parker on the floor of Winona's bedroom, working in a child's inept fashion with a pair of those blunt-bladed scissors made for small people.

Toby pushed one of the tiny vehicles up the alleyway of bare wood between the wall and the hall runner. He defied custom by not simulating the sound of an engine.

Reinhart asked: "That wouldn't be a Rolls-Royce, would it?"

"Why do you ask?"

"You're not making any engine noise. They used to say about a Rolls-Royce that it ran so quietly the only sound you heard was the ticking of the dashboard clock."

"Ticking?" asked Toby. "Was there a bomb in it?"

Reinhart thought for a moment. "Clocks used to tick. That was before they were digital."

"I can tell time on the ones with hands!" Toby announced with pride. "We learned that in school."

The telephone rang. He answered the one beside the door.

"Carl?" It was Helen Clayton. "I thought you'd want to know why Grace Greenwood has been out of touch. It seems she made a suicide attempt yesterday."

"Oh?"

"Lovers' quarrel! Can you imagine that? She got this girl to move in with her, you know, after working on her for weeks. Just like it was a *guy* and a girl. And they didn't get along, so this girl was going to walk out on her, and Grace took an overdose of sleeping tablets. Of course she claims it was by accident: it was dark, and she got the wrong bottle or something. What surprised me though is that it was Grace who did this and not the other dyke. Grace is always the boss."

"Not in this situation," said Reinhart.

"Excuse me?"

He said: "I guess even authoritative people have someone who knows their number."

"Dykes!" said Helen. "God in heaven. I guess fags have got nothing on them." She said this with a hint of female pride, the old-fashioned kind that predated the recent phase of feminine activism: the sort that had been characteristic of his mother, a roughhewn woman who despised the aims of femlib as being degenerative of the authority she had acquired singlehanded.

"I guess they're all human," said Reinhart, but without piety. He got a grip on himself. "Thanks, Helen. I *am* interested in that information."

"I've got my own source," said she.

"No doubt male?"

"Now, now," Helen said. "Do I ask you to explain everything?"

"I'd be glad to."

"I'll bet," said Helen. She seemed to think his life more enterprising than it was.

"Maybe we can get together again soon."

"Let me call you about that," said Helen. "Al has to go in the hospital for another operation. That means I'll have to spend a lot more time at the motel office."

"Al's Motel?"

"Didn't I mention it? Al's my husband. He's been disabled for a while and in a wheelchair, but he can run the office when he's not in the hospital."

"I'm sorry to hear about his trouble," Reinhart said. He cupped his hand around the mouthpiece, so that Toby, up the hall, would not hear him. "Do you mind my asking? Did Al know we were there the other day?" Helen couldn't understand his whisper, and he had to repeat the question in a somewhat louder voice.

She answered: "He knew *I* was there. I don't think he saw you. I didn't tell him your name, Carl, if that's what's worrying you. I'm not a pervert."

"I hope things work out for him at the hospital," said Reinhart, with real feeling.

He had just hung up and was starting for the kitchen when Winona came in. His instantaneous emotion, which came and went like a flash of light, so swift it might have been imagined, was one of repugnance. In guilty compensation he went to her, seized, and hugged her.

She seemed ill at ease with him. Her trunk was rigid.

"Dad," she said. "How are you?"

"I'm fine, Winona. How are *you?*"

"I'm all right," she said defiantly, almost angrily. She went into the living room and dropped with a funny shoulder movement onto the sofa, as if she were a little girl again.

Reinhart followed her. She was wearing a long skirt. He liked that. He was bored with those eternal jeans.

"Daddy," she said, "Mother's been in touch with me. It seems she's out of the hospital. She claims there was nothing wrong with her at all, that there was no reason for me to call the police, that there was no reason for the police to call the ambulance, and so on down the line, and she intends to sue everybody involved."

"How much more money does she want you to give her? Do you have anything left after paying Blaine for her supposed treatment?" Reinhart ground his teeth.

"Ah, well . . ."

At just that moment the doorbell rang, with a marked effect on Winona. Reinhart was annoyed to be interrupted just as he was about to talk turkey with her.

When he opened the door, he saw Genevieve, showing what he knew from experience as, by intention anyway, a sweet smile.

"Hi, Carl." She had undergone an alteration in appearance: something, some neatening, by cut or comb, had been done to her hair. She also seemed to be better dressed, or perhaps it was merely that today she was not wearing that old green coat. All in all, it was an improvement.

Reinhart blocked the doorway with his large body. "Just what can I do for you, Genevieve?"

She continued to grin. "You're not going to ask about my trouble the other day, the emergency trip to the hospital, et cetera?"

"No," said Reinhart. "I don't have the slightest interest in it."

In what would seem an instant of genuine admiration, Genevieve said: "Carl, if you had always been the mean son of a bitch you've turned into in your old age, I'd probably have stuck by you."

"Thank God, then, my change came too late." Reinhart sighed to dramatize his sense of tragedy averted, but in point of fact he too now grinned. Bantering with Gen was a sadomasochistic entertainment, but sometimes even yet he could remember when they had been, though for all too short a term, comrades.

"Are you going to invite me in?"

"Why should I?"

"For old times' sake." Her morale had been raised by something or other—perhaps the commotion she had caused last Monday. At any rate she did not hint at the beseeching note, alternating with the spiteful, culminating in the vicious, which had characterized her style at the shopping mall.

Reinhart stepped out into the corridor, closing the door behind him. "This is Winona's apartment and not mine, and in fact she's here at the moment. She just told me you had an idea of suing all the poor devils who responded to your fake emergency the other day, including her! I recognize that threat to be as false as your breakdown itself, and I warn you if you say anything to make her feel bad, you will be given a ride out the door on the toe of my shoe."

Genevieve raised her hands and said: "O.K., O.K.!"

Reinhart sighed again and ushered her through the door.

"Winona!" he called in warning when he reached the entrance hall. "It's your mother."

He gestured towards the living room, then stepped ahead of Genevieve and led her in.

Winona, however, came from the bedroom hallway, behind them. "Mother," she said.

Genevieve now wore the kind of curled lip that she wished, but not ardently, to be taken as a polite smile. For a while she ignored her daughter absolutely and instead surveyed the room.

It had dawned upon Reinhart shortly after setting up his domes-

tic partnership with Winona years before, when she was still a
teenager, that his daughter had a taste in furnishings and their
arrangement that was markedly superior to that of her mother—
though indeed he recognized his own gifts in that area as being
minor: he could not, for example, have said why a chair bought by
Winona invariably had a unique agreement with the situation in
which she deployed it, or how her hand, to all appearances even
careless, could throw a bouquet of flowers into a vase, touch them
here and there, and place the vessel at just the precise conver-
gence of all reasonable sightlines in the room and furthermore in
that corner which most profited from new color.

Whereas Genevieve's sense of decor, if it could even be so
termed, was unfailingly pedestrian. Indeed, very much like Reinhart's own, it seemed to him in all frankness, and that would have
been quite O.K. had not the woman, sporadically throughout their
years together, been vociferously interested in interior decoration
and aggressively vain about each of her successive versions of the
living room, imposing them on their neighbors (envious wives,
indifferent hubbies) at lavish holiday open houses, which added
even more to the bills Reinhart had to pay from the proceeds of
whichever will-o'-the-wisp he was chasing at the moment in "business."

His ex-wife now completed the circuit of eye and at last brought
her vision to bear on her daughter.

"Oh, Winona," she said, the name shading away in a fervent
sigh. "Oh." She threw a loose wrist towards the nearest wall, presumably to indicate just everything. "It's certainly *you*, every inch
of it."

"Thank you," said Winona, who, Reinhart could have sworn,
was turning pigeon-toed and concave-chested before his eyes.

His command applied to them both: "Sit down."

But Genevieve, as he might have known, turned suddenly and
walked to the windows at the far end of the room, those which
overlooked the river. For an instant he couldn't remember whom
this action reminded him of, and then he could: Grace Greenwood. But one thing about Gen: she had never seemed dykey. You
could say that for her.

Reinhart suddenly remembered the children.

"Where'd the boys go?"

"To take a nap," said Winona. "They were all tuckered out."

Reinhart asked: "What did that cost you?"

Genevieve whirled suddenly and came back. She pointed a finger at Reinhart. "The security in this building leaves something to be desired. I walked right in past Stepin Fetchit. I could have been a criminal."

"He could see you were harmless," said Reinhart, knowing she would hate to hear that.

Genevieve exposed her front teeth in a snarl, but it was a parody, and she seemingly remained in her good mood. "I suppose you're wondering why I came here?" She took a seat at the other end of the couch from Winona and leaned back against the cushions. "Call it pride."

"Pride?" Reinhart hospitably gave her the expected cue: she was after all a guest in this house.

"I didn't handle myself too well the last time you saw me." She stared at him. "But who among us is always at the top of his form?" Her grin turned dirty. "I can mention certain episodes that would scarcely be flattering to you!" And for only the second time since entering did she look at Winona. "And you too, God knows. Don't get me started."

"Genevieve." Reinhart spoke in quiet menace.

"O.K.! O.K.!" She crossed her legs and leaned forward over her knees. "I came to say good-bye."

This time it was Winona who did the courteous thing. "Where are you headed, Mother?"

"*California,*" Genevieve said decisively, slapping her top knee as she leaned back. "I should have done that long ago, but the time never seemed ripe. But now's the moment. Oh, I know it."

Reinhart stood up. "I'm sorry, Genevieve. Where are my manners? Would you like a cup of coffee or a drink?"

"Carl, did you hear me? I'm getting out of your hair for good." Genevieve spoke vivaciously, uncrossing and spreading her legs in an almost indecent movement even though she was wearing slacks. "I'm remarrying."

Winona stood up. "If you'll both excuse me . . ."

"No, Winona, I won't," said Reinhart. "I have some things to talk over with you when your mother leaves."

His daughter sat down.

His ex-wife shrugged and said: "I can take a hint. I just wanted you to know that I'm riding high again."

Reinhart stood up. "So it would seem, Genevieve. No doubt your prospective husband is a wealthy and powerful business- or professional man."

"You don't believe me, do you, Carl?"

Reinhart said sincerely: "I shouldn't have said that, Genevieve. I apologize. The fact is that it's none of my business."

She rose from the couch. "You tell her she can come home now."

"You mean Mercer?"

"Yeah, the society girl." Genevieve snorted and turned to her daughter. "Good-bye, Winona. Be sure to let me know when *you* meet Mister Right. I'll come back for the wedding with bells on!"

Reinhart snapped his fingers. "I'll bet you're going to San Francisco. Isn't that where your pansy brother Kenworthy has lived for years?"

Genevieve looked stoically at the floor, then flung her head up sharply. This had been a gesture of her father's. "I know you think you've given me a devastating shot," she said. "But I didn't come over here for petty bickering." She put her hands on her hips. "Let me put it to you straight: I *have* got an opportunity out there, but I'll admit I'm strapped at this moment. I need the price of the fare —one-way only, I assure you."

Winona went to the sideboard and opened the drawer in which she kept the big flat checkbook used to pay the household bills.

"That's to Los Angeles," Genevieve said. "And better add enough for cab fare. That airport is supposed to be miles from town."

Reinhart said: "Just a minute, Winona." He asked Genevieve: "She just the other night gave Blaine a sizable sum that was supposed to be spent on you. Is that all gone already?"

"Oh, God, Daddy," wailed Winona. "Let's not have a scene." She opened the checkbook and groped in the drawer for a pen.

"I'm just trying to establish the truth," said Reinhart.

Genevieve said: "It seems to me that's your lifelong complaint. It ought to begin to occur to you that life is just a collection of stories from all points of self-interest."

Winona ripped the check from the book, folded it in two, and gave it to her mother.

Genevieve said defiantly to Reinhart: "You expect me to unfold it and examine it, don't you? You haven't ever thought I had any class."

This was a phony attack. From the first it had been Genevieve who was the snob.

"If you say so," was the best he could come up with. Besides, he was longing for her departure.

She stood up. "Well, now you can all rest easy. I'm leaving for good. You won't see me again."

"Mother . . ." Winona murmured feebly.

"Good-bye, Genevieve," said Reinhart. Staring at her, he began to walk towards the door.

His ex-wife looked stubborn for a moment, but then she shrugged and followed him. At the door she took a kind of stand.

"I caught you on TV, Carl. You have a lot of nerve, I'll say that for you."

Reinhart opened the door.

"If you could of found that kind of gall years ago you might have made something of yourself. What a con artist you are! Remember Claude Humbold? He couldn't hold a candle to you. Cooking! What do you know about food aside from being a glutton?"

As real-estate salesman for Humbold just after the War, Reinhart had met Gen for the first time. She was Claude's secretary.

She went on now: "And that boogie-woogie bugle boy, Splendor Mainwaring. The two of you were inseparable. Frankly I always thought you were a couple of qu—" Without looking back she called: "Oops, sorry, Winona."

Reinhart took her by the shoulders and steered her firmly out into the corridor.

She made no resistance, but when he took his hands off her, she said: "What would happen if I screamed bloody murder? You know you can't push women around any more."

"I'm sure that Winona would cancel payment on the check. For another, I've got a lot of friends in this building, including the owner's daughter."

Genevieve's transitions were breathtaking. She went from the onset of rage through a crooked, perhaps crazed simper, into a broad grin. She threw her open hand at Reinhart. "Congratulations, Carl! Put 'er there!"

He didn't understand this, but he shook with her anyway. "I hope things work out for you in California." He suddenly remembered how frail her shoulders had felt under his fingers. "If they let you out of the hospital you must be in good health."

"I'm all right. I've got plenty of steam left. I just need a break."

"And you've got one waiting in California, right?"

"That's right." Her eyes darkened with suspicion. "Don't you worry about me, fella. Maybe I'll take a leaf from your book and try television. At least I wouldn't be any worse than you. And that's the TV capital of the country, not a tank town like this." She winked at him. "A TV chef, huh? I'll bet you think you're King Shit."

"You have a way with words," said Reinhart. Nevertheless he walked her down to the elevator. He suddenly felt reluctant to let her go. "Hey, Gen," he said, "remember Jack Buxton, the actor? Didn't we see him together lots, in the old days, in the old movies?"

"He kicked off yesterday. Good riddance. He was always a real scumbag. I happen to know, through some friends who are high in Chicago law-enforcement circles, that Buxton was arrested once for molesting an underaged boy, but the charges were dropped because the kid's family didn't want the publicity of a trial."

"Buxton?"

Genevieve wore her tough-guy grin. She spoke in fake sympathy. "Aw, and he was one your idols too, wasn't't he?" She shook her head. "My, my. I wonder what that says about you."

"For once, can't you put aside that malicious crap?" he asked. "I saw the man die, yesterday at the TV station. I was the last person to talk with him while he was still conscious. It's really strange to remember that I started seeing him in movies when I was still a boy in high school, forty years ago, and then through the

War. I even saw him at the Onkel-Tom-Kino, a German movie-house in Berlin! And then in the early Fifties, remember, before we got our first television, we'd go to the Regal on Friday nights? After we did have the set of course, we watched all his old films from the Forties and Fifties. I think that by that time his career had faded . . ."

"Jesus Christ," Genevieve said in contempt, *"who cares?* He was a forgotten ham actor and also a pervert, his pictures were stupid garbage, and if he suddenly dropped dead, it was probably as a result of an overdose of drugs."

"I wasn't really thinking of him personally. I was thinking really of the recent past in what?—entertainment, publicity, or what-ever: that funny illusionary plane of existence which one is in when watching TV or movies, where a Jack Buxton is a recogniz-able figure. It's a shock to have it proved, and in a brutal way, that there is a real man who has served as a pretext for an image which consists of impulses of light."

Genevieve punched the button for the elevator. The doors opened immediately: the car had been waiting. She said: "You haven't changed. You've never learned: if you're going to be an ass-kisser, then you ought to at least kiss the asses of winners."

She gave him the cocky World War II salute that in fact Buxton had specialized in cinematically. Was this a conscious parody or coincidence?

"Good-bye, Genevieve."

"So long, sucker." She stepped into the elevator and the doors closed behind her.

Reinhart stood in position for a moment. Despite his relief at any departure of hers nowadays, he felt as though it were a historic occasion, marking the end of something that should be ended.

He returned to Winona. Already she seemed distracted by other matters.

"Do you think that Genevieve alone is to be blamed for the trouble between Blaine and Mercer?"

"Well, it's a theory." Winona frowned. "I wonder if the boys are asleep. Because if they aren't, I want to go to my room and get something."

Reinhart spoke from experience. "No, it's the other way around:

you should go in if they *are* napping and stay out if not. Sleeping kids aren't bothered by intrusions, but they tend to obstruct you when awake." Apropos of nothing he asked: "Winona, you know our neighbor Edie Mulhouse, well—"

"That creep. Has she come around looking for me?"

"She's not so bad," said Reinhart, feeling, with this wan defense, like a traitor. "Did you know she's the daughter of the owner?"

"The owner of what?"

"This apartment house. You know, the Mulhouse Corporation."

Winona shrugged indifferently. "If you say so. Excuse me, Daddy, I think I'll just check on the boys, according to your theory." She went down the hall.

Reinhart went to the kitchen. His larder needed replenishment. He began to draw up a grocery list, but heard Winona's good-bye shout from the door. This seemed rude of her. He came out.

"You're not leaving already?"

She put the suitcase down. "I really have to . . . You were sure right about the boys: they didn't even wake up when I got this off the high shelf and dropped it."

"I wish you would ask me to do things like that," Reinhart chided. He looked at the suitcase, and then at her. "Have you made your permanent plans yet? Of course, at the moment Mercer and the boys are still here."

"You mean, will I be coming back?" She smiled in a fashion that was meant to be helpful but looked uneasy. "Gee, Daddy . . ."

"I'm not trying to pry, believe me."

"I know you're not. . . . It's just that . . ."

Reinhart picked up the suitcase. It felt empty, but then women's clothes weighed nothing. "I'll go down to the car with you. By the way, I still have your Cougar. Do you need it?"

Winona shrugged. "Not really, and you do."

As they went along the hall he asked about Grace. "I heard she was under the weather. Is that true? Because I have a couple of matters to discuss with her."

"She's fine," Winona said quickly. "I'll remind her to call you."

"She *is* at home, then? I don't want to disturb her. I can wait till she's back at the office."

"She'll call you," Winona said firmly.

They went silently down in the elevator, and then, past a gravely smiling Andrew, out to the front walk. Winona led her father down the street a way and stopped at a glistening vehicle. Reinhart had not kept up on the latest makes of cars in recent years, but there was no mistaking a Mercedes. This one was colored beige. Winona unlocked the trunk. The interior was a kind of handsome little living room.

"A rich dwarf could make his home in there," he joked as he put the suitcase therein. "Grace just buy this heap? She got rid of her Imperial?"

Winona smirked uncomfortably. "I miss you, Daddy." She kissed his cheek, got into the gleaming car, which was obviously brand new, and drove away.

The telephone was ringing as Reinhart returned to the apartment. He took the instrument just inside the door.

"This is Blaine. Put Mercer on the line."

"Blaine! God Almighty, you had us worried. Where have you been?"

"I asked if Mercer was there." Same old Blaine.

"Well, she and the boys have been staying here, but she's not in at the moment."

"When did she leave? How long has she been gone?"

"That I can't tell you, Blaine. She was here this morning when I left, at about eleven. I got home I guess an hour ago."

"You were out all that time?" Blaine asked in outrage. "Were the boys home alone?"

As usual Reinhart was stung. "For God's sake, you vanish for three days without a trace, abandoning your wife and kids, and then you have the nerve—"

"Are you senile? Vanish? I've been out of town on business, but I've called her every day. I called earlier this afternoon, but nobody answered."

"I was here all last night," said Reinhart. "The phone never rang."

"I talked to her in the afternoon!"

"Where are you now, Blaine?"

"At home. I just got back from Detroit. I took the night plane the other evening after seeing you and Winona."

"Why don't you come over here now? Your life is your own business, but I seem to have become involved in this part of it. I want a better understanding than I have." His son remained silent. "Blaine, did you hear me?"

"All right," Blaine said sullenly. "I'll come."

"All right, then. Maybe Mercer will have returned by that time." But Reinhart spoke this into a dead wire: his son had hung up in his usual graceless style.

Reinhart had not had the heart today to so much as look into the bedroom currently being used by Mercer, and before going out that morning he had shaved, etc., in Winona's bathroom, the one at present assigned to the two small boys, who were neater than their mother.

Now however, distracted, he went for a pee in his own bathroom, with its wastecan overflowing with those female items of volume but no substance, such as wadded Kleenexes, discarded cotton balls, ex-tampon tubes. He washed his hands, planning to carry them wet to the kitchen and dry them on paper towels: none of cloth was available. If Mercer had showered today, she perforce used one from the heap of soaked terry-cloth on the floor between the toilet and the wall—unless of course she simply swathed her wet body in his thirsty-fabric bathrobe, which she had commandeered on arrival and never yet surrendered.

He shook the excess water from his fingers and glanced briefly at his face in the mirror. A note was Scotch-taped to the glass.

> *"Dad"*—
> *I had to go away—can you run boys home—or wait til B. gets in and hell do it.*
>
> > *sincerly,*
> > **M.**

When Blaine arrived, a half hour or so later, Reinhart assured him that the boys, still napping, were fine, but that Mercer had not yet returned. Meanwhile they might have a conversation in the living room, over a good stiff drink if Blaine would state his pleasure.

His son stared at him, shrugged, marched in, and took one of the modern chairs that faced the couch. He rejected the repeated offer of a drink. He pointed to the sofa. Reinhart hesitated for a moment, and then, deciding this was hardly the moment to resist Blaine's bullying in meaningless matters, took a seat where directed. (He thought he could see a faint stain on the cushions where Mercer had vomited, but that may have been a trick of light; the beige rug showed a blond patch, which was now more or less covered by the coffee table.)

He opened his mouth to speak, and Blaine said: "No."

"But—"

"No, Dad," Blaine said curtly, "you don't know anything about it."

"I just wanted to say about Mercer—"

"I don't want you to say anything about her," said Blaine. "That's what I mean. You don't know what you would be talking about."

"I'd be the first to admit that," Reinhart said. "I don't claim any powers of analysis. Even at close quarters I've found her an enigma."

"Is that all you were going to say?"

"If," said his father, "that's all you want me to say." He would have to seek another means by which to introduce Mercer's note.

Blaine rubbed the right lobe of his nose with a thumb. As a gesture it was out of character. He sighed, lifted both hands, and brought them down on his thighs. He stood up. "I'd better get the boys."

Reinhart put out an arm. "Could you stay for a meal? You just got back from a trip, and your children haven't eaten since lunch at their schools." He rose. "Let me rustle something up."

"I just can't spare the time. Some people are coming in from out of town. I really must get back—"

"Sit down, Blaine," Reinhart said, gesturing. "I can understand how a man will protect his pride, especially from other members of the family, but there comes a time. . . . I'm hardly in a position to score off you. My failings are public knowledge, and your sister has only recently made her confession, though nowadays her ways would not necessarily be called even a weakness. The point is that no human being is without places of sensitivity."

Blaine's sneering smile was not attractive. "Well, thanks, Dad. When I need some help you can be sure I'll apply to you."

Reinhart drew the note from his pocket and handed it over.

Blaine glanced quickly at the message, balled the paper, and thrust it in the pocket of his pin-striped suit-jacket.

"I'm sorry," said Reinhart.

Blaine arched his eyebrows. "For what?"

"Doesn't that mean she's walking out?"

Blaine shook his head. "Certainly not. She had an appointment, that's all. Probably one of her classes. She takes various courses. She did some modern dance, studied playwriting, even went to a class called 'The Police and the Public,' at the Catholic college over in West Hills. I think it's admirable for a person to explore their potentialities."

"I think I really should tell you," Reinhart said, grimacing, "a couple of times recently Mercer turned up over here, somewhat the worse for wear, as if more than drunk. Does she take any kind of medication?"

Blaine looked at him. "She has a full life. She has lots of her own friends. I say, more power to her." He stood up abruptly, wrinkled his nose, sniffed, and spoke. "I really must leave."

"Your mother was here earlier. She got some more money from Winona. Is she really going to California?"

Blaine nodded briskly. "Of course. If she says so. I have never known Mother not to carry things through."

"Same is true of you, Blaine," said Reinhart. "You actually are quite impressive at it."

Blaine turned and marched back to the bedroom to get his sons. Before long he reappeared, followed by two small stragglers, each of whom carried a Matchbox car. Blaine held the one valise that served both boys: the smaller you are, the lighter your travel. In the pocket on the right round of his little jeans-clad butt Toby carried the bandanna given him by his grandfather. It was too big for the pocket, and most of it dangled. When Reinhart came to say good-bye, he snatched at it.

"Somebody's going to steal your tail," he said.

"No, they're not!" Toby cried in his contrary style, but when Reinhart turned to address Parker he saw, from the side of eye, that the senior grandson was furtively tucking the bandanna in.

"Well, Parker, it's been nice having had you on board," said Reinhart, and did not dwell on the ceremony of parting, for a child of that age is like a cat about such matters and won't meet your eye.

He opened the door and told the boys: "Run down and punch the elevator button. The bottom one."

"I know!" said Toby. He got the jump on his brother, but Parker's flying sneakers were close behind.

"But don't get on the elevator until your father gets there!"

"I know!" said Toby.

Reinhart spoke to Blaine. "I really enjoyed having them. I got to know them a little better. They're nice boys, Blaine. Any time I can serve as baby-sitter . . ."

Blaine looked lofty. "Of course a nanny would be the answer." He did not go so far as to assume a British accent, but still, he was a remarkable fellow.

When they had left Reinhart went to gather up the dirty laundry, stuffing to the limit two pillowcases. He took these down to the basement, filled two washers, dropped into the respective slots the requisite coins, and was on his way back to the apartment, there to wait until it was time to return and transfer the wet wash to the dryers, when he encountered Andrew, the doorman, who was just coming off his shift. He hadn't spoken anything beyond the commonplaces to Andrew since the day that Mercer had left the building clad only in a towel. Reinhart had not seen any great reason to bring the man up to date on the subject of his daughter-in-law. Andrew had no doubt seen worse in his years of service.

"Home to supper," he said now, remembering that he himself was all alone this evening.

"Yes, indeed," Andrew said with obvious satisfaction. "I'll say good evening to you, Colonel."

"Say, Andrew," Reinhart said, turning back after they had passed each other. "It was only today that I discovered that the landlord's daughter lives right here in the building." He laughed lightly at his ignorance.

"I expect you mean Edie Mulhouse," said Andrew. "But she is

Edwin Mulhouse's child. He just works as a bookkeeper for his brother Theodore M., who is the one who has the money."

Reinhart looked up and down the basement corridor, seeing no one. "Edie's a very nice girl, but I don't think she's found herself yet."

The doorman maintained an expression that might be seen as benevolently detached, and Reinhart understood it as the mark of the professional.

"Sorry," he said. "I was just thinking out loud, not asking your opinion of a tenant."

He said good night to Andrew. After two more trips down to the laundry room, one to transfer the clothes to the dryer and the second to fetch the load back home, he fell into the kind of dispirit which sometimes even claims a cook, and he made his own supper childishly on a peanut-butter sandwich and a glass of milk.

He was lonely, but it was at least a relief to have his room back. He made up a fresh bed, and after having taken a leisurely shower and dried himself with a fluffy fragrant towel, he put on the television set and inserted himself between the fresh sheets. If he ever made any money, he wanted to get himself one of those remote-control gadgets. As it was, he did not dare to do more than nap fitfully throughout the evening, for fear he would fall into a sound sleep and stay in it till morning. Yet climbing out of bed and going across to extinguish the set was just enough to keep him awake for any subsequent hour.

When finally he had nevertheless cranked up sufficient courage to undertake the mission, at about one A.M., had already swung his feet down onto the bedside rug, the late-late movie came on, starring Jack Buxton.

CHAPTER

18

Reinhart was half asleep when he answered the phone.

"Carl? You're not still in bed?"

He covered the instrument as he cleared his throat. "In fact I am, Grace." Only in recent years would he have had the nerve to make that sort of admission. When younger he would have denied the charge had it been made at five A.M. He squinted at the electric alarm clock on the bedside table. "It's hardly seven thirty."

He had stayed awake last night for the entire Buxton film, for once not the kind of action movie with which the man was usually associated, but a romantic comedy, probably the only one he ever made. It wasn't bad: a kind of hygienic bedroom-farce-cum-mistaken-identity caper, co-starring a cream-faced, retroussé, wry but cheery young actress (who had never been seen again) and featuring a supporting cast of benevolent zanies, the inordinate Slavic concert pianist, the stuttering maître d'hôtel, the effeminate hotel clerk, and the fluttering middle-aged lady wearing a hat and, for some unexplained reason, speaking in an English accent. Movies were better then.

Grace was saying something. Reinhart came back on the line and overrode her voice. "I'm glad you called finally, Grace. I've been trying to get hold of you for several days. First, the TV show went well, I thought. At least so the studio people told me." She tried to recapture his ear at this point, but he said imperiously: "No. Let me finish. Then I found a little café up in the country that serves an extraordinary chili con carne, homemade, made in fact on the premises. I think that Epicon should maybe consider it as a product to can and sell to the public. It's a different concept of the dish from the other canned versions you can buy—your own Pancho Villa brand, for example. And this is an example of the kind of thing that I think Epicon should try to go in the direction of, whether or not this chili works out: namely, the interesting and, if possible, unique product that would deserve the name of gourmet, instead of the line of more or less fake stuff offered at present."

Grace cried: "Carl! I think you were just pretending to sleep just now, weren't you, you sly dog? You've got the jump on me." But she seemed in a good mood: perhaps Winona had trained her to acquire a taste for a certain amount of bullying from anyone named Reinhart. "Listen for a moment, please! The *Eye Opener* folks are looking for you."

"You mean the TV show?"

"Sure! This is a comedy of errors. You're not listed in the book—"

"That's because of Winona," said Reinhart. "It's her phone, really, not mine."

"And that wouldn't have mattered ordinarily, because they could have called me for the number, but in point of fact I was laid up for a day or so and not in the kind of communication with the office that I usually maintain."

"I hope you have fully recovered," Reinhart said, in a ritualistic expression.

Grace went on: "I had neglected to put your number on my wheel, so my secretary couldn't help—"

"Yes, Grace. Go on." The fact was that his "employment" had been merely her private project, a feature of the cajolery of Winona. "But what did they want?"

"Only to say that you were sensational, old boy!"

"Pardon?"

"You were the hit of the show, Carl, and they got tons of calls and letters asking for more. All raves, buddy."

"Is that right?"

"It's your image, Carl: knowledgeable, but all wool and a yard wide. You're plain folks. You don't talk down to anybody, but you

have your specialty down cold. That's what they're saying over at
Channel Five! See, when it comes to food, everybody's got to eat.
You become too partisan about a certain kind, though, you lose a
lot of people, or if you get too fancy-pants. On the other hand, as
a nation we've passed beyond the simple meat-and-potatoes
phase. Well, that was my idea in bringing your expertise into
Epicon in some way, except that for a little while I couldn't figure
out just the right way to maximize what either one of us, or the
firm, would get from it—"

"Did they, the people at the *Eye Opener Show*, have any plans
to put me on again?"

"That's the whole point, mister! They want to give you a regular
daily spot to cook up something on the air! You're on the threshold
of stardom, Carl. Now here's our idea—mine, just now, but the rest
of the board will go along with me, I can promise you that. To have
our own man on television every day, who would turn that down?"

"You mean Epicon will sponsor me?"

"That's the most popular of the wake-up shows in the local
markets, outdrawing even the network programs of the same
type. They get a damned stiff commercial rate, but hell, you'll use
our food products, clearly marked, and I'm getting us into cookware these days. Did you use that copper-clad fry pan I sent over
to the studio the other day? Unfortunately I couldn't catch the
show."

"That skillet was junk, Grace. The copper's just for aesthetics:
so thin it looks as if applied with a paintbrush. That's the kind of
thing I disapprove of, along with bottled hollandaise sauce." He
got out of bed. "And if I do this show, I won't be bound by an
obligation to use anything Epicon sells. Most of your line is crap,
Grace, whether you know it or not."

"Come on, Carl," said Grace, with no diminution of enthusiasm.
"I don't mean for a minute that you would be standing by with
your finger in your ear while everybody else collected the bucks.
You'd be an integral part of it, on a percentage of the increase in
sales, et cetera. We wouldn't be asking you to do charity work, big
fellow."

Her style was remarkably reminiscent of several male con men
with whom Reinhart had been associated in past commercial ventures; beginning with Claude Humbold the frenetic realtor in

whose office, so many years before, he had met Genevieve. A practice of them all had been to talk money incessantly while never delivering a cent.

"Apparently that's what I've been doing thus far, Grace."

"Now, Carl, you know I've been under the weather. I'm back now and full of beans. You'll be paid well for these one or two little things, of course, but what I'm talking now is big bucks."

"I'll have to speak to the *Eye Opener* people first."

"I think we ought to make our deal before you go to them," Grace said. "I really do, Carl. I don't want to lean on you, but after all it really was me who saw your potential. As I recall, you practically had to be dragged out of your home kitchen. I mean, if you're going to make a *career* of it, don't you think I should get a *little* credit?"

"It's true that at one time I would have thought that way," said Reinhart. "But now I don't." And as if that were not blunt enough, he added: "You've got enough from me. Think about my chili suggestion. I can always take it elsewhere."

Grace whistled low and said: "I'll tell Win she's a chip off the old block. Don't go away mad, Carl. I think we can do business. If you insist, though, call Billy Burchenal at Five. He's the producer of *Eye Opener.* He'll be at his office till noon." She gave the number.

Reinhart took his pajamas off and nakedly crossed the hall to the bathroom, having learned that trick from Mercer. But it *was* one of the advantages in living alone. After showering, he had some coffee and toast. He should have been ravenous the morning after dining on peanut butter, but he was too excited to be hungry.

At last the time reached a decent hour to call Burchenal, he hoped.

The producer answered his own line, perhaps because it was Saturday.

"My name is Carl Reinhart. I was supposed—"

"Carl, hi. You're a hard man to find. Could you possibly zoom over here this morning, say by eleven, and we can get this deal wrapped?"

Reinhart chuckled to relieve his nervousness. "You don't waste time, do you, Mr. Burchenal?"

" 'Burch,' please. Sixth floor, six-oh-two. I'll give your name to Security downstairs." He hung up.

A quarter-hour later Winona called her father.

"Daddy, you're going on TV? Isn't that great?" She giggled.

"It might be," said Reinhart. It helped to have someone else's enthusiasm to play off. "I don't know, though. I'm not a professional cook, let alone a performer." He waited for and got Winona's loving protests. "We'll see. I haven't talked to them yet. I'm going over there this morning."

"That reminds me," said Winona. "This is a thing I know something about. You've got to get yourself an agent to do the negotiating of the deal."

"Oh, yeah?"

"A show-business person, though, not the kind of agency I have, which is for models."

"Shouldn't I wait until I get a little farther along in my career —if in fact I have a TV career?" Yet this talk was thrilling to him.

"Noo," his daughter said forcefully. "*Now* is the time to set the pattern: you wanna talk turkey from the beginning. Otherwise they'll try to screw you."

Reinhart wet his lips. "Really, Winona . . ."

"Sorry, Dad. That just slipped out."

"Huh? Oh. No, I meant, gee, the whole idea of my being a television performer is so startling if I think about it, that I'd probably do it for a while for no payment whatever." He did not add that he had performed a few jobs for Grace in that fashion, including even one TV appearance. "Let me just go and talk to the producer first and hear his proposition. I'll consult with you on the deal I'm offered, I promise."

"Some of the models here have done some acting work. One of them has a small part in *Song of Norway* at the dinner theater in the Lemburg Mall."

"Jack Buxton was in that, wasn't he? The actor who died the other day?"

"Gee, I couldn't say," said Winona.

"Didn't we ever watch him together in old movies on TV when you were a kid?" Reinhart asked, softening in nostalgia. "We had some good times, didn't we, baby? Remember the popcorn I used to rush out to make at commercials? And those enormous Dagwood sandwiches we'd eat?"

Winona took in air. "I can't even listen to that kind of talk without going up one size." She sighed out. "I gave up a lot for my career."

"Is that right? You mean you still have to discipline yourself?" He couldn't believe it; she was sweetly trying to make him feel good. He adored his daughter. He changed the subject. "Don't tell me you are working today too."

"Not me," said she. "Grace went to her office, but I'm still in bed."

He regretted having asked the question, but within a trice recovered when Winona added: "My room is practically soundproof, and anyway you know what a heavy sleeper I am. I didn't hear her go out, but she just called me now with the good news."

"Blaine came over not long after you were here yesterday and got the boys," said Reinhart. "He refuses to acknowledge that anything is wrong with Mercer. What can I do? I don't want to interfere, but I'm worried about the boys' being neglected."

Winona cleared her throat. "I've talked this thing over with Grace." She waited for his objection: he understood that, but none would be forthcoming. Did not Grace by now have the status of an in-law?

"And?"

"First, the shrink I told you about is a prerequisite. Don't blame me, Dad! I didn't say it!"

"Look, Winona, I'm not against anything that works."

"Then Grace thinks she might find something for her at Epicon."

"A job?"

"Maybe part-time anyway."

"You know, that's a damned fine idea," Reinhart said. He saw no reason to add that it would probably be unpaid unless Mercer spoke up. The fact was that he did think it a splendid thing to try on for size: his daughter-in-law *was* a college graduate after all, which was more than he could say for himself. Given a certain kind of employment, she might even learn to spell most common words.

"Do you miss me, Daddy?"

"You know I do. But I also recognize that this is a transitional time, Winona. Besides, we probably know all there is to know about each other at close quarters. Now there's a whole new perspective for us both, looking back and forth across town."

"Who can say where you might be living a year from now if this TV thing pays off as I think it might? Heck, you might be picked up by one of the big networks and go to New York or the Coast."

"I'm trying not to have delusions of grandeur," said her father. "I used to be addicted to such fantasies while not bothering to see whether there was any solid ground beneath me when I came down. No, Winona, I'm the sort of guy who does better by looking at the eggs in hand rather than at the soufflé to come. I'm a cook and not a waiter: I'm better at making things and letting someone else take over from there. I'm going to try to remember that if I do get on TV regularly, and keep from being too much of a ham."

"I beg to differ with you, Dad!" Winona protested. "I think I know something about an allied field. Modeling after all is performing too. You have to have *presence*. You can't think first of what would be your natural good taste. I worry only that you might be too modest!"

"My, oh, my," said Reinhart, "but aren't we anticipating?"

After some endearments he hung up. He had used the phone more in the current week than in the previous twelvemonth. No doubt the practice would continue if he went into show biz. He must cultivate the quick, sure style of Billy Burchenal. . . .

Who, an hour later, turned out to be a tall thin man of indeterminate age: i.e., his tight, curly hair was very light gray, yet his face, with a synthetic-looking orangey tan (but which must have been real, for why would a producer wear make-up?), looked hardly more than thirty-five. He wore a tieless blue shirt with epaulets and sat behind a desk that was strangely, but for two telephones, bare. The blue walls of his office, however, were crowded with certificates: awards apparently, citations of merit for public service, and the like.

"Hope you don't mind ruining your Saturday morning," Burchenal said. "I come in then to get a little work done without being interrupted by *that*." He pointed at the nearer phone. "Brain-work, I mean. I've been sitting here now trying to come up with a name for your spot, a catchy name for Debbie and Shep to say. You'd be surprised at how effective a name can be. We've always called it the Cook Spot, but that's when it was the guest chefs. We need something to call attention to your unique contribution."

He had neither shaken Reinhart's hand nor asked him to sit down. Burchenal himself was standing behind his desk.

Reinhart said: "You know my real first name is not Carl, but Carlo."

"For God's sake," said Burchenal. "That's perfect: *Chef Carlo Cooks.* What a perfect name! It's foreign, but you're all-American in looks. You won't scare anybody. That's what the viewers loved about you the other day—show you the letters if my secretary were here—you made it clear, and you made it look easy. They thank you for that. They know it isn't really easy, but they are grateful to you for letting them lie to themselves. This can be a big first step for you, Carlo. There's a tremendous turnover here. Faces change week by week. Most of them go on to bigger things. We're monitored incessantly by the big networks. Despite what you might hear, the youngsters are a drug on the market. An older personality, who is furthermore a new face, can attract! There's no doubt about it."

Burchenal's style in person was notably different from his speedy, bare-details manner on the phone. Suddenly he made a humorless smile and flattened both hands on the desk top. "Now what we can pay, with a restricted budget of the kind we have, is —we don't get prime-time commercial money, obviously, and the craft unions are ferocious. I mean, Carlo, you have to revise downward any idea of getting rich that early in the morning." He ran a finger under his nose and looked sternly at Reinhart, this time meeting his eyes, though actually looking through them. "We can pay fifty per spot, and we'll give you a spot every day unless exceptional circumstances arise: you know, like the Pope coming to town and we get him exclusively, or something."

Reinhart grunted.

Burchenal said: "I talked to Greenwood this morning. I'm afraid nowadays you can't get away with the kind of blatant promotion she would like, for example using a lot of things that are boldly labeled with trade names, and if the spot becomes a permanent feature, you'll have to sever your official connection with Epicon: we can leave that in the gray area to begin with. We'll see how things go."

"Then I'll be only trying out at first?"

Burchenal showed his palms. "That's true of everybody, including me. No, I'm *with* you, Carlo, all the way, but think of life: nobody lives forever. That's also true, in condensed form, of television. I think you've got tremendous potential, but I have to be careful. We'll try you for a couple of weeks to start, O.K.?" Now and only now did he sit down.

"My daughter told me to get an agent before I agreed to anything," said Reinhart. He half expected Burchenal to be offended by this statement, and added, apologetically: "She's a professional model."

But the producer nodded in agreement. "That's essential. You also will have to join AFTRA."

"The performers' union? Gosh."

Burchenal stood up again and leaned across the desk to offer a handshake. "I hope to see your man on Monday then. But can I assume meanwhile that we have a deal in spirit?"

Reinhart shook with him.

The producer said: "I've got a personal motive in all this: the lady I live with could use a few cooking lessons. Jesus! She can burn water."

"Then take a turn at the stove yourself," said Reinhart. "You'd probably amaze yourself. It's a thrill when something turns out well."

Burchenal squinted at him. "Cooking as therapy?"

"I don't care much for the term. Having the natural need and the ability to make something doesn't have to be justified. Of all the things that have been said to be exclusively human—thinking, which can't be proved one way or the other; use of tools, but doesn't a simple-minded chicken make a tool of the gravel he takes into his crop?; laughing, but people who have owned pets for many years swear their furry friends can grin at those who can see —of all the activities of human beings, there is one thing that they alone, in all the world, do, and that is: cook the food they eat."

Burchenal said: "Carlo, you're a philosopher."

"Naw," said Reinhart. "I'm better than that! I'm a cook."

Burchenal repeated that he wanted to see Reinhart's agent on Monday and predicted that *Chef Carlo Cooks* would begin a week later.

When Reinhart got back to the apartment house, he stopped off in the lobby to collect the mail, if any. The box yielded a utility bill and a circular announcing the opening of still another supermarket in yet another local shopping mall. In the past he had been wont to study the latter sort of announcement for bargains in short ribs, pork shoulder, Florida grapefruit, etc., and would tear out the redeemable coupons, with an eye to saving a few pennies for Winona—though if she caught him at this practice, she would fondly denounce him for it.

Dammit, he would miss his daughter, with whom he had lived for all her twenty-five years on earth!

He boarded the elevator. As the doors closed he lowered the hand which held the mail, and a blue envelope slipped from a fold in the supermarket circular which had concealed it and fell to the floor of the car. It was addressed to him and its stamp had been cancelled yesterday. But by now the elevator had reached the fourth floor. He went into the apartment, threw the bill and the circular on the telephone table, and, strolling through the living room to the window that looked down on the river, opened the blue envelope with his thumbnail.

> *Dear Mr. Reinhart* [he read],
>
> *First, can you forgive me for not having the courage to make this apology either in person or on the telephone? Notice that I am apologizing for even the manner of my apology, which is a compounding of my habitual style, which is boring even to me, and what must it be to anyone else?*
>
> *I am an utter and contemptible fraud. I am not the daughter of the owner of this house. I work at a dreary job of no distinction, and otherwise I read a lot. I hardly ever drink anything containing alcohol. Therefore it would not be strange that several glasses*

of beer would make me obnoxious. But what is hu-
miliating to remember is that at the time of my
prevarication I had had nothing whatever to drink.

I don't know how to atone for my conduct this
afternoon except by promising to avoid you in fu-
ture. I am not being false when I say you are the
finest man I have ever known and that I shall remain
in your debt.

Yours respectfully,
EDITH MULHOUSE

This was written in black ink on the blue paper, in a fastidious,
yet graceful hand.

Reinhart refolded the letter and put it on the coffee table. He
went to his liquor cabinet. Champagne was the drink of celebra-
tion, but he had none at hand. Looking through the bottles, he
came upon the good bourbon he had bought for Grace, which had
gone untouched that day, only two weeks before, when she had
come for brunch. Could anything be more appropriate for him to
drink now than two fingers of Jim Beam? Did he not owe all his
success to his daughter's lover? He brought a tumbler and some
ice from the kitchen.

During Reinhart's lifetime the world had changed so thoroughly
that were a Rip Van Winkle to have awakened after a sleep of any
twenty years he would be able to make use of none of the experiences, convictions, or even faculties in his possession at the moment he shut his eyes.

While sipping the bourbon, slumped on the couch, shoes off and
stockinged feet propped on the coffee table, he began to get hungry, this time for a very particular and celestially simple menu: red
meat, yellow sauce, golden potatoes, green vegetable, red wine.
The best way to get this right was to make it oneself: top round
of beef, sauce béarnaise, julienne potatoes, undercooked green
beans, and as big a Burgundy as you had the money to buy. A
chunk or hunk of meat, to be sliced thin and served in overlapping
strips napped with sauce, and not an individual steak to be attacked whole. But maybe rather Bordelaise sauce? But that would
require shallots, if you could find them, and a marrow bone, and

he had forgotten whether he still had on hand, in the frozen state, a supply of the jellified essence of beef stock called *demi-glacé*, which he liked to use in the brown sauces. The green beans should be left whole except for the tips and plunged into as large a volume of boiling water as could be managed, taken out when still crunchy . . .

He picked up Edie's letter and reread it. Naw: he remembered her in the supermarket. He had better go shopping alone.

CHAPTER
19

Next morning Reinhart felt an urge to acknowledge with gratitude that rise in his fortunes that could not be narrowly ascribed to Grace Greenwood, that part which was divine or at any rate not rational—for example, Buxton's collapse could not have been foreseen—and not belonging to a sensible faith which offered graven images for this purpose, e.g., a Golden Calf, he turned towards the humanitarian effort.

Unless crops could be sown and brought to harvest in a fortnight, it was unlikely that Brother Valentine's flock at Paradise Farm had any more to eat now than when Reinhart and Blaine had made their visit.

Reinhart now got out the strip of brown paper from his wallet and dialed the out-of-town number.

"Center Café!"

"Marge? Carl Reinhart—I had your chili the day before yesterday?"

"My God," shouted Marge. "I never thought I'd really hear from you."

"Here I am. I'm going to be on morning TV starting in a week."

"I'll sure be watching, if you tell me when and where."

"Sure," said Reinhart, "and I'm proceeding with the idea about marketing the chili. But what I'm calling about at the moment is, do you suppose you could make up several gallons of the chili by say eleven this morning? Along with an appropriate amount of the pinto beans and rice?"

"It's already simmering," said Marge. "Boy, you must *really* like that stuff."

"Oh, the order will be take-out. I guess I'd better organize some big containers. I doubt that you keep any gallon-size on hand, do you?"

"I'll have my husband pick up some at the Kentucky Fried Chicken in the mall."

"The police chief?"

"He'll run them over in the cruiser, so don't you bother."

In the basement garage Reinhart saw Edie's yellow Gremlin in her slot across the way. As it happened, last night he had cooked and eaten his celebratory dinner alone. He had phoned her several times throughout the early evening, but there was no answer. He had an impulse now to slip a friendly note under her windshield wiper, but decided against doing so lest the look of the folded paper, as she approached the car, give her a fright. Complaint? Obscene letter?

When Reinhart arrived in Brockville the main street was somewhat busier than it had been on his earlier visit. Persons were coming and going at the delicatessen, and only one parking space offered itself in front of the Center Café. Four vehicles were at the curb in that block, two of them pickup trucks. Sunday was an active time out here.

Inside the restaurant were six or eight male customers, most of them at the counter, though two heavy-set middle-aged men in suits and ties were having a solemn and what might even be seen as a conspiratorial discussion in the remotest of the booths: a romantic interpretation might present this as skulduggery-hatching by two provincial politicians.

Marge was serving a hot sandwich to a muscular young fellow across the back of whose chino shirt some trade name was embroidered in red.

"Looks good," said Reinhart. "Is that roast pork in its own gravy?"

Marge colored slightly when she saw him. "I got your order all ready to go. All's I have to do is fill the buckets with the chili, which I've kept hot on the stove in back, and I got the rice and beans too."

"I thought you might not be open on Sunday," said Reinhart. "But I see you have quite a good business."

"Oh, sure," Marge replied, wiping her hands on a wet cloth she found beneath the counter. "You'd be surprised how many people work on Sunday. I don't get much of the Sunday-dinner family trade that my folks used to have though. Families now head mostly for the fast-food places."

"But I was thinking about you doing everything here yourself. You're open seven days?"

"Close early on Mondays, though," said Marge. "I guess I'm crazy, but it's been a tradition to keep the Center Café open. Maybe that's gonna change soon, though."

"Hey, Marge," said the recent recipient of the hot sandwich, "when do I get my mashed potatoes and applesauce?"

"Lenny, you're too heavy as it is," said Marge, shrugging an apology to Reinhart. She seized a little bowl and, using a spring-levered ice-cream scoop, filled it with potatoes and then dampened them with more of the gravy, which by its light-brown color suggested it was the real stuff, from an actual pork roast and not a can.

He saw the roast itself, or one of them, on the steam table. "That's fresh ham, isn't it?" he asked Marge.

She was filling another small bowl with what would certainly seem to be, from its spicy fragrance and coarse texture, home-made applesauce. "These bums needn't think they're getting loin for these prices."

Lenny, tucking into his sandwich with a fork, smirked at this jibe. A name was embroidered over his left pocket: interestingly enough, it was not "Lenny," but rather "Bill."

Reinhart said: "They're lucky. Loin doesn't have nearly as much flavor." He followed Marge, on her beckon, through the swinging doors into the large old kitchen: a very clean and even spacious place. A bony man of indeterminate age, aproned and with sleeves rolled high, was washing dishes at some sinks on the far wall. Nearer was an enormous stove in black metal trimmed in shining steel—with none of the white porcelain of home appliances: this was the real thing.

"French chefs call their stove a 'piano,' " said Reinhart. "It must be a thrill to play a tune on that one."

"A lot of folks would think it's plain hard work," said Marge, "but I enjoy feeding people." She seemed a bit melancholy.

"I see you have some help anyway with the dishwashing."

Marge lumped her tongue on one side of her mouth. "We could use a machine. Bob does a good job, though." She paid the compliment in a loud voice. Then, with Bob's back still turned, she pantomimed to Reinhart the lifting of a bottle and the gulping at its throat.

Two capacious steel stockpots sat on the stove top. Marge took one of the candy-striped Kentucky Fried Chicken tubs from a stack on a vintage butcher's block (with side-slots for an assortment of black-handled, gray-bladed knives in all sizes and a surface that remembered a history of the cleaving of bloody meat: things like this were poetry to Reinhart).

"I'll fill the buckets now, if you are in a hurry to get going. Or would you want to try the fresh-ham special first?" Again he saw her color slightly. She was still a bit shy with the big-city big shot she believed him to be.

Someone out at the counter was shouting for her: "Hey, Marge!"

"To hell with them," said she.

"Get out there and take care of your people," said Reinhart. "I can do this. And I really would like to eat here, but I think I'd better get this chili to where I'm taking it, or they won't have it in time for lunch."

By the time he had ladled three buckets full she was back.

She flipped her thumb at the swinging doors. "My husband's back there right now, in the booth, talking with a gentleman who wants to buy this place."

Reinhart put down his ladle. He felt as though personally wounded. "You don't mean it. Not the Center Café?" It was perhaps an absurd excess of emotion with regard to an obscure eatery he had never seen until the day before yesterday. But it was already precious to him.

"Fact is," said Marge, "I've been losing money for some years. If I raise the prices too much I'll lose the customers I've got. But my costs have more than doubled over the past ten years. I'm not getting any younger. Let's face it, the place has only sentimental value for me."

" 'Only'?" Reinhart asked indignantly. "What's worth more?"

"Well, I don't mind telling you, I will miss the old joint." Marge wiped her hands on a damp cloth and yelled in the direction of the dishwasher: "Hey, Bob! I can use some glasses."

He turned, showing a nose like a berry, and said: "Sure, Marge." He began to find tumblers in the soapy liquid before him and rinse them with hot water in the adjoining sink.

"What's this guy want to do with it?" Reinhart asked. "Have his own restaurant?"

"Storage space." Marge got a bucket and began to fill it with the pinto beans and rice from the other stockpot. "Cheaper to buy a place like this than to build something or even, would you believe it, cheaper than renting over a couple of years. I got quite a lot of space all told. There's a storeroom out back, and of course the second floor is empty: used to be an apartment where we all lived when I was a kid. He's got a business over at the mall: home improvement, paint and wallboard and stuff, and has to keep a big inventory."

Reinhart had been thinking. He picked up the ladle again and gestured with it. "Marge, you don't know me at all, and if you did, you might not trust me anyway. But do you suppose you could hold off on this sale for just a little while? I'll tell you why: *maybe* I can come up with a better offer. A week from Monday I'm going on TV regularly, with a spot on the early-morning *Eye Opener Show*. I've been in touch with the Epicon Company, where as I told you I'm a consultant, about the idea to market the chili. If I have any kind of success on television, there's no limit to what might be possible. What occurs to me is something along this line: what if I became involved in the Center Café? Maybe buy into it in some fashion? Become your partner, under an arrangement whereby either one could buy out the other if it didn't work?"

For the third time Marge colored slightly. It occurred to Reinhart that she might have a kind of crush on him, she who was so rough-and-ready with her customers. She was probably not used to this sort of attention. She claimed the ladle from him and began to fill more chicken buckets with chili.

"My gosh," she said. "I just don't know what to say."

"If you could just hold off on making a deal with anybody else for a few days." Reinhart gestured. "Some interesting ideas have begun to occur to me. You said your main business was early in the morning. I'll bet you serve really great traditional Midwestern breakfasts: country sausage, farm-fresh eggs, flapjacks, hashbrown potatoes, ham steak . . ."

Marge was nodding shyly. "I serve a nice oatmeal in wintertime, with cream and brown sugar, and usually I get a chance to make my own doughnuts and coffee cake."

Reinhart sighed. "Generally nowadays the last place you can find real food is in the country!" He accepted a filled bucket from her. "What I have in mind is that you would continue to handle the breakfast for the working guys on the early shift, but maybe on Sundays from say about this time of day until three we might do a brunch together. All your great classic dishes, to which might be added an English mixed grill with kidneys, lamb chops, broiled tomato, and so on, and maybe chicken crepes and some form of seafood, say shrimp quiche or individual soufflés. We might attract people up from the city, especially in the oncoming warm months." He took the bucket to a counter and fitted on the cardboard disc that was its top.

"Maybe we could start like that, and if it went over, we might think of doing something ambitious with dinners—again on the weekends, at least at first. We could have an interesting menu. What I'm thinking of is a simple one, with only a few main dishes. Say two really good down-home American classics, country ham and red-eye gravy and deep-dish chicken potpie, and then maybe I could try my hand at a dish or two, maybe veal Orloff or poached fish in season. No doubt one must always offer steak in addition, but that would make only five or six dishes, with a few appropriate opening courses and a dessert or two."

Marge put down the container she had just filled and leaned against a counter. "Whew," said she. "I'm getting a little dizzy. Things had been getting more and more quiet for years, and then all of a sudden this now."

It looked as if between them sufficient food had been tubbed. Reinhart now fitted the rest of the tops on the buckets.

"This is all speculation as yet," he told her. "But I'm not talking completely through my hat. A big executive in the food business is practically a member of my family, and I really am going to start appearing on television. If you could just hold off for a while on the selling of this wonderful place to some guy for a warehouse, maybe I'll be in a position to talk turkey about an arrangement that would work out for us both."

"It's true," said Marge, "that a lot of trade would come to a restaurant operated by a TV chef." She was grinning as if to herself: he could see that he had successfully corrupted her, whether for good or ill. He wondered whether he was himself corrupt in supposing he might get Grace to back him in this venture.

He and Marge proceeded to quarrel about the bill for the chili, he of course wanting to pay and she refusing to accept his money. Bob the dishwasher suddenly stopped his work and slipped through the door to the outside.

"There," said Marge, mock-reproachfully, "you've got Bob all worried. He'll have to take a drink to calm down."

"But for all my talk," said Reinhart, "it might well be that nothing will come of any of these ideas, and until something positive actually happens I want to pay as I go." He gave her the money and then shook her hard, sinewy hand. "I hope we'll be able to call each other partner one of these days."

Marge gave him a crinkly smile. "I'd like that." She steered him to the door through which Bob had slunk, as if it were more convenient to go out past the garbage cans and along the narrow passage between the buildings to reach his car parked at the curb out front. He suspected that for her own reasons she did not want to attract her husband's attention.

"Where does Bob go for a drink on Sunday?" He had half expected to see the dishwasher lurking, with brown-bagged bottle, in the alleyway.

"Over to the cellar of the delicatessen," said Marge. "It's his sister and brother-in-law run the business."

"Everybody's related to one another in a village like this," Reinhart noted admiringly.

When they got to the car, he unlocked the trunk and put the

buckets therein, arranged in a snug fashion so that they would not be likely to overturn.

"Well," said Marge, "I guess there's certainly enough there for anybody to decide whether it's good."

He realized that she assumed he was taking the chili to be tested by the people at Epicon, and he saw no point in disabusing her: explaining would have taken too long.

"On the other matter," said Reinhart. "If you could just—"

"It's my old man who's so all-fired anxious to sell," Marge said. "You know how it is when you're married—I don't see a ring on your finger, but you must have been married once to have a great big fine-looking daughter like the one you brought the other day." She waited for his response.

Reinhart was sure he had given the last name when introducing Edie, but such was the power of the expected.

"Which one was your husband, out there in the booth? I didn't think either one of those fellows was wearing a uniform."

"The fatter one," said Marge. "He won't wear the chief's uniform on Sunday. He's got a lot of niceties like that." It wasn't clear whether she was being ironic.

"I'll be in touch," said Reinhart.

He drove the twenty miles cross-country to Paradise Farm and parked near the barn, as before. From the trunk he took as many buckets as he could carry in one big embrace and walked around to the rear of the house. Distracted by a need not to spill the chili, he did not digest the fact that no other cars were visible on the property, but as he stood on the little step and shouted helplessly at the closed back doors, screen and wooden, he began to wonder whether anybody was there.

Suddenly a known face appeared behind the glass panel and peered disagreeably out at him: it belonged to Brother Valentine, AKA Raymond Mainwaring. After an instant the hostile expression changed to neutrality, and Raymond turned the key in the lock, opened the inner door, then unfastened the latch on the screen door, and pushed it open.

Reinhart by now was in some worry as to the buckets of food, which had begun to feel uncertain in his grasp. He remembered that they had probably not been made waterproof to hold fried chicken. He rushed to the kitchen table.

"This is lunch," he said, freeing himself of the load. "There are a couple more buckets in the car. I'll go get them."

But Raymond lifted a beige palm and spoke wearily. "Too late."

Again Reinhart had been slow to notice a lack. This time it was people who were missing. Aside from Raymond and himself there was no one in the kitchen.

"Do you mean—?"

"That's exactly what I mean," said Raymond. He pulled a chair away from the table and sat down upon it in slow motion. "Paradise Farm is now a community of one."

Reinhart took a chair for himself. His first thought was selfish: all this chili and rice & beans. But then he asked Raymond what had happened.

"I was on television." Raymond wore an expression that probably was a cruel grin, but he didn't have the right face for it; he merely looked puzzled. "I was investigative-reported." His look turned certifiably peevish. "The world has too many people in it whose profession is to interfere with the plans of others."

"That's probably true. . . . What happened, were you accused of something?"

Raymond tightened the flesh around his eyes. "No, *I'm* clean! But to be investigated is to be guilty in the eyes of some people." He pushed out a bitter chin. "They left, all of them. Either on their own or some relative came and hauled them off. All of a sudden Paradise Farm became a potential Guyana and I was working up to be a Reverend Jim Jones."

"I'm really sorry to hear that," Reinhart said. "The farm sounded like a good project to me as you sketched it out." He looked at all the buckets of food. "Well, you and I can have lunch anyway. How about some chili con carne, beans and rice?"

Raymond winced suspiciously at him. "That wouldn't be your idea of darky food?"

"Come on, Raymond, don't be rude. The other day you told me you didn't have anything to eat here. Now I've brought something, and nobody's here to eat it." Reinhart got up from the table and poked into the wall-hung cabinets and counter drawers until he found two plates and two forks. He opened a couple of the buckets and served them each a hearty portion of beans and rice covered with the chunks of beef in their thick sauce.

"Try this." He put a plate in front of Raymond.

The younger man took a morsel of chili on the end of his fork. He made a face after chewing it briefly, but he did not spit it out. "Where'd you get this? It's certainly not very good."

Reinhart ignored the complaint. "Did the young people too leave because of just the TV thing?" he asked, beginning to eat from his own plate. But the chili wasn't as good today; of course it was tepid.

"There actually weren't any young people as yet," said Raymond. "I misrepresented that situation. I was anticipating. I intended to make an appeal to youth, and I assumed that they would answer it. But the fact is that in the short time we had been under way, I could get only older people, retired persons, and widows. That was one of the things that caused a certain suspicion about my motives, I suppose. It was obvious that the older people couldn't do the heavy work of running a farm, especially since most of them were urban types."

"You know what I forgot to bring?" asked Reinhart. "The beer! Though it *is* Sunday. But I've got connections with a little deli and could have bought some under the counter, I bet."

Raymond looked along his dark nose. "I don't use intoxicants," he said disapprovingly.

"Well, for me water just doesn't do the job with something of this persistent a flavor." Nevertheless he got up and searched the cupboards, without any help from his host, until he found a glass. But when he turned the Cold faucet and then, unrealistically, the Hot, nothing came from either.

Raymond at last said dolefully: "There's a well here, with an electric pump. But in fact the power has been turned off owing to failure to pay the last bill."

"Then," Reinhart said, "it's just as well I didn't try to heat this food. Isn't there anything to drink around here?"

Raymond got up. "There's another well outside, with an old hand pump." He rose and led Reinhart out the door, the latter bringing along the glass.

The warm light and gentle breeze were of the kind that could make failure even worse, Reinhart well knew from personal experience: sometimes good weather was a mockery and rain a balm.

Raymond walked straight and rigid in his denim work-clothes. He was as tall as Reinhart, though more slender; taller than his late father. Behind the barn was an ancient rusty horse trough, with a pump at one end. Raymond seized the long iron lever and began to move it up and down.

Reinhart held his glass at the pump's mouth. "Has this thing been used lately?"

"Once for washing a car."

Reinhart decided that further questioning would be offensive, and therefore, when after much squeaking the water suddenly gushed forth in a rust-colored flow that immediately overwhelmed the waiting tumbler and wet his sleeve to the elbow, he turned as if in a certain disorder owing to the flood, and with his back to Raymond, got rid of the glassful without tasting a drop.

"Thanks," said he, coming around after this sequence was at an end. "What's next for you now, Raymond?"

The young man looked expressionlessly at the dripping pump. "That's the obvious question."

"Do you mind my asking, how did you come to be at this farm? Do you own it or what? Granted, it's none of my business."

Raymond answered in a neutral, noncritical fashion: "You're curious about only the financial arrangements? You have no interest in my beliefs?"

"That's not tr—" Reinhart began, but caught himself. "Yes, I suppose it *is* true. It's too important a subject on which to tell diplomatic lies." He was still holding the water glass and was therefore preoccupied physically with it: funny how you can't find a decent way to get rid of certain things at special times. "My idea of such matters is that they are private. I generally feel a certain disdain, perhaps unfairly, when I hear on TV that some celebrity has been 'born again.' But I think what I dislike is not his faith, which is none of my business, but that he is telling the public about it. But that's a Christian obligation, I suppose." He suddenly appealed to Raymond: "Would you mind if I put your glass down here?" He pointed to the base of the pump. "I'll take it back to the kitchen in a moment."

"The fact is," said Raymond, himself preoccupied, "I always believe in what I stand for. I don't repudiate my basic beliefs of a decade ago, which are not really incompatible with what I believe now. But I seem to have a gift for falling in with persons whose motives will not bear scrutiny. For example, certain of my supposed political comrades were common thugs and are today still serving time for criminal acts for which their ideology was a hypocritical mask." He kicked some dirt and stared into the horse trough. "Leave it to me to walk right into what was really another version of the same thing."

"You don't mean some political movement was in back of Paradise Farm?"

"No," said Raymond, shaking his finely made head. "Some financial movement. What I mean by 'same' is in the lack of moral principle. To the people who handled the money Paradise Farm was only a tax write-off."

Reinhart grasped the handle of the pump and gave it a few experimental thrusts and recoveries; already the water had receded too far to be induced so easily to flow again.

Raymond went on: "Of course I was aware of the situation, but I assumed that I would be allowed to develop the project along the lines I explained to you on your earlier visit, successful but losing money for the early years and thus achieving everyone's purpose. But then eventually being able to pay for itself, at which point the original backers would turn it over to us, having accomplished not only their financial purpose but also having done a good deed as Christians or Jews or humanitarian atheists for that matter."

"There was a change of plans?"

"They got cold feet when that investigative reporter, that black girl, began to sniff around."

"Oh, yes. Molly Moffitt of the Channel Five News Team." Reinhart was now one of her colleagues, in a sense. "I've got some connection with that station. Maybe I could help in some way, anyhow find out just what's going on?"

"Too late for that," said Raymond. "Paradise Farm is finished. This place has been sold. Molly told me that. It's sold to some Arabs. And not just this immediate farm, but a great part of surrounding acreage."

Reinhart dry-pumped a few more times. He was dying of thirst, but didn't want to take a chance on rusty water. "Are we going to see people riding through these fields on camels?"

"I doubt that any actual Arab has ever been here," said Raymond. "They have agents who do all this purchasing, and I doubt that they have any immediate purpose for the land. Molly tells me that they simply buy everything they can."

"Speaking of Channel Five," Reinhart said, "what I should have mentioned is that I have a job there, as of Monday a week. You could leave a message for me there. I hope you keep in touch, Raymond."

The young man looked at him. "My father always spoke well of you."

"I wanted to ask, if you don't mind: is your dad's body still frozen?" How bizarre this question would have sounded to a casual passer-by; but Raymond's father, Reinhart's friend Splendor Mainwaring, had been cryogenically embalmed ten years before.

Raymond's expression was for a moment exquisitely sensitive, and then it returned to the stoical. "I couldn't afford myself to keep up those annual maintenance charges. Furthermore, the belief in bodily resurrection is at odds with my faith. Finally, those people who did the freezing inspired little confidence."

Still, there was something unfortunate, something awful, in— what? Burying the body, cremating it, thus ending all hope, quixotic though it might be, that eventual thawing and revival would take place?

"I understand," said Reinhart. "But it depresses me to—"

"Oh." Raymond was suddenly in tune with him. "Yes, of course, the body is still frozen. It is with others at a scientific facility in southern California, where research in cryonics continues."

Reinhart picked up the glass he had put down. "I'll just take this back indoors."

But Raymond took it from him. Without warning he smiled in a smug way. "I can make a better chili than that."

Reinhart smiled. "You can?"

"Surely. With chocolate."

Reinhart raised an eyebrow.

"Unsweetened, of course," said Raymond. "As in *mole poblano.*"

"That's interesting," Reinhart said. "I think chili con carne is supposed to have been invented in Texas, but it was certainly based on Mexican cuisine, so what you're suggesting makes sense."

"Oh, it's not my own fantasy. It's a standard on the menu at the Ten Gallon Hat. I cooked there for three or four years."

"The restaurant downtown? I've never eaten there." Reinhart was excited. "I've got this project in mind, buying an interest in an old existing small-town kind of restaurant in Brockville and keeping the good old stuff on the menu, but adding terrific things from other cuisines, all fine dishes, nothing fake, but very ambitious when we wanted to be. We could in fact do anything we wanted. There's a wonderful woman who owns it; it's been in her family for years. She'd retain half ownership. I'd want her to. I don't know anything about the restaurant business."

Raymond was not being ignited.

Reinhart suspected why. "Oh," he said, "what I meant was, if this thing gets going, would you like to be associated with it?" Raymond looked somewhat aggrieved. "I don't mean to offend you. What I meant was, if you didn't have immediate plans to start another religious colony."

Raymond shrugged. "I'd like to get back to cooking, in fact. I think it's probably the best profession for someone of my personality. But, frankly, what I don't care for is going in to some nice simple little place in the country and transforming it into a chic eatery designed to attract adulterers and sodomites from the city."

"All God's children have to eat," Reinhart said. "Look here: if I'm not able to work something out, this restaurant is going to be sold to some local businessman for storage space—after forty or fifty years of being open seven days a week. Did you ever hear of the gangster John Dillinger? He ate there!"

"Don't tell me," said Raymond, "you want to put a bronze plaque on his booth, and submachine guns will make up a prominent part of the decor?"

"I think you're ribbing me now, Raymond."

The younger man stared at the barn for a moment. "Is this offer in atonement?"

"Atonement?" Reinhart scowled. "What does that mean? Something about your father?"

Raymond turned his head back. "Something to do with your son."

"Well, what?"

"You don't really know that he was one of the backers of Paradise Farm?"

Reinhart shook his head slowly but with weight. "No, certainly not. But he did say, that time we visited, something about his church being a sponsor. Of course, one must understand that Blaine is a fanatical believer in the religion of money." Suddenly he felt defiant, and he stared at Raymond with spirit. "But am I my son's keeper? After all, did he not suggest that I myself move in here?"

Raymond said: "At that time there was really going to be a Paradise Farm. I don't accuse him of deliberate deceit, and it doesn't seem to be the case that he and his partners broke the law."

"It was just a crappy thing to do," Reinhart said. "No, a downright lousy thing to do. But look here, Raymond, maybe we can get this other project going: Paradise Restaurant: the idea, anyhow. I don't think Marge would want to change the existing name, which is classic: the Center Café. Isn't that great?"

CHAPTER
20

When Reinhart returned from the country and saw the little yellow Gremlin still in place he tried to reach Edie by telephone. He tried several times again throughout the succeeding two hours, but there was no answer. He began to worry about her.

He first went down to the lobby mailboxes to find the number of her apartment and then to the fifth floor, West wing. He had rarely been in that section of the building, which, extending really towards the northwest while the river at this point wended southwestwardly, was to some degree the Other Side of the Tracks.

He found 516W and pushed the button. . . . No response. He drummed upon the metal face of the door.

"God *damn* it," cried a petulant voice within.

That certainly did not sound like Edie. Reinhart shrank in embarrassment: he had obviously got the wrong apartment.

But then the door opened and there, in bathrobe and traditionally toweled hair, stood his friend. On seeing him, Edie gasped and actually began to hurl the door shut in his face. It seemed a reflex action. She caught herself, stepped behind the jamb, and bending her body so that Reinhart could see only her towel-framed face, was probably about to apologize.

But he spoke first: "I've been calling you since last night. At first I thought you were out, but your car's been in the garage all day."

She flushed within the environment of white terry cloth. "Maybe something's wrong with my phone."

Reinhart grinned at her. "You sounded pretty rough just now, when you didn't know who was pounding on the door. I think I have just seen your sweet side." She grew pinker. This was the day when he made the girls blush, but he was not complaining. He decided to go for even more color. "You look very pretty in that outfit."

But this seemed a gaffe. She paled quickly. Obviously he was deficient in eloquence when standing in a corridor and addressing this kind of young lady, though he had been telling the truth. She was a nice big pink girl wrapped in white.

But she was saying solemnly: "Last night I wouldn't have been here, because I was at work."

"On Saturday night?" Reinhart nodded to take the harsh edge off his incredulity. "Where do you work, Edie?"

She answered in that ingenuous or ingenuous-seeming style in which a statement is made a question: "A bowling alley?"

Reinhart said: "Look, I'm sorry to have bothered you. I see you're doing your hair or whatever. I just wanted to check on whether you were—"

"You don't believe me, do you?" she suddenly asked boldly. "I work nights as a cashier in a bowling alley. The pay's good, since it's hard to get people, even men, to work at night. That gives me my days to myself. And my hours are the kind you wouldn't know where they went anyway: five to midnight."

Reinhart shifted from one foot to another. "Well, as I say, I was just trying to get in touch to . . ." It seemed bad taste here to mention her apologetic letter, standing in the hallway, speaking to a young woman wrapped, even unto her head, in terry cloth.

Edie said: "I don't work tonight. Sunday and Monday are my weekend."

"Uh-huh."

"Of course, a lot of bowling goes on on both those days, but I've got to get off sometime."

"That's true," said Reinhart. He was beginning to feel stupid, but he was as yet unable to do anything decisive. "Probably you'll be doing a lot of reading, then."

"Pardon?"

"You mentioned you did a lot of reading."

"Oh. Oh, yes, that's true."

"I used to be more of a reader when I was a young fellow," said he. "I got away from it in later years, I don't really quite know why. Unless you count cookbooks." He exposed the palms of both hands. "When you've lived a long time, you find it hard to explain where the years have gone and what you did in them and why and why not."

Edie lifted her shoulders and let them fall, while smiling sympathetically. Winona too was invariably in sympathy with him, but she was his daughter. There were more differences than similarities. He thought here of Winona because he was trying to make some sense of his interest in Edie.

"I'll tell you why I especially wanted to get in touch with you last night: I wanted to invite you to have dinner with me, to celebrate my getting a regular job on TV."

Her reaction to this was to disappear for a moment back of the door, perhaps to collect herself. After all, she had been the only person in his circle of women, other than Genevieve (who had naturally insulted him on the matter), to have watched his triumph in replacing Jack Buxton, or at least to tell him of it.

When she returned to view her eyes were pink. She thrust a hand out of her robe. "Congratulations."

Her fingers were almost as long as his own and her palm almost as broad, but her hand was virtually weightless. The flesh of women is not as dense; in addition Edie was too shy to insinuate the least movement in her hand; it was up to him to do with it as he wished.

He shook it gently and returned it to its owner. "Thanks. I realize now that you wouldn't have been able to accept the dinner invitation anyhow." He supposed he was smiling foolishly. "I hope you enjoy your day off." He began to leave. He could not explain why, more than four decades too late, he was behaving like a schoolboy.

Edie suddenly spoke in a bell-clear voice. "Why don't we have dinner together tonight?"

Reinhart was released from his strange paralysis. He turned back eagerly—and found, or seemed to find, that Edie had embarrassed herself and vanished behind the door.

He addressed the empty space. At his angle he could see nothing significant through it, and he wanted badly to look at the interior of her apartment. But he did not dare to touch the door. "Last night I was going to cook. But maybe you'd rather go out tonight?" He remembered that in the code that obtained in the time of his young manhood it was considered ipso facto illicit for a woman to be alone with a man in *his* home, though for some reason quite O.K. for them to be together, unchaperoned, in hers. But like so many practices that once seemed preposterous, this one, when viewed from afar, could be seen to have had its use: the establishing of probabilities; a girl who visited a man alone would probably "put out," or in any event not be offended by a "proposition."

Edie came back into view, her hands at her towel. "The thing is," she said firmly, "it's my turn to entertain you."

Reinhart looked down at her slippers. They resembled huge bearpaws and were covered with long synthetic fur.

"All right. Thank you. I like your slippers."

"Do you know what they're called? Abominable Snow Shoes. I'm not kidding!" She was laughing with white teeth. She seemed in perfect health, but that was a routine condition with the young.

"Well," Reinhart said, making a type of bowing movement, "I'll see you later, then?"

"Would seven be O.K.?"

"Perfect." He started away, then turned back. "May I bring something? Wine? It's Sunday, but I always have some on hand."

The suggestion seemed to startle her. "Oh, no. No, thank you."

Reinhart went back to his own apartment. He feared her rejection of the offer meant that he would get no wine with dinner, whatever the dinner might be. Edie knew nothing about food and did not herself drink wine. God! It had been years since Reinhart had eaten a meal he had not himself cooked or at least ordered from a restaurant menu. He really dreaded being at the mercy of someone else's table. . . . That was what happened to you as you grew older: your habits became all-important; you could sleep only in your own bed and watch TV only with the sound set at a certain volume. As a boy, when Reinhart had to surrender his room to a relative and sleep on the living-room sofa he was overjoyed with the sheer novelty of it. So had he been hopeful when as young marrieds he and Genevieve went to eat at someone else's house. He could not remember ever before having been invited to dine at the table of a single girl: such an experience, back in his day and milieu, would have been unique.

What time was it now? . . . Only five o'clock? He wasn't cooking this evening. He had *two hours* to get through! He went to the liquor cabinet and poured a generous measure of Scotch, iced and watered it in the kitchen, and took it to the bedroom. He switched on the television set atop the dresser. . . . A sturdy woman wearing a billed cap was bending a putter. Sunday afternoon and ladies' golf, of course!

He reclined on the bed, nape against headboard, Scotch cradled in two hands at his navel. He watched for a while, but the upholstered bodies no longer had their old appeal. He went to the set and roamed the dial. Tennis would hit the spot today, with younger legs under pleated skirts. This was not a concupiscent taste: he was interested in relative levels of vigor.

But no more female athletes of any sort were available at the moment, which belonged, on one channel—indeed, his own Channel Five—to stock cars speeding around an asphalt oval and on another to two undersized Latin American prizefighters who pounded each other furiously without apparent damage to either. On "public" television a hirsute young chap was talking rapidly to a bald-headed middle-aged man about—by gosh, about the upcoming Jack Buxton Film Festival! . . . But apparently it was not to begin for a while. At the moment what one got was a discussion between these two fellows, who werely oddly paired: the hairy youth spoke like a hoodlum, the bald-headed critic was peevishly effeminate. At the moment the latter was saying: ". . . *really* think that's *true?* Oh, come *off* it." To which the former replied: "Chroo? Of cawss! Wadduhyuh think, I'm loying?"

Reinhart discovered that his Johnnie Walker was missing: a ghost had drained the entire glass while his attention was elsewhere. He returned to the bar and got a refill onto the same, or much the same, ice.

He was restless. He showered again and made an entire change of clothing from the skin out, though he had put everything on fresh that morning. He must make arrangements with a professional laundry to do his work. As a TV personality he could hardly be seen trundling his wash down to the basement. The job could alter his life in many ways. He might be recognized on the street. One of the local papers had a show-biz gossip column. Could he ever afford to be seen with Helen Clayton? "Which TV chef is consorting with an invalid's wife?" Your life is not your own when you get into the public eye.

A good deal, but by no means all, of these reflections were ironical: it is amusing to mock oneself when things go well. And when one has waited so long for success that one has forgotten what is being awaited, there is a limit to the swelling of one's head. But he *was* impatient for Monday to come, after all these years, and therefore while waiting first for sufficient time to pass before he could go down and eat Edie's probably overdone and surely wineless meal, he drank more Scotch than he should have, certainly more than he would have if he himself had been cooking. It anesthetizes the palate, you know (he said to himself in the bathroom mirror), really belongs in the after-dinner range, an interesting and worthwhile potation, surely, but its place is postprandial.

He winked at his large visage and added: "Listen to the epicure, who was himself reared on well-done meat and vegetables boiled to death and served dry. Who when in France as a soldier looked for whores and not meals. . . . Who, hoohoo, is now drunk for the first time in many years." Not helplessly. His stride was straight enough, and when speaking to himself at least, he could not hear that his tongue was getting stuck behind his teeth.

But his emotions were intensified. Suddenly remembering that he had nothing to take to Edie, who had spurned his offer of wine, he decided to go out and find a florist who was open. This was not the kind of shop normally accessible on Sundays, but the alcohol evoked from Reinhart a stubborn determination to leave no mall unturned.

This was a splendid aim, but in point of fact the same spirits had caused his sense of time to be deranged. It was 6:55 when he looked at the bedside clock. He brushed his teeth once again, put on his blazer, checked it insofar as he could for lint (but living alone, one must forget about a certain area in the back of garments being worn; Grace could now perform inspection service for Winona, he himself had no one), and left the apartment.

Edie was certainly a conveniently placed friend. He would now have been in no mood to visit someone by car.

He reached her door and pushed the buzzer. She was quick to answer this time. No doubt the Scotch had something to do with his vision, but Edie looked even taller than usual. Before crossing the threshold he tried to figure that out and at last saw that she wore high heels.

"I'm sorry to say," he confessed, "I'm empty-handed."

"Good," said Edie, beckoning him into her home. She wore some kind of soft white blouse and an ankle-length figured skirt. This seemed an occasion for her. She was fairer of hair this evening, and her eyes had . . . whatever. More make-up, certainly, but—

"That's what 'karate' means, incidentally," said Reinhart, interrupting his own process of observation. "In Japanese. *Kara*— 'empty.' *Te*—'hand.' " He smiled into Edie's limpid eyes. "A bit of the useless information I've accumulated throughout the many years of my life." For some reason he was delaying a survey of the apartment, staying just inside the door.

"Won't you come down here?" said Edie, who had gone ahead and now spoke from a slightly lower situation. She was in the living room, which like his own was one step down from the level on which one entered.

Reinhart stepped jauntily down to join her. Half the room, that half towards the large window, was a kind of greenhouse full of standing or hanging plants, which seemed to exude freshness and verdant moisture, as the sun radiates warmth and light. Reinhart's sensibility lacked in the horticultural faculty, and he had never before felt this effect from vegetable life. Nor was Winona, though a deft hand with cut flowers, a grower of plants.

"Now I see what's wrong with my apartment," he said. He went to the window, or at any rate as close as permitted, and looked out through the greenery. The view, especially at this fading time of day, was none too vast, being mostly of an angle of the building, with only a glimpse of the river, as if one were looking illicitly through a chink. Yet living among these plants one would feel no deprivation.

"I wish I knew enough about the subject to discuss it with you," said he, "but I don't think I've tried to grow anything, with the exception of lawn-grass some years back, since the scrawny little tree we used to be given annually on Arbor Day at school—which always died. I've thought about starting some herbs in windowsill pots, but I'm still too shy."

Edie invited him to sit down. Comfortable facilities were available: a sofa upholstered in tan-flecked brown, a chair or two, modern but capacious and genial. He chose the couch, where he could expand in any direction. When he sat down, he was looking across at a long low bookcase, pleasantly variegated with spines in various hues. He thought he might ask Edie what she read, but when he looked for her, she was gone . . . but not far. Back of a counter, at the top of the room, was her kitchen.

She soon returned with a glass of sherry. He could not remember that he had been asked, but perhaps he had. She found a little knee-high table at the end of the couch and brought it near him.

"Are you all right?"

"Me?" asked Reinhart. He smiled at her. "Sit down, why don't you?"

She chose the rust-colored chair.

"Come sit on the couch," Reinhart said. "I want to talk to you like a Dutch uncle, as they used to say. . . . And don't worry that simply because I've had a few drinks I will behave improperly. I have always been what the American lower-middle class thinks of as being a 'gentleman,' which is to say, a prude with respectable young ladies."

Edie smirked at this statement, but she did not blush. She sat down on the couch, at just the right distance from him: not so close as to embarrass, not so far away as to offend. But she sat tentatively, towards the edge of the cushion, as if she might rise. She was now wearing an apron, a merry one, in colorful stripes.

"Ah, you're cooking," said he. "Well, I won't detain you."

"And am I nervous!"

"Please don't be." He started to get up. "Why not let me do it?"

"I want to do it myself," Edie said. "I think I *can* do it, and when I invite a guest, I *should* do it."

This was a new aspect of her, or at any rate one he had previously not given her an opportunity to show. Her manner in her own domicile was very different from that she displayed when abroad. And how right she was to feel strength here: it was a warm and wonderful little cave. The rug was the color of peach preserves. In the embrasure of the window a geranium was blooming redly: one of the few plants in all the world that Reinhart could identify offhand. A hanging pot was blossoming in white stars. He still retained the aftertaste of Scotch, which was not altogether pleasant, yet he was not really sorry he had drunk so much. He felt in a vulnerable state, but well protected here.

She returned with one little bowl of small, withered black olives, the sort that are cured in fragrant olive oil, and another filled with smoky salted almonds.

When she was back in the kitchen Reinhart called up-room: "Are you going to tell me what the bill of fare is?"

"Maybe I shouldn't, so that if something doesn't turn out well I can change it!" She looked up from her work, across the counter. "Are you ready for more wine?"

"Not yet, thanks."

"Isn't it drinkable?"

"It's superb, a lot better than I can usually afford."

Edie came back. Her apron's stripes included Reinhart's favorite combination of turquoise and navy.

"This is just a delightful apartment," he said. "It makes one feel good just to sit in it."

"It could be bigger. What you see is all there is, except for the bathroom of course."

"It's just the right size for a person living alone, I'd say." He finished his wine but held onto the glass lest she take it and leave for a moment. "Mine will probably be too big now. You see, Winona has moved out. She's gone to live with a friend, a woman friend, and it's high time she came out from under my wing, to tell you the truth, and lived with someone of her own age, more or less." He looked at Edie with feeling. "I'm misrepresenting that. I'm acting as if it's Winona who needed me, rather than what is true, the other way around: she supported me for a good many years. I kept house, of course, but she was the one with the career."

"I'm sure you were just biding your time," said Edie. She put out her hand for his wine glass.

He surrendered it. He was becoming aware of a sort of motherly force immanent in her. When she returned, he said: "I confess I had a bit to drink before I came up here. I was nervous on general principles, and then I was feeling a funny reaction to getting the new job, a mixture of elation and maybe megalomania and greed —and most of all, disbelief. But then I remember that I did step in to fill the breach left when Buxton had his heart attack: I did it, off the cuff, ad lib! Yet even that gives me mixed feelings. Maybe I've wasted my life. Maybe I should have been a performer of some kind from the beginning, studied acting or even tap dancing or whatnot."

Edie had not sat down this time. She said, in her new maternal style: "I think you're wrong about wanting to be anything other than you've been." She went back to her work without his feeling that she had left him: that was a true art, but apparently unstudied.

"I hope you're aware," he said, "that it's all I can do to stay out of your kitchen, but I know what goes on in mine and how I hate to be watched." There were times when you just had to plunge your hands in to the wrists, so to speak, or retrieve something edible from the floor or scrape off charrings or mask raggednesses with sauce or garnitures. But if the error had been to put too much salt in solution, you might be in real trouble, though you could try boiling a raw potato in the liquid. Over the years one learned a lot of tricks. These would make nice little bits for the show. Already he was thinking professionally.

> *Q. If by accident some hardboiled eggs got mixed up with uncooked ones, how could you distinguish each from each without breaking any?*
>
> *A. Simply spin each egg on its side. The cooked one will spin in uniform revolutions, whereas the raw egg will wobble erratically.*

Edie came to him. "Dinner is ready."

He got up and said, face to face: "We're about the same height when you wear those shoes."

"What a relief," said she, "to be able to wear heels without making someone feel lousy."

"You mean men? I thought that had changed nowadays."

"You can't change biology," said Edie. "Most men are bigger than most women. If you're not like most people, then you are in a special situation. You can't just say it isn't true."

She led him to the counter between living room and kitchen. Two places had been set there for a meal, with wooden-handled eating utensils of stainless steel and blue bandannas for napkins. Each setting was on its own island of a straw mat, bound in blue fabric. As Reinhart sat down Edie went behind the counter and with a big wood spoon and fork served spaghetti and sauce, already combined, from an earthenware casserole onto painted plates of similar crockery.

Accepting his, Reinhart noted with approval that it had been prewarmed. He asked her if he might at least pour the Valpolicella, which was already uncorked.

"I see you have a glass for yourself."

She put her own plate onto the counter and came around to the eating side and took a stool. She lifted the glass he had just poured.

"I'm all right now," she said. "I'm drinking wine."

"I didn't mean—"

Edie touched her glass to his. "To your health."

It was a fine and simple and unexpected thing to hear.

"To yours, Edie."

The spaghetti sauce proved to be a rich *ragù bolognese*, a far cry from the scarlet acidity of Naples, made from ground beef and pork, bacon, and chicken livers, simmered in beef stock and white wine. Edie had found the recipe in a book.

"Why," said Reinhart, "this is the best thing of its kind. Did you just happen to have all the ingredients on hand?" It was really a rude question, as he recognized when he had put it. But her transformation from the awkward creature she had hitherto been into this gracious hostess, the accomplished cook, the lovely young woman she was at present, could not be taken as a routine event. Perhaps some of it was due to his altered perception, but if he was drunkenly upgrading her now, he had soberly failed to appreciate her previously.

"Let's just say that I was planning something, for sometime," said she.

Reinhart grinned at her over his wine. The Valpolicella was as pretty on the palate as its name was in the ear.

"Edie, all I know of life tells me you cannot always be as sweet as you have thus far been to me, but I'm shamelessly enjoying it at the moment." He went on in what to him was a logical progression: "I have lived with my daughter all her life, and yet I had no inkling of . . . what shall I call it? Her darker side? If by 'darker' what is meant is not evil but a kind of moral toughness. Winona can be, well, rude of course, but beyond that . . . not exactly cruel —though I suppose she could be that, too, outside my experience —but 'forceful' would probably be an accurate word."

Edie had stopped eating to listen even more attentively than usual.

He asked: "You know her only to chat in the lobby?"

Now she seemed guileless again. "I'd seen her pictures a lot. You know how it is when you see a celebrity, you feel you know them."

"It was awfully arrogant of her, though, on the basis of that slight an acquaintance, to want to borrow your car."

"Oh, I don't think so!" She took a sip from her glass. There was that about her mouth which suggested the curve of a stringed musical instrument.

She went behind the counter.

After a while Reinhart said: "You, Miss Mulhouse, are making a spinach salad with a warm dressing of bacon and vinegar." He saw that the minced bacon had previously been rendered of its fat; the skillet was now being reheated on the stove behind her as Edie thin-sliced some plump white mushrooms.

When she took away the dinner plates and served the salad, he said: "The mushrooms are definitely an asset. I have previously known only the purist version: all green, except for the flecks of bacon, though there are those, I believe, who sprinkle on chopped hard-boiled egg, but that is almost entirely an aesthetic effect." He winked at her. "Forgive me for the shop talk."

"Don't stop," said Edie. "I really like to hear it."

"Judging from this meal, in composition and execution, you know quite a bit about food already. It's the kind of simplicity that comes only with gastronomical sophistication. For some reason you were deceiving me, with your talk of living on hot dogs and hamburgers."

Edie stared at him. "I swear that I just got all these things out of a book."

"Nothing wrong with that. It's exactly how I learned to cook seriously."

"But this is the first time for me," she said, with a mixture of shyness and something else, perhaps defiance: as if she were talking of a sexual experience. "I've never really cooked anything before, except maybe a fried egg."

Reinhart nodded sagely. "You see how easy it is."

"Is it really O.K.?" asked Edie. "Or are you just saying that?" She proceeded to give him an intimate feeling by chiding: "You are always being too easy on me."

"Winona says the same thing." Reinhart brought his fingertips together. "Can I help it if I like girls?" Now Edie sighed cryptically. "Look," said he, "the Center Café in Brockville? I was out there again today. It's become an obsession with me to think of acquiring it somehow. It's a fantasy and will probably never come to reality, but I've started anyway to assemble a staff of kindred souls. Would you want to be part of it in some fashion?"

"Me?" Edie drew back on the stool. She seemed genuinely startled.

Reinhart touched the Formica counter with his forefinger. "You're a cashier by trade, are you not? Am I wrong in thinking that if you could practice your profession at a bowling alley, you could do it at a restaurant, where at best the traffic would be lighter? . . . Mind you, this is all theoretical at the moment. I am not even considering how we could earn a profit. Marge has been losing money."

Edie received this information inscrutably and then went around to the kitchen, opened the freezer compartment of the refrigerator, and removed an ice-cube tray. She looked into it and winced, agitated it slightly in her hand, and winced again.

"Something didn't jell?" Reinhart asked.

"Pear sherbet. I'm afraid I flopped at that."

"No, you didn't. It just hasn't had time to freeze. It takes a while." That was the very dessert he had made for the uneaten brunch to which Grace Greenwood had been invited.

"Would you like to have coffee in the living room?"

He was not unhappy to be relieved from sitting on the stool, which was a jolly perch at the outset, but even when younger, with his length of body, he liked at certain points during a meal to lean against the back of a chair.

"I'll pass up the coffee, though, if you don't mind. I have acquired the kind of equilibrium between food and drink that caffeine might unbalance." He went in to the couch. "Why don't you sit down and tell me about yourself?"

Edie took off her apron. In the living room she chose a chair some distance from him. She looked at him and said levelly: "I'm not gay."

Reinhart had not been prepared for this statement. Of an unusually generous supply of possible reactions he chose in effect to shrug it off. "Neither am I." He had brought his glass of wine along, and now he drank some.

Edie said almost fiercely: "I'm not criticizing anyone who is."

"I know you're not," said Reinhart. He raised his glass to her, but lowered it without drinking. "I must tell you, Edie, that I suspect you do everything well, but you pretend to be defenseless. You must be aware that that's an old-fashioned style. It's the one I have always preferred, though having had not only the other kind of mother but also the other kind of wife."

"Sometimes," Edie said, "it seems at first you are making fun of me, but then I realize you're not."

"That's right. I'm not. I don't ever make fun of anybody." He put his glass down and got to his feet. "I think I'll leave now, though it is awfully rude to eat and run. But I'll tell you why I think it's necessary: on the one hand, I think I desire you, but on the other I dislike the *idea* of lasciviousness in a man of my age—if what I feel is that. I have just been separated from a daughter who is only a year older than you. Maybe what I feel is really a simple longing to be in the presence of a young woman to whom I'm closely attached, and since you're not a relative by blood, I crave some other kind of intimacy."

Edie remained seated and looked up at him with deep blue eyes. "Are those good reasons for leaving?"

"Then how about cowardice?" But she laughed at him. "All right, then, I'll just take a nightcap, but first I have to go to my own apartment for a moment. I have to make a phone call. Business. . . ." He put his hand out, and she gave him hers. "Don't go anywhere."

"Not me," said Edie.

He took the stairway down to the fourth floor. Inside the apartment he found he had to look up the number in the public book: Winona had taken the personal directory from the drawer in the telephone table. He wished she had also taken that etching full of hairy lines.

"Grace, Carl Reinhart."

"Aha."

"May I speak to my daughter?"

"She's not here at the moment, Carl."

"Not there?"

"That's right," Grace said tartly. "She went to the movies."

Reinhart looked down into the living room, but the light was too dim to see the little clock above the liquor cabinet. "She's out alone this time of night?"

Grace snorted. "She's with Ray!"

"Ray?"

"My son. He's in from California for spring vacation."

Reinhart had never heard of this person before, but he felt that courtesy required him to fake it. "Oh, yes, *Ray*. He's in the last year of college, isn't he?"

"Last year of law school!" crowed Grace. Her voice had very clearly taken on an unprecedented tone of affection. This too was new to Reinhart. He had never heard her use it with reference to Winona, but there are all forms of human emotion, and he himself had certainly experienced many of them.

He said sincerely: "I'd like to meet him."

"You would?" Grace asked, incredulous for a moment, and then she recovered: "I want you to! Which night's good for dinner? It's on me this time. But you pick the restaurant. You're the expert.

Make it fancy. We've got all kinds of celebrating to do. Did you know that tomorrow I become president of Epicon?"

Reinhart congratulated her. "And I have a new idea I want to talk to you about in the area of food," said he. "How about Tuesday night for dinner?"

"I'd better check with Ray first. He's seeing my ex, his father, one night this week. . . . Good to talk with you, Carl. When should Winnie return the call, tonight still or tomorrow?"

"I'll call her tomorrow," said Reinhart. "It's nothing crucial."

"Sleep tight," said Grace, in what would appear to be a certain affection for *him*. Well, he had never thought her the world's worst.

As he rode the elevator up to Edie's floor Reinhart understood that Winona's absence at this moment was another piece of the good luck he had been enjoying lately. How fatuous had been the impulse to ask her whether she could permit him to have a girl friend younger than herself. Of course she would have refused! Winona was a notorious prig. Who would want any other kind of daughter?